Those who Return

Ruth Rodgers

For John & Jonalyn –
enjoy!
Ruth R.

Those who Return

This book is a work of fiction. Although based on historical events and including persons who lived at the time, these events and characters are used fictitiously. Any resemblance to any person living or dead is coincidental.

Printed by Island Blue/Printorium Bookworks, Victoria, British Columbia, Canada

ISBN: 978-1-9991596-6-5

Front Cover Image: *Return Home*, Charmaine Bayntun, 2022

Author Image: Erin Banit

Also by Ruth Rodgers

Sunshine Coast Series:
Those who Wander (2019)
Those who Stay (2020)
Those who Return (2022) is the third installment in the author's Sunshine Coast series. Though exploring similar themes and time frames, *Those who Return* is not a direct sequel to *Those who Wander* and *Those who Stay*, the first two books in the series, and thus can be read as a stand-alone novel.

This Fair Land (2021)

All books available as ebooks and print on demand at Amazon.ca

"Who is the custodian of my freeborn rights, if not the government of my native land? Who is the protector of my own chattels from looting, if not the laws of this land? Who is the sponsor of my dreams, of all the hopes and plans, the confidante entrusted with what lies ahead of me, if not my own, my native land?"

Muriel Kitagawa, *This is My Own*, 1985

This book is dedicated to the Nikkei, who stayed loyal to their adopted land even when it was trying its hardest to reject them.
I'm so glad you stayed.

Glossary of Japanese words and phrases used in this book

ani*:* eldest brother

atama no kuroi keto: "black-haired white trash" a slur applied to Nikkei who supported Canada in the war, made by those who supported Japan

auto*:* out (as in baseball)

bushido: "the way of the warrior" or the samurai tradition; also called the *le* way

dekasegi: sojourners; emigrants who came to Canada for a time to gain wealth, intending to return to Japan

deru kugi wa utareru: "the nail that sticks up gets hit" (i.e. blend in, don't do anything to get noticed); this aphorism also underscores the Japanese culture of collectivism. Individual effort and pride are discouraged; contributing modestly to the group's success is praised.

dojin: North American indigenous

ganbarum da zo: "let us not give up!" also ***ganbari ya*** ("don't give up!")

haha: mother (informal, 'Mom')

haiku: a Japanese form of poetry, typically with a 5-7-5 syllable form

hakujin: whites/Caucasians; also *keto* ('whiteys') in slang

hashi: chopsticks used for eating

hibachi: a small, charcoal-fueled barbecue

ianjo: a 'comfort station' (i.e. a brothel) with *ianfu (*prostitutes) provided to the Japanese military during WWII

ikebana: a Japanese type of flower arranging

issei: first generation emigrants from Japan to other countries (in this instance, Canada)

jaakuna hito: evil one

kakigori: flavoured shaved ice

kamikaze: divine wind; Japanese fighter pilots who flew their aircraft directly into their targets, achieving their destructive aim through their own suicide; exemplifies the 'death before surrender' attitude of the Japanese military during WWII

kimono: traditional Japanese women's garment, worn with an *obi,* a wide sash tied with an elaborate knot

kodomo no tame ni: "for the sake of the children" (we must endure)

kusa wake: "those who part the grass/blaze the trail for others to follow"

-kun: dear one, a suffix attached to a name to express affection

kuyō: a Shinto ritual burning of origami figures to honour the ancestors

nihonjin: Japanese, people of the rising sun, used by very early immigrants to Canada to describe themselves

nihongami: an elaborately rolled and pinned traditional Japanese hairstyle

nikkei: persons of Japanese descent living outside of Japan

nisei: second generation, children of issei

musume: daughter

obasan: aunt

obaasan/obaachan: grandmother

oji: uncle

okaasan: mother (formal); also used for mother-in-law

pauru gai: the Powell Street neighbourhood in Vancouver (Japantown)

sansei: third generation, grandchildren of issei, children of nisei

sayonara: goodbye

sefu: safe (as in baseball)

shikata-ga-nai: "it can't be helped" (i.e. accept things and move on)

shirofugen, ojochin, shirotae, akebono: types of Japanese flowering cherry trees

sutoraiku: strike (as in baseball)

takoyaki: a deep-fried filled dumpling

tamahagane: jewel steel; a highly refined steel used for samurai swords and other uses

tennōheika banzai: "long life to the emperor!"

Tonari Gumi: the Japanese Canadian Volunteers' Association in Vancouver, B.C., who run an elders' housing unit, *Sakuro-So*

tsukune: chicken meatballs

wa: group strength

zori: thonged sandals made of reeds or straw; worn with *tabi*, socks with a separate big toe

PROLOGUE

Winnipeg, Manitoba 2000

Michelle wasn't sure that her grandmother Asami was going to be able to stay calm amid all the noise and activity of the party that the family had planned for her hundredth birthday. Her attention span was very short these days, and sometimes she fell asleep in the middle of a conversation. But Michelle's mother Isabel had insisted that they go all out, and who was Michelle to deny the frail old lady her celebration? At least Isabel had agreed to hold the party in the nursing home's recreation room, so if Grandma got tired or overwhelmed, they could return her to her room quickly and without fuss.

For the moment, the elderly woman seemed calm. She sat in her wheelchair, gazing quietly out at the snow falling steadily onto the nursing home's small but tidy gardens, her tiny body almost swamped by the bright pink dress Isabel had bought her for the party. Michelle thought the strident colour of the dress made her grandmother's face looked more sallow than usual, but there was no arguing with her mother.

"Can I get you a cup of tea, Grandma? The party won't start for an hour yet. Or maybe you could have a little nap first," said Michelle gently, being sure to speak into Asami's good left ear. The old woman smiled and reached up for Michelle's hand. She ignored the offer of tea but raised her face to speak clearly to her granddaughter.

"Is Kenji coming today?" she asked, her almond-shaped dark eyes bright under her still-thick white hair and eyebrows. Michelle frowned.

"Kenji?" she asked. "I'm sorry, I don't know anyone by that name."

Asami shook her head in impatience. "Kenji, Oji Kenji, your uncle. You know him!"

Michelle shook her own head. "I have no Uncle Kenji, Grandma. You must be thinking of someone else."

The old woman became agitated, her voice rising. "Kenji is my son, my Kenichi! Don't tell me you don't know him! He was born in 1926, eight years before your mother. Where is he? I want to see him on my birthday!"

At that moment, Isabel came in, clicking her tongue to see her mother flustered and upset. "Ma, what are you getting all bothered about? Michelle, what have you been saying to your grandmother?" she demanded in a sharp tone.

"Nothing at all, Mom. She is demanding to see an Uncle Kenji, but I don't know who she's talking about." A guilty look flashed over her mother's face, an expression so rare that Michelle was astonished. Mom never admitted guilt about anything! Any problem that arose was someone else's fault. Isabel had always been quick to place blame and make sure everyone heard about it.

"She's just confused," said Isabel. "Ma, come now, it's almost time for your party. Never mind these silly questions."

"But Isabel," the old lady demanded, refusing to be distracted, "where is Kenji?" Michelle saw her mother frown in impatience, but then she paused, biting her lower lip and shooting a sharp glance toward Michelle. After a long moment, she seemed to come to a decision. Crouching down in front of her mother, Isabel reached out to gather the old woman's hands in her own. With a tenderness that her daughter had rarely seen, Isabel looked into her mother's wrinkled face and spoke quietly.

"I don't know where Kenji is, Ma. He disappeared when we were all sent to East Lillooet during the war, do you remember? Perhaps he still lives, but we have not heard from him since that day. I have looked, Ma, I have, but I have not found him."

Asami's face crumpled. "He is not here?" she asked sadly, tears leaking from under her wrinkled eyelids.

"No Ma, but many others are coming to wish you happy birthday. You are a hundred years old today! Not many people can say that, eh? Did you see the greeting you got from the Prime Minister? Isn't that special?"

"Prime Minister!" said the old woman in disdain. "What good was Mr. William Lyon Mackenzie King to me when we lost everything, hey? Where were his greetings on the day we were forced out of our homes? What did he have to say when the English men took your grandfather's strawberry farm?" She pushed Isabel's hands away. "I don't want any greeting from him."

"It's not from Mr. Mackenzie King, Ma, it's from that nice French-Canadian Mr. Chretien. Remember he came around one day, shaking everyone's hand? He spoke to you then, I'm sure you remember."

"No," said Asami shortly, turning her face away, "I do not remember, and I don't want to." Isabel glanced up at Michelle, her face worried. Asami could be stubborn. What if she refused to attend her own party, after all the trouble they'd gone to? Michelle crouched down as well.

"Did you know, Grandma, that the bakers have made a large chocolate cake for the party?" Her grandmother had a sweet tooth and a weakness for chocolate. Michelle was relieved to see the old lady's face brighten.

"Does it have chocolate icing?" she asked querulously. "I only want it if it has chocolate icing."

"I think so," said Michelle. "But to be sure, shall we go and look? I think they may have put your name on it, too. Let's go see if they spelled it right, shall we?" Her grandmother nodded eagerly, the previous conversation seemingly forgotten. As Michelle turned her grandmother's wheelchair, she looked pointedly at her mother over the old woman's head.

"Yes, I will tell you--later," Isabel whispered reluctantly, looking away. Michelle nodded and said nothing. Her mother had chattered on and on about the internment experience during her fight for redress. How could she have totally omitted the fact that her brother had disappeared during it? Something wasn't right here...

PART I

1880
Esquimalt, Vancouver Island, British Columbia

Haruto Sato crouched in the hot and noisy bowels of the Japanese Navy's steamer corvette *Tsukuba,* passing a hand-rolled cigarette to Kai Kuryu, who squatted beside him. Kai sucked in, causing the end of the cigarette to glow brightly, illuminating his thin face with the long laugh lines bracketing his mobile mouth. Sighing out a billow of smoke, Kai passed the cigarette to Tamio Hirata, who nearly ignited his bushy eyebrows with the flame; Tamio then handed it to Hiro Sawamura, the smallest of them, who took barely a breath of the now short stub before passing it along to Masao Sugaju. Hiro was younger than the other four and he didn't really like the taste of tobacco, but he pretended to inhale so the others wouldn't mock him. Masao raised a sardonic eyebrow at him as he took the butt, and made a show of inhaling deeply and luxuriously, causing the others to laugh while Hiro cast his eyes down, embarrassed. Turning his head to blow out a long streamer of smoke, Masao carefully ground out the final stump of the cigarette against the ship's wooden hull and looked at his friends.

"Well? Are we going to do it?" he asked. The others looked sideways at each other. They were all barely twenty, second or third sons, and had signed on to this steam corvette as naval trainees back in Hiroshima prefecture. It had seemed like such a good idea at the time.

Times were very hard at home. During the long Tokugawa regime that followed the destructive wars of the samurais, conditions for almost everyone had been bad in Japan. The small local prefectures were grouped into regions ruled by the powerful shoguns, and their overlords' demands seemed never-ending. The local daimyō, the feudal lords, encouraged the growth of cottage industries such as weaving, silk production, the making of tatami mats, and the growing of cash crops such as cotton as well as the ubiquitous rice, but this did not ease the wrenching poverty of most of the common people. The country's rigid regime of isolation was enforced by the shoguns, and the people became passive and resigned. It seemed nothing would ever change. It was best to accept fate and carry on as best you could.

The unforeseen arrival of Admiral Matthew Perry of the United States Navy in Edo Bay in 1853 had shaken Japanese culture to its core. Perry used the might of his four heavily armed warships to force the shoguns to sign the Treaty of Kanagawa, which favoured the foreigners and broke the shoguns' control over Japan. When young Emperor Meiji was set up as a figurehead in 1868, he replaced the corrupt Bakufu administrators, and briefly there was hope that conditions would improve. Compulsory education and military conscription offered, it seemed, routes to improvement. But soon it became clear that this new system was as onerous as the old one. In less than a decade, increased taxes and falling rice prices caused many farmers to lose their lands. Families and whole prefectures fell more deeply into poverty. Even the growing of cotton, which so many had invested in, failed to save them. Local products were replaced by cheap imports from India now that foreign trade had come to their shores.

When the Navy had come recruiting, the young men's families had encouraged them to enlist. Perhaps they would make a career in the service. At least it was one less mouth to feed at home. Ready for an adventure, the five friends had boarded the *Tsukuba* with eager hearts.

It hadn't been at all what they'd hoped for. The duties were both boring and onerous, their superior officers harshly demanding. They were treated as the very lowest of the low, almost as slaves, given all the worst jobs. The novelty of swabbing decks and emptying slops had worn off within hours. The seemingly endless ocean had swiftly lost its fascination. The five had taken to whispering about alternatives.

Now they were nearing Esquimalt, the British harbour at the edge of the fledgling city of Victoria, on Vancouver Island in the young Dominion of Canada. The boys had no idea what it might be like. No one they knew had ever visited Canada. They had heard the older sailors saying that this was the first time a Japanese ship had come to Esquimalt. But surely, they'd said to one another, anything had to be better that staying on the *Tsukuba*. And they couldn't go home in disgrace. No, better to jump ship and see what they could make of themselves in this huge and undiscovered land.

"But what will we do? How will we feed ourselves?" asked Hiro, always the most timid among them.

Haruto shrugged his stocky shoulders. "I assume there will be fish in the ocean and the rivers. We know how to fish. We will not starve." Indeed, all four had grown up on the shores of Setonaikai, a broad inland sea on the Strait of Shimonoseki that divided the main islands of Japan. More than the Japanese who lived inland, they had been exposed to sailors from other cultures who had found their way through its waters long before Admiral Perry had brought the world to their doorstep. Those of Hiroshima prefecture were a bit more worldly, a bit less insular, as a result. Perhaps this was why the five friends had left their homes so readily and were even now considering a move that might sever their connection to their homeland forever.

"Yes," agreed Kai, "but perhaps we should take a few hooks, lines, and nets with us—nothing much, nothing that anyone would notice was gone..."

They looked at one another and nodded. They would go tonight as soon as it grew dark but before the order for lights out.

They slipped away so easily that Haruto kept looking behind himself to ensure that they weren't being followed. The huge ship had docked in the harbour without incident, and the officers had all made their way into the town, chattering excitedly among themselves in a quite uncharacteristic way. Haruto supposed that even officers got excited about a new experience, on the other side of the world. He was grateful that their anticipation made them careless. No one saw the five slender figures who climbed over the side of the ship away from the harbour lights and swam silently toward the quiet estuary on the far side of the harbour, carrying their small haversacks high upon their backs.

When they reached the lagoon, they pushed their way through the thick reeds bordering its shores, disturbing nesting waterfowl and alarming frogs, who croaked and jumped off their perches with splashes that seemed to echo across the water. Terrified that the racket would attract attention, the five scrambled up the shallow banks, running crouched over into the enormous evergreen trees that surrounded the water. Haruto twisted his neck to gaze up into the darkness. He couldn't see the tops of the trees despite the glow of the lamps from the harbour. How tall were they? Their trunks were huge. It would take many, many men linking hands to encircle their circumference. Haruto had never seen trees anywhere near this size. Most trees on the Japanese coast had been cleared away many centuries ago to make way for rice paddies. The sharp and resinous scent of the giant trees surrounded them now, and the deep carpet of their needles was soft underfoot as they ran.

Once they were far enough into the forest to feel safe from any eyes looking out from the ship, they stopped and huddled at the base of one of the big trees, shivering in the warm early summer air in their wet clothing. They giggled a little, amazed that they had made their escape, but sensibly quieted and settled in to await the coming of the dawn before venturing any further into the dense woods.

Haruto didn't think he would be able to sleep, alert as he was to any signs of pursuit, but suddenly a shaft of sunlight warmed his closed eyes. He blinked, lifting his head from its cramped position on his chest and looking around. The other four were still sleeping. Hiro had toppled over sideways and lay with his arms wrapped defensively around himself. Kai leaned against the tree trunk beside Haruto, his cheek scored by its deep furrows, and Tamio leaned against the other side of the same trunk. Masao was flat on his back, his long thin arms outflung in an attitude of total relaxation. Haruto shook his head, marveling at his friend's ability to ignore their danger. If they were caught, they'd be flogged and probably sent home in disgrace and without their wages.

He shrugged his shoulders, trying to loosen the stiff muscles, and struggled to his feet, only to freeze in alarm. Through the palisade of towering trees, he could see a figure walking nearby. It was a single man, about their own age, carrying a simple net in one hand and a woven basket in the other. His skin was brown, and his hair was black. He wore it long, tied back by what looked like twisted twine. The fellow seemed oblivious to them as he made his way to an opening in the reeds on the shore and walked into the shallow water.

Haruto eased his way to his feet as silently as he could and stepped softly to a position from which he could watch, a few yards away from the others. Within moments, it seemed, the young man had scooped up a netful after netful of small silver fish and popped them, still wriggling, into the basket. Next, he bent and dug into the mud, coming up with large clams that he added to his basket. As he stepped out of the water, he paused, listening and swiveling his head, eyes narrowed, scanning the trees. Haruto winced, realizing that his companions had woken and were talking quietly. He turned to hush them, but the moment he moved, the young native saw him. They both froze, staring at one another.

After a moment that seemed to stretch to eternity, the young man spoke, but Haruto could make no sense of the words. They didn't sound threatening, and the man made no move toward him, but Haruto could only shake his head and spread his hands out, palm up, in the universal gesture for non-hostile intent.

"English?" asked the man, the word heavily accented. Again, Haruto shook his head. He knew the word—it was the name of the language spoken by the foreigners who had come to his country. But that was just about all he knew. The man frowned but after a moment, he gestured to the fish in his basket and mimed eating. "Hungry?" he asked. This Haruto understood. He nodded but made no move. The man smiled and beckoned him. "Come," he said. "Enough for you." But Haruto gestured in turn, indicating the four others who had now stepped up to join him, wide-eyed and silent. He looked back and raised his eyebrows—enough for all?

The brown-skinned young man laughed. "Yes," he said and beckoned again. "All come."

Haruto looked at his friends. "He seems friendly enough," he said. "And I am hungry, aren't you?" Hiro shook his head, stepping back and looking ready to run, but Kai, Tamio, and Masao nodded.

"We can always run if we have to," said Kai. "But he does seem friendly, and I am hungry too."

The five of them gathered up their belongings, meagre as they were, brushed off the needles and forest debris clinging to their still-damp clothes, and walked warily up to the young man, who turned and walked off through the trees. With an anxious glance at each other, the Japanese followed.

Their guide walked for only about five minutes and then broke out of the forest into a clearing. Haruto was astonished to see a whole community of people. Large rectangular buildings of wooden planks were arranged in the clearing and dozens of people milled around and among them. He saw men, women, youth, and children dressed simply in skins and garments that appeared to have been woven of reeds or bark or—in the case of the smallest children—completely naked. Wide brimmed woven hats of a conical design sat on many heads, shading the high-cheekbones and wide mouths of the wearers from the bright sun now rising above the morning mists. Strings of fish propped up on arrangements of sticks smoked over low burning fires, while others were drying in the sun on flat rocks, guarded from the inquisitive crows by groups of shouting children.

Over one fire, tended by an old woman, a tightly woven basket was suspended. As Haruto watched, the woman maneuvered some hot stones out of the fire with several sticks, then scooped them deftly into the basket, which sent off an aromatic steam that set Haruto's mouth to watering. Their guide beckoned them again, and squatted down beside the old woman, adding the clams he had gathered to her steaming basket, and setting the basket of fish down beside her. He stood, turned to the Japanese, and gestured broadly at the settlement. Then he tapped his own chest,

"Lkungen," he said, again sweeping his arm to indicate the whole group of people. Haruto nodded, understanding that this was the name of the people living here. He tapped his own chest and gestured at his companions.

"Japanese," he said carefully in English. It was one of the very few words he knew in that language. His own people called themselves Nihonjin, the people of the rising sun. Then he touched each of his companions' arms and said their names, ending with himself. "Hiro, Kai, Masao, Tamio, Haruto." Their guide nodded and smiled, then tapped his own chest.

"David," he said. Haruto's face expressed his surprise at this obviously English name. The guide shrugged, unable to explain that in the past forty years, his people had come under the influence of the Oblate missionaries, who had converted them all to Catholicism and given them Christian names. David also couldn't explain that their community, once over a thousand, had been diminished by smallpox and other diseases to just over two hundred. What the Japanese youths were seeing in this clearing was all that remained of his people. To the English, they were known as the Songhees, as close as the newcomers could come to pronouncing Stsangés. This was really the name of only the group of Lkungen who had made first contact with the British when Fort Camosun was built by the Hudson's Bay Company in 1843, but his people had given up trying to explain the intricacies of kinship and caste to the foreigners, and simply accepted the name. There were too few of them now to maintain all the divisions anyway.

The formal introductions over, David gestured for them all to sit beside the fire and served them each a wooden platter of steaming clams and the little fish, which he fried quickly in strong-smelling grease in a cast iron frying pan, a much-prized trade with the English settlers. Haruto and his friends were accustomed to eating their fish raw, mixed with rice, but they were too hungry to hold back. Haruto found the texture of the fish strange: dry, oily, and flaky rather than moist and tender, but nevertheless he enjoyed it very much. Unable to express their gratitude in any other way, the young men emptied their plates, wiping them clean with the hunks of flat bread offered to them by the silent old woman, who revealed neither surprise nor curiosity about their unexpected arrival at her hearth.

When they had finished, David rose from his place and indicated that they should follow him. As they walked through the community, Haruto marveled at the many novel things surrounding him. He saw tiny babies strapped to stiff cradle boards on the mothers' backs, their soft skulls bound tightly to the boards. Haruto wondered that the little ones didn't struggle to get free, but the infants seemed utterly content, gazing around them with bright black eyes. Women and girls carried baskets brimming with berries of several types that Haruto didn't recognize.

As they approached the largest of the plank buildings, they stopped, and David gestured to the intricate carvings on the corner posts. Through gestures and words that they didn't understand, he managed to suggest that the carvings represented the gods of his people. They nodded respectfully and bowed their heads as they passed through the wide doorway. Inside it was dim, the darkness relieved only by light filtering down through holes cut for the exit of smoke from the hearths spaced regularly down the centre of the large space. In the morning's early summer warmth, the hearths were cold, their fires unlit. The walls were lined with wide shelves heaped with blankets and furs, obviously sleeping bunks, and every few yards a skin or blanket had been hung to divide the space and provide a modicum of privacy between what Haruto assumed were family groups. In a larger central space near an open door for light, several women were working at looms, weaving thick blankets that seemed to be a combination of two types of wool and the soft downy under feathers of ducks. When two woolly white dogs chased each other through the space, Haruto made the connection: one of the types of wool in the blankets was obviously from the dogs. The other looked more like sheep or goat, he thought. A few women were twisting long strands of what appeared to be tree bark into long ropes, which they then braided together in tight patterns. Others were working at separating the layers of long sheets of bark, folding and stacking the soft inner layer and shredding the outer layer into fine fibres.

Farther away from the communal houses, a group of men worked at hollowing out a huge log with adzes and flint blades. It was obviously going to be a boat, but of a type the Japanese had not seen before. One man sat sharpening the blades against a whetstone. When he slowed in his work, looking around, one of the boat builders spoke sharply to him and slapped him hard across the head. Haruto flinched. *But why should I be surprised?* he thought to himself. *Everywhere there are masters and servants. Why should it be any different here?*

The five Japanese stayed in the Lkungen community for some days, hoping that their Japanese masters would be unlikely to look for them there. Everyone made them welcome, and the children found it greatly entertaining to teach them English words for common objects, falling about laughing and kicking their legs when the Japanese struggled to copy words containing the letters 'R' and 'L'—they often confused the two. It was embarrassing, even though the elders chided the children for making fun of them. Hiro especially blushed in shame at his failures, but it was clear that they all had the same difficulty. Those two sounds simply did not exist in Japanese, though they did have a sound that was somewhere between the two, as in Hiro's and Haruto's names. Try as they might, their mouths simply could not form the English sounds correctly. They also struggled with 'B' and 'V' sounds, frequently replacing one with the other, but with practice they could make themselves understood. They all worked hard at learning the language; if they were to stay in Canada, they would need to be able to communicate. Kai showed a surprising talent for English, but shy Hiro mostly left it to his companions to speak for him. As their English grew, they eventually understood that they were not the first Japanese to come to these shores, a fact that both disappointed their hopes of being the first of their people to explore the new world and reassured them that it was possible to survive here.

David and some of the other young men also spent time teaching the Japanese to fish with scoop nets. They identified the fish in the reed beds and in the rivers, as well as drying on the racks, and soon Haruto could differentiate among the five types of salmon: coho, chum, chinook, pink, and sockeye. He learned to spear the fish using the long-shafted harpoon fitted with a bone hook, or throw out a line with a baited hook, not so different from the way he had fished at home. In gratitude, he gave David one of the precious *tamahagane* steel hooks he had filched from the ship and showed him how to prepare raw salmon for eating. The Lkungen didn't have rice, but Haruto dried some seaweed from the shore, and rolled chunks of the salmon in it, making a sort of sushi. David offered some roasted camas root to eat alongside, which the Japanese enjoyed more than the floury white potatoes that the Europeans had taught the native people to grow.

On their second day, Kai befriended a group of young women who were whipping some berries in a wooden bucket to a froth. When they offered him a taste, he almost spat it out—it tasted like soap! He thought perhaps they were teasing the foreigner but shortly afterwards a crowd of children came along and eagerly dipped their fingers into the bucket. Kai politely refused any more of what was obviously a treat for these people.

The five young men were grateful to the local people who had sheltered and befriended them but by the second week, they were getting restless. They were eager to seek their fortunes on their own.

1882
New Westminster, British Columbia, Canada

Haruto finished coiling his lines and looked out toward the open ocean, shading his eyes against the late afternoon glare off the sea. The five of them had fished here in the mouth of the mighty Fraser River for several years and had become adept at catching the salmon that were so plentiful in these waters as they migrated to sea as younglings, and again when they returned up its tributaries to spawn. David of the Lkungen people had taken them along on the newest canoe's maiden voyage and had shown the Japanese the best fishing grounds across the strait from Vancouver Island, up the mighty Fraser River to the new town of New Westminster on the Burrard Peninsula. They had stayed here ever since, making a homesite of sorts on the shore close to the forest, and selling their catch for other foods and necessities in the town. The English settlers viewed them with some suspicion but tolerated their presence and were eager to buy their fish for the salmon cannery that had been established there a dozen years before. Some of the white fishermen complained that the Japanese were unfair competition. With little power to bargain, the young men took whatever price was offered by the English settlers, which was often less than was paid to the white fishermen for their catch. It was an uneasy relationship, and Haruto had begun to push his friends to consider moving on.

Today's catch hadn't been very good, however; it was obvious that a storm was coming. Haruto could see indigo clouds boiling up on the horizon. The light on the river had become the flat gray that presaged rain, and the wind had picked up substantially in the last hour. It was time to seek shelter. As he turned to gather his nets, however, Haruto's keen eyes picked out the white of sails downriver. It was clear that the vessel was struggling in the fitful winds, and Haruto called out to his companions, pointing to the boat tossing on the rising waves.

As they watched the boat come closer, they realized that those aboard had decided to run it up the river to shelter from the full strength of the storm. Haruto admired the skill with which the sailors handled the boat, tacking toward the shore where they stood watching. When it became clear that the vessel was headed their way, the five young men strode deeper into the waves to catch hold of the lines thrown from on board, helping to guide the small vessel safely to shore.

When they were close enough to make contact, Haruto was shocked to see that the two men aboard were Japanese! These were the first of their people they had seen since jumping ship in Esquimalt two years before. Once the small fishing boat was close to the beach, the newcomers jumped out and, assisted by Haruto and his friends in wordless cooperation, they hauled the vessel out of the waves to safety on the beach just as the storm broke over their heads.

They all ran through the drenching rain toward the shelter of the trees, and Kai beckoned them to follow as he led the way further in, to the rude shelter the five of them had built. Once they had crowded into the small space, Hiro set to work to start a fire in the pot-bellied stove they had installed to cook their food and warm themselves over the cool winter months.

"Welcome!" said Masao, nodding to them. "I am Masao Sugaju, and these are Haruto Sato, Tamio Hirata, Hiro Sawamura, and Kai Kuryu."

"Thank you for your help," said the larger and older of the two men, his handsome face creased in a smile. "I am Manzo Nagano and this is my partner Uwakichi Shimamura. We were fishing off Whatcom, in Washington State, but in this storm, we were blown off course up into Canadian waters."

The men took off their wet outer clothing and sat down to share the hot tea that Hiro had quickly prepared. As they shared stories, Manzo revealed that he'd been away from Japan for five years. He'd left a British ship at New Westminster, the very port where they now sheltered, back in 1877. For a time, he'd fished in the Fraser with an Italian partner, then worked as a logger before teaming up with Uwakichi to fish for halibut off the American coast.

"We are doing well," he said, "and I am hoping to settle back in Canada soon. I'd like to open my own fish cannery, perhaps on the Island. Why should we be paid less for our catch than the white fishermen? Why not can it ourselves?"

"Would you be canning salmon?" asked Masao. At Manzo's nod, he continued. "How about salted salmon? That's one thing I really miss here in Canada. I bet you could export it to Japan—there's always a demand for it back home." Manzo smiled.

"That's an excellent thought. Perhaps I should take you on as a partner to manage my exports!" he teased. Masao didn't smile back.

"In fact, I wouldn't mind going home if I had a steady job that would support my family," he said. "We do all right here with our catch, but it's hard to make enough money to send back to Japan. Our families could use more help." Manzo sobered, then looked around at the five younger men. "Do you all feel that way?" he asked. "I'd have thought young men such as you would be eager for adventure in the new world!"

Hiro shrugged shyly. "I'd go home if I was sure to find work," he said softly. The other three shook their heads, looking at their friends in surprise.

"I didn't know you felt that way," said Haruto to Masao and Hiro.

"I want to stay in Canada, though I, too, would be glad of a chance to send more money home and make my way here—something more than a shack on the shore!" Kai and Tamio nodded in agreement.

Manzo looked at Uwakichi, who shrugged. It was clear that the older man was in charge of their partnership venture. He sipped thoughtfully at his tea.

"What if we worked together?" he asked after several moments. "We could pool our catch from the boat and from the shore and when we are established, we could look at setting up a cannery. I know just the place in Victoria..."

1893
Victoria, Vancouver Island, British Columbia

Haruto gave Tsuya Nagano her packages and bowed briefly to her with a smile. Manzo's young wife blushed, ducked her head, and scuttled out of the J.M. Nagano & Company food store. Haruto watched her go with bemusement, as always amazed at her silence. Manzo—who now called himself Jack—had returned briefly to Japan in 1886 to marry the seventeen-year-old, returning in triumph with her. Tsuya had arrived in a sumptuous silk kimono, her hair arranged high on her head, but it hadn't taken her long to adopt the Canadian women's bustled dresses and elaborate hats. Nevertheless, she didn't lose her Japanese reticence, and even after seven years of marriage, Tsuya barely spoke outside their home. Now that she was finally pregnant with their first child, Haruto barely saw her. Jack seemed satisfied with her, however, so Haruto asked no questions

Jack had made good on all their dreams. His experiences as a fisherman, a carpenter, and a logger had all been useful as he established his small cannery on the outskirts of Victoria. The products had proven popular with the small Japanese population of the city—mostly single men, homesick for the tastes of their native land and for the sound of their native tongue—and, just as Masao had suggested, also in great demand back in Japan. Masao and Hiro had returned to Hiroshima prefecture and become the Nagano company's agents there. Tamio, Kai, and Haruto had stayed in Canada and were now established in the cannery in various roles. To his own surprise, Haruto had found that he enjoyed working in the small food store Nagano had built onto the cannery. Kai had found his calling as the manager of the cannery; his easy charm made him a favourite with all the workers, and he was also the best at defusing the jealousy and disgruntlement of their white neighbours. Tamio was happy to continue fishing; he'd taken over the partnership of the fishing boat with Uwakichi, though they had both Anglicized their names to Tom and Ken. The English seemed to resent having to twist their tongues around the unfamiliar names, so the nicknames they came up with were often adopted by the men just to make things easier. Haruto was considering changing his name to Harry, but for now he was sticking with Haruto.

The door opened and Jack himself came striding in. He had a handful of letters that he waved as he came up to the counter.

"One from your mother," he said. "I'll mind the store for a few minutes—go off and read it in peace."

Haruto nodded in gratitude, taking the thin envelope with him into the back storeroom. Seating himself on a stack of enormous bags of rice, he carefully tore it open and slid out the fine paper covered in his mother's beautifully formed characters. The news from home was mostly unchanged; they suffered under the current conditions and were grateful for the money he sent on a regular basis. Toward the end of the missive, his mother included an oft-repeated refrain.

"It is past time you married," she wrote, as she had in every letter in the previous three years. But this time her comments were more pointed and Haruto read on with growing dismay. "I have been impressed by Sakura Shishido, from the Wakayama prefecture. She is the niece of our neighbour, whose sister married and moved to Wakayama to join a family of charcoal-makers. She is only sixteen, but it takes time to arrange the marriage and permits for her to emigrate, so if you are amenable, we will have a photo of her taken for you. Please have one taken of yourself and send it as soon as you are able..."

Haruto stopped reading and raised his eyes to the roof beams criss-crossing high overhead, where a few swallows twittered and preened. He gave a deep sigh. He supposed that he couldn't hold out forever. Ever since he had become established enough to send funds home regularly, his mother had been harping on this topic. Yes, it was true, he was now thirty-three years old, past the time most Japanese men married. But it wasn't as if he was old! There was plenty of time. His lips twisted wryly—not according to his mother there wasn't.

He wondered about the Shishido girl. Sakura—it meant cherry blossom. For a moment, Haruto was awash in memories of the swirls of pale pink blossoms that blew from the trees in his homeland in late spring. The village had festivals dedicated to the delicate beauty of the flowers. He wondered if this girl was as beautiful, as fragile as the bloom for which she'd been named. Sixteen seemed impossibly young but it was only a year younger than Jack's wife Tsuya had been when they married. He supposed he could go to Japan and choose his own wife, but it was such a long journey, and he was a bit surprised to realize that had no real desire to return to his homeland. When the five of them had left Japan, their plan had been to be *dekasegi*, sojourners, ones who traveled for a time, made lots of money, and then returned to take up their traditional roles. But Haruto had grown to love this new land. He loved its mountains, its forests, its teeming oceans, its opportunities. He knew that he had become truly an *issei*, an emigrant, and expected that he would stay in Canada for the rest of his life.

But he wasn't so changed as to think of marrying a non-Japanese woman—certainly not! The white women he saw here in Victoria were too big, too loud, too fair, too...everything! No, he wanted a small, quiet, dark-haired Japanese girl, a wife whom he would understand and who would understand him.

Very well, he thought as he resumed reading his letter. *I will have a photograph taken and send it to my mother. I am sure that she will choose a suitable bride for me, as generations have done before. I just hope that she chooses someone with a sense of adventure!*

Six months later, Harry—as he had finally decided to call himself—perched on another sack of rice and opened another letter. After the last one, he had obediently dressed himself in a sober suit of clothes in Western fashion, with a starched white wing-tip collared shirt and a dark tie. He'd brushed the waves of his thick hair into as neat a style as he could manage, applying a hair oil sold in the Nagano store to hold it in place above his broad forehead while the photographer fussed behind his huge camera. Harry had stood straight and stared into the lens with a serious expression. He had to convince Sakura—or, more importantly, her parents—that he was a good prospect. It wouldn't do to smile foolishly or slouch in the photo. Harry didn't think the result was too terrible, and he'd sent it off in the next post. Apparently the Shishidos agreed that he looked acceptable, for they'd allowed their daughter to send a photo and a letter in return. The small photo slipped out as Harry unfolded the thin sheets of rice paper covered in delicate handwriting. He was startled to realize that the letter was written in English!

Harry stared at the black and white image of his prospective bride's head and shoulders. Sakura was dressed in a patterned silk kimono. Her thick black hair, Harry was glad to see, was rolled back simply from her face, not teased high in a fashionable but, to his eyes, ridiculous pompadour. He was also glad that she had not powdered her face or applied the thick ceremonial make-up as some hopeful brides did. Sakura's brows were finely plucked but straight. Her mouth was firm, and Harry judged it as not too wide nor too small—just right. Her dark eyes looked calmly into the camera, neither fearful nor aggressive. Her jaw was strong but feminine; just at the edge of her kimono, Harry could see a small dark mole on her neck. Suddenly his mind conjured an image of placing his lips just there, and he was disconcerted by the rush of heat that filled him at the thought. He had waited so long to take a wife and had sometimes wondered if he ever would. He'd lived among men for so many years, seeing only Western women other than Tsuya, and he'd almost forgotten how beautiful the women of his homeland could be. This woman was no delicate cherry blossom! Sakura looked energetic, determined...and very beautiful.

Wrenching his eyes from Sakura's compelling gaze, Harry picked up the letter. He was impressed that she had been educated, had learned English well enough to write it. This was a rare skill in Japan and made her a very attractive prospect. The ability to speak, read, and write

English would serve her well if she came to Canada. Harry didn't want a wife who would be hidden away as Tsuya was; he wanted a partner who could help him achieve his ambitions. In recent months, Harry had begun to dream of moving on from Nagano's. Jack had been very good to him, and he'd learned a great deal, but Harry wanted to see what else there was in Canada for an ambitious young man—well, still youngish, anyway.

As he read her letter, he was more and more convinced that she would be an excellent choice. She listed her skills and accomplishments with modesty but no simpering. She expressed an interest in learning about Canada and making a home there, and she sounded unafraid of the challenges. By the time he reached her flowing signature, Harry had made up his mind. He would write back immediately and ask his mother to begin the long process of readying Sakura to come to Canada. They would be wed by proxy, and she would have to be entered into the official family records as a Sato for a full year before she would be permitted to emigrate to Canada. Harry pictured her moving into his family home and sitting with his mother and sisters, stitching the linens for her dowry. Now that he'd made the decision, he could scarcely wait to meet her. Folding the letter back into its envelope but placing Sakura's photograph safely in a small pocket inside his jacket, Harry stood up and went in search of writing materials.

1896-97
Galiano Island, British Columbia

Shielding his face from the heat and glare with his free hand, Harry reached out with his long rake and pulled the sticks of burnt alder from the rocky depths of the pit kiln. He arranged them onto the stone hearth and quickly covered them with ash, clay, and sand to cool, just as Sakura, who had renamed herself Sara, had taught him.

Harry sat back on his heels, poking gently at the heap of cooling charcoal, thinking about his wife of a year. He smiled to himself, re-living the day she'd arrived at the Victoria dock...

He'd recognized her instantly as she stepped off the ship, head high and elaborate kimono gleaming in the weak sunshine. She spotted him immediately and, far from holding back in modesty, she walked toward him as fast as her elevated patten shoes would allow, her eyebrows knitted and her expression stern. The minute she was close enough for him to hear, she called out to him, astonishing him with her audacity.

"Have you brought me a dress?" she demanded in English. Harry was startled into speechlessness, and simply held out the carefully folded Western-style dress, hat, parasol, and shoes he had bought as instructed in her last letter. She took them from him and shook them out for inspection. Nodding her acceptance, she looked around for a place where she could change into her new finery. Harry ushered her into the room he'd rented nearby, his head full of visions of the upcoming wedding night. Still without saying a word, he backed out and closed the door, leaving his new wife to change, and stood outside, twirling his hat in his hands.

Ten minutes later, she emerged, stunning him with her transformation. Gone was the Japanese maiden who had stepped off the ship. She had donned the bustled dress and re-arranged her hair to accommodate the large hat he'd provided. On her small feet were dainty boots laced to the ankle. She twirled the lacy parasol over her shoulder and her face was illuminated by a warm smile.

"Hello Harry," she said softly. "Thank you for the clothes. Now I am hungry. Is there somewhere we can go to eat?"

That first exchange was to set the pattern of their marriage. Sakura had told him she'd decided that her English name was to be Sara, and from that moment he had never referred to her as anything else. If her demands were met, Sara was a model of sweetness. The minute he crossed her, however, she would glower ferociously and pelt him with angry words until he retreated in dismay. She was utterly committed to becoming as Canadian as possible, and insisted that they speak only in English, even to each other.

"It is the only way that we will succeed here," she said. "If we are too different, the *hakujin* will find us threatening." *Hakujin*—meaning whites—was one of the few Japanese words she still used. She also frequently quoted the Japanese aphorism *deru kugi wa utareru,* meaning 'the nail that sticks up gets hit,' to justify her determination to blend into white society as much as possible.

Harry was bemused by the strength of her opinions and the energy of her movements. Sometimes he would simply sit and watch her as she whirled from task to task. He was hugely impressed by her education, her intelligence, and her clear focus, and he was not inclined to contradict her. Even if he had been, the warmth of his memories of what Sara provided in the privacy of their room at night would have kept his mouth shut. He had no wish to anger his new wife into denying him the considerable pleasures of her bed.

When Jack Nagano met Sara, he quizzed her on her knowledge of the charcoal burning her family was famous for in her Wakayama home. The high heat generated by well-burned charcoal was ideal for soldering shut the cans of fish at the cannery, and Jack was always seeking out new sources of it. Sara put her nose in the air and informed Jack that her father was the acknowledged expert on a process that was almost five thousand years old and that she, Sara, also knew all there was to know about it. Jack just laughed at her haughtiness and immediately asked Harry to set up a charcoal burning operation on a piece of property that he'd recently purchased. The land was on nearby Galiano Island, where there were ample supplies of the required rock, sand, and clay as well as numerous alder trees for raw material.

So here he was, living on an island in a hastily built one-room home and making as much charcoal as he could by carefully following Sara's instructions. She had told him to burn the sticks until their ends were as shiny as mirrors, and to wait until a tapped piece rang like struck metal before raking the heap out of the kiln.

Harry knew how valuable the results of his labour were. Properly prepared charcoal was integral to Japanese life and was thus highly valued. Its purity meant that it burned without steam, lending a crisp skin and juicy texture to meat cooked over it on a *hibachi*—a small barbecue. Bags of it were laid in the foundation of houses in Japan to regulate humidity and prevent rot. Its moisture regulating properties also made it useful for plant growth when mixed with the soil, boosting the yields of water-heavy plants such as lettuce and cabbage. It was added to rice while it cooked, to make it fluffier, and even incorporated into soaps and toothpastes for its purifying qualities. It was most famous, however, for the role it played in the forging of Japan's famous samurai swords and armour. A highly protected secret method using iron sand and charcoal was necessary to achieve the high temperatures required to forge this jewel steel, this *tamahagane*. Repeated layering and folding steps shaped the resulting metal, ensuring its strength and beauty.

The process required many tonnes of the very best and purest charcoal and the making of it was a sacred art. Sara's family was revered for their knowledge and skill, and her pride was well earned. She had boasted to Harry that her family could trace their lineage back to the thirteenth century, when they had provided eight hundred tonnes of charcoal for the casting of the massive bronze statue of the Kamakura Daibutsu Buddha. The image of the god towered almost forty-four feet high and had taken over two years to complete. Harry was impressed, wishing he had been able to travel to the Kanagawa Prefecture to see the famous statue while he was still in Japan. He sighed a little, holding out his hand to test the temperature of the heap of cooling charcoal. It was unlikely that he'd ever see it now. His future was here, in the New World.

He didn't mind making charcoal. It was always interesting to learn a new trade and he had never shirked hard physical work, but it was a little lonely working away in solitary concentration day after day. Sara helped harvest the alder saplings and sewed the coarse burlap into sacks for the charcoal, but otherwise she was occupied in growing vegetables, milking their cow, and feeding their few chickens, preparing the meals, and sewing the many household linens and clothes they needed. He'd noticed that she was also sewing a baby layette and hemming many cloth diapers, but so far there was no sign that she carried a child. Harry was too shy about women's matters to inquire. He assumed she'd tell him when there was something to tell.

When Jack Nagano came to pick up the bags of charcoal later that week, he was accompanied by a boy of about ten years. The lad leaped off the boat and helped to drag it up onto the stony beach and then began unloading stacks of empty charcoal bags, all seemingly without any direction from Jack. Harry raised his eyebrows, indicating the boy with his chin as Jack came within earshot. Jack grinned and spread out his hands, palms up.

"I brought him for you," he said, and Harry's eyebrows climbed higher. "He's sort of an orphan, came from Japan last year with an older brother. The brother died in an accident at sea, and Jiro Suzuki here can't go back to Japan on his own. He's too young to make it on his own here, as well, but he's a hard worker and reliable. Thought you could use a little help, maybe."

Harry frowned, watching the boy struggle with the heavy bags. He wasn't sure how much help the slender child was going to be, and his expression must have shown his skepticism, for Jack leaned in and spoke more quietly in his ear. "To tell the truth, the boy needs someone. Since my Tsuya died, well, I've had my hands full with the baby, you know, but I couldn't just abandon the lad. You'd be doing me a favour, Harry, and—look—maybe I can raise the price I pay for each bag of charcoal a bit, to help cover the costs of keeping him..."

Harry tilted his head, watching the boy. He felt sorry for Jack. He and Tsuya had tried for so long to have a child together, and then Tsuya had died of a milk fever soon after their infant son, George Tatsuo, had been born. Harry knew that Jack was planning to find a new wife next time he traveled to Japan, and that he wasn't in a position to take on another child. It would be nice to have some help with the charcoal burning and to have a little company during the long days. He wondered what Sara would say, though.

"Let's go have some tea," he said, and Jack's grin widened. He knew who needed to be convinced.

Jiro seemed to understand that he was on trial. He bowed politely to Sara, who stared at him suspiciously as he entered their simple home. Then he sat down quietly in a corner and listened respectfully to the adults' talk. Harry could see Sara's eyes straying to him every few moments, and the slight frown that creased her forehead as she took in his thin frame and sad eyes. When she suddenly rose and cut a thick slice of milk bread, and even added some of their treasured wild strawberry jam to it, Harry knew that he didn't need to say a word to persuade her that the boy needed mothering. When she held the tempting snack out to Jiro, the boy's eyes widened, and his mouth gaped.

"For me, mistress?" he asked in a whisper. At her nod, he reached out for it and crammed it into his mouth, his eyes closing in bliss at the sweet treat. Sara's tongue clicked, and she turned to Jack.

"Whose child is this?" she demanded. "Why are they not feeding him properly?"

With a serious expression, Jack launched into Jiro's sad tale, emphasizing the poor child's aloneness and grief over losing his brother, his only family here in Canada.

"I have been doing what I can, Sara-san, but you know, I am only a man..."

Sara gazed at Jiro as he continued chewing his bread and the men wisely stayed silent. Suddenly she turned to Harry with a determined expression.

"He can stay here and help you with the charcoal," she said. Harry shook his head.

"Sara, it is too much to ask you to take on another's child. You have enough to do, looking after me and our house..." He allowed his voice to trail off as he gestured around the house, indicating all the things his wife had to do. Sara flapped her hand, dismissing his concerns.

"He needs a mother," she said, and that was that. Harry avoided looking at Jack, knowing that he would break into a smile if he did.

Jiro proved more helpful than his small frame suggested, and Harry soon came to rely on the boy for the myriad small tasks involved in charcoal making. He was even tempered, if a touch serious, which Harry attributed to the loss of his brother. As the months went by and the boy's skinny ribs were covered by a layer of plump flesh, Harry made it his mission to make the child smile. In the quiet evenings, he would carve small wooden toys for him from chunks of the ruddy arbutus trees that grew all over the island: horses and dragons and soldiers in elaborate samurai armour, all for the pleasure of seeing Jiro's solemn face light up with happiness. The child treasured these small gifts and each night he tucked them carefully into the lidded box Harry had made for him.

Sara treated Jiro carelessly, seldom revealing how fond she was of him, but her affection was betrayed by how often she would bake an extra cake or heap the child's plate with his favourite rice dish. For his part, Jiro worshipped Sara, following her with his eyes as she moved about the kitchen and jumping to help whenever she beckoned.

As a result, it was Jiro who first noticed Sara's thickening waistline. He became morose, his smiles gone, not even playing with his treasured toys in the evenings before the fire. Harry tried to cheer him up with a newly carved captain of the guards. He was disappointed when Jiro thanked him respectfully and set the new toy in his box, shutting the lid.

When they were out at the charcoal kiln the next morning, Harry asked him directly about his sadness.

"Are you missing your brother, then, Jiro? Or are you sick? What ails you?"

Jiro looked at him with dolorous eyes and Harry was appalled to see big tears rolling down the boy's sallow cheeks.

"I am sad, Harry-san, because soon I will have to leave here and go back to sea, or to the cannery."

"But why would you have to do that?" Harry asked, frowning. The thought was surprisingly upsetting. He had grown very fond of the lad. Jiro hung his head and Harry had to lean close to hear his miserable whisper.

"Soon Sara-san will have her own boy and she will not want me anymore."

"What?" exclaimed Harry, rearing back in shock. "Her own boy? What do you mean?"

"Or little daughter," said Jiro, nodding sadly and wiping his wet cheeks with the back of a grimy hand.

"Sara is with child?" Harry said wonderingly, oblivious for the moment to the boy's misery in his contemplation of a child of his own. Then he looked again at Jiro and rushed to comfort him. "But why do you assume that you must go when the baby comes? Jiro, you are our boy now, you will be a big brother to the coming child. You cannot go away!"

Jiro's small head came up and he looked deeply into his foster-father's face. "You will not send me back to Mr. Nagano?" he asked tentatively. "I may stay here?"

"Of course!" said Harry heartily, throwing an arm around Jiro's still-thin shoulders and pulling him close. But even as he did so, he had a guilty pang—would Sara agree? *She must*, he told himself. *I am the man of the house. I will make the decision. Perhaps if I say I will build her a new room on the house, for Jiro—or perhaps a nursery for the baby. A baby!* he thought again, caught up in the wonder of it.

In the end, he need not have worried. Sara confirmed her pregnancy and they celebrated together. Confronted with Harry's determination to keep Jiro in their household, Sara merely nodded as if it was obvious. Harry found his shoulders sagging in relief and he rushed to offer to extend the house nevertheless, a plan that brought a sweet smile to his wife's face. Jiro's joy at this evidence of their affection was a wonder to behold. He wept when they said he should change his name to Jiro Sato, to formally be their adopted son. He fairly glowed with happiness and rushed to assist both Harry and Sara with every small task he could find. He even put on a growth spurt, stretching up until he reached Sara's shoulder. Harry watched the two of them happily, well-satisfied with his little family.

The rains of winter were in full spate when Sara's time came. Despite her calm demeanour, Harry had fretted and worried for weeks. A few families from Sara's own home prefecture of Wakayama had established a fish salting operation at the north end of the island, almost seventeen miles away. But at their end of the island, at the foot of Mount Galiano, there were no other women, let alone a midwife.

"I will be fine," said Sara confidently. "It is a natural process, after all. If a dog can whelp by herself, surely I can manage it." Harry wanted to believe her, but he eyed her growing belly with unease.

At first, the pains were gentle, and Sara smiled through them. But as the hours went by and the baby did not come, she grew less sanguine, and Harry's anxiety intensified. Jiro stuck close, watching Sara with enormous, fear-filled eyes as she rolled back and forth across their thin mattress in pain.

Suddenly Sara let loose a wild screech of anguish, rearing up to rock on her knees, the sweat pouring from her face. Harry looked at Jiro and saw his own panic reflected in the boy's face.

"I must get help," Harry said, making to stand up from his crouch, but Sara reached out to grip his hand, moaning.

"No, no, don't leave me!" she panted. Harry looked at Jiro in desperation, and the child leaped to his feet.

"I will go!" he declared. "I will find a woman at the saltery and bring her back to help Sara-san." Harry was torn: he didn't want to leave Sara with only the boy to help if the child came, but how could he send this lad out into the wild night, to run through the woods for miles in the dark? He thrust his hands into his thick hair, leaving in standing up in wild disarray, squeezing his eyes shut in indecision. No good answer came to him.

He opened his eyes and looked again at his wife, curled up in misery on the floor. Finally, he turned to Jiro, who was poised by the door. "Go!" he said, wondering as he did so what terrible outcome might come of his decision. At his word, the boy thrust his feet into his shoes, grabbed his thin jacket, and ran out into the pelting rain.

The minutes seemed endless to Harry, who watched in horror as Sara writhed and howled. Nothing he did seemed to help, and he was reduced to sitting near her, crooning helplessly. It would take many hours for Jiro to reach the saltery and return with a woman in tow, but it was their only hope. He was startled, then, when the door opened not two hours after the boy's departure.

The lad's drenched form appeared, followed by the close-wrapped figure of an old woman, but not a Japanese woman. It was a member of the Penalakut, a native Coast Salish group that used the island mostly as a summer fishing camp. Few of them stayed through the winters, so Harry could only think it a miracle that the boy had somehow stumbled across their camp at this time of year, and even more that he had somehow made them understand the need for help.

"She says she will help!" gasped Jiro, gesturing to the woman, who came in wordlessly and proceeded to take off her layered wraps and wide-brimmed woven hat. She turned to Jiro and Harry and gestured for them to leave the house.

"No men!" she said in heavily accented English. "Bad luck!" Harry hesitated, reluctant to leave Sara with this stranger, but the old woman herded them both toward the door. "Go!" she said, and the two of them fled into the rain.

They huddled under the wide eaves of the house, teeth chattering, heads down, flinching at the screams they heard from inside. It seemed an age before the door opened a crack and the old woman's face appeared, her solemn expression unchanged. She beckoned them inside and stood silently against the wall.

One look at Sara's face told the tragic story. Tears poured down her cheeks and her eyes were clenched shut. In her lap lay a child, but its skin was grey and its limbs unmoving. Harry dropped to his knees beside her and reached out to touch the flaccid flesh.

"No," he whispered, "no..."

Beside him, Jiro whimpered and hid his head in Sara's sodden skirts.

"Wrong way," said the old woman. "Too long coming. I turn, but too late."

"I don't understand," said Harry, and Sara opened dark eyes filled with pain.

"The baby was positioned the wrong way in my womb, bottom down instead of head," she grated. "That's why he wouldn't come out. She," here she jutted her chin at the old native woman, "turned him around but it was too late. He was dead when he came out." She looked at Harry and fresh tears spilled from her eyes. "I'm so sorry, Haruto. I was arrogant. I thought I could do it all by myself." She hung her head. "I was wrong."

Harry's heart broke to see his confident wife so defeated and was startled by her use of his Japanese name. "No, no, it is not your fault," he said, stroking her sweat-dampened hair. "Perhaps he would have died no matter what you did, even if we had arranged for help." Sara just shook her head sadly, letting her lank hair fall forward to cover her face.

"If I not turn, both die," said the Penalakut woman harshly, but then her tone gentled. "What name?" she asked. "Must name before burial."

"Sara?" asked Harry, but she just shook her head again. He thought for a few moments. "How about Umichiro? The words for the sea and first son? He will rest here forever, far across the sea from our homeland. But he will always be our first son." She gave a choked sound but nodded. Harry reached out and gently took their dead son from her arms, marveling at how something so near weightless could carry such a heavy weight of misery. He gazed into the tiny face, so perfect, so still, and brushed his fingertips over the wet slick of hair that straggled across the infant's pale scalp. He bent to place a gentle kiss on the cool forehead, and then wrapped the blanket around the tiny form. Stifling his grief, he went out into the cold winter rain to bury his firstborn child.

1908
Haney, British Columbia

Harry stood up from his hoeing and stretched to ease his aching back. He lifted his wide-brimmed hat and wiped the sweat from his forehead. Looking down the row of leafy green strawberry plants, he smiled to see his eight-year-old daughter Asami valiantly poking at the moist spring soil with her cut-down hoe, unobtrusively watched by Jiro, who hoed much more productively nearby. The child was such a blessing. After Umichiro's still birth, Sara had tried again and again to carry a child but lost each one months before term. The series of miscarriages had disheartened them both and Harry had been alarmed to see his formerly vibrant young wife slipping into despondency.

One day as they were cutting alder saplings to burn as charcoal, Jiro—by then a tall adolescent of thirteen-- had suddenly stopped work and spoken emphatically to his foster-father.

"We must move to where there are other women," he'd blurted out, seemingly without context. Harry had blinked at him in incomprehension. Was the boy already looking for a wife? Jiro's expression showed his impatience with Harry's slowness.

"For Sara-san. She needs to be with other women who can advise her, support her, help her to have a baby." Harry had nodded. Now that the thought was voiced, it seemed obvious. Why hadn't he thought of it earlier?

"Yes," he'd said approvingly. "I think you are right, Jiro. I will discuss the idea with Sara. Perhaps we could move to the saltery at the other end of the island. I'm sure I could set up another kiln there…" But Jiro had shaken his head.

"No, no, we should move away from the island, go to the mainland where there are more people. She needs company, more things to do."

"But…what would we do? How would we make a living? Mr. Nagano relies on our charcoal," Harry had protested. Jiro had obviously been thinking about this for some time.

"Someone else could come and take over the kiln. We could teach them how to make the charcoal. We could go back to the Fraser River, maybe buy a boat and fish, or maybe farm. When I first landed, I saw white men clearing the land and planting vegetables. The soil looked rich and good for growing." His young face was intent. "Back in Japan, my family grew strawberries. I don't remember very much, but I'm sure I could learn…" Harry had smiled at his earnestness and clapped a hand on the boy's shoulder.

"We will consider it. I will talk to Jack and see what he says."

Sara had brightened so dramatically at the idea that Harry knew he needed to make the move for his wife's sake. They agreed that farming would be better than fishing; Sara hated the idea of Harry and Jiro being away at sea for weeks at a time. At first, Jack Nagano was a little put out at the idea of having to replace him, but when Harry and Jiro had agreed to train someone new before moving away from the kilns, he had reluctantly agreed to the plan.

"Now Harry," he'd said, pointing at the younger man, "don't let those *hakujin* talk you into leasing the land. They'll say it's free for seven years, but what they won't tell you is that unless you can clear it all and build a house within that time, you'll lose everything you've done—the land goes back to them, and they sell it to someone else as nearly cleared. In the end you'll have given them free labour for seven years and have nothing to show for it! The acres they'll sell to a Japanese are the worst ones, the ones filled with giant stumps and swampy places. It takes years and years to clear, backbreaking work, no time to do anything else! No, what you need to do is this: put down a deposit, take out a mortgage on the land—the interest rate is about 6% just now—and pay it off as quickly as you can. It seems harder, but you'll own it outright. You can clear it slowly, plant it up as you go along and start making a return right away."

Harry's face had showed his dismay. "I do not have enough savings to pay a deposit on the land," he'd said quietly. Nagano had smiled.

"I will loan it to you. You can pay me back once you are settled and making a return on your produce." Harry had hated to take the money from Jack, but this was the Japanese way: everyone helped each other so that everyone survived. He had nodded and the two had shaken hands.

Jack had introduced Harry to Jiro Inouye—a recent immigrant and another second son, as his name revealed—from Saga village. Mr. Inouye was a graduate of the Law Department of Waseda University, an educated and clever man who felt that the key to success in Canada was to integrate, to become, as he said, *kusa wake*, those who part the grass, blaze the trail, for the ones who will follow. He had bought twenty acres of land in Haney, about thirty miles upstream from the mouth of the Fraser River, not too far from where Harry and his friends had fished when they first arrived in Canada, and he wanted to clear it to plant strawberries. Haney was on the high side of the river, had deep fertile soil, and a wonderful view of Mount Baker across the border in Washington State--so much like Mount Fuji back in Japan. Mr. Inouye had agreed to sell a few of his acres to Harry for a good price if they could agree to work together to clear all the acreage. In the end Harry had been able to purchase five acres, and after two years all of it had been planted to strawberries.

It had indeed been hard work, as Jack had warned, and Sara had laboured right alongside Harry and Jiro. But there were other Japanese families living nearby, and the company of women seemed to be a balm to her troubled soul. She still bore the emotional scars of her lost babies and dashed hopes, but Harry accepted these. He even admired them as evidence of her resilience and strength. To him, the sorrow that lurked in her eyes, the body that was no longer as lithe and responsive as when he'd wedded her—these were like the veins of gold that showed where a broken porcelain vase had been lovingly repaired in the art of *kintsugi*. The Japanese revered the results of wear, even breakage, as part of the eternal process and beauty of life. Sara's signs of age and loss were something to be cherished, not hidden.

When she again fell pregnant, they hardly dared to believe that this time she would bring the baby to term. Harry had insisted that she be under the care of a midwife from the start, that she rested and ate good food. As her time approached, Sara had stayed in their small cedar slab house, reclining on the straw-stuffed mattress, and trying not to fret. The neighbouring women had cared for her, bringing food to their door each day.

When their daughter was born in January of 1900, Sara was attended by the midwife, and all their hopes were fulfilled when the rosy-cheeked infant slid into the world, bawling lustily, just as the sun rose. They decided to call her Asami, Japanese for 'morning beauty.' Harry had expected Sara to choose an English name, but his exhausted wife had shaken her head.

"I have learned, Harry, that I need to honour and respect my Japanese heritage. I was arrogant, believing I could leave all that behind and reinvent myself. I know now that I need the help of my people. Yes, we must learn to be Canadian, as Asami is and always will be, but we must not forget our Japanese ancestry either. She will be called Asami, always, to remind me."

The child had become the light of their lives, with a sunny, happy personality and robust good health. Jiro had taken his role as honorary big brother very seriously, appointing himself as Asami's protector and constant companion.

That brotherly devotion had been useful last year, when the family had traveled to the growing city of Vancouver to meet the ship carrying some cousins of Sara's from Japan. As Harry stood watching his daughter and adopted son toil among the rows of strawberries, he remembered the frightening incident...

In the years since Harry had moved his family back to the Fraser

River delta, the influx of Japanese to Canada had increased. He had heard that there were now about eight thousand Japanese in British Columbia, and the *hakujin* were pushing back against the rising number of Asians, both Japanese and Chinese. Economic conditions were tightening, and the success of the Japanese fishermen was seen as 'unfair competition' by many of the white and Indian fishermen on the Pacific Coast in both Canada and the United States. Some activists cited the case of Australia, who had put into place an Immigration Restriction Act in 1901 in support of a 'white Australia' policy that was gaining favour there. The activists wanted Canada to put a similar law in place.

On September 5th, 1907, an anti-Asian riot broke out in Bellingham, Washington, just to the south, and the incident was widely reported in Vancouver's many newspapers, both English and Asian. Unbeknownst to Harry, the ship carrying Sara's cousins to Vancouver was only one among several arriving from China, Japan, and India that week. Tempers were running, stoked by a newly formed Asiatic Exclusion League. Rumours were circulating about a planned attack on the Asian neighbourhoods of Vancouver, but Harry dismissed them as just that—rumours.

On September 7th, the Satos were staying with Harry's old friend Kai and his family in what was known as 'Little Yokohama,' awaiting the arrival of the steamer *Monteagle* the next day with their Japanese kin. Kai had moved to the city the previous year to manage a new restaurant that the ever-entrepreneurial Jack Nagano had opened. It was a sultry day, unusual for September in British Columbia, and they had spent much of it enjoying food and drink on a balcony overlooking the narrow street. As evening came on, a cooling sea breeze picked up, carrying the sounds of many people gathering not far away. According to an English-language newspaper someone brought in, the Exclusion League had organized a public meeting and a parade, complete with a marching band.

At first, they could hear little, just an occasional cheer or the unintelligible rise and fall of an impassioned speech, but suddenly there were many people in the streets in nearby Chinatown, the sound of smashing glass, and running feet. Harry realized that there was a real threat, and he insisted that everyone go indoors. He and Kai ordered the women and children to stay in the apartment while they went out to investigate. Jiro pleaded to go with them, but Harry ordered him to stay behind. The twenty-one-year-old was fiercely devoted to Sara and Asami, and Harry trusted him to protect them, if necessary, despite his still-slight build. The young man frowned but nodded his agreement.

As Harry and Kai reached the street, they saw a knot of angry men carrying a flaming effigy. As it came nearer, they saw that it was of the Lieutenant Governor James Dunsmuir, who had tried to uphold the right of Asiatics to enter Canada. It was clear that the mob was out of control and that they had wreaked considerable damage on the shops of Chinatown. Harry and Kai joined a group of Japanese men who had gathered in the street, gesticulating excitedly and speaking over one another.

"We must defend our homes, our families," shouted a tall man whom Harry recognized as the owner of several businesses nearby. Most in the group nodded tensely in agreement. "Gather what weapons you can and come back here—quickly, before they reach us!"

Within minutes, they had reconvened, carrying bottles, clubs, and boards hastily torn from fences. One young man held a wicked-looking knife, and an unusually burly fellow, who apparently worked as a bodyguard to a local big-time gambler, had an ancient samurai sword.

"We must not let them get into Japantown," said the one with the knife. "We are not cowards like the Chinese—see, they have hidden behind their doors, and look what these *keto*, these whiteys, have done to their homes, their businesses! We must chase them out!" Heads nodded and fists were raised, but the elders shouted anxiously, "Don't kill anyone! It will make it worse for us!" The younger men ignored their pleas, shifting restlessly and shaking their weapons angrily.

At that moment, a front runner from the angry mob appeared at the top of the street, shouting. "Down with Japs! Japs go home! British Columbia belongs to the British!" Within seconds, it seemed to Harry, this lone rioter was joined by a screaming knot of others. The intruders ran straight at the small group of Japanese, thinking them defenceless.

But they were not defenceless. Led by the samurai-wielding bodyguard, the men charged towards the mob, screaming "*Tennōheika Banzai*! Long life to the emperor!" Startled by this unexpected show of force, the rioters hesitated. Seeing that the Japanese held weapons and were clearly prepared to use them to defend their territory, the insurgents turned tail and ran back the way they had come, entangling with those who had rushed up behind them. Emboldened by this reaction, the Japanese men continued their charge, and soon the rioters were the ones being chased in disarray, back through the ruined streets of Chinatown, back out of the Asian district altogether.

Once they had run off the intruders, the Japanese retreated to their own district, but for the rest of the evening they patrolled the streets, running off a few rioters who thought to sneak back and destroy property under cover of darkness. When Harry and Kai returned to Kai's family apartment around midnight, the women were full of praise for Jiro, who had thrust a broom at a would-be invader who had tried to come up the stairs, chasing him off. It was some hours before they felt secure enough to retire, and even then, Harry's sleep was disturbed; he was repeatedly startled awake by unfamiliar sounds and lay listening tensely for any signs of further intrusion.

The following day, they learned that the Chinese of Vancouver had gone on strike in retaliation for the damage done to their homes and shops. This caused considerable hardship to the white community, as many of them employed Chinese cooks, laundry staff, and nursemaids in their homes and businesses. When the steamers *Cassiar* and *Comox* berthed, all the Chinese staff walked off, leaving the ships unable to resume their routes.

The Japanese stayed on the job even after they discovered that one of their Japanese language schools had been burned to the ground sometime during the night. They were somewhat mollified by the news, published in the *Province* newspaper, that Prime Minister Sir Wilfred Laurier had sent a telegram to Vancouver's Mayor that read, "His Excellency the Governor General has learned with deepest regret the indignities and cruelties to which certain subjects of the Emperor of Japan, a friend and ally of His Majesty the King, have been victims and he hopes that peace will be promptly restored and all offenders punished." Kai smirked when he read it aloud.

"Ha!" he said, slapping the newspaper, "the Governor General knows that his country relies on the trade agreements they have with Japan! He cannot afford to anger the emperor by mistreating his subjects here in Canada!"

It had taken six days for the Chinese to go back to their jobs, Harry remembered. Kai had told him that several weeks later a government man named William Lyon Mackenzie King, the Deputy Minister of Labour, had come around tallying the cost of the damages inflicted on the properties in Japantown. Kai seemed hopeful that those whose homes or stores had suffered in the riot would eventually receive some compensation. But the atmosphere in the city had remained tense for months.

In response to Mackenzie King's reports, Prime Minister Laurier had sent the Canadian Minister of Labour Rodolphe Lemieux to Japan to negotiate an agreement with the Japanese Foreign Minister, Tadasu Hayashi, to restrict Japanese immigration to Canada. Under the terms of the 'gentlemen's agreement' that they had agreed to, the Japanese government voluntarily limited the number of Japanese emigrants traveling to Canada. The agreement restricted the emigrants to no more than four hundred per year, and only women married to those already established in Canada could come.

This news had dismayed the many Japanese bachelors, who had been struggling for years to save enough money to go to Japan to select a bride. To circumvent the new limit—and out of fear that if they returned to Japan, they'd be conscripted into the military there-- more and more men had chosen wives based on an exchange of photos, as Harry had done, and scores of new 'picture brides' began to arrive. Their arrival had 'civilized' the sometimes-rough culture of the Japanese settlements, reducing the amount of drinking and gambling, and producing baby after baby to swell their ranks.

Now Harry replaced his hat and gazed out over the broad strawberry fields, nodding with satisfaction. The rows stretched away from him, filled with healthy green foliage tended by over a dozen men, women, and children. Haney had grown, and the small Japanese community had collaborated to ensure that they all succeeded. Their strawberries were much admired and sought after in the markets and grocery stores of Vancouver. In the winter seasons, the men laboured at local logging or shingle bolt camps, worked at the canneries, or continued to clear their acreages. Things were improving, and Harry was optimistic for the future, even though Sara had not had any further children after Asami's birth.

As his little girl ran toward him, holding out an enormous double strawberry, he smiled. How could a man complain when he was so blessed?

When Harry and Jiro arrived home as the spring sun tilted towards the western horizon, they found Sara standing outside, chatting enthusiastically to a Japanese man Harry had never met. Asami, whom he'd sent home to her mother hours ago, swung on Sara's hand, bored by all the adult talk. Harry leaned his hoe against the doorframe and wiped his calloused hands clean on a large handkerchief pulled from the pocket of his trousers.

"Welcome, I am Harry Sato," he said, and reached out his hand to the prematurely balding young man with the shaggy eyebrows.

"Yamaga Yasutaro," said the man, bowing respectfully as he shook Harry's hand in the Western fashion. "I have come to Canada on the advice of Mr. Inouye. I read his articles in the newspapers in Japan and was persuaded to come to seek my fortune."

Harry laughed and shook his head. "Well, if you figure out how to make a fortune here, do be sure to let me know!" he chuckled. "The work is hard, Mr. Yasutaro, and the profits are slim. But come, let us go inside and have a glass of sake. You can tell me all your plans."

As Sara prepared their simple evening meal in the simple one-room dwelling that housed the family, Yamaga spun out his dreams of one day owning thousands of acres of golden wheat on Canada's prairies.

"But Mr. Inouye suggested that I begin by growing strawberries and other fruit here in the Fraser Valley. He also gave me your name, as someone who could give me an idea of how to get started."

Harry gave the younger man the same advice Jack Nagano had given him about buying rather than leasing land. He explained how newcomers cleared the land in the winter months, working at shingle bolt camps or other general labour in the summer until they'd cleared enough land to plant out. Yamaga nodded, listening closely.

"When you fell the trees, buck the lumber into three-foot shakes and cover your walls and roof with them," continued Harry, explaining how to build a rough shelter and gesturing to his own as he explained. "Use the long straight poles for the studs and rafters. It gets cold here in winter, so make the walls double, with a layer of paper in between to keep out the drafts, you see?"

"But how do you clear the stumps of the large trees out of the fields?" Yamaga asked. "I have never seen trees so large. It must take a large blast to clear them!"

"Most of us cannot afford the stumping powder to blow them out of the ground," explained Harry, "so we dig as far as we can go underneath the roots with mattocks, then light a fire in the hole and keep it going until the stump is hollow and can be pulled down."

Yamaga's expression was skeptical, and Harry grinned. "Yes, it takes a long time—sometimes weeks—and you have to keep that fire going. As I said, it is hard work." He drained his cup of homemade sake and offered to refill the younger man's cup. "Yes, hard, hard work—but there is opportunity here, too. More than back in Japan."

"That is what Inouye-san said to me," Yamaga said, accepting the drink with a nod. "He said that we must be pioneers, who make the way for others."

Harry nodded and raised his glass. "Welcome to the ranks of the *kusa wake*, Mr. Yasutaro."

1914
Haney, British Columbia

It took four years of grinding labour before Yamaga was able to save enough to purchase ten acres not far from the Sato farm. He was determined to have a thriving farm before sending for a picture bride from Japan, but it took much longer than he expected. Over the years he learned much from his neighbours and became close friends with the family.

He was moaning about the delay one early summer evening at the Sato's home as he shared an evening meal yet again. Sara shook her head at him.

"Do not complain," she said sharply. "You must wait until you are sure you can support a wife! Remember Mrs. Kawamoto, over in Hammond, how she had to take her three oldest children back to Japan last year and leave them with her parents! The profits from her husband Sansuke's farm could not support them all."

Yamaga dropped his head in the face of her rebuke, "I know," he said, "but it is hard to wait." He looked up with a hopeful expression. "Things are getting better, though. Our strawberries are commanding better prices, and now we have the Nokai Hall in the old school building, where the farmers can meet and discuss strategy."

"Yes," said Harry, nodding. "Don't be too hard on him, Sara. Yamaga has done wonderful things, getting the farmers to work together. You know it is important that we do so, as the *hakujin* farmers are not happy with our success. Persuading the Agricultural Association to allow Japanese on their board was an important step forward. We must work together for everyone's success."

"Hmph," said Sara grudgingly, and ladled more soup into Yamaga's bowl. As he smiled up at her, there came a commotion at the door and Jiro Inouye and his wife Kane burst in.

"There has been an assassination in Europe!" Inouye said. "It will mean war!"

"What?" exclaimed Harry and Sara together. Harry noticed that young Jiro's face had lit up and he frowned at the young man. War was not a cause for excitement! But inwardly he sighed. Dreams of glory came easily to a young man. He remembered.

"What does assa…assassa..what does that word mean?" asked fourteen-year-old Asami, her spoon suspended in front of her mouth. She turned to her father, who sat beside her. "Why would it mean war? Will there be war here, Papa? Will soldiers come to our house? Will you and Jiro have to go and fight?" She dropped her spoon back into her bowl and her lower lip trembled a little.

"No, no, little one, no soldiers will come here. This is happening far, far away, in Europe across the sea. And I am fifty-four. Too old to fight." He saw a look of relief pass over Sara's face, but then her expression darkened as she looked at Jiro.

For the rest of the evening, they pored over the newspapers the Inouyes had brought, discussing the likelihood of war being declared because of the shooting of Archduke Franz Ferdinand, the heir to the powerful Austro-Hungarian Empire, and his wife Sophie, by Serbian nationalist Gavrilo Princip. The balance of power in Europe, already strained, had exploded in the wake of the disaster, and nations were lining up on either side of the conflict.

"Surely Japan will side with the Entente Nations—Russia, France, and Britain," said Jiro, whose eyes were intent.

"Perhaps, but we are Canadians now," scolded Harry. "Japan's decisions will not affect us."

"But Canada, as a Commonwealth nation, will have to fight for England, will it not?" rejoined Jiro, looking to Mr. Inouye, whose opinion he respected above all others. The older man nodded slowly, glancing sideways at Harry.

"Yes, yes, it is likely. But perhaps it will not come to that..."

Jiro sat back with a look of satisfaction, but he said no more.

Just as Mr. Inouye had predicted, war broke out in Europe, and the news became worse and worse. For the remainder of the summer and into the fall, everyone gathered every evening at the Farmer's Hall to peruse the Japanese language papers and discuss the war.

Japan did indeed enter the fray early on, seeing an opportunity to expand its power in the Pacific. In the first week of what came to be known as the Great War, Japan agreed with the United Kingdom that they would enter the war if they could take and hold Germany's Pacific territories. On August 7th, England officially asked Japan for assistance in destroying the raiders from the Imperial German Navy in and around Chinese waters. Japan sent Germany an ultimatum a week later. This went unanswered, so Japan formally declared war on Germany on the 23rd of August. Only two days later, when Vienna refused to withdraw the Austro-Hungarian cruiser SMS *Kaiserin Elisabeth* from Tsingtao, Japan declared war on Austria-Hungary, as well.

The Japanese Navy, only loosely controlled by the civil government in Japan, rapidly occupied German territories in the Far East. By early September, they had taken all of Germany's island colonies in the Pacific. Already fired with enthusiasm for the success of the Japanese navy, Jiro was jubilant when he read that they had attacked German ships with airborne bombs, even though the attack on the *Kaiserin Elisabeth* and its accompanying gunboat *Jaguar* was ultimately unsuccessful.

Then the news came in September that the Japanese Red Cross Society had put together three squads, each composed of one surgeon and twenty nurses, and dispatched them to Europe on a five-month assignment. When they heard this, some of the *hakujin* farmers expressed grudging appreciation for Japan's assistance in the war effort and their attitudes toward their Japanese Canadian neighbours softened a little. However, as the demand for supplies grew, the price of strawberries rose all the way to twenty-one cents a pound, an unprecedented high, and the other farmers resented the success of their Japanese neighbours. More and more white farmers began to plant their acreages to strawberries, and the Japanese farmers watched worriedly as the market was glutted with fruit and prices fell. Relations between the two groups soured again.

1915
Haney, British Columbia

Jiro had been reading the English language newspapers as avidly as the Japanese ones, and he knew exactly when the Canadian government started recruiting soldiers across the country. Night after night he lay sleepless, thinking about how and when to sign up. He knew Sara and Harry would try to dissuade him, so he planned to slip away without discussing it. He'd leave a note, of course, so they'd know where he'd gone. Every time he envisioned them finding that note, however, he could see the look of disappointment that would appear in Harry's eyes, the fear that would tighten Sara's mouth and, most of all, the anguish that would show on little Asami's face. She would not understand why he wanted, no, needed to go, why he felt this burning drive to prove himself, to extinguish forever those looks of contempt and the derisive laughter that followed him whenever he went to town and crossed paths with the young white men. Just yesterday, when he'd been lounging against a storefront across from the recruiting station in Haney, three fair-haired white boys had strolled past and noticed him there. One had nudged the other and gestured at Jiro, laughing.

"Hey look, fellas, the Japs have sent reinforcements all the way to Canada! Maybe he's a spy, whaddya think? Ooh, we'd better watch our step, in case he thinks we're Krauts, eh?"

Jiro had turned away and slipped inside the store, but it was no use. Whether he ignored them or stood up to them, the result was the same. Laughter or anger, the message was the same: You aren't one of us. You don't belong here.

Jiro didn't care whether he fought for Canada or Japan. Neither country really wanted him, he felt. He knew that Sara and Harry loved him. They had never for a moment suggested that he should make his own way, or that he wasn't welcome in their home. And Asami—well, no real brother could have loved a little sister more. The thought of her sorrow was the only thing holding him back. But aside from them, he had been rejected. No, it was up to him to make a name, a place, a life for himself. He longed to follow *bushido*, the way of the warrior, adhering to the samurai precepts he had read about. If he had to be different, well, then, he would find a way to be different through an ancient and honorable tradition from his own culture.

Trying to sleep on a cold early winter night, Jiro made plans. He'd heard a rumour that the Canadian Japanese Association was setting up military training in Vancouver. Many Japanese men were keen to volunteer, to prove their loyalty to Canada, but some did not speak English and were thus reluctant to sign up with the regular troops. This all-Japanese Canadian unit provided a perfect solution, and Jiro had made up his mind to join. As the December winds rattled the thin walls of their tiny home on the fields, Jiro squeezed his eyes shut and burrowed more deeply into his insufficient blankets. *Right after Christmas*, he told himself. *I'll go then, I will…*

1919
Haney, British Columbia

Asami checked her appearance in the tiny mirror tacked up on her bedroom wall one last time. At nineteen, she was still small, but her figure had finally begun to blossom, and she thought that her face was looking a little thinner, more mature. She turned her head to one side and then the other, assessing the effect of her new, short hairstyle. Her mother had been furious when Asami had returned from town one day with it bobbed to her nape, but the new look was all the rage and it looked right with her new dropped-waist, layered-skirt dress. Harry had frowned ferociously at the length of the dress and the amount of leg it showed, but Asami had persuaded him that all the girls were wearing similar styles and he had grudgingly agreed to it, as she had known that he would. Her father always tried to be the harsh disciplinarian, as Japanese fathers were meant to be, but he failed every time. Asami knew that she could persuade him to anything she set her mind to—though she tried to resist the temptation and felt a little guilty when she succeeded in wrangling him over to her side. No, in this family, it was her mother Sara whose word was law. Asami knew better than to try to wheedle anything out of her!

Satisfied, she turned back to slide her feet into the new pointed-toe shoes she'd bought to add the finishing touch to her outfit. If only the rain would hold off! Asami glanced out the small window Harry had installed in her bedroom when their new house had finally been built, almost ten years after they'd settled in Haney. It still wasn't very large, but at least it was bigger than the tiny one-room shack that had housed them all for so many years. Asami loved having her own bedroom instead of a curtained-off box bed, and she still thrilled to the silky feel of the pale pink satin bedspread she'd received for her birthday this year.

Relieved that no rain clouds were on the horizon, Asami closed her bedroom door and went down the hall to the kitchen, glancing into the empty bedroom adjacent to hers as she passed it. Her stomach lurched a little as she gazed at the two single beds with their smooth spreads. Soon—tonight!—Jiro would enter this room, throw his kit bag onto one of those beds, sleep beneath its cover. She could hardly believe it. She had missed him so much!

Her adopted brother had gone to Vancouver on New Year's Day, 1915 and signed on to train as a soldier. Asami had sobbed into her pillow for weeks and weeks after he'd gone, and she'd spent most of her days staring across the empty winter fields, as if by strength of will alone she could conjure up his slight figure, make him return to her. But finally, he began to send letters, and these slender threads of contact soothed her a little.

The training was hard, he'd said, but he was proud to be doing his part. When his two months of basic were complete, he was bursting to join the fight. When the army in British Columbia refused to allow any of the Japanese trainees to join their regiments, he was livid. Impulsively, he had jumped on a train with a group of other young men from his training camp, and they'd persuaded a recruiting officer in Alberta to accept them. Asami had known that this was what Jiro wanted, but she couldn't chase away the horrible images of her brother killed or maimed on the battlefield—images that haunted her dreams and gave her many long wakeful hours at night. A letter in 1916 warned them of his impending departure for the front in France and told them to expect fewer letters from then on. Indeed, they had received only two more letters in the following two years, heavily redacted with broad black lines where the censors had hidden potentially sensitive information. The little that remained was hardly comforting, other than to confirm that he was still alive. Asami, raised a Buddhist, found herself praying to Buddha, Jesus, any God she could think of, to spare her beloved brother. She doubted that anyone was listening, but she prayed anyway.

By the time the war finally ended in November 1918, fifty-four of the original two hundred Japanese Canadian volunteer soldiers had died at the front, and 92 had been wounded. They had fought in major battles such as Vimy Ridge, Hill 70, the Somme, and Passchendaele, and thirteen were awarded Military Medals for Bravery. The community hoped that those who returned as war veterans might be able to persuade the Canadian government to allow them to vote—a privilege still denied all Japanese in Canada, even those born there.

But now all that fear, all that anxiety, all that sorrow, was behind them. The Entente Forces had won, Germany and its allies were crushed. Today, the soldiers were coming home after nine months of anxious waiting while the troops were demobilized and transported back to Canada. It was a day for celebration, an unprecedented joining of Japanese and *hakujin* in gratitude and recognition of their mutual cause for joy. Harry had helped build the thirty-five-foot-high arch that was now soaring over the entrance to the Hammond, Haney, and Whonnock Fairgrounds entrance. Asami and her school friends had helped the older women decorate the large exhibition hall with flags from the allied countries, wreaths commemorating individual soldiers and battalions, and bowls and bowls of hothouse flowers. Nearly 1800 people were expected to attend, and Asami knew she'd spend most of her day scurrying between the kitchen and the long tables that had been arranged to seat up to 600 people at a time in three dinner shifts, serving traditional Japanese dishes and less familiar Canadian fare. She hoped her new shoes wouldn't pinch.

Asami entered the kitchen, where her mother was pinning her broad-brimmed hat onto her graying hair. She looked up and took in Asami's stylish appearance, and a frown creased her face.

"You will be cold, with those flimsy layers," she said and when Asami rolled her eyes in disbelief—thinking just how warm the hall would be with all that hot food and all those sweating bodies—her mother took another tack. "You will spill food on your new dress and your feet will hurt in those narrow shoes." Asami huffed an exasperated sigh.

"Perhaps you are right," she said. "Perhaps I should change into the dress I wear when I am thinning the strawberries, and my old boots." Sara smiled reluctantly, coming to place her hands on her daughter's thin shoulders.

"You look very pretty," she said grudgingly, but still she fussed a little, adjusting the neckline of the dress and tsking a little over its length. Asami reached out and held her mother's hands still, looking into her eyes.

"So do you, *Haha*," she said, using the Japanese term she rarely voiced, preferring to call her mother Mama, as her school friends did their mothers. She was rewarded by a softening of Sara's expression, and she squeezed the gnarled hands with their enlarged knuckles. "Can you believe that in just a few hours we will see him, that he will really be home?" she said excitedly, letting her mother go and spinning a little in place.

"Not if we don't get going," came her father's voice at the door. "Come now, get in the truck or we will be late!"

As they climbed into the rickety old farm truck that they used to gather the products of their fields, Asami perched uncomfortably between her parents, squeezing out of the way every time her father had to change gears with the stick shift. She wished they had a shiny new car, something to show off to her friends. But the thought faded in her excitement over the events of the day. This wasn't a day for wishing—this was a day to give thanks.

Asami reached out to place the last steaming pot of rice on the long table. As she stretched to centre the covered bowl on the snowy tablecloth, a loud cannon blast startled her so much that she almost dropped it. Hissing in relief that she had not spilled the rice all over the table, Asami looked up to see the double doors of the hall swing wide, and a crowd of people stream into the space. There was no seating plan, so Asian and white diners sat side by side, taking the first available seats. The noise level was stunning, as excited voices echoed off the rafters high above and bounced around the wooden floor and walls, and a jaunty brass band continued to play outside.

Asami had only moments to observe the crowd before a bowl of *tsukune*—meatballs made with chicken-- was thrust into her hands, and a firm hand in her back propelled her toward the nearest table to serve. From that moment until hours later, when all the eager diners had finally been satisfied, Asami had not one second to do more than remove empty serving vessels and replace them with filled ones. She kept looking around, hoping to catch a glimpse of Jiro, but he must have been placed among the uniformed men seated at the far end of the hall. All she could see was a stretch of dark and fair heads bent over their food.

When the last diners had left the hall, Asami sank into an empty seat. Her feet did indeed hurt abominably, a fact she'd never confess to her mother. But she had managed not to soil her new dress. Hearing a loudspeaker calling everyone's attention to the platform that had been built outside, she stood up and removed her apron. Discarding it on the chair behind her, Asami scurried outdoors. She'd planned to stand with her parents, but they were nowhere to be seen among the throng standing in a loose semi-circle facing the platform.

The band was playing again, but when Senator Taylor stepped up to the microphone, they finished with a flourish and the musicians filed off the stage, their polished brass instruments gleaming in the August sunshine. The Senator spoke at some length, congratulating the local soldiers on the part they had played in the victory, and encouraging roars of patriotic approval with his rousing words. Asami hopped from foot to aching foot, trying to see over the taller people who crowded in front of her. As Senator Taylor's speech wound down, she slipped between the bodies blocking her, finally making her way to the edge of the crowd, where she found an empty crate. She upended it and stepped on top, ignoring its wobble as she put her weight fully on it. Finally, she could see the stage clearly.

As Asami craned her neck, she spotted her mother and father, standing together near the front of the crowd. She could see them only in profile, but she noticed how stooped her father's body had become. *Well,* she reasoned, *he is almost sixty, and he has worked hard all his life*. Nevertheless, it saddened her to see his crooked stance. Beside him, her mother stood straight and tall, her arm looped through her husband's elbow, and Asami took comfort from her indomitable presence.

Senator Taylor made his final remarks and shook hands with Major Donald Martyn, a local teacher and realtor who'd been quite successful in rising through the ranks of the army. The Senator stumbled a little as he left the platform, but Asami didn't notice; she had eyes only for the columns of soldiers making their way to the front. Row after row of khaki-clad men marched into place and stopped in unison, stomping their right feet and crisply saluting the Major, who stood above them saluting back.

A lump rose in Asami's throat as she scanned the small block of men, both Caucasian and Asian. She knew that most of the over two hundred Japanese Canadian volunteers had come from this area. So many had not returned. She stared hard at the backs of the men's heads, trying but failing to pick out Jiro. Where was he?

The Major began calling the men up, one by one, to receive a silver medal recognizing their service to the British Empire. As each one made his way up the stairs, across the platform, and then back to the block of soldiers, Asami's anxiety grew. Why was her brother not there? As the Major's list passed the names beginning with S and moved to the Ts, her heart pounded. Surely they would have received a telegram if Jiro had been killed? Her friend Yua's brother had been killed in action, and she'd seen the black-bordered telegram that had been delivered to their door with the news.

She watched her parents, seeing the signs of a bewilderment that mirrored her own. Just as Asami decided to hop down off her crate and join them, seeking explanation and reassurance, the crowd shuffled to make room for an additional column of soldiers who were coming through. Some made their slow way with crutches, their empty trouser legs pinned up to the ankle, the knee, or higher. Others had neatly shortened sleeves. But a dozen soldiers at the end of the line had bandages wrapped around their heads, covering their eyes, and as these came into view, each man with his hand on the shoulder of the soldier who marched in front of him, Asami moaned in disbelief. For there was her brother, Jiro, his slim frame reduced to sticks, the skin of his face blistered beneath the bandages that swathed his eyes. *No! Not blinded!* It was the worst thing she could have imagined. *Almost better that he had died*, she thought wildly, only to retract the thought immediately. *No, no, blinded is better than dead, of course it is.*

She had heard of the horrors of poison gas, as had everyone. Used first by the Germans at Ypres, it had been quickly deployed by the British forces as well, and it was the use of mustard gas by the American forces, who had only entered the War in its final year, that some said had been the deciding factor in overcoming the enemy forces. The stories in the news had focused only on its role in achieving victories for the allied nations, never on the horrifying effects of the gas, but Asami knew that blinding and lung damage were two of the most common.

It had somehow never occurred to her that Jiro could have been wounded. She'd only ever feared his death and had naively assumed that if he wasn't killed outright, he'd come back unchanged, the kind, smiling brother she'd loved and depended on all her life. This—scarecrow, this shambling, stumbling wreck of a man—how could this be him? She shut her own eyes in horror, which immediately caused her to lose her balance on her precarious perch. She tumbled off, falling to her knees in the dust. She stayed there, looking on in grief as her brother was led gently up the steps to the platform, where Major Martyn spoke about the price paid by so many volunteer soldiers, and pinned the silver medal on the uniform that hung slackly on Jiro's emaciated form. Another soldier came to guide Jiro down the steps and over to Harry and Sara. Asami could see the tears streaming down her father's face, but Sara's face was resolute. She reached out to Jiro, enfolding him in her arms and guiding him away. The second soldier went with them.

Asami blinked and blinked, watching until they disappeared into the crowd, willing it all to be a bad dream. But she knew it wasn't. Wiping her dusty hands over her face, making grimy smears in the wetness on her cheeks, she forced herself to her feet. Ignoring the state of her beautiful new dress, she walked slowly forward, seeking her family.

By the time Asami reached the truck, Jiro and the other soldier were in the open back. Her mother was striding towards the hall, obviously coming in search of Asami so that they could take Jiro home. She took a cue from her mother's calm expression and swiped the tears from her eyes before calling out.

"Mama," she said, "I'm here." Sara's look of relief at seeing her steeled Asami's spine. She needed to be strong, for her parents, for her brother. Sara came and took her by the shoulders, gazing into her face.

"You saw," she said. Asami nodded. Whatever her mother saw in her face obviously satisfied her; Sara squeezed her shoulders silently and then let go. "Come," she said, turning away. "Let us get your brother home and then we will begin."

Begin what? thought Asami, but she knew, really. Begin to plan the rest of Jiro's life, their family's life. Begin to rebuild this shattered young man, this broken boy.

She climbed up into the box and sat down beside her poor, maimed brother, touching him gently on the arm so as not to startle him.

"Jiro," she said softly. "It's me, Asami. Welcome home, big brother." He didn't turn his head toward her, but his hand reached out to find hers, and he held it tightly. She squeezed back, then reached with her other hand to wipe away the tears sliding out from under his bandages.

"Are you in pain?" she asked, and he shook his head.

"Nothing like at first," he croaked out. "Bearable, now. But I am totally blind, Asami. No light, no shadows, nothing but darkness. They tell me it may get better with time, but..." his voice cracked, and the tears flowed more swiftly. On his other side, the stranger who had accompanied him from the stage passed over a large cotton handkerchief, pressing it into Jiro's hand. Her brother's mouth smiled tremulously as he mopped the wetness from his cheeks and chin.

"Asami, this is my friend Hoshi Tasaka. Without him, I wouldn't be here at all. He hung onto me after the gas attack, got me back to base."

Asami leaned forward to see the young man, who reached across Jiro to shake her hand solemnly, bowing slightly from the waist. She liked that he treated her as an adult, not a child.

"Thank you," she said. "Thank you for what you did for my brother. We are in your debt."

"No, no," he replied, shaking his head. "Jiro covered my back many, many times. There are no debts between soldiers," he said.

She was silenced by his modesty, and simply sat back as her father started the truck and they moved off down the potholed track. The ride home was taken in silence; no-one knew what to say, where to start. Asami just held her brother's hand tightly and hoped that would speak for her.

When they reached home, Asami realized that Jiro would need to be guided, as he had never been in this house. He could not stride into his new room, tossing his bag on the bed, as she had imagined just a few hours ago. Asami bit her lip as she watched him climb down from the truck with some difficulty, stretching out his toes to touch the ground before sliding tentatively off the tailgate.

"There is a path, and then three steps up to a porch," she murmured to him, adjusting her pace to his. She placed his hand on the railing adjacent to the steps as they reached it, and at his nod she stepped up with him. Her father opened the door for them, and Jiro smiled slightly.

"I'll soon get to know that squeaky hinge, Pa," he said humorously as they passed into the house. Asami was heartened to hear him make a joke.

Everything takes him so long, Asami thought several hours later, watching Jiro feel his way hesitantly toward his bedroom. She had never appreciated how important vision was to, well, to everything you did. Eating, walking, even conversing with someone—it was all managed through sight. She had been grateful to Hoshi, who had eased the way through the evening as they struggled to reacquaint themselves with Jiro. His blindness was an obvious, enormous change, but he had also gone through the hell of war, had seen, and done, felt and heard horrific things they couldn't even imagine. Asami came to realize that she had been silly to expect her brother to simply 'come back' as if from some holiday. She didn't know whether it was better to ask about his experience or pretend it hadn't happened. Jiro responded to direct questions, but he had trouble initiating any conversational topic. Asami realized that, without being able to see them, he couldn't know what they were thinking or doing.

When the setting sun had shone directly onto his face, she

had stood up, meaning to close the window blind, but he'd heard her movement and forestalled her.

"No, leave it," he'd said. "I can't see it, but I can feel it. The warmth is nice." Harry choked a little at that and turned his face away so they wouldn't see his tears.

Now, as Jiro made his way toward the bed, one foot tapping ahead of him to find its edge, Sara held Hoshi back at the door for a moment, handing him some fresh towels.

"How long can you stay with us?" she asked quietly. "When must you return to your own family?" Hoshi's face was sad.

"I have no family in Canada," he replied. "But I will not intrude upon you..."

"No!" said Sara quickly, "that is not what I meant. I hope that you will stay as long as you like. We are so grateful for your help, for what you have done for Jiro." Hoshi bowed his head to her and took the towels, closing the bedroom door behind him. Asami saw her mother's shoulders sag as she turned away, and her step was slow.

1920
Haney, British Columbia

As summer slipped into autumn, Hoshi stayed on, becoming an integral part of the household. In only a short time, Asami found that couldn't imagine the family without him. His laughing mouth, his twinkling eyes, his tenderness and quiet care for Jiro, the way he teased her in a way that was somehow never hurtful—she couldn't bear to think of his ever going away, and she held her breath any time the subject was raised.

Over the long winter, Jiro gradually discovered tasks that he could do to help. It made him feel less of a burden and helped to keep the demons that plagued his nights at bay. Both Jiro and Hoshi sometimes cried out in the darkness, thrashing and weeping, reliving the days of horror and despair in the trenches of France or Germany. When this happened to one of them, the other would reach out in comfort, speaking quietly. Asami was glad to note that the nightmares had become less and less frequent, but if left to himself, Jiro still tended to sit, silent and lost, his hands idle in his lap. The sight tore at her heart and she redoubled her efforts to include him in her activities.

They all worked together in the spring, planting out the new Superb everbearing strawberries that had been introduced a few years ago. Harry talked with the other farmers, and a delegation went to Washington State to learn all about this new variety of fruit. Whereas regular strawberries fruited heavily in spring to early summer, and then almost not at all until the following year, these new plants had a slightly more modest yield in spring, then a short rest period, then another good harvest from late summer into fall. The advantages were clear, and most of Haney's strawberry growers had plowed up their fields and replanted them with either Superb or Progressive berry plants. These two cultivars seemed to thrive on the valley's sandy, low nitrogen soil, and Harry was cautiously optimistic about the increased yields they would bring.

Asami and Hoshi bent over the hills of soil, tucking in the round-leaved plants, and snipping off the long-stemmed runners to direct growth to the crowns, chatting easily. Jiro walked slowly between the hilled-up rows, scattering a thick mulch of straw to keep the plants clean and moist. They'd found that if he walked carefully, straight ahead, he could keep to the paths quite well. Watching him, Asami could almost persuade herself that he could see, but she knew this was an illusion. Her brother had become better at navigating the house, and rarely tripped or bumped into things anymore. But at the dinner table he still had to tap his fingers from side to side to find his *hashi*, his chopsticks. Asami had to bite her lip to prevent herself from helping. She knew it was important for him to be as independent as possible.

Asami and Hoshi hoed between the rows of strawberries, chopping off any runners snaking out onto the mulch, rejoicing to see the little white flowers that promised fat berries appearing on each plant. It was a glorious day, the first truly warm day of early summer, with a warm blue sky brushed by a few wispy clouds high overhead, and Asami enjoyed the gentle warmth of the sun on her shoulders as she worked.

When they finished, they went in for a cool drink and then Hoshi insisted that Asami throw the baseball to him so he could practice his batting. She tried to refuse—her pitching skills were awful—but he persisted until she laughingly gave in.

"But Jiro, you have to come out with us," she said. "You've been inside for too long today and it's beautiful outside!"

"Yes, yes, all right," Jiro answered from his seat at the kitchen table where he was shelling early peas for Sara. "Let me finish these first, though."

Swiping his fingers through the bowl to ensure he hadn't missed any pea pods, Jiro stood and made his way to the sink, where he rinsed the tender green peas and set the bowl on the drainboard.

"All right, I'm done. Go get your glove, 'Sami."

They set a chair for Jiro at the edge of the scruffy lawn adjacent to the strawberry fields. Farmers—and their wives-- had little time to keep decorative gardens, but Sara insisted on maintaining a small space next to the house for vegetables and flowers for the house. She had also planted a weeping cherry, beloved by all Japanese and the young tree was just finishing its annual bloom. The grass beneath it was covered with fallen pink blossoms and the branches above were leafing out in pale green slivers that caught the light.

"Give me your best throw," called Hoshi, swinging the wooden bat to loosen up his shoulders. Baseball had been introduced to Japan in the 1870s by an American teaching English at the Kaisei Academy in Tokyo. It had quickly become Japan's favourite sport, and Japanese Canadians were equally enamoured of it. Local teams and leagues were springing up all over now that the war was over and the young men—those who had survived—were home.

"Come on Asami, pitch a fast one," shouted Jiro, grinning. Feeling the sun on his face, he slipped off the band of cloth that covered his eyes, enjoying the warmth on his closed eyelids.

Asami rolled her shoulders and tried to remember all the instructions both Jiro and Hoshi had told her over and over. She stood facing Hoshi with her legs shoulder-width apart, her arms raised to her chest level and the hand holding the ball nestled in the bulky leather glove on her left hand. She was far from mastering all the various throws—Hoshi's descriptions of curveballs and screwballs, sliders, two-seam, four-seam, knuckleballs, and the disgusting-sounding spitball had simply dizzied her. She'd be lucky to even get the ball to where Hoshi stood, still swinging the bat, let alone perform some fancy pitch. If she was honest, she'd admit that she didn't really enjoy baseball. But she did enjoy being out here with the two young men, on this beautiful day. So, she'd do her best.

Shifting her weight and swinging her right arm behind her, Asami stepped forward and threw the baseball towards Hoshi as hard as she could. To her amazement, it flew straight at him, and he swung at it, connecting with a crack like a rifle shot. However, it wasn't a solid hit. The ball veered off sharply to the side, spinning crazily—directly toward Jiro where he sat under the cherry tree.

"Jiro!" Asami screamed, "Watch out!" Even as the words left her lips, she knew how futile they were.

And yet…at her cry, Jiro's eyes flew open, and he dodged…in the right direction to avoid being hit by the speeding ball!

PART II

1925
Vancouver, British Columbia

Asami shut the door behind her on the tiny apartment above the noodle shop, touched her hat to ensure it was secure, and ran down the narrow stairs out into the autumn sunshine of Princess Avenue. Her footsteps tapped out a quick rhythm as she passed the Ohori Fruit Store, hurried north to Alexander Street, and turned left. It wouldn't do to be late on her very first day of teaching at the Japanese Language School.

As she scurried along, nodding to the acquaintances she passed, scattered memories flooded her mind, reminding her of all the changes that had brought her to this day and this place.

After that day under the cherry tree, Jiro's sight had slowly, slowly returned. It still wasn't perfect, but with thick glasses he could navigate well enough and even read a little. He'd been able to return to working in the strawberry fields and his strength and confidence had grown. Asami smiled to herself, picturing her beloved brother—for so she always thought of him—working in the fields with her aging father. In his mid-sixties, Harry Sato still toiled among the strawberries every day, his gnarled fingers clipping the runners or gathering the soft fruit.

Jiro's recovery had changed many things. As it became clear that Jiro no longer needed Hoshi's help, Hoshi had begun to speak of moving to Vancouver and buying a fishing boat. His family, he said, were fishermen in Japan, and he missed the life. Asami had been devastated at the thought of his leaving. She had become more than used to his presence in their family. Indeed, she had come to love him. She tried to hide her feelings, fearing rejection, assuming Hoshi saw her only as Jiro's little sister.

That had all changed one day out in the strawberry fields, where they were harvesting the spring berries. The memory was vivid in Asami's mind even today, five years later. She suspected that she'd remember it until her dying day...

Hoshi had announced at breakfast that he'd found a suitable boat, a real beauty, and he planned to go into the city to look at it the following day. Asami's heart had plummeted, and her expression was morose as she worked down the row. Her movements became slower and slower as she contemplated life without Hoshi's kind eyes, his gentle laugh. Tears gathered in her downturned eyes and splashed onto the strawberry plants. Suddenly a hand intruded into her view, holding out a clean white handkerchief. She looked up to find Hoshi beside her and straightened awkwardly, embarrassed that he'd found her weeping. She hid her flaming cheeks in his large handkerchief, wiping her eyes and blowing her nose.

"What is it, 'Sami? What is making you so sad?" Hoshi asked quietly.

"I don't want you to go!" she blurted out, then was immediately horrified by her admission, especially when it was met by a long silence. She dared not look at his face.

"Would you...would you consider, I mean..." Hoshi voice faltered, and at that she looked up, a flash of wild hope lighting her heart. He drew a deep breath and began again, looking into her eyes. "Would you come with me, Asami, as my wife?"

Before she could reply, he rushed on. "I don't have much, but I hope to do well fishing. We'd have to start out small and you'd probably have to find work, at least at first..."

She stopped his nervous flow of words by flinging her arms around his neck. "Yes, yes!" she cried, but just as quickly she stepped back. "If my father and mother approve, of course," she amended.

Things had moved quickly after that. Harry and Sara had indeed approved, and Jiro was overjoyed that his dearest friend was to truly become part of his family. Their wedding had been modest, and immediately after it they had moved to the city. Hoshi had bought the fishing boat and found another fellow to work with him. They'd found the little apartment in the heart of the Japanese district of Powell Street and set up housekeeping.

Asami had enrolled in Japanese language lessons at the Language School for herself at first. Although she spoke some Japanese, both Harry and Sara had insisted that English be the primary language at home, believing that successful assimilation into Canadian society required it. Once in the city, however, Asami had found that very few of the older residents of the Japanese Canadian enclave spoke English. She'd realized that she needed to be fluent in both languages.

The Language School had been established in 1906 under the guidance of the Japanese consul at the time, a Mr. Morikawa. Japan was concerned that the children of emigrants would lose their Japanese language and culture. As many of the residents of Japantown still intended to return to Japan or send their children back there some day, it was deemed critical that there be instruction in their heritage. At first the school had also taught other subjects such as mathematics and history, but after the war, they had decided to focus solely on instruction in the Japanese language. Japanese Canadian children now attended the local public schools, where they learned English—and *hakujin* culture—very well. Many of the *issei*, the first generation of immigrants, feared that this second generation, the *nisei*, would forget Japan altogether.

The school had become a natural gathering place for neighbourhood organizations and events in the years since the war, and there was talk of building a larger building to accommodate the school and a community hall. In the meantime, however, Asami had learned Japanese so well that the school had offered her a position as a teacher. Today she would begin.

The low sun was gleaming through the trees when Asami made her way back home in late afternoon. She walked much more slowly than she had in the morning, scuffing the leaves underfoot and enjoying the remaining warmth in the air. She hummed the little tune she'd used to teach the Japanese numbers to the children in her classes today. They had done well, and she looked forward with new confidence to tomorrow. Asami allowed herself to daydream for a moment that someday she might be allowed to teach in an English public school, as Hide Hyodo had been hired to do at Lord Byng school in Steveston just three years ago. The Japanese community saw Hide's hiring as a breakthrough for their people's acceptance in British Columbia, even though she was only permitted to teach the Japanese children in the school.

Asami ran up the narrow stairs to their apartment and reached out with her key to open the door. She was confused to find it already unlocked and frowned as she pushed it gently open. She was sure she had locked it when she left this morning.

"Hello?" she called out as she stepped in. Perhaps her parents or Jiro had come on an unexpected visit—they had keys to the apartment. But it was her husband's voice that answered her and Asami's frown deepened. Hoshi should be out fishing for days yet! Why was he here?

"Hoshi! What are you doing at home? Are you hurt? What's wrong?" She hurried to pull off her coat and hat and sit down beside Hoshi on their small sofa. The expression he turned to her froze her heart. Something was badly wrong.

"Is it my father?" she whispered, fear tightening her throat. Hoshi shook his head and silently held out a crumpled piece of paper. She took it and smoothed it out to read the official looking seal and words typed there.

"What? The Ministry of Fisheries has revoked your fishing license? But why?"

Hoshi's normally genial expression twisted in disgust. "Because Japanese fishermen are too good at fishing," he said harshly. "The *hakujin* and the *dojin*, the Indians, have complained that we represent 'unfair competition' for them. They say we will overfish the stocks, not leaving enough for them."

Asami listened quietly. She knew that Japanese fishermen had held more than half of the British Columbia fishing licenses when Hoshi had first applied for his in 1921. In the years since then, fewer and fewer annual licenses had been issued to Japanese, but until today Hoshi had still been authorized each year. There had not been any talk about falling fish stocks in other years.

"When did you receive this?" she asked.

"The Fisheries boat came by our fishing grounds and issued these revocations to every boat there! All of us are barred from fishing for the rest of the season and I don't think we'll get a license for next year. I think they've taken back about a thousand Japanese licenses altogether. Asami, I don't know what to do! We cannot survive on your teaching wages."

Asami reached out and took his hand. "We'll find a way, Hoshi. If we must, we'll move back to the strawberry fields. My family will not abandon us, you know that."

Hoshi shook his head. "I don't want to do that. Your parents sheltered me for months after the war. It is time I made my own way, Asami. Can't you understand that?"

"I can," she said softly, squeezing his hand. "We will find a way," she repeated. After a moment she spoke again. "Could you sell the boat?" she asked tentatively. She knew that boat was his pride and joy, but, if he couldn't fish…

Hoshi's face crumpled and he turned away from her so she wouldn't see his eyes fill with tears. "And then what?" he asked fiercely. "That money would only support us for a short time. I must find other work!" He stood up and began to pace around the small space.

Asami bit her lip. She knew how hard it would be for Hoshi to give up his dream of fishing. He loved the work and was very good at it.

"What about Hasting's Mill?" she asked. She had heard people saying that the huge old Mill, just a few blocks away at the bottom of Dunlevy Street, was slowing down, but she also knew it was still the world's largest manufacturer of toothpicks. Toothpicks! What a comedown from life on the open ocean, captain of your own boat. She hated to even suggest it, but what could they do? They had to think of something, and Hastings hired many, many Japanese. The men were often groups from the same prefecture in Japan, and one of them—the one who spoke the best English—would act as a 'boss,' a liaison between the company and the men. The shabby rooming houses of Powell Street were crammed to overflowing with these single young men. Asami had heard that the box beds were stacked to the ceiling in each crowded room, and that as one man rolled out to go to work, another returning from his shift would take his place in the still-warm sheets. With tight restrictions on Japanese immigration into Canada now in place, there were far more young men than families. It took many months—even years—before the men earned and saved enough to send for a 'picture bride' from Japan, just as Asami's father had done with her mother Sara. Times were hard in 'Little Tokyo,' as the Anglos called it—and their life was about to get harder, she feared.

But then Hoshi grabbed his jacket off the hook by the door. She saw him sigh deeply and straighten his shoulders.

"You are right," he said. "I must face reality. I will go to the dock and see if I can find a buyer for my boat. Then I will go to see the manager at the mill." He tried to smile reassuringly at his young wife. "You are right, Asami. We will figure something out." He went out and closed the door quietly behind himself. Asami sagged back on the sofa. *Why did this have to happen today of all days? I wanted to tell Hoshi all about my first day, and he didn't even think to ask me. Of course he didn't, with this shock. But it would have been nice…*

1926
Vancouver, British Columbia

"I'm going, Hoshi! I won't hear another word!" Asami said and frowned darkly at her husband. "I'm fine, absolutely fine!" Hoshi tipped his head and raised his eyebrows, gazing at his wife's hugely swollen belly. Asami's due date had come and gone a week ago, but still the baby showed no interest in coming into this world. All this week Asami had meekly stayed quiet, resting with her feet up, allowing others to wait on her and, in truth, she had been glad of the chance. She felt as big as a whale and the summer's heat hadn't helped her swollen ankles.

But today—August second—she would *not* stay at home. The entire Japanese population of Vancouver—and hundreds of others—would be at the Powell Street baseball field to cheer on their favourite team to the Terminal League Championship.

The Asahi baseball team had been around since 1914, when five young men from Shiga Prefecture had decided to form a Japanese Canadian team. Three Kitagawa brothers--Mickey, Yo, and Eddie--had invited Yasomatsu Nishizaki and Tom Matoba to join them. Their manager, Matsujiro Miyasaki owned many businesses along Powell Street, and was nicknamed Basha Matsu, or horse carriage, for his many endeavours. There had been only two other Japanese teams in the Vancouver area at the time, but the Mikado, Yamoto, and Fuso teams had formed just after the Asahis, and together the six teams formed the Diamond League. At first the Asahis hadn't won many games. But slowly, slowly, over the years, they'd gotten better and better. It helped that the Asahis had access to the Powell Grounds diamond for almost unlimited practice. The other teams had to share space with schools or other community organizations, but the Powell Street neighbourhood was devoted to the Asahis and made sure they had lots of time and space for practice.

Baseball was a glue that overcame many differences in the Japanese Canadian community. Opinions on assimilation versus isolation were deeply divided, mostly along religious grounds. Those who had converted to Christianity tended to send their children to public schools, teach them English, and do their best to integrate into Canadian society. The Nationals insisted on staying as Japanese as possible, and resisted attempts to Canadianize. But everybody loved baseball. Whether they yelled strike or *sutoraiku*; safe or *sefu*, out or *auto*, everyone was passionate about the game.

Basha Matsu was hungry for a bigger win. He wasn't satisfied for his team to beat other Japanese Canadian teams. Oh no. He wanted his Asahis to beat the Anglo teams. He knew they had no chance at outhitting the *hakujin* players. They were far taller, far heavier, with much longer arms and much more power behind their hits. No, the Japanese Canadian team would have to out-think, out-strategize, out-play their opponents, and Basha wanted them to be ready to do just that.

The canny manager had come up with a strategy that came to be known as 'brain ball.' It was focused on defense and made strategic use of bunts and squeeze plays to get the maximum number of players to home during each inning. The team practiced it until it was second nature to every player. It required smooth and dedicated teamwork—no individual grandstand hits, no star pitching—and it suited these players perfectly. The Japanese Canadians all believed deeply in the concept of *wa*, of group strength, where each one's individual strengths blended with those of all the others for the best result for everyone. They also, however, saw the battle between the pitcher and the batter as exemplifying the heroic struggles of the ancient samurai. Baseball was an ideal game to satisfy deeply held cultural values.

When the day finally came that the Asahis were condescendingly challenged to play the Anglo teams, the results astonished everyone. Al Moser, known as 'Stringbean' for his gangly height, who played for the rival Downtown Patricias Anglo team, complained that the Asahis could win a game without a single actual hit. The Asahi players were already small, Moser whined, and then they crouched down at the plate as well, making the strike zone as small as possible. Their carefully placed bunts would drop the ball in the most awkward possible place, just in front of home plate, so that both pitcher and catcher would run for it, often colliding as they scrambled to scoop it up and throw it to first base before the Asahi player reached it. However, the speed of the Japanese Canadian runners made it unlikely that the ball would reach the base before the runner, and in the meantime the Asahi players on second and third bases would have run as well. Again and again the Asahis made this play, maddening their larger opponents. But the Anglo players never seemed to learn the lesson, never seemed to be able to suppress their own desire for the big hit, the home run, enough to emulate their smaller opponents.

The Asahis had played—and beaten—the Japanese American teams across the border in Seattle in 1918, and eventually won against their Caucasian teams as well. After winning the championship in that league in 1918, the Asahi had returned to playing only in Vancouver in the City League. In 1921, they traveled to Japan and became the first visiting team to ever beat the Keio University players. Overall, throughout their tour of the homeland they won eleven games, lost ten, and tied one. Satisfied that they had 'played even' with their Japanese counterparts, the Asahis returned to Canada and kept moving up in their local league.

Their big leap forward had come in 1922, when manager Basha

Matsu was replaced by former player Harry Miyasaki, who scouted very young players in Sunday School Leagues and groomed them over the years to be stellar team players. He even saw the potential in one-handed George Tanaka, who despite his handicap became one of the team's most reliable pitchers.

Over the years the team's accomplishments gained them not only hundreds of adoring Japanese Canadian fans but, increasingly, *hakujin* fans as well. Nevertheless, the players were always aware of the fragility of approval from Caucasians in an atmosphere of simmering racial unrest. They were careful to show unfailing courtesy and a commitment to fair play. They never protested the umpire's calls or became angry at a defeat. When a dispute erupted over a white umpire's call against the Asahis at a game in the late summer of 1922, it was belligerent white fans who jeered the call and hustled the ump to his car after the game, telling him never to return.

Harry Miyasaki was determined to build a league-winning team, and he worked hard to achieve it. It took him five long years. But now here they were, in August 1926, about to play the final game against the Mount Pleasant team in what had been their best season ever. Despite some controversy in the first half of the season when this same opposing team had been unable to field enough players and yet had refused to forfeit the game, the Asahis had won the first half of the season and had an 8-1 win-draw record in the second half. Everyone fully expected them to sweep to victory today, and Asami was determined to be there to celebrate with everyone.

"Very well," Hoshi said, bowing to the inevitable, "but you'd better bring a parasol. The sun is very bright out there even though it's not very hot today." Asami obediently pulled the dark blue parasol with its ruffled edge, her favourite, from the umbrella stand by the door and smiled at her husband.

They made their way down the stairs and along the thronged streets to the field at the corner of Dunlevy and Powell Streets. Powell Grounds wasn't much to look at: really, it was just a scruffy little urban park with an irregularly shaped outfield, a stony infield, and clumps of sage growing up along the edges of the baseball diamond. A barrier of wobbly wire netting had been erected behind home plate and in front of the primitive dugouts at first and third bases where plain wooden chairs had been set out for the players. Some stands for spectators had also been built, but they were nowhere near large enough to accommodate the crowds of spectators that often numbered into the thousands. People simply stood in a loose ring all around the diamond, though they'd sometimes have to step aside as a player charged after a fly ball. But the park was the centre of Japanese Canadian activity in Vancouver, and

Asami loved it. She'd never become a big fan of the game itself, but she loved the feeling of togetherness, of belonging, the positive energy and the pride generated by sitting among her neighbours and friends as they watched the game and cheered and groaned in chorus.

Harry and Sara and Jiro, visiting for the big game, had gone down to the grounds early to save seats in the stands, while Hoshi had tried to persuade Asami to stay behind. Harry smiled with no surprise as Asami struggled to climb the steep bleachers to them. He had known it was useless to argue; his daughter wouldn't be separated from her family on this exciting day.

Asami squeezed in between Jiro and Harry, reaching out to take her father's hand in an affectionate gesture. He nudged her gently with his shoulder.

"No keeping you at home, eh? Baby will just have to wait." Asami laughed and nodded as she wiggled and squirmed in a vain attempt to get comfortable on the hard wooden seat. *Should have brought a cushion*, she thought, annoyed that she hadn't thought to do that. She glanced down the row and saw Hoshi gazing north to where the roof of Hastings Mill was just visible through the trees. She sighed a little, knowing what he was thinking. He had managed to get a job at the mill and had done well, moving up to a boss position within a year. But he still longed for the open seas, she knew. The enclosed spaces and constant noise of the mill wore on him, and he was worried about rumours that the mill might be sold or even shut down. She wished there was a better choice. But now, with their first child due—overdue!—was not the time to be destabilizing their source of income.

As the players streamed onto the field, she forgot her minor pains and Hoshi's worries. The crowds roared in excitement as play began.

When the Asahis came up to bat at the bottom of the first, they quickly gained three runs achieved by a combination of two consecutive walks, a sacrifice bunt, an error by the Mount Pleasant team, and a timely hit that sent the fans into a frenzy of cheers. Asami surged to her feet with the rest of the crowd, yelling, but as she sat down again, she felt a strong pang low in her belly. She stretched her back up straight, trying to relieve it, and after a moment it passed. *Just been sitting still too long*, she decided, and forgot about it.

Southpaw player Kenichi Suga, nicknamed Ty after legendary American pitcher Ty Cobb, was the Asahi's most impressive pitcher, and he held the opposing team hitless to the fifth inning. Asami tried to concentrate on the game, but those pesky pains kept distracting her and as the Asahis came back up to bat, a truly wrenching pain caused her to cry out. The sound could have been lost in the noise of the crowd, but Asami's mother had been watching her daughter for some time, and she heard the cry. She reached over her husband and tapped Asami's hand.

"Come," she said, standing. "It is time."

"What?" gasped Hoshi. "The baby's coming? Now?" His mother-in-law nodded briskly.

"Help me get her down," she said. Jiro and Harry took Asami's elbows, and the family began edging their way past everyone's knees to the edge of the stands. A few tskd or grunted irritably as their view was obscured, but most saw Asami's pregnant belly and assisted her to navigate the awkward space. Halfway down, Asami was overwhelmed by a pain stronger than any so far, and she stopped, head hanging and knees buckling, as those around her supported her through the contraction. When it was over, many hands helped to hustle her down the remaining steps to the ground.

They had taken only few steps away from the stands when Asami felt a gush of wetness spread down her thighs, soaking her skirt and dripping onto the dusty ground.

"Oh no," she cried out in embarrassment, thinking she had wet herself. Her mother gathered her in her arms, steering her away from public view into the shadows beneath the stands.

"It's not what you think," she whispered. "It is the birthing waters. We must get you home..." But Asami couldn't make sense of her mother's words buzzing in her ear. Wave after wave of wrenching pains rolled over her without surcease, taking all her attention. Her knees buckled and she knelt in the striped light beneath the bleachers, moaning and rocking.

"I can't, I can't," she groaned. "The baby's coming, I can feel it!"

Sara turned to her son-in-law. "Find the midwife," she snapped. "She's bound to be here somewhere." Hoshi gaped at his mother-in-law but at her sharp gesture he turned and fled back to the stands above them.

Harry and Jiro pulled off the light jackets they wore and spread them upon the ground, Harry hastily sweeping his foot over the space to clear it of stones first. Sara helped Asami lie down, but she writhed and bucked, unable to lie still in the pain of her travail. Above them, the oblivious crowd wailed and cheered, stomping their feet on the wooden boards, dislodging dust that sifted down onto the trio below them. Asami coughed and her father handed her a clean white handkerchief to cover her mouth.

Though it seemed like hours to Asami, it was only moments later that the midwife appeared by her side. The woman had been visiting Asami every few days for the past weeks and knew her well. A quick check confirmed Asami's assertion that the birth was near.

"No time to move her," she said. "We'll just have to do our best here. Hoshi, go ask the ball boy for a pail of clean water and any clean cloths he has on hand. Quickly! I don't think we have long…"

When Hoshi returned, carrying the water and cloths, he found Asami half sitting up with her father and brother supporting her shoulders from behind, her knees raised. Her mother crouched next her, holding her hand, and whispering encouragement.

"Thank you, Hoshi. You and Jiro should step away now," said the midwife, but Asami cried out, "No, no, don't leave me!" so Hoshi knelt and reluctantly took her other hand, and Jiro stayed where he was. Hoshi dared not look at what the midwife was doing between his wife's legs! But if her father and brother could stomach it, well, then, so could he.

Hoshi couldn't believe the sounds coming out of his usually genteel wife's mouth. She groaned and wailed and grunted, sounding more like an animal than a woman. Her face was bright red, and her hair was a sweaty mass on her shoulders. Hoshi was terrified and he could see that Jiro was too. His friend's eyes were stretched wide behind his thick glasses. They exchanged panicked glances over Asami's head.

Surely Asami would die of this much pain! Why had he agreed to having children? He'd had no idea of what was involved in bringing them into the world. As the minutes ticked by with no discernable progress, Hoshi prayed to every deity he could think of to save his wife. He couldn't believe how calm the midwife was, or his in-laws. Couldn't they see that this was killing Asami? Why didn't they do something to help her?

Suddenly the midwife spoke urgently to Asami. "All right, now, no more pushing. Stop, stop, hold, pant like this." She demonstrated a quick breathing rhythm that sounded like 'ha-ha-ha' and Asami copied her, tongue peeping out, looking like a puppy on a sweltering day.

"Good, good," said the midwife, doing something complicated with her hands that Hoshi couldn't understand and didn't really want to see. "All right, the head's out and I've got the shoulders turned. Now, one more good, steady push, that's it, good, come on, keep pushing…"

Above their heads a massive roar sounded, startling them all. As the Asahis claimed the Terminal League championship with a 5-2 win over Mount Pleasant, Hoshi's son burst into the world like a miniature ball player sliding into home plate.

And so, in honour of the Asahi star pitcher, they named him Kenichi.

1931
Powell River, British Columbia

The sun poured in and splashed across the breakfast table as Hoshi, Asami, and little Kenji, as he was nicknamed, sat eating their breakfast on a warm July morning. Asami was focused on preventing their five-year-old son from pouring the entire pitcher of maple syrup over his single pancake, but Hoshi was reading the out-of-date newspaper that had come in from Vancouver last week as he absently forked his own stack of well-soaked pancakes into his mouth. Pancakes for Sunday breakfast, made by Hoshi, had become a well-loved ritual in their home and Asami looked forward to waking up to the enticing smell of fresh-brewed coffee and frying bacon each week. It was the one day of the week that Hoshi didn't have to rush off to the Powell River Pulp and Paper Mill or to other errands, and she luxuriated in the chance to sleep in a little and be waited upon.

"Well, here's good news," Hoshi said, laying the paper down and pouring himself more coffee—a Canadian habit he'd become very fond of. "The Dominion has finally agreed to allow the Japanese Canadian soldiers who fought in the war to vote in both provincial and federal elections. So that means me, I guess, and Jiro."

"Oh, that is good," said Asami, reaching over to wipe Kenji's chin yet again as a rivulet of sticky syrup threatened to drip onto the tablecloth. "What about your family members?"

Agitation about the franchise had a long history among Japanese Canadians. It was the clearest signal from their country that they didn't belong, that they were not really accepted as Canadians. As far back as 1903, Tomekichi Honma had tried to get the law changed. He had fought for the provincial franchise through the British Columbia Elections Act and won his case in the B.C. court, and then in the Supreme Court of Canada when the province appealed the lower court decision. Unfortunately, the province had one more trick up its sleeve. It appealed to the Judicial Committee of the Privy Council of England, an obscure body that typically had little to do with Britain's Canadian colony, but which still held the ultimate authority over Canadian laws. Sadly, they upheld the province's right to discriminate specifically on the basis of race, without regard to a person's citizenship status. So Japanese Canadians in British Columbia—and Canada as a whole--were left without the vote.

As Asami and Hoshi knew well, Japanese Canadian men had volunteered within days of the outbreak of war in 1914. Both Hoshi and Jiro, though they volunteered and trained in B.C., had to make their way to Alberta to find an active battalion that would accept them. In the end, over two hundred Japanese Canadians managed to be deployed overseas, and, as their own family was very well aware, many had not returned, or had returned maimed. There could be no doubt that these men had given equal service, yet the government continued to refuse them the most foundational right of a citizen—the right to vote.

Delegations from the soldiers had made appeal after appeal to the government in the years since the war ended in 1918. Now, it seemed, persistence had finally paid off. Thirteen years on, the veterans had been granted the franchise.

Hoshi glanced back at the article as he sipped his refilled cup. "No," he said, his expression reflecting his disappointment, "only the veterans themselves, and only for their lifetimes. Not their families, not their sons after them."

Asami clicked her tongue and shook her head. When would Canada come to terms with its multi-racial citizenry? She had been born here. Canada was her home, the only focus of her loyalty. She'd never been to Japan and perhaps never would go there. Her musings were interrupted by a chuckle from her husband.

"Here's another little bit of good news, though," he said, reading aloud. "*Shige Yoshida, of Chemainus on Vancouver Island, has formed the first Japanese Canadian Boy Scout troop in the British Empire. Barred from joining a local troop five years ago, he has studied on his own by correspondence and earned the highest possible rank, resulting in a warrant from the Boy Scouts of America granting him the right to form his own troop.* So maybe there's hope for you yet, Kenji, my son. Would you like to be a Boy Scout someday?"

"Are they the ones who wear the funny hats and shorts and go on long hikes in the woods?" asked Kenji, swiping another pancake off the platter while his mother's attention was elsewhere.

"I suppose that's as good a description as any," laughed his father.

"Then, yes, I would like to be a Scout," said Kenji decidedly. "I like being in the woods."

"Don't put ideas into his head, Hoshi," said Asami, deciding to ignore the extra pancake that had appeared on her son's plate without permission. "You know the local troop doesn't let Japanese Canadians in."

"Not yet," Hoshi replied. "But maybe with Yoshida's success, they might reconsider."

Asami shook her head, unconvinced. They had moved to Powell River, a hundred miles north of Vancouver, in 1927 when the Hastings Mill had finally shut down. The old mill building itself, a landmark from Vancouver's earliest days and one of the few buildings to survive the 1886 fire that had leveled the young settlement, had been slated for demolition after the company closed. It had been saved through the efforts of the Native Daughters of B.C. Post No. 1, barged to a new site at the foot of Alma Street, restored, and opened as a heritage museum just this past January.

This reverence for the old building was nice, Asami had thought at the time, but she wished as much attention had been paid to the fate of the hundreds of workers displaced by the closing of the mill. Still unable to get a fishing license, Hoshi had searched for a job that would allow him to support his family. He'd heard that the pulp and paper mill in Powell River, which had opened in 1912 as the first company making paper in western Canada, was hiring. He had begged an old fisherman friend to take him up the Strait of Georgia that snaked between Vancouver Island and the mainland of British Columbia, following the rocky shoreline of what was now dubbed the Sunshine Coast for its many annual hours of sunny weather.

Landing at Powell River, he'd been overwhelmed by the sight of the huge factory, its towering smokestacks belching dark clouds into the clear air. As the boat neared the wharf, Hoshi had been amazed to see men carrying enormous rolls of paper on their shoulders from the plant down to the dock. He couldn't imagine how they hoisted those rolls up—they must have weighed hundreds of pounds each! He later learned that the owners, two brothers named Dwight and Anson Brookes, had built a huge dam across the narrow Powell River in 1910 to generate a wealth of hydroelectric power. It was an ambitious enterprise that overcame several near disasters to become very successful, and the company had built a town around the mill, including a school, a hospital, and social and recreational facilities, to house its many workers.

The Company, as it was always called, needed workers with a wide skill set. Log sorters, lumber graders, sawyers and filers, jigger men, stone sharpeners, cooks, acid makers, blow pit operators, tinsmiths, blacksmiths, patternmakers, bricklayers—all of these were needed to make top quality paper and newsprint. The bosses didn't care about the race of its workers, only that they did their jobs effectively and didn't cause trouble. Hoshi, with his experience as a mill boss at Hastings, had soon found work, but it was difficult and dangerous work.

Asami knew little about the process, though Hoshi had described the steps to her. She knew that before logs could be made into paper, they had to be debarked and cut to size to fit the grinders. The saw blade used to accomplish this step was enormous--over 64 feet long and 16 inches wide. Nothing was wasted: a conveyor carried the bark and other wood refuse to the steam plant for burning; smaller logs were put through the chipper to make chips for the sulphite mill. Next, the sized logs were loaded into mechanical grinders and pressed against rapidly revolving grindstones. At the end of this step, the pulp emerged, hot and thick as porridge. It was then diluted with water and run through screens to remove splinters and excess fibre before being pressed into paper. All these processes involved huge machines and rapidly moving parts. There were lights and horns that went on when the machines broke and automatic showers that went on right away in case of fire or spill, but they still had plug-ups, and inevitably men got hurt. The whole community had learned to listen for those ominous sounding horns, to stop what they were doing and run up to the plant to see who had been injured.

Asami had been sad to move so far away from her parents and brother, but she understood that they had to go where Hoshi could find work that made use of his skills and experience. She'd found seven other Japanese wives in the Company town, most of them recent immigrants to Canada via the picture bride system, only two of them speaking any English at all. Asami soon found herself acting as an unofficial teacher. It soon became clear that none of the Japanese working at the Company would ever be allowed to progress beyond their manual labour jobs, but it offered a steady paycheque and a decent place to live, in one of the tiny houses the mill had built to house its workforce. Everything was controlled by the Company—the banking, the post office, the town's municipal government, the social activities. As long as you agreed with all their policies and kept your head down, life was tolerable. But you wouldn't want to be noticed or be seen to be 'disagreeable.' Asami had become good at keeping quiet.

Kenji was enrolled in the local school this year, where for the first time he was surrounded by white children with only a few from different cultures. Asami viewed this with mixed emotions. It was good that he was exposed to many white Canadian children and was fluent in English, but sometimes she wondered if he was losing the Japanese side of his heritage, so far from his grandparents and the Japanese Canadian community of Powell Street. She did her best to provide a balance, making Japanese food sometimes, or explaining Japanese stories, but she wasn't sure how much good it was doing. Just last night, for example, she'd told Kenji a bedtime story about Daruma the protector, a fabulously ugly monk with a red coat who brought great good luck. She'd described the custom of throwing dried soybeans out the doorway on Setsuban, the festival of seasonal division in early spring, to cast out Oni the ogre and protect the household. Kenji seemed to find these stories incomprehensible. He'd asked her to read *The Little Engine That Could* instead.

After breakfast, Hoshi offered to take Kenji for a walk to the local park. Asami knew he was hoping to find a few friends for a game of pick-up baseball, and she smiled as she waved them off. Once the breakfast dishes were done and a load of laundry put into the sink to soak in soapy water, Asami stole a few minutes to glance through the latest edition of *The Digester*, the monthly Company newsletter. As always, she turned first to the page of jokes—it never failed to make her smile. Today's first joke, however, made her roll her eyes.

"What do you do?"
"I keep house, scrub, scour, bake,
wash dishes, cook, do the laundry,
iron, and sew."
And the census taker listed her:
~ Housewife—no occupation."

A few pages on, there was an article about Powell River's early history, and her smile reappeared at the mention of strawberries.

And how, one is often tempted to remark, was the supply of fresh milk obtained in those days of high-pressure construction? Today the local requirements are met daily by a number of small but well-equipped milk merchants in our suburbs, who deliver their product straight from the cow to the consumer. In 1910 the fresh milk came in cans and strawberries and cream were seldom seen, except on the cover of magazines or in the imaginations of fertile - brained residents. By 1912 a partial supply of this precious liquid began to percolate about the townsite. On the present site of the bowling green, Joe Errico had established his ranch, and by severe discipline and tactful advances managed to coax an inadequate supply of milk from a couple of worldly-wise kine, both of whom were conscious of their superior elevation in this world of milk substitutes.

Asami sighed, thinking longingly of the bowls of fresh strawberries and thick cream the family enjoyed so frequently on her parents' farm back in the Fraser Valley. It was one of the many things she missed. She flicked another page, glancing at the sink and deciding the clothes needed another few minutes' soak. On page five she gazed at the photo of the candidates for Paper Queen, to be chosen at the annual Elks Labour Day picnic. She couldn't help but note the pale faces and fair hair of all the girls in the running. Powell River might be tolerant of other races for the sake of the Company, but no Japanese Canadian girl was likely to find herself chosen for the local beauty contest.

The *Editor's Notes* page caused Asami to sigh yet again. There was no avoiding talk of the worsening economy, triggered by the stock market crash of 1929. People were whispering that they were in for a full-blown Depression. The Editor urged the populace to buck up.

We are wrestling today with another period of depression. "There has never been anything like this," we cry—and inform our neighbor, who informs his neighbor—and soon everyone believes it. There have been periods of depression before. And each generation had its calamity-howlers who magnified the situation far beyond its real limits. Yet the men and women of these other periods conquered gloom and panic. Were they of stouter hearts and more stubborn in adversity than we?

One more page, Asami promised herself, but the laundry was forgotten as she turned to page fifteen and got caught up in the story of the *Komagata Maru*, the steamship full of East Asians from India that was denied entry at the port of Vancouver for two months in 1914.

How many Powell River residents remember the famous Komagata Maru, *and the international furore her entry into the Port of Vancouver: on May 21, 1914, raised? This incident was outstanding in the history of Vancouver, and no greater excitement has ever prevailed in Vancouver harbor than during the month in which the* Komagata Maru *and her 376 Hindus opposed local immigration officials in the now memorable "Battle of Burrard Inlet."*

When the Hindus on board SS Komagata Maru *arrived at the quarantine station at William Head on the evening of May 21, 1914, they innocently commenced a controversy which focussed the eyes of the world on Vancouver, and only ended two months later when they left here without having set foot on Canadian soil.*

Immigration officials refused the East Indians admittance on the ground they had not received a clean bill of health at Moji, Japan, their last port of call and that an order-in-council provided that all Hindus entering Canada must come to this country direct from India. It was pointed out the Komagata Maru *was chartered at Hong Kong. Officials also stated they had heard reports that the immigrants were practically destitute, few possessing as much as $100.*

Captain Yamamoto of the Japanese ship declared the British Consulate at Moji had told him it would not be necessary to get a bill of health as the vessel had previously been given a clean sheet at Hong Kong and Yokohama. Gurdit Singh, leader of the party, stated that as the Hindus were British subjects they should be immediately admitted to Canada. He retained Mr. J. E. Bird, well-known Vancouver lawyer, to fight his case.

The Komagata Maru *entered Vancouver harbor on the afternoon of May 23 and anchored in the stream. In the meantime, the unusual situation attracted attention of the whole world to Vancouver. A number of prominent newspapers, including the* London Times, *dealt with the matter editorially, and discussions of the pros and cons of the situation became more and more frequent. Several attempts were made to take small parties of Hindus off the vessel, but these were foiled by the close watch kept by immigration officials.*

Instead of being speedily solved, the case became more and more complicated as official red tape gradually worked itself into a tight knot about the Japanese ship and her passengers. Ottawa was notified, Vancouver Hindus held indignation meetings, and their brethren aboard the ship went on a brief hunger strike. It was eventually decided that the twenty-two East Indians who had resided in British Columbia previously should be allowed to land, but the official door was closed to the remainder. Gurdit Singh then wrote indignant letters to King George and appealed to Lord Hardinge, Viceroy of India at that time. A reply from the latter told the Hindu leader he could expect no aid from that source. Several days later an attempt was made to move the Komagata Maru *to another berth in the harbor, but the Hindus, thinking they were about to be taken back to Japan, refused to allow the sailors to raise steam.*

Annoyed by continual demonstrations of the Orientals, the City Council at this time passed a resolution favoring ejection of all Asiatics. It was then announced the Court of Appeal had rejected Gurdit Singh's plea, and the Hindus would have to leave Vancouver as soon as possible. They showed no such inclination, however, and on July 20th the cruiser Rainbow *and approximately 1,000 soldiers of the Irish Fusiliers and the Sixth Regiment were called out to suppress the Hindus if necessary.*

Their services were not needed, however, for on the afternoon of July 23 the vessel and her dark-skinned passengers sailed out of the harbor, after a stay of more than two months. Thus terminated one of the strangest immigration tangles ever staged here.

Asami, who had been fourteen at the time and airily uninterested in local politics, had only the vaguest memory of this event, but the newspaper's review of it now caused a very different reaction. How clearly the anti-Asiatic message came through, she thought. They were 'dark-skinned Orientals' and the implication of the refusal to grant entry was that they were somehow 'unclean' and that the Japanese assurance of good health wasn't to be trusted. Asami snorted, thinking about how her parents had expressed horror when they learned that Anglos actually washed themselves in the standing water of their baths. The Japanese custom was to use hot water, soap, and soft cloths to wash their bodies while standing on a platform adjoining the bath. Only once they were entirely clean would they enter the deep bathtub itself and sink down into the steaming water to relax among family members or friends. No-one would sit in the bath water with dirty skin—to do so would be disgusting. Judging by their contrasting smell, Asami would wager that most Japanese Canadians were far cleaner than some of their English neighbours. But, of course, she thought, prejudice had nothing to do with the facts of the matter, did it?

Speaking of cleanliness—Asami folded the newspaper and rose to her feet to tackle the now well-soaked laundry.

1934
Powell River, British Columbia
Kanagawa Prefecture, Japan

Kenji's little sister's birth in January of 1934 wasn't anywhere near as dramatic as his arrival had been. For one thing, this time Asami knew more of what to expect. She'd been saddened by several miscarriages in the years between the two children but remembered her own mother's history of loss and knew that it was not an uncommon experience. She and Hoshi had been so thankful when this pregnancy progressed totally normally, and that she had a nice clean, modern hospital in which to give birth. No baseball stands this time! The birth, however, was the only easy part of the little girl's infancy.

Baby Ichika, whose name meant one thousand flowers, slid into the world with a frown and seemed determined to disapprove of everything from that moment onward. She screamed constantly with colic, and nothing would soothe her but to be tied onto her mother's back and carried everywhere. Carrying infants in this way was common in Japan, Asami knew, but her Anglo doctor advised against it, and the local housewives gave her disparaging looks when they saw her packing the baby on her back.

"You'll just spoil her, you know," one matron with tightly permed grey hair in the grocery store checkout line had advised Asami this warm spring morning.

"And you'll weaken her legs," added another woman.

Asami pretended not to speak English, but it was hard to hide her flaming cheeks as the two women went on to discuss her foreign ways, tsking as they gave her sideways looks. The cashier, who knew that Asami spoke perfect English, kept her eyes averted and her expression stony as she checked the few items through. These days, Asami tried to keep her store purchases to a minimum. The Depression continued, though due to its foreign exports, the Company had managed to stay afloat and keep most of its workers employed. Nevertheless, prices continued to rise, and it was hard making ends meet each week.

By the time she reached home, Asami was totally out of temper, having told the two women off in her head all the way up the hill. She was partly consoled to find that Ichika had fallen deeply asleep on the walk to their small but comfortable Company house. She slid the baby carefully from her back into her crib, holding her breath until she was sure Ichika was going to continue sleeping. Then she tiptoed out of the room, closing the door firmly but silently behind herself. She hoped she'd have an hour or so at her sewing machine.

She'd been thrilled to find a new Singer machine under their tiny

Christmas tree last December. She'd had no idea that Hoshi had been saving for months to purchase it for her. It made such a difference to be able to stitch up all their clothes so fast! She felt almost guilty at the ease it provided, remembering her mother squinting by lamplight every evening after working on the farm all day, endlessly making work and school clothes for them all. Asami found that she quite enjoyed embellishing Ichika's little rompers and jackets with ruffles and trim, things she would never have added to Kenji's boy clothes.

As she went towards her small sewing alcove in their living room, a packet of letters was pushed through the mail slot in the front door. She scooped it up on the way and stopped, intrigued by the spiky writing on the topmost letter. It was not from her mother or father, nor from Jiro. No, the stamp was unfamiliar, and the thin blue onionskin paper of the envelope spoke of air travel from somewhere far away. She lifted it to her nose and sniffed. Was that a distant echo of cherry blossoms she smelled, or just her imagination? She turned the letter over to find a return address in Kanagawa prefecture. Who was writing to them from Japan?

The envelope was addressed to Hoshi, however, so she propped it up on the tiny table next to the door and moved on to her sewing, her mind full of speculation.

By the time Hoshi came home, Asami could hardly wait for him to open the letter. She stood with Ichika on her hip, swaying side to side to keep the baby amused, at the same time listening to Kenji as he played with his few simple toys in the bedroom he shared with his sister. At eight, he had little interest in Ichika, but he tolerated her presence and the demands she placed on their mother. As long as his father took him out for long hikes or baseball games, Kenji was content.

Seeing his wife's curiosity, Hoshi obligingly slit the envelope open with the dragon-headed silver letter opener that was one of the family's prized possessions, having come to Canada with Hoshi so many years ago. His eyes scanned the single flimsy sheet of paper, reading the columns of Japanese characters left to right. When he had read it through, he looked again into the envelope and pulled out another slip of paper with an official-looking seal on it.

He looked up at Asami, his eyes wide with surprise.

"Well, I never thought I'd see this day!" he said. "My mother has sent us passage to go to Japan for a visit!"

"What, all of us?" asked Asami in astonishment. That was a very costly gift! "Why…I mean, why now?" she continued.

Hoshi's expression sobered. "My father is unwell—dying, it seems. My mother wants him to see me again before he dies, and she wishes to meet her grandchildren."

Asami raised her eyebrows. They had, of course, sent a

marriage announcement when they wed, and birth announcements for both children, but this was the first time her mother-in-law had ever acknowledged their existence.

"Can you get the time off work?" she asked, and Hoshi nodded slowly.

"I think so," he replied. "I am owed some holidays and the Company does allow time off for family bereavement. This will be instead of that, I guess. If it's not enough, I'll have to take the time without pay. I think we have to go..." He looked up to see her nod.

"Of course we do," she said, feeling quite excited at the prospect of such an adventure.

Asami was overwhelmed by the size of the Canadian Pacific's *SS Empress of Japan* as it towered above her at the Vancouver dock, its two masts and three belching steam funnels scraping the blue late April sky. They had made all the arrangements for travel as quickly as possible, and now here they were, only a month later, about to walk up the steep gangplank to this enormous liner, which would get them to Yokohama in a record ten days. Ichika was in her usual place, tied securely on Asami's back, and Hoshi had Kenji by one hand as he hoisted their one heavy suitcase in the other.

They took their place in the short line and made their way to the purser who stood at the top of the ramp. Kenji's eyes were wide as he stared up at the man's crisp white uniform. The purser looked at their tickets.

"Hmmm, steerage, eh?" he said, looking the four of them over. He leaned in a little and whispered to Hoshi conspiratorially. "Tell you what, there are a few third-class cabins empty on this voyage. For an extra fifty bucks, I could get your family into one of those. You'd be a lot more comfortable, and you'd have access to the third-class dining room. Better food and plenty of it..." He winked.

Hoshi looked at Asami, who shrugged. They did have the cash with them, although it represented a large part of their savings. She wasn't sure if this upgrade was at a fair price or not. After a moment of hesitation, Hoshi agreed, and a small wad of bills surreptitiously changed hands. The purser smiled broadly as the bills vanished into his pocket.

"Welcome aboard the *Empress of Japan*!" he said, raising his voice and waving his hand expansively. "Please make your way to Cabin 3F in the third-class section. Just follow the signs."

As they walked down the softly carpeted hallway and opened the door to 3F, Asami was glad they'd paid for the upgrade. The cabin wasn't large, but it was nicely kitted out with two sets of bunk beds and a tiny sink. She knew that in steerage, they would have had to share washing facilities and a large open bunk room with many others. She luxuriated in the idea of having this lovely private space all to themselves for the next ten days.

"Mama, I'm hungry," said Kenji, predictably.

"All right," Asami replied. "Let's quickly unpack and then go and find this dining room the purser mentioned."

Along the way, they peeked into the men's and ladies' washrooms, staffed by welcoming stewards and stewardesses, and marveled at the pristine showers and bathtubs provided. They weren't Japanese-style soaking tubs, but Asami decided she could wash herself and the children in a shower before soaking in one of the gleaming porcelain tubs. They stepped out onto the wide decks, covered above by the decks of the upper-class accommodations, and gazed back at the Vancouver dock, hardly able to believe that they were really going to sail away across the ocean in just a few hours.

Smoking rooms, billiard rooms, a reading lounge—even a small ballroom—amazed them as they continued to the dining room. There, they were graciously conducted to a small family table that featured seats fastened to the floor with a mechanism that enabled them to swing all the way around. Kenji was delighted with these and was only distracted from twirling by the arrival of the plentiful, hot, and fresh food. There was a selection of Japanese -style food available on the menu, no doubt to satisfy the requirements of their frequent Asian passengers, but Kenji only wanted Canadian food—a hamburger and French fries. He was even more excited when the waiter added a side dish of American ketchup to the order—a rare treat.

The ten days passed quickly, it seemed, with many enjoyable experiences on board the great steamship. It was with some reluctance, then, that Asami saw, for the first time in her life, the shores of Japan approaching. The harbour at Yokohama was overwhelming, crowded with both passenger ships and thousands of freight vessels, large and small. She was also a bit anxious about meeting Hoshi's family and found herself practicing her Japanese in her head as they made their slow way toward the gangplank connecting them to the dock.

Her fears escalated as Hoshi waved and pointed out his family waiting up ahead. A more traditional-looking matriarch could hardly have been imagined. Instead of the modern dress Asami herself wore, the tiny older woman was wrapped in a traditional ankle-length kimono with a wide *obi* sash. On her feet were *zori*, thonged sandals made of straw, and divided *tabi* socks. Her long hair was rolled in a complicated *nihongami* style, held in place by ornate ivory combs. *Uh-oh,* thought Asami, *I have a feeling that she's not going to approve of the length of my dress or my high-heeled shoes! Hoshi should have warned me.* But she realized that her husband would have had no way of knowing what his mother expected, so long after leaving Japan himself.

"*Haha*," said Hoshi respectfully but without warmth, bowing deeply to his mother. He turned to greet the tall, thin man standing next to his mother, wearing an elegant double-breasted Western-style suit and a bowler hat. "*Ani*," he said with another bow. Asami understood that the man was Hoshi's older brother, Yoshitaro Ichirou, meaning first son. Hoshi had explained to her that in traditional Japanese families such as his, the oldest son inherited everything, including jurisdiction over his younger brothers and sisters. This was the reason why Hoshi had emigrated to Canada—there would be no land or wealth for him from the family even when his father died. Although the samurais were long gone, abolished in the 1868 fall of the shogunate, some of the wealthier commoner families like the Tasakas tried to cling to the old ways. Hoshi turned to introduce his family.

Asami bowed to her mother-in-law. "*Okaasan*," she said, handing over the gift she had brought, an *obi* sash she had hand embroidered. Mrs. Tasaka's eyes were solemn and she did not smile even as she accepted the gift. When she turned to the children, however, her expression softened.

"Welcome, my grandchildren," she said in Japanese. Kenji looked up at his mother in confusion. He only knew a few words in Japanese and this strangely dressed old lady scared him.

"Say hello to your grandmother, your *Obaasan*," said Asami gently, and Kenji mumbled something that approximated the word. Ichika, held in Asami's arms, merely stared, sucking her thumb. Mrs. Tasaka reached up and yanked the child's thumb out of her mouth with a sharp word Asami didn't recognize but which was obviously a criticism. Ichika frowned ferociously and promptly replaced the thumb. *Oh, this is going to be a battle, I fear,* Asami thought to herself, *but I suspect that Ichika will be equal to the contest!*

They made their way through the throngs of people to a gleaming black sedan car, a Toyota Model AA, newly launched in Japan. With obvious pride, Yoshitaro swept open the doors and settled them in the back seat after carefully tucking his mother into the passenger seat to the left of the driver's seat. Hoshi had told Asami that his brother was one of the majority shareholders of a company called Precision Optical Instruments. One of the company founders, Tikashi Mitari, had deconstructed a German Leica camera and decided that he could make a Japanese version, which he called the Kwanon. As they drove, Yoshitaro boasted that the new camera would sweep the international market as soon as it was released, making him a very wealthy man.

Sitting quietly in the back seat, Asami thought of how hard Hoshi worked every day in the paper mill and found herself feeling resentful of the traditional Japanese family structure. Why should all the family wealth go to only one child, with nothing given to Hoshi or his two younger sisters? She tried not to feel envious of this sleek man, with his fancy car, but it was difficult.

When they reached the family home, Asami's envy grew. Even though she knew that Japan had been influenced by several important Western architects in recent years, including America's Frank Lloyd Wright, Yoshitaro's large home was classically Japanese. It was a sprawling wooden structure with the classic soaring roofs of temple architecture and as the group was ushered inside, Asami saw that the rooms were divided by sliding panels and rice-paper covered partitions. There was very little furniture, and only tatami mats covered the floors. It was elegant and spacious, and Asami couldn't help comparing it to their tiny Company home back in Powell River. She tried to tell herself that she preferred the coziness of their little house.

Interçepting Hoshi's meaningful glance, Asami removed her shoes and found slippers to fit from among the many arrayed by the front door. She took Kenji's shoes off and let him remain in his sock feet. He stayed very close to her, which was highly unusual. They were conducted to their rooms, where Asami busied herself changing Ichika and settling Kenji for a rest. Hoshi disappeared with his mother and brother to visit with his bedridden father.

When he returned, his expression was sober.

"How is he?" asked Asami quietly, for both children were asleep.

"Very near death, I believe," said Hoshi and sat down beside Asami on the edge of the bed. He took her hand in his, a rare gesture for him. Asami frowned. What was going on? In the next moment she found out.

"Asami, he...he wants Kenji to stay here in Japan, to be adopted by Yoshitaro."

Asami gaped at him. "Why?" was her first question, quickly followed by another. "What did you tell him?" Hoshi spoke again, his eyes on their entwined fingers.

"Yoshitaro has been married twice—his first wife died young—and neither of his wives has conceived a child in ten years. As eldest son, he will inherit all the family's wealth, as you know. But he must have an heir and the family has concluded that, well, that he is not able to produce a child of his own. If he dies without an heir, all the family's holdings will revert to the state."

"That's ridiculous!" said Asami, trying to keep her voice down.

"Surely it would go to you, or your sisters." But Hoshi shook his head.

"No. Many things have become Westernized since the Great War, but not the laws of inheritance. They still follow the *Ie* way—the samurai way. Kenji can only inherit if we allow Yoshi and Eiko to adopt him."

"And what did you say?" she asked again, fear climbing into her throat. Surely, surely he would not allow this to happen! Kenji was their child, their little Canadian boy, born under the baseball stands of Vancouver! They could not give him up, leave him in Japan! She snatched her hand away from her husband's. He raised his head and looked into her eyes.

"I told them we would talk about it. Asami, many Japanese Canadian families send one or more children to Japan for a time, to learn Japanese ways. They come back to Canada eventually, most of them. It would be a tremendous opportunity for Kenichi. As the sole heir, he would inherit all this," he waved his hand at the large home surrounding them, "and all Yoshitaro's wealth. He would be far wealthier than he could ever be in Canada."

"You don't know that," Asami replied quickly. "His life in Canada could go in many directions." Her eyes narrowed. "Did you know this was why we were given tickets to come here?" she asked in a savage whisper, feeling betrayed. But Hoshi shook his head.

"No," he said softly. "I had no idea about the situation." He paused. "Will you at least think about it?" he asked after a moment.

She shook her head. The idea was inconceivable. Then she was struck by another thought. "Why would he have to stay here?" she asked. "Can't he be named heir even if he lives in Canada?" Again, Hoshi shook his head.

"No. The family would require him to stay here, to learn about Japanese culture, and become fluent in the language. It is unclear whether a Canadian citizen would be able to inherit an estate here, so he may have to become a Japanese citizen. And he must be formally adopted by Yoshitaro to inherit, not be his nephew."

"That's barbaric!" Asami hissed.

"It is practical," said Hoshi sadly. "It is the way Japanese families, and their wealth, are preserved in Japan. And there's another thing, Asami. If we agree to this, the family will pay us a generous stipend. It would make our lives much more comfortable and enable us to give Ichika a better life."

"So, we'd be *selling* Kenji, then?" Asami sneered. Hoshi grimaced but did not reply.

He stood. "I said we would talk about it. We do not have to give them a decision now, but we must choose before we go back to Canada."

"That's a week away!" Asami said. She also stood. "But my

answer will still be no, Hoshi. I am not giving up my son." Her husband just gazed at her unhappily, saying nothing, and Asami knew with a lurch of terror that the decision would not be hers to make.

As might have been expected, the revelation of the true purpose of their visit soured the entire experience for Asami. She was not taken to meet Hoshi's father, which was just as well, she thought. She wasn't sure if she would have been able to hold her tongue about this crazy scheme to leave Kenji behind—to essentially sell him to Yoshitaro and his meek wife Eiko. She found herself watching her little boy closely. She no longer trusted her in-laws, or even her husband, and had nightmares in which they spirited Kenji away somewhere that she couldn't find him.

She saw that Eiko followed Kenji hungrily with her eyes and stayed near him wherever they went, and despite her opposition to the scheme, Asami did develop a reluctant sympathy for the woman. She could imagine what it was like to desperately want a child and not be able to conceive, having heard stories from her mother about the many tragedies and disappointments they had suffered before Asami had finally been born. How she wished Sara was here now, to help and advise her. Nothing in her life had prepared her for such a decision.

The tension grew as the week went on, but still Asami refused to discuss the matter with Hoshi. On one of the last days of the visit, the family went to the Cherry Blossom Festival, a huge celebration of spring in Japanese culture. A vast park in Yokohama was dedicated to the trees, and on this warm day in early May it was thronged with people enjoying the beauty of the millions of delicate pink flowers dangling overhead and carpeting the grass. Japanese music wafted through the air and the mood was festive. Asami thought again about her mother, whose Japanese name, Sakura, meant 'cherry blossom' but who had insisted on changing it to Sara to be more Canadian.

Asami watched Kenji race around, kicking up fallen blossoms with his young cousins, the children of Hoshi's sisters. He was laughing, carefree, clearly enjoying himself. It occurred to Asami that no-one had asked *him* what he wanted. He wasn't an infant—he was eight. Hardly old enough to understand the entire implications of the idea but nevertheless...she started toward him, thinking to broach the topic casually, but at that moment the older of Hoshi's sisters, Hina, sidled up to her.

"May I speak with you?" Hina asked quietly, and Asami nodded. *Now what?* she thought. *Some other mysterious secret no-one has told me?*

"I know that my *ani* has asked you to allow him to adopt Kenichi. I am sure that this is troubling to you." Asami nodded again, not trusting herself to speak of the anguish in her heart. Hina continued. "I am wondering if you know that there is an alternative," she almost whispered, darting glances to where the men strolled nearby. Asami glanced at her and raised her eyebrows. Hina tucked her hand through Asami's elbow and drew her slightly away, as if to admire a particularly large tree smothered in dangling blooms. As the two women ducked underneath the enveloping canopy, the distinctive musky scent of the flowers surrounded Asami, almost dizzying her. Was there a way out of this dilemma?

"My father could adopt my husband, his son-in-law, as his oldest son," Hina said so quietly that Asami had to strain to hear. "Then he would inherit, and our son after him."

Asami frowned. Subtleties were at work here. Such a move would disinherit Yoshitaro, wouldn't it? And if that was a possibility, then... "If that's possible, couldn't your father also decide to recognize Hoshi as the oldest son?"

An irritated expression flashed across Hina's face. *Ah,* thought Asami, *she didn't expect me to figure that out! She was counting on me to grasp at any alternative to giving up Kenji!*

"Yes," admitted Hina. "But you would all have to move to Japan in that case. I did not think you would wish to do such a thing. You are proud Canadians now, are you not?" There was a slight sneer in her voice as she asked this.

"We are," said Asami, walking out from under the almost-cloying scent of the blossoms. She drew in a deep breath of fresh air and kept walking away from Hina. What a tangled web this was! There were no good choices here.

Later, as they all sat on blankets and ate the picnic lunch Yoshitaro's cook had packed for them, Asami arranged her little family at the edge of the gathering. Hoshi sat near his mother, assisting her. Asami settled Ichika to nap in the shade and sat down again, close to Kenji. As they ate, Asami leaned close to her little boy and spoke quietly to him.

"Are you having fun, my son?" she asked, swallowing hard to quiet the quaver in her voice. Kenji tipped his face up to grin up at her.

"Yes," he said. "It is nice to have cousins, others who look like me, to play with. I didn't know how much fun that would be. And no white boys jeering at me, calling me Jap, laughing at the tilt of my eyes..." His soft little boy's lips trembled a little and Asami's heart broke. He had not complained about this at home, perhaps knowing that there was little his mother could do to help. She swallowed again and steeled herself to ask the next question.

"Would you...would you perhaps like to stay here in Japan, go to school with your cousins?" she asked and watched his face light up.

"Could I?" he asked, "That would be great!" Now for the hardest question.

"What if that meant staying with Oji Yoshitaro and Oba Eiko?" Kenji frowned, not understanding. "If Mama and Papa and Ichika went back to Canada, and you stayed here with them?" Now Kenji's eyes grew wide, and he gripped her arm.

"You would leave me here?" he asked, panicked. "Go home without me?" Asami could not bear the terror in his eyes, so she tempered the message.

"Perhaps, just for a little while? To go to school and learn all about Japan?" she said. "You could come back to Canada later."

Kenji's breathing was rapid. For a moment he looked away, his narrow shoulders heaving. Then he looked at her again, tears swimming in his eyes. "Why?" he demanded. "Have I been very bad? Do you and Papa not want me anymore?"

"Oh Kenji-*kun*, no, no, that is not it at all. We love you dearly and it would be very, very hard for us to leave you here. But, you see, Kenji, your Oji Yoshitaro has no son, and in Japan it is the oldest son's son who must carry on the family name. They wish you to be the oldest Tasaka grandson, and eventually be the head of the family. For this to happen, you must stay in Japan and learn how to do that."

Kenji was quiet, looking at the many family members around them and struggling to swallow his tears. After a few moments, he spoke again, and now his voice was thoughtful.

"Does Papa wish me to do this?" he asked.

"Well, yes and no," answered Asami. "He would miss you terribly, as would I, but he feels an obligation to his family, too. It would be an advantage to you, certainly, as you would grow up in a wealthier family and go to a more prestigious school."

"But why would we not all stay in Japan?" Kenji asked. "Why must it be only me?" This was the question Asami had hoped to avoid, for it was not easily answered.

"Ah, Kenji. I am Canadian, not Japanese, as is Ichika. This is not our home. And Grandma and Grandpa Sato are in Canada. I cannot live so far away from them."

"But I am Canadian too!" the boy protested.

"Yes," his mother answered. "You are. It would mean making a choice, for the good of your father's family." She paused. "What if we had a trial period? What if you stayed for a year, to see if you liked it? If you didn't, then at the end of the year you could come home to Canada, and us."

Kenji was silent for a long time. His small hand crept into hers and clasped it tightly. She waited, swearing to herself that if he said no, she would take him home, no matter what everyone else wanted. She would not force her son to do something he did not want to do.

"You promise?" he whispered, and she could hear the tremor in his voice. He was trying so very hard to be brave. "You promise I can come home after a year if I want to?"

She put her arms around his slight body and whispered into his ear. "I promise," she said and prayed that she would be able to fulfill that promise if needed.

1939
Powell River, British Columbia

Since leaving Kenichi behind in Japan, Asami had become much more attentive to Japanese affairs. Four times a year, she received a stilted letter from her son, saying he was fine, he was doing well at school, he missed them but was willing to stay where he was. The only parts of each letter that sounded like the little boy she remembered were his enthusiastic narratives of baseball games he'd played in or watched. These letters caused deeply confused emotions for Asami. Of course, she was glad that Kenji was doing well and not pining away for his Canadian family, but as each year passed, she felt him grow less and less connected to her. Would she even recognize this almost-teenager? What was his life like now? So—she pored over the few Japanese newspapers she could find and nagged her Japanese Canadian neighbours for any news they heard.

It was easier these days to follow events of interest to Japanese Canadians since the establishment of the English-language newspaper *The New Canadian* in 1938. Asami read it eagerly, grateful to editor Tom Shoyama and the many dedicated writers who established themselves as "The Voice of the Second Generation." The paper was focused mainly on events in Canada, but it also reported on items of interest from Japan.

As a result, Asami knew that Japan was growing more and more militant. Ever since the war ended, there had been competing voices arguing about the best path forward for prosperity. Some, such as the American-educated idealist Nitobe Inazō, were convinced that diplomacy would be best. His motto was 'peace through mutual understanding' and he was one of the founding members of the post-war League of Nations, dedicated to preventing another catastrophic war.

Others, championed by Shidehara Kijūrō, took a business-like approach. The way to avoid conflict, Shidehara said, was to make peace more profitable than war, and the best way to ensure that Japan prospered was to engage in trade. He had strongly objected to Japan's take-over of the Chinese state of Manchuria in 1931, arguing that it was too expensive and difficult to maintain a conquered puppet state, as the re-named Manchukuo was. Instead of invading, it would be better to support China in establishing a stable government, one that would engage in ongoing and profitable trade with Japan.

But these days the dominant voice was Ishiwara Kanji, an ardent militarist who had led the breakaway forces that had taken Manchuria. His faction had only the loosest connection to the central Japanese government, and as far as Asami could tell, he and his armies did whatever they wanted. Kanji believed that a second world war was not only inevitable, but desirable. He envisioned a global unification, with the Japanese at the helm, and saw the United States as their most dangerous opponent. When the League of Nations refused to recognize Manchukuo as a legitimate state, Kanji convinced Japan to withdraw from the League. Since then, he had achieved more and more influence. Asami feared this man and his vision for Japan. It seemed he was determined to lead his country into major conflict. When Japan had renewed its aggression against China and carried out atrocities in the city of Nanking in 1937, she had trembled to think what that might mean for her son and the rest of Hoshi's family.

Not that conditions in Canada were all that much better for what were now being called the Nikkei, persons of Japanese descent living in other countries. In 1936, the Nikkei had put together a delegation to Ottawa's Special Committee on Elections and Franchise Acts of the House of Commons, to argue for the right to vote for naturalized or Canadian-born Japanese Canadians. The group included Minoru Kobayashi, an insurance agent; Edward Banno, a dentist; SJ Hayakawa, a university lecturer; and Hide Hyodo, the female teacher who had been the first to be allowed to teach in a *hakujin* school in British Columbia. The newspaper reports of their presentation to the Special Committee had included many expressions of surprise at how fluent they were in English, a remark that caused Asami to roll her eyes. For heaven's sake, the Nikkei been in Canada for decades. Many of them were born and educated here—in fact, many of them didn't speak Japanese at all! When were white Canadians going to realize that the angle of someone's eyes didn't necessarily tell you anything about them? The delegation was listened to politely, but the Committee deferred the decision to the jurisdiction of British Columbia who, of course, declined to make any changes whatsoever. It was a great disappointment.

As Asami opened this week's edition of *The New Canadian*, however, all thoughts about obtaining the right to vote in Canada flew out of her head. For the headline told her that Adolf Hitler, the leader of Germany's Nazi Party, had invaded Poland. As much as she hoped otherwise, Asami very much feared that the first step toward General Kanji's desired second world war had just been taken.

1940
Powell River, British Columbia

Isabel Tasaka dashed out of the door of her kindergarten class, proudly waving the page of colouring she'd completed that day. She was happier in school now that her mother had agreed to change her name from Ichika.

"The other kids called me Itchy Cat," she'd wailed after her first day. Asami (hiding a smile at the aptness of the nickname for her rather irritable and fiercely independent daughter) had sighed and agreed that perhaps a more Canadian-sounding name might be better. Together they had settled on Isabel, and from the second day on, Isabel had insisted that everyone call her that. Now hardly anyone remembered she'd once had a different name, and Isabel was glad. Things were hard enough these days, with all the grown-ups whispering in corners and looking worried about the war. Lots of her classmates' fathers and older brothers had signed up as soldiers and Isabel wondered why her father hadn't gone as well. Not that she wanted him to go, exactly, but some of the kids sneered at her and said that her dad couldn't be a soldier because he was a Jap. Isabel didn't know what that word meant but it sounded mean.

She ran toward the gate in the fence surrounding the school, where her mother always waited for her, but today there was a stranger standing with Asami, and Isabel skidded to a stop a few feet away. Who was this tall teenager with his awkwardly fitting suit and short haircut?

Asami beckoned to her, and Isabel approached them slowly, hiding her colouring behind her back.

"Ichika, come here," her mother called sharply, "Stop dawdling!" Isabel scowled at the use of her old name. Why couldn't her mother remember to call her Isabel? She hated being called Ichika. She scuffed her feet and held back until all the other kids had streamed out of the gate, chattering excitedly to their mothers. Finally, when almost everyone else was gone, she walked slowly forward. The boy crouched down in front of her and smiled.

"Hey little sister," he said softly. "Don't you remember me? It's Kenji, your brother. I've come home from Japan."

Isabel frowned. She knew she had a brother in Japan, of course, because her parents talked about him all the time. Kenji this, Kenji that, as if whatever he did was more important than anything she did. And now here he was, right here in her hometown. Probably her parents would forget she even existed.

"Give your brother a hug!" remonstrated Asami. "Aren't you happy to see him?"

Isabel turned her face away. "I don't know," she mumbled.

"I've brought you some presents," said Kenji, and Isabel glanced at him from the corner of her eye.

"What kind of presents?" she demanded.

"Oh well, you'd better come home and see," Kenji said, grinning and standing up. "Or maybe I should give them to some other little girl."

"No!" said Isabel, turning to face him. "You said they were for me!"

"And so they are," he said, and she allowed him to take her hand. "Come on, let's go find them."

Isabel was thrilled with the porcelain doll dressed in a pink silk kimono, her hair dressed high in a geisha style and tiny zori sandals on her feet over divided socks, and the delicate doll-sized tea set. She thanked her brother hurriedly and then raced to her room to play with her new treasures. She could hear the murmur of her mother's and brother's voices coming from the kitchen, but she tuned them out.

"I can't believe you are really here," Asami said again, gazing raptly into her son's face and reaching out to touch his hand softly. "Now, tell me properly—why *are* you here?"

Her son shrugged in the infuriating way fourteen-year-olds have. "I wanted to come home," he said, his eyes downcast, his fingers fiddling with the wrappings from Isabel's gifts that lay on the table between them. "Aren't you happy to see me?"

Asami blew out an exasperated breath.

"Of course I am! But Kenji, that is not the whole story. It can't be. Your Oji Yoshitaro adopted you and I know he fully intended for you to stay there and inherit the family lands. Why would he let you come back to Canada just because you 'wanted to'?" Kenji's cheeks reddened a little.

"We—we had a disagreement," he said, his eyes still on the table.

"What about?" asked Asami, wondering if she was going to have to drag each detail out of her reluctant son. Kenji's eyes came up to hers and his expression was defiant.

"The war," he said. "Oji said that Japan was a great military nation that would soon rule the world, and that I should be proud to be Japanese. He said I should join the junior militia and hope to be a soldier one day." Asami sat back, astounded.

"He said that, that they would soon rule the world?"

Kenji nodded, then straightened and leaned toward his mother, his tone now earnest.

"Mama, he said that Japan is about to join with Germany and Italy against the Allies! He expected me to be proud of that, to be part of a country going to war with my homeland! I am *not* Japanese; I will *never* be Japanese! I am *Canadian*, and if I fight at all, it will be for *my* country, against the fascists!"

"I don't expect he was very happy to hear that," said Asami, struggling to manage the terror this information evoked.

"No, he was not. In fact, he locked me in my room, swearing that I'd stay there until I admitted the error of my ways. He said that no son of his would refuse to fight for Japan..."

"And, of course, you told him that you *were* no son of his?" guessed his mother. Kenji nodded, looking away again. "So, how did you manage to get aboard a steamer to Canada?" she asked, but she had a suspicion.

"Oba Hina came when Oji was out and gave me the ticket. She gave me money—that's what I used to buy these things for Ichika, on the ship. She even paid for the taxi to take me to the dock." Asami nodded. With Kenji out of the running, Hina was free to press her goal of having her husband adopted into the family as the heir, and their sons after him. The old man was long dead, but Yoshitaro, now the head of the household, could adopt Hina's husband as his son. She didn't think Hina would have deliberately harmed Kenji, but this rift between the boy and his adoptive father probably seemed like a golden opportunity to clear the field.

"Did Oba Eiko know about this?"

"Maybe," Kenji said, his cheeks flushing again. "She was always kind. She understood that I was homesick all the time. I...I think she saw me sneaking out the back door with Oba Hina, but she turned her face away. She must not have told Oji, because he didn't chase after me. I think she probably made him think I was still in my room, until it was too late to catch me."

Asami stood and stepped over to her son, bending to put her arms around him, her cheek laid on top of his tousled hair.

"Kenji, Kenji, why did you not let us know that you were unhappy? Every letter we got said you were fine and that you wanted to stay! I would never have left you there if I'd known you were so sad."

A stifled sob broke from the boy, and his thin shoulders shook. "Oji always told me what to write and checked my letters. And I...I was trying to be brave, to do what was expected of me. Sometimes it was all right, at school, playing sports. But I never stopped missing you and Papa and even baby Ichika, annoying as she was!" He gasped a chuckle through the tears now coursing down his cheeks. "I wanted you to be proud of me, and Oji told me over and over that he was sending you money for my staying in Japan. He said that I had to stay so you could have a better life." His arms crept around his mother's waist, and he turned his wet face up to hers. "I'm sorry, Mama, I'm sorry. I tried to do what was best for everyone but I...I just couldn't say I'd fight against you!"

"Of course you couldn't. You did the right thing. I am just glad that Oba Hina was willing to help you get home."

“So, you won’t send me back?” Kenji gulped, his eyes fastened intently on hers.

Asami hugged him closely and spoke into his ear. “No one will ever send you away from us again, my dear son. When it comes time to leave us, it will your choice and no one else’s.”

1941
Powell River, British Columbia

Kenji's report of Japan's intentions proved true within weeks of his unexpected return to Canada. In late September, Japan formally made a Tripartite Pact with Germany and Italy, and the war expanded from Europe to the Pacific. By vowing to protect the signatories from attack, the three countries were warning the United States, which had so far remained neutral in the conflict, to stay out of the war. Asami could not imagine how the tiny nation of Japan thought it could stand up to America, but she knew little of military strategies. She was just fervently glad that her boy had returned home before everything changed.

War was the major topic of conversation everywhere, of course. In the grocery store, at the line-up to pick up children from school, in the paper mill. It was also, inevitably, talked about at home, and little Isabel was heartily sick of all the long faces and sad tones. Tonight, Papa had told them that a special committee of the war cabinet of the Canadian government had decided that Japanese Canadians could not join the armed forces, because there was 'strong public opinion against them.' Isabel imagined a huge wooden cabinet with toy soldiers all locked up inside because nobody liked them. But if the new law kept her father and newly rediscovered brother at home, she was all for it. She couldn't understand why everyone else thought it was so terrible. It had been lovely to have Kenji home over Christmas, because he played with her and took her sledding on her new sled on the snowy hills above the town. It was January now, but she wanted to go sledding some more. She didn't want him to disappear again.

The snow had mostly melted in March when the tall man banged on their door. The loud sound startled Isabel, who had been nodding off over one of her books, all cozy and warm under a blanket on her bed. She knew she was supposed to be practicing her reading, but she kept being distracted by her geisha doll's sleek kimono. It was so nice to stroke it, but it did sometimes make her feel a little sleepy. But now she wasn't sleepy at all. Who was knocking so loudly on their door on a Saturday afternoon?

Isabel crept out from under her blanket and stepped softly along the hallway. She peeked around the door frame toward the front hall, where Papa had just opened the door to a big man in a bright red coat and a black hat with a wide brim. Isabel knew who he was—a policemen, one of the ones they called 'arsyempy,' which seemed a very funny name to her, especially as it included a word that Isabel knew was rude, but everyone said it so it must be right. Papa politely invited the officer into their home, but the man shook his head. He held a clipboard with lots of papers on it and was asking Papa questions about who lived in the house. Papa told him about himself, giving his full name Hoshitaro Tasaka, and the date of his birthday. Isabel giggled to herself. Did Papa think the officer was going to give him a birthday present? Then Papa gave Mama's name and birthday too. That was funny. Maybe the whole town was going to have a big birthday party?

The officer nodded and touched his fingers to the brim of his hat and turned to go. Isabel dashed out into the hallway.

"Wait, wait! I live here too, and my big brother Kenji! We want to go to the birthday party too!"

The officer looked sternly at Papa. "Is there someone else over sixteen living here? It's an offence to withhold information, sir!" he said.

"No, no, my son is only fourteen," said Papa, almost bowing in his eagerness to be polite.

"Oh, very well, then," said the policeman, and turned away. At the last moment he looked back, and his stern expression softened. "I am sorry about this, sir. We—the RCMP--have told the government that we have no concern about the Japanese Canadians who live here on the coast but, well…in a time of war, you know…" His voice trailed off, and he touched his hand to the brim of his hat again before walking down their front path. Isabel saw him striding up to old Mr. Ohashi's house three doors down.

"Why don't the people in the next two houses get to come to the birthday party?" she asked her father, who looked at her in bewilderment. "Is it a special party only for people who look like us?"

Her Papa hoisted her up in his strong arms, a rare treat she loved even though she was *almost* too old for it now. "What birthday party, my little Izzie?" he asked, tickling her tummy.

"The one that the arsyempy is organizing, of course! Why else would he have asked when your birthdays are? But how come it's only for grown-ups? I want a party too!"

"And you shall have a party, my little *musume*, when your birthday comes. Let's see, when is that? I seem to have forgotten…is it in July? October?" He tipped his head as if thinking deeply.

"Papa! It is in January, you know that! Just a few months ago! I turned seven!"

"Ohhh, so we just had a birthday party for you, then, did we?" her father teased.

"Well, yes, but if everyone else is getting one, I want another one. Why *was* that policeman asking about your birthday, Papa?"

Her father's laughter faded, and he put Isabel down on the floor.

"It's nothing, nothing. They just want to know where all the Nikkei live, that's all."

"But why? Why just us?"

Her father shook his head sadly. "I don't know, Ichika, I don't know." And he looked so troubled that for once Isabel didn't remind him not to call her by her old name.

Spirits were low that summer. It was clear that the Nikkei were under suspicion, but nobody said or did anything other than gathering their information. Everyone continued to follow the war news avidly. When hints of the atrocities visited upon the Jews began to leak out, Asami was horrified.

"How could people do such things?" she whispered to Hoshi as they lay sleepless in bed one hot Saturday night in July. "Just for being different—they would take their homes and belongings, force them into camps, kill them? How can the world hold such hatred and evil?"

"I know," said Hoshi, gently stroking her hand where it lay on the sheets between them. "But I think it is rarely just because the others are different. That is just the excuse. It is because someone wants what they have, is jealous that they have more." He fell silent, thinking about how he had lost his fishing license because the *hakujin* and *dojin*, the Indians, saw the Japanese immigrants as 'unfair competition.' *Competition, yes,* he thought, *but why was it considered unfair?* The Japanese immigrants certainly hadn't been given any advantage by anyone—on the contrary, they'd had to work a lot harder to earn enough money to buy their boats and fishing gear.

"It is so sad. Everything is so sad," Asami said, sighing. "Let's take a picnic up to Powell Lake tomorrow, let the children have a swim, forget about the war for a day."

"Yes, that's a good idea," said Hoshi, glad to turn his mind to something more pleasant.

The next day was another hot, sunny one, so they packed a hamper, gathered a picnic blanket and towels, and followed the winding trail through the forest to Powell Lake, a deep glacial lake that had been enlarged when the dam to power the paper mill had been built on the river. They followed an old logging rail line and as the peace of the forest surrounded him, Kenji remembered his joy during the long hikes his father had taken him on as a small boy. How he had missed this Canadian wilderness! When Isabel complained that she was tired of walking, Kenji cheerfully piggybacked her the rest of the way.

They stopped at a remote but lovely spot for swimming near an old shingle slide. They could still see scattered blocks of lumber, sections of trees that had been chopped into quarters, ready to be split into shingles, and floated down a chute toward the mouth of the river. Some of the swampy parts of the trail were still covered in planks the loggers had put down, and Kenji marveled at how well preserved the thick slabs of cedar were, despite being submerged every winter.

After eating their picnic, they changed into swimming clothes and entered the clear, cold water. It was rumoured that this lake was so deep that some of the original salt water from millennia ago still lurked far below. Goat Island, a mountain drowned by the melting glaciers of old, lifted its massive granite head not far offshore and Kenji challenged his father to swim to it.

They reached it almost in tandem, with Hoshi touching the rocks of the island just ahead of his son. Laughing, they hauled themselves out and basked for a few moments on the warm rocks, warming up. Suddenly a shower of small pebbles struck Kenji's shoulder and he looked up to meet the flat gaze of a yellow-eyed mountain goat perched precariously on a ledge far above. Its thin black horns jutted aggressively from its head, ending in lethally sharp points. Its creamy white coat hung in shaggy tatters in the summer heat but was still so thick around its legs that Kenji laughed aloud. It looked as if it was wearing baggy pants. The goat stared meditatively, chewing, for a moment more, then evidently decided the men were no threat. It turned and, with a leap that made Kenji gasp, moved to an even narrower ledge higher up. Within another moment it had disappeared around a tumble of rocks.

Still staring after the goat, Kenji was startled to see the head, then the torso, then the long bare legs of a man appear. It was a *hakujin*, a white man, sporting a thick moustache but little else. In one hand he carried a large camera, and in the other a cigarette, which he now raised to his lips, blowing a thin stream of smoke from the corner of his mouth. Gazing about, he spotted the two Nikkei far below him.

"Oh hello!" he bellowed, seemingly unperturbed by his state of near nakedness. "Lovely day, isn't it?"

They looked back up at him, nonplussed. Without waiting for a reply, the man scrambled down to where they sat, leaping almost as agilely as the goat. When he reached them, Kenji realized how very tall the man was. The fellow towered over both Kenji and his father, but his face was wreathed in a genial smile. He reached out a hand to shake both of theirs, saying, "Ozzie Stevenson, photographer. Pleased to make your acquaintance, gentlemen." Kenji and Hoshi shook hands, bowing slightly as well, not sure what to say to this unexpected arrival.

Undeterred by their reticence, Ozzie gently waved his camera. "Trying to get some shots of the young rams fighting for top dog status—

well, top goat, I guess," he said. "Very dramatic at this time of year. As are the views—spectacular from the top. You should come up!"

Kenji couldn't imagine how the man had managed to get to the island with his expensive camera. How on earth had he kept it dry? He couldn't resist asking the question and Mr. Stevenson laughed.

"Oh, I didn't swim, old boy! I have a small canoe on the other side, around the point there." He waved in a vague direction. I've made a camp on a flat rock there, planning to stay a day or two while the clear weather holds. You can pretty much stay on this island for as long as you like if you're a decent shot and don't mind eating goat meat most days. Water's great to drink, there are plenty of fish, and you can always find a few berries and greens to vary the diet. We—the fellows in the mountain climbing brigade--come here at least once a summer. Wonderful spot."

"There are others who climb?" asked Kenji, intrigued.

"Oh yes, a few. Albert Adams—he's the best goat hunter of all of us—and Percy Lockie—we call him PR, best climber by far—and Roland Simmons. We all work for the Company, of course—but we get out climbing as often as we can. I mean," he said, waving his sinewy arm at the peaks surrounding them, "there they stand in all their majesty, just asking to be explored! How could a man resist?" He smiled at them again. "Sure you won't come up higher? No? Well, I'll be off then. Enjoy your swim!" With a brief wave the man stretched out his long legs in several great leaps and disappeared from their sight.

Hoshi and Kenji looked at each other and laughed. What an unexpected meeting! Kenji quite envied the man and his carefree outdoorsy life. He'd love to do such things someday!

The happy memory of that lazy summer day had long faded when terrible news came in early December. For more than three years, tensions between the Japan and America had been rising. When Japan had invaded China in 1937, committing terrible atrocities in Nanking, the United States had passed economic sanctions against them. They had also provided economic support to the Chinese forces trying to resist the Japanese. While the Americans had hoped that the embargoes would convince Japan to halt its expansionism, instead they convinced Japan to stand its ground, angered by continued Western interference in Asian affairs. To Japan, war with the United States seemed inevitable if it hoped to maintain its status as a major world power.

The previous spring, the United States had made Pearl Harbor, in Hawaii, the main base for its Pacific Fleet. The Americans didn't expect the Japanese to attack them there, some 4,000 miles away from the Japanese mainland, so the naval base was relatively undefended. But on the morning of December 7th, the Japanese Admiral, Yamamoto Isoroku, hit Pearl Harbour with a surprise attack from the air.

Everyone in Powell River was horrified to hear on the radio that the Japanese bombers had hit all eight American battleships, sinking four and damaging four others. They had destroyed or damaged more than three hundred aircraft and killed some 2400 Americans in the attack. Overnight, it seemed, Japanese Canadians, whether *issei* immigrants, naturalized Canadians, or *nisei*, Canadian born, became the face of the enemy for Canadians. The small number of Nikkei families in Powell River turned to one another in fear and trepidation. What would happen next? They did not have to wait very long to find out.

1941
Powell River, British Columbia

One day. That's all it took. In concert with the other Allied countries, Canada declared war on Japan on December 8th. Under the War Measures Act, the government passed Order-in-Council P.C. 9591 which required all Japanese nationals and those naturalized after 1922 to register by February 7th with the Registrar of Enemy Aliens.

"Enemy aliens?" exploded Kenji when he read this in the next morning's paper. "Anyone who has been here since 1922 is no longer a foreigner, let alone an enemy! They are loyal Canadians! Surely they cannot do this?"

"It seems they can," said Hoshi quietly. "Luckily this order does not apply to anyone in this household, so it is best if we say nothing about it." He cast a quelling glance at his son, who subsided with an inarticulate grumble.

"But there are things that will affect those we know," said Asami, still reading the front page of *The New Canadian*. "The Canadian Navy is impounding all Japanese fishing boats immediately, twelve hundred of them, it says."

"Why would they do that?" demanded Kenji, his anger flaring again.

"Because they fear that the Nikkei fishermen will cooperate with Japan to spy or assist in enemy actions," said his father. "It is understandable that such fears would arise in the wake of such a horrific attack. No one feels safe anymore when the Americans can suffer such an unexpected and stunning defeat."

Kenji stared at his father, open-mouthed. "They really think some poor fisherman is going to attack Canada?" His father shrugged.

"Fear is not rational, my son. We must accept that these things happen in wartime. The less we object, the clearer it will be that there is nothing to fear from us. Then things will improve." Then he frowned and continued. "However, boats cannot be stored for long without damage. I hope the government lets the fishermen have them back soon, or they will be worth nothing." He turned to Asami. "Perhaps it is a good thing that I was unable to get a fishing license all those years ago! We would be losing our livelihood today."

She nodded absently, still reading. After a moment she looked up, her eyes wide. "It is worse than we thought! All Japanese language schools have been closed. All insurance policies issued to Nikkei have been cancelled! They are accusing the Nikkei of 'fifth column activity'--which is apparently a term coined in the Spanish Civil War in the 1930's--meaning subversive actions here in Canada intended to aid the

Japanese in winning the war! And they have shut down the other two Japanese newspapers. *The New Canadian* will now publish in English and Japanese so they can communicate government orders to the Nikkei population of British Columbia. These are serious actions, Hoshi. I fear things will get worse, not better. We must write to my parents and Jiro, make sure they are all right."

Asami's prediction proved correct. Little more than a week later, another Order-in-Council, number P.C. 9760, required *all* persons of Japanese origin, regardless of citizenship, to register. The newspaper reported that there were approximately 23,000 persons of Japanese descent in Canada, of which over 75% were Canadian citizens, either Canadian born or naturalized after three years of residency. No one seemed to think it wrong that Canadian citizens were to be required to carry an identification card, with a photograph and fingerprint, on their persons at all times.

Hakujin newspapers were filled with unsubstantiated rumours and tales that grew wilder and wilder, especially about the supposed actions of Japanese Americans in Hawaii. It was said that they were deliberately blocking roads—although this was later proven to have been a simple road accident. They had concealed machine guns in their farm trucks! They had sabotaged fighter jets! They had set up signal fires in an arrow pattern to guide Japanese bombers in—though these were revealed (in a tiny correction later buried in the inside pages) to have been innocent brush fires set to clear fields. It was only with the greatest reluctance that the papers later reported that, in fact, not a single Japanese American had been accused of any wrongdoing whatsoever. By that time, it was too late anyway. Canadian newspapers quoted these wild stories as fact, and embellished upon them, reporting that "B.C. Japs held rejoicing parties when Hong Kong fell" and that "openly sympathetic residents were predicting a Nipponese invasion of Canada." One member of the House of Commons declared that he was sure that the Japanese residents on Canada's coast were planning to guide the invaders to strategic points from which they could "make the whole of British Columbia a battleground." The rhetoric was hot and relentless. 'Once a Jap, always a Jap' became the rallying cry. The few dissenting voices—including that of the Canadian Army's own Vice-Chief of General Staff, Major General Maurice Pope, who stated that the army saw "not the slightest menace to national security from Japanese Canadians" --were drowned out by the hysteria. Prime Minister Mackenzie King expressed concern that Japanese Canadians might stage riots that would motivate repercussions against Canadian prisoners of war being held in Japan. Evacuation began to gain popularity as a preventative to all of these imagined actions. Calls for internment of all Nikkei from the west coast became louder and louder.

The news item that brought tears to Hoshi's eyes, however, was the one reporting that the eternal flame on the top of the Japanese Canadian War Memorial, the one built in 1920 to commemorate their contributions in the Great War, had been extinguished. He thought about Jiro's long suffering, and his own difficult experiences in the war. They had been proud to fight, proud to defend Canada. Now that seemed to mean nothing. Only their racial origins mattered.

1942
British Columbia

After a very subdued Christmas during which the Nikkei in Powell River stayed huddled in their homes, January brought more shattering news. Yet another Order-in-Council created a 100-mile 'protected area' on the coast of British Columbia from which male 'enemy aliens' were excluded. Posters were tacked up, requiring any who were so classified to report to the RCMP office immediately, for deportation away from the coast. It was said that they were being sent to work camps in the northern interior of the province. Asami whispered a thankful prayer that her father, Hoshi, and Jiro, were exempt—they had been naturalized long before 1922. But her relief was very short-lived.

On February 7th, the order was changed: it now required *all* male Japanese Canadian citizens between the ages of eighteen and forty-five to be removed from a 100-mile-wide zone along the coast of British Columbia. Asami panicked. Her father was almost eighty-two. He could not manage his farm all alone. As a disabled veteran, would Jiro be allowed to stay with him? For that matter, what would happen to the farm itself? She wrote to her mother repeatedly but heard nothing. She was afraid to travel to the Fraser Valley for fear of not getting back home, and long-distance calls were now prohibited to Japanese Canadians, so her worries about her family grew more frantic by the day.

Her only consolation was that Hoshi's manager had told them that there was a possibility that Hoshi might be allowed to stay with his family. How this might happen was unclear, though it seemed some payment was being talked of--but for the moment they were allowed to stay in their home. Perhaps Jiro would also be allowed to stay with her parents?

It was a time of terrible uncertainty and fear. No one knew what to believe. There seemed to be nothing to be done to protect themselves or plan for the future. Some of the Japanese Canadian men from the mill disappeared, presumably to the work camps, and their wives and children were left with no source of income. The tiny community banded together, sharing food and other resources.

Only a few weeks later, the news got worse yet again. On February 24th, a third Order-in-Council empowered the Minister of Justice to control the movements of *all* persons of the Japanese race in the protected coastal area. It became clear that all Nikkei--men, women, and children--were to be removed. But to where? Rumours flew and seemed to change each day. They were all going to the work camps. No, they were to be moved to deserted ghost towns in the interior and housed for the duration of the war, but they had to leave all their belongings behind. No, they were all going to be housed somewhere in Vancouver. No, they were all going to be sent to Japan! No, they were going to internment camps to build their own houses, with their own money.

Some of these rumours proved to be true. Most of the men were rounded up and taken by train to the work camps, but still Hoshi was allowed to stay at home. One day he found out why.

"The bosses at the mill say that some men will be allowed to move with their families to a place in the interior, where we will build a new town, called a 'self-supporting community.' But only if we have the means to pay for our own transportation, our food, the materials to build our houses, everything. If so, it seems we can go to the town of East Lillooet."

"And do we have enough?" asked Asami, trembling. Hoshi nodded wearily.

"It will take all of our savings, all the money I set aside from when Kenji was with my brother in Japan, but yes, we have just barely enough, I believe."

"And what of the families who cannot pay?" she asked. He rubbed his eyes, his face a picture of sadness.

"They can go to work on sugar beet farms in Alberta if they choose to. But in many cases, the men will go to the road camps in the north and the women, children, and old men will be taken to the ghost towns in the interior, the abandoned mining towns: New Denver, Lemon Creek, and others. I don't know how they will be supported, how they will survive…" His voice trailed off and he raised anguished eyes to his wife. "I did not think that Canada would treat us this way! I know it is wartime and everyone is fearful but, to force us to leave everything behind, to keep us in camps…this I did not expect."

"Is there anything else to do but submit?" asked Asami, her heart breaking to see her husband so disillusioned. He shook his head.

"No," he said. "We must obey, not cause trouble. *Kodomo no tame ni.* For the sake of the children, we must endure."

But one of those children Hoshi and Asami were trying to protect had other ideas. While little Isabel was simply fractious, not understanding why she couldn't go to school or play outside with her friends, Kenji burned with a rage that consumed his every waking thought. He hated Japan, hated what they were doing, hated the impact on him here in Canada. He had thought he had successfully left that country and its expectations behind. He was Canadian! He had no loyalty to Japan whatsoever! At the same time, he was fearful. Yes, he had been born in Canada, but his Uncle Yoshitaro had formally adopted him when he was in Japan. His parents now simply ignored that, as if it had never happened. They would never send him back, they had promised. But what would the Canadian government say about it? Would they consider him to be Japanese, an enemy? Would they send him back there to fight alongside those he considered his enemies? Would they separate him from his family, send him to a work camp despite his being only sixteen? He lay sleepless at night, alternating between hot rage and icy fear. What could he do? Where could he go to hide from the authorities?

They had learned that each of them was to be allowed one suitcase, and that they could take additional household goods equivalent to 150 pounds. Asami had already decided to take her sewing machine, and her best cast iron skillet. Those two things alone made up much of the allowable weight. Cameras and radios were not permitted, as they could be used for 'spy activities,' or so it was said. They were told to be ready to go at short notice—perhaps as little as an hour.

Asami instructed Kenji to pack a bag, to be ready to go. He lay awake one more night, trying to think rationally about his options. He couldn't ask his mother, or his father. They would just reassure him, tell him to stay with them and hope for the best, keep quiet, not make a fuss. But Kenji could not do this. He could not, *would* not submit to being treated in this way! It was wrong, could they not see that? They had to refuse, resist, not meekly obey! He imagined himself as the hero of one of the stories he read each week in *The New Canadian*, a Nikkei hero who felt like an outsider, a misfit, but who strove endlessly for a better life. Finally, he made up his mind.

He pulled out his heavy canvas duffle bag and stuffed it with carefully selected items. Into it went a selection of warm clothing and a raincoat but hidden between these was a large package of matches stored in a tightly sealed glass jar, a smaller skillet that his mother had left behind and a spatula to go with it, a plastic tarpaulin rolled up tightly, and a warm blanket. He couldn't think of how to get a pistol, but he did manage to fit in a small collapsible fishing rod, a box of hooks, and a sharp knife, a plate and a bowl, as well as one spoon and one fork. He hoped that, in the fuss of preparing to leave, his mother would not be counting the cutlery. As he packed, Ozzie Stevenson's words kept replaying through his brain: "You can stay here for about as long as you want..." He would go to Goat Island. No one would find him there.

For the time being, he kept silent about his intentions and didn't even argue about preparing to leave. While his mother accepted this change of attitude gratefully, Kenji caught his father casting a few suspicious looks his way. When he returned a bland expression, Hoshi turned away, his brow furrowed, and said nothing.

The tense days and nights ticked away with no news of the rest of their family until there came another banging on the door in the pre-dawn light of March 15th. The red-coated officer said tersely that it was time for them to leave and instructed them to go down to the town dock. Wrapping themselves in their warmest clothes—for who knew what was to come?—the family lifted their suitcases and trudged down the hill in the drizzling rain. Only little Isabel protested, but her complaints were mostly about being roused from sleep so early and the cold rain that drenched her as she followed her mother, dragging her steps.

As they approached the dock, the lights from the steamer dazzled their eyes. Outlined against the flickering glare were the few remaining Japanese Canadians from Powell River—fifty-one in all, women and children and a handful of old men. No other family had managed to come up with the necessary funds to stay together, and the other women cast jealous glances at Hoshi and his household as they joined the group.

A large group of families from the McNair Company's shingle bolt camp up at Khartoum Lake huddled together as a separate group. The owner, Nat McNair, was standing nearby, twisting his hat in his hands, tears in his eyes. It was clear that he hated having to give up his Japanese Canadian employees, some of whom had been with him for generations, for evacuation. But there was little he could do, no matter what his personal feelings were.

Dick Andrews was also on the wharf to offer silent support. This wealthy mining magnate, whose family had made their fortunes by trading in Japan and Korea, had foreseen the war. Following his intuition, he'd built his family a lavish lodge on Twin Islands to the north where they were hunkered down for the duration. He'd recently been investigated for the number of radios he'd had installed in the lodge, even on his big yacht. Knowing his history of Asian connections, the RCMP had suspected him of spying for the Japanese and ripped out his largest radiophone before the radio technician who had installed it, Jim Spilsbury, could tell them that the equipment could not be used to communicate outwards. But rumours were hard to quell and even now people looked sideways at Dick as he stood, smoking his pipe, on the Powell River dock.

Kenji watched for his chance. He helped his mother get Isabel aboard and passed her the box of kitchen utensils and the sewing machine. Just as the boat began to rev its engines, he said, "Oh, I'll just go help Mr. Ohashi. He's having trouble getting his suitcase on board."

"All right, but hurry, Kenji, the boat is leaving!" his father said, trying to move all their belongings under the meagre shelter afforded by the overhang on the deck of the boat.

Kenji took a last look at his father's harassed face and whispered a prayer for his forgiveness as he moved away. He hoisted his duffle bag and faded into the shadows of the harbour buildings. Everyone's attention was on the boat as it cast off and began to move slowly away from the dock. Before his mother could discover that he was missing and raise an alarm, Kenji slipped away, sliding between the buildings, and running, crouched down, into the trees. By the time the steamship *Lady Cynthia* rounded the point, he was well up the forest trail, heading as fast as he could for Powell Lake.

1942
Aboard the S.S. Lady Cynthia, west coast of British Columbia

Asami huddled beneath the overhand, hugging little Isabel as close to her as the child would allow. The little girl squirmed and twisted, refusing to be confined, as usual. At just eight, she was still small, but her thin frame was wiry and strong.

"Let me go, Mama. I want to go find Kenji."

Her mother's head came up sharply. "Why? Where is your brother?"

"I don't know," said Isabel irritably. "That's why I want to go find him."

"Hoshi? Where is Kenji?" Asami called to her husband as he stood near them, attempting to provide a little shelter from the blowing rain. He turned, his hand shielding his face.

"He said he was going to help Mr. Ohashi. I'll go find him," Hoshi replied. He pulled his coat collar up around his ears and trudged away. Isabel tried to dash after him, but Asami held her tight.

"No, I need you to stay here, Isabel. I don't want you getting lost as well!" Isabel scowled, but when her mother pulled a leftover Christmas candy out of her pocket, she took it eagerly and settled down to enjoy the treat.

Minutes passed. The candy was long gone, and Isabel was whining to be allowed to go look for her father and brother when Hoshi came back, his face anxious in the dim light.

"I cannot find him," he said in a low tone. "Mr. Ohashi says he never saw him at all! I have searched the whole boat, and no-one has seen him since we left the dock."

Asami frowned. "He must be here somewhere! Where else would he be? We must ask the officers to help us look." She struggled to stand, her muscles cramped from crouching in the cold and damp. Hoshi took hold of her arm and bent to whisper in her ear.

"No! We must tell no one that he is missing!" he hissed.

Asami looked at him in puzzlement, her heart beating hard. What could he mean? Why should they not ask for help? Hoshi's face was clenched in fear and worry.

"I think…I fear…he may not have come with us," he whispered urgently. "If this is so, we must not alert the police. They must not go searching for him! If they catch him, they will put him in jail or maybe send him to a work camp."

"But…but where can he have gone?" Asami asked, bewildered.

"I don't know," Hoshi replied, "but I suspected that he was planning something."

"Why didn't you stop him, then?" demanded Asami, her voice rising as panic set in. "Where is he? He is only a boy, Hoshi, he can't be on his own!"

Hoshi squeezed her arm. "Hush, wife. Yes, he is a boy—but he is not a child. Asami, we made a bad decision for him once and forced him into it. I will not do the same thing again. Who knows, perhaps he is right to run and hide? Perhaps we should not accept this indignity so quietly. I don't know what is right. Kenichi is sixteen years old, old enough to make up his own mind. He is not on the work camp register, so they will not be looking for him unless we alert them. We must keep this to ourselves." He paused, looking down at his small daughter, who was gazing up at her parents, her eyes wide. He crouched down and took her thin arms gently in his hands, looking seriously into her face.

"Isabel—Ichicka, my daughter—your brother has left us to find his own way, do you understand?" Isabel nodded solemnly, for once listening intently and not fidgeting. "It is very important that we not talk about Kenji where anyone will hear. We must keep it a secret that he is not with us. Can you do that?" Isabel's lower lip trembled.

"Never talk about him again, Papa?" she asked in a whisper, tears starting from her eyes. "But why did he leave us? Doesn't he love us anymore?"

"We will remember him together, just our family," said Hoshi. "And I am sure he still loves us, my little one, just as we still love him. But he is very angry about being forced to leave our home and go live somewhere else."

"Are you angry too, Papa?" Isabel asked. "And Mama?"

Her father sighed deeply. "Yes, I am a little angry too, and so is Mama. But sometimes, it is best just to obey, even if you do not agree. Like when your teacher wants you to do something you don't want to do—you know it is better to do as she says, rather than get into trouble, yes? The policemen—the RCMP--they are authorities over grownups, like teachers are authorities over children. We must do as they say and not make a fuss. Kenji should have come with us today, but he did not. We do not want anyone to know that he ran away, so no one will go looking for him and get him into trouble. Do you understand?"

Isabel was silent for several long minutes, thinking. Then she raised her face to her father's. "Okay, but can I keep my geisha doll that Kenji gave me?" she asked.

The sun had risen but was still behind the mountains when they stopped briefly at Saltery Bay to pick up six more Nikkei from Egmont. Asami and Hoshi had managed to find a spot inside the steamer, and they sat quietly, warming up and trying to keep Isabel occupied to prevent her from asking more questions about Kenji. Mostly she seemed content to play with her doll, to her mother's relief. Asami's belly was a roil of emotions, alternating between pride in her son for having the courage of his convictions and dread that he would either be caught or perish somewhere in the wilderness. He had always been an outdoorsy boy, and relished adventuring in the forests. But hiking for a day was one thing; surviving alone for—who knew how long it would be?—that was another thing altogether. Nevertheless, there was nothing she could do. Hoshi was right. They must give him a chance to escape by keeping quiet about his absence. There was no one they could trust back in Powell River to go look for him, and no way of returning there themselves. She would just have to hope he was all right.

By the time they reached Pender Harbour, the rain had stopped, and the sun was casting a weak light. Hoshi shepherded his family out onto the deck to catch a breath of air. Ten more passengers—it looked like three families--were lined up on the dock to board, their suitcases crowded around their feet.

In contrast to the sad scene in Powell River, where only a very few *hakujin* had come out in the cold dark morning to see their neighbours off, here the shore was lined with what seemed to be nearly the whole population of this small community. Asami was surprised to see white women weeping copiously.

"They seem sad to see them go," she remarked to Hoshi.

"Yes," he replied. "These families have been in this community for several generations, and they helped the *hakujin* to set up the fish canneries. I have heard that they are well liked here."

Asami nodded, gesturing to where a tawny-skinned *dojin* woman with shiny black hair, wearing a nurse's uniform, was embracing a pregnant Nikkei woman who was about to board the steamer. "That poor woman," she said, "having to be packed off to God knows where, about to have a baby. Poor all of us, packed up and shipped off like cans of sardines, with no recourse, no chance to prove our loyalty." She shook her head, feeling conflicted. As a fugitive, Kenji would face many challenges, but at least her son would have a fighting chance at freedom. Perhaps he had been right to flee, as Hoshi had suggested. Perhaps if they'd all refused to go, the matter would have been re-thought. As the new group of Nikkei boarded the boat, she looked around at all the sad, resigned faces, and wondered.

Eight more joined them at Sechelt, a large group of forty-four at Wilson Creek, nine at Gibsons Landing, then a final old man at Port Mellon. By the time the S.S. *Lady Cynthia* chugged her way out into the swirling grey waters of Howe Sound, seventy-eight Japanese Canadians crowded the small steamship, hemmed in by red-coated RCMP officers with stony expressions and rigid spines.

Few children cried or played. Few adults spoke. It was eerily silent--as if they were already gone.

1942
Vancouver, British Columbia

The resigned silence continued as the Nikkei were guided from the steamer into the backs of trucks and open wagons at the Vancouver dock, though the cries of infants and whines from cranky children were increasingly heard. The late winter light was fading, and a chill wind sprang up as the various vehicles pulled up at the gates of Hastings Park, a large facility on the outskirts of the city that was usually used for the region's annual agricultural fair, the Pacific National Exhibition or PNE. Hastily erected wire fencing with a row of barbed wire at the top surrounded the site. It looked a far cry from the place where folks came in the summer to lick ice cream, take a ride on the Big Dipper, and peruse homemade jams and local vegetables.

As the families climbed stiffly down, the RCMP officers brusquely separated them into groups: men to one side, and women and children in another. Hoshi tried to object.

"No, sir, there is some misunderstanding. My family will be going to East Lillooet together! See, I have this document..." He waved the paper he'd kept safely in his inner jacket pocket, but the officer ignored it.

"That'll be sorted out later," was all he said. "Now go where you are told."

Hoshi had only time to exchange a frantic look with his wife, and then he was swept aside into the milling group of men. Asami called out to him as he disappeared.

"Soon! We will be together soon! Do not lose hope!" she called, clutching Isabel's hand tightly and trying to stifle her tears for the sake of her daughter.

The women and children picked up their meagre baggage and were herded inside a vast metal building. As they passed through the enormous double doors, a nauseating stench hit them like a solid wall. The children cried out in disgust, and the women snatched handkerchiefs out of their pockets to cover their noses. The warehouse-like space stretched hundreds of yards away from them, filled with row upon row of roughly built narrow wooden bunk beds made up with stiff grey horse blankets and thin pillows over mattresses stuffed with scratchy straw. Down the edges of each row ran narrow trenches, and it was these that made Asami realize the source of the horrible smell. This was a livestock building, built for cows, pigs, horses! The trenches were for the run-off of the manure, and that was what they smelled. Perhaps some attempt had been made to clean the building, but the stink was still overwhelming, and Asami was appalled at this unhygienic place where they were expected to live—for how long? *Is this truly how they see us?* she thought, tears now rolling unchecked down her face. *As no better than beasts, to be penned up like this, in such a place?* She spared a moment's thought for Kenji, somewhere in the forest—alone and perhaps lost—but free, in the open wind and surrounded by the comforting scents of the woods. Would that they had all gone with him!

But there was no time for regrets now. She moved to the space pointed out to her by an officious man with a clipboard and set her bags down on the upper bed. She picked Isabel up and set her on the lower bunk, then took off her filth-caked shoes before guiding the girl under the insufficient blanket. Isabel was whining about being cold and hungry, and Asami dug several warm sweaters from Isabel's own little suitcase and pulled them over the child's head. She also unpacked a knitted shawl from her own bag and laid it on top of the bedclothes.

"There," she said. "Soon you will feel warmer. Now, can you stay right here on this bed while I go and see if I can find out about supper? Do not go running off, Isabel, you must promise me, yes?"

"Yes, Mama," the child replied, unusually obedient, and Asami patted her shoulder as she turned away.

"I will be back very soon," she said. She went back to the big doors, now closed, and approached the officers guarding it, their shiny pistols in heavy leather holsters obvious on their hips. "Excuse me," she said softly, and one turned his head. "My daughter is very hungry as we have been traveling all day, since before dawn. Can you tell me where I can get something for her to eat?"

"Supper will be in an hour, in the dining room in the next building," the officer said gruffly but not unkindly. "She'll have to wait until then."

"But..." Asami began. She stopped. It was clear from the man's expression that this was to be her only answer. She turned away, making her way back to her allotted space. As she approached, her heart began to pound, for Isabel was not on the bed! Her little shoes were also gone.

Asami looked around frantically. "Isabel!" she called, "where are you?" She looked at the woman curled up on the bunk next to theirs, a mere three feet away. "Did you see my little girl leave?" she asked, her voice hoarse with fear. The other woman silently pointed further down their row. Asami gasped her thanks and scurried in that direction.

She kept calling out as she went, terrified sobs building in her chest. As she was reaching the far end of the building, almost despairing, she heard Isabel's faint reply.

"Come see who I found!" the child's treble voice called out. Asami ran toward the sound, and a cry broke from her throat when she saw Isabel tucked up in another bed, with an older woman sitting beside her. The woman raised her head, and Asami sobbed aloud.

"Mama!" she cried and collapsed into Sara's welcoming arms,

Isabel's disobedience swept aside by a tide of relief at being reunited with her own mother.

It didn't take Asami long to learn that her parents' experience had been much the same as her own. The strawberry farm had been confiscated, and Harry and Sara rounded up along with Jiro.

"Jiro is with Papa?" Asami gasped, relieved. "Oh, I am so glad. I thought they might have sent him to one of the road camps!"

"No," Sara said, "The officer who came said to us said that Jiro's limited eyesight would be a handicap, make him worthless to them—worthless, that's what they said!" She shook her head angrily.

Asami bit her lip. It was surely an insult, given that Jiro had managed to work the farm for years with his damaged vision. Yet she was glad that he had not been sent to the camps, that he was here to help Harry, whose strength was failing. She hoped that Hoshi had found them in the men's section.

"What will happen to the farm?" she asked, setting aside her worries about their menfolk.

"We were told that it would be held and managed by the Custodian of Enemy Alien Property—what a terrible title!--a man appointed by the Canadian government. The land will be rented out to *hakujin* farmers, and the proceeds are meant to go towards our support during our internment. A Nikkei representative, Mr. Kishizo Kimura, is on the committee so I suppose he will protect our interests as best he can."

"And have they said where you are to go?" asked Asami. Her mother shook her head.

"Then we will ask for you to accompany us to East Lillooet!" she exclaimed. Sara smiled.

"That would be wonderful, to be together. I do not know if they will allow it, though."

At that moment a clanging noise echoed through the huge hall, and people came through shouting for everyone to line up and proceed to the dining hall for supper. Asami scooped up Isabel and took her mother's hand as they joined the line-up. She was astounded by the number of women and children—thousands, it seemed—who crowded towards the doors.

In docile rows, they crossed into the next huge space and seated themselves at long tables, jostling only a little to find seats. The meal that was slapped down unceremoniously before them by harassed-looking white staff members was a far cry from the vegetable-rich, flavourful food to which they were accustomed. A small piece of overcooked chicken breast was slathered with a spoonful of pale gravy, already cooling and congealing, accompanied by a thin slice of white bread scraped with a layer of greasy margarine. A tiny spoonful of canned peas, barely heated, sat on the side of the plate. Water was the only beverage, and Asami's request for milk for Isabel was met with an unfriendly stare.

"Milk at breakfast only," grunted the server, and hurried away.

Most of them were still hungry after finishing the meal, but another bell warned them that it was time to return to the main building. Asami hugged her mother before making her way to their own bunk bed. She changed Isabel into her nightgown, and they lined up yet again to use the communal washroom, cleaning their faces with the scratchy washcloths provided. Asami saw that there were only ten shower stalls for all the women in this building, and she thought angrily about how difficult it was going to be to keep themselves and the children clean. There were no shower curtains across the stalls, no privacy despite there being twelve-year-old boys among the children housed with their mothers. It was unconscionable! She took Isabel into the next room to urinate before sleeping and was appalled all over again; the 'toilet' was nothing more than a trough to squat over, with water running down it, carrying everyone's filth along to a drain. The smell was horrendous, and Isabel refused to even try. Asami gave up after a weak attempt to persuade her. By the time they returned to their beds, the little girl was stumbling with weariness, and she fell asleep within moments of being tucked in, her geisha doll clutched in her arms.

Asami slid beneath the blanket on her own bed, shivering. The enormous building had been designed to house animals, not humans. The few stoves that had been added around the perimeter did little to warm the space, and only the collected heat of the many bodies in the building made it tolerable. She closed her eyes and tried to relax, but the sounds of all the women, moaning in grief, snoring, speaking in low voices, singing quietly to fretful children, echoed around her. Her chest ached and she could not stop the tears from flowing yet again. What was to become of them? And where was her son? She whispered a quiet prayer that he was somewhere warm and dry this cold night.

1942
Powell Lake, British Columbia

Kenji's exultation at getting away without detection carried him for the first part of his hike, and the effort of making his way through the trail, overgrown from the winter past, kept him warm. He made good progress and arrived on the shore of Powell Lake as the warmth of the rising sun was lifting a thin layer of cold mist from its mirrorlike surface.

He halted and shrugged off his heavy pack, rotating his tired shoulders and sighing with relief. He'd made it! He looked carefully around and listened intently, but nothing could be seen or heard save the flash and knocking of a large pileated woodpecker nearby. He had stopped at about the spot where they'd made their picnic last summer, but after a few moments he lifted his pack again and walked further along the shore, seeking the small dock and—he hoped—the boat that Mr. Stevenson had mentioned. The dock wasn't far away, just around a jutting point of land, but there was no boat to be seen. Kenji stopped, staring at the empty dock stretching out into the still water. He had counted on there being a boat to get him to the island. He realized now that his hope had been naïve. No one would have left a boat out all winter, to be savaged by the winter rains and snows and wild animals. But the vision of it, sitting there waiting for him, had been so strong! *Wishful thinking, I guess*, he thought.

Now what? The water was far too cold to swim, and he'd never manage to keep his bag dry even if he did dare it. He chewed his lip, considering his options. Well, he wasn't going to eat goat anyway, as he had no gun, and he supposed fish could be had from the lakeshore, or the dock, just as easily as from the island. There didn't seem to be anyone around, so it was probably safe enough to camp on the lakeshore, almost as safe as the island would have been, he reasoned. No one was going to be coming to the lake until summer, and by then—well, by then he'd have thought of something. That was months away.

He turned away from the disappointing sight of the empty dock and trudged back around the point to his original starting place. He remembered a large cedar with wide boughs where they'd sat in cool shade to eat their picnic. It would make a shelter from the rain just as well. Sure enough, when he found the tree, the area beneath its overlapping branches was dry and carpeted by tawny twigs of aromatic cedar.

Kenji unpacked the tarpaulin he'd brought and draped it over the lowest branches, creating a sort of tent, and set out to unpack and organize his small array of tools and utensils. Next, he gathered a pile of twigs and small branches and carefully arranged them as his father had taught him. He pulled his jar of matches out of his pack and was relieved to find them dry. He'd need to make sure they stayed that way! The dried remains of ferns made excellent kindling and he soon had a crackling small fire going, which immediately made his little campsite cheerier. He'd packed some food—a bag of dry rice and cans of beans, a bit of bread, a box of porridge—and a chunk of cheese carefully cut from the block at home well before they left, so his mother wouldn't notice. He'd thought of bringing some cans of tuna and salmon, but he'd been confident of his ability to supply himself with fresh fish and added more cans of beans instead.

As he sat alone, eating bread and cheese, he was optimistic. He felt quite proud of himself and how he had planned and executed his escape. And here he was—safe, dry, and fed. He hoped his father would be proud of him as well—but then he thought guiltily of how sad and scared his mother would be now, having surely realized what he had done. Gazing into the cheerful little fire, he had a sudden impulse. Taking his battered wallet from his pants pocket, he pulled out the identification card he'd been issued along with all other Nikkei in British Columbia. He gazed at his own likeness and pondered the fingerprint on the back of the card. His expression hardened as he read 'Japanese' on the card. *I am CANADIAN*, he thought angrily, *not Japanese*. He flicked the card into the flames and watched with satisfaction as it blackened and curled before crumbling into ash. Feeling a spurt of triumph at this small defiance, he lay down and pulled his blanket over himself for a rest. Within minutes his eyes had closed, and the soft sounds of the forest faded from his mind.

When he awoke the sun was low, almost behind the mountaintops ringing the lake, and his fire was out. He scurried to gather more fuel for the fire, astonished at how quickly it had been consumed, and worryingly aware of how quickly the temperature was dropping. No time to fish for tonight's supper now; he'd have to make do with bread and cheese again. He pulled on all the warm clothes he'd brought and huddled before his little fire as the night grew dark around him. Before he knew it, he'd eaten all the fresh food he had carried in—on the very first day! He'd have to fish tomorrow for sure or go hungry.

Despite his easy drift into sleep in the afternoon, now Kenji found that slumber escaped him. The night seemed full of frightening noises. Attracted by the smell of his food, some small animal snuffled around his campsite and was only prevented from chewing into his bag of rice because Kenji shouted, frightening it off. After that he found himself thinking about bears and wondering if they'd still be hibernating or beginning to wake up, ravenous and looking for food. Every noise in the darkness became the shuffle and pad of large paws, and Kenji found himself sitting with his back to the comforting mass of the tree trunk, gripping his sharp knife and staring out beyond his fire. Its flickering brightness seemed but a small bulwark against the vast darkness of the forest.

At some point he fell asleep, for he awoke in the thin dawn with his neck awry and his knife loose in his lap. His fire was out, and a cold drizzle fell, wetting all his fuel. Cursing loudly—something his mother would have deeply disapproved of—Kenji got up, stretching to ease the ache in his back and the cramp in his shoulders. He rubbed his hands roughly over his arms and jumped up and down, trying to warm his muscles. Happily, his makeshift tent had kept him and his pack mostly dry. He shrugged on his rain jacket and went in search of dry fuel, searching underneath the low spreading branches of the giant trees surrounding him.

He managed to get his fire going again, close to the front of his tent. He sat beside it, staring up anxiously, hoping no sparks would set the tarp—or the tree he sheltered under—afire. He decided on beans for breakfast and was relieved to find that the can opener he'd bought a few weeks ago and stuffed into the bottom of his duffel bag was still there. *I'd really be in a fix if I'd lost that*, he thought. He scraped the beans into the skillet and warmed them over the fire, finding that he had to stir them constantly to prevent them sticking and burning. He was so hungry that he could scarcely wait until they were lukewarm before wolfing them down.

Feeling a little better, he took the skillet down to the lakeshore and scrubbed it roughly clean with the spatula and his fingers. As he went back to his campsite, he realized he'd forgotten to pack a towel or cloth or anything to dry the pan—or himself, for that matter. He had thought about eating, of course, but somehow the details of keeping himself and his belongings clean hadn't occurred to him. He hadn't packed any soap either. A niggling sense of worry began to grow in his stomach: what else had he forgotten? He shrugged the feeling away, deciding to go fishing. Everyone knew that fish bit more in the rain.

It took much longer than he expected, but eventually Kenji had hooked two small trout and was huddled under his tent, gutting and cleaning them with his knife. The frypan was again propped over the fire, heating, and he laid the small, filleted fish on its hot surface. When they immediately began smoking and scorching, he identified another thing he'd forgotten to pack—oil or butter or any kind of fat for frying. As a result, his lunch was a combination of blackened and raw fish. It was vastly unappetizing, but he was too hungry to care. As he swallowed the last scraps, he realized with a sinking feeling that he'd have to do the whole thing over again if he was to have meat at supper. Or—maybe he could just boil up some rice and get more fish tomorrow. It was raining more heavily now and the thought of going back out to stand motionless on the shore, waiting for a bite, was daunting.

Rice, yes, that would be all right. It would be filling, anyway. He examined the bag closely to make sure last night's small marauder hadn't chewed it open. No, it seemed all right. He opened it carefully and looked around for a pot to pour some into—and found himself staring blankly. He'd brought the skillet for frying, but hadn't remembered until this minute that dry rice needs a lidded pot to absorb the water it was cooked in. He'd seen his mother do it a thousand times, but as he'd never done it himself, he hadn't thought it through. His heart sank and he had no idea how to solve this lack.

After a few minutes' fruitless thought, he shrugged. It would be beans again for supper, then.

So the days passed slowly and with great effort. It was far more difficult to keep himself warm, dry, and fed than Kenji had imagined it would be. But at least the constant effort gave him less time to think, and he was grateful, for he was surprised to find himself very lonely. So many times, during his difficult years in Japan, when he was treated at best as an outsider and at worst as a target for bullying, Kenji had longed for the quiet and solitude of the Canadian woods of his childhood. Now that he was surrounded by the forest's vast emptiness—of humans, at least—day after day, he found himself wishing instead for the sound of his mother's quiet voice, or even Isabel's whining. He also wished he'd thought to pack a book or two. The long nights began to wear on him, and he watched anxiously for signs of spring.

He'd solved the problem of the lack of a rice pot by laying his one plate over the skillet while it boiled the rice in water, which worked well enough but meant he had to cook his rice before he could cook anything else, such as fish or beans—and the rice contained not a few hard grains that had escaped the steam each time. He'd tasted a few woodland greens and berries, but it was too early for most, and he was too afraid of poisoning himself to attempt any he wasn't absolutely sure of. As a result, his diet was an unvarying menu of fish, beans, and rice for the most part. He lost weight and began to feel a bit weak.

Fears and worries began to gnaw at him. How long could he survive out here alone? And what would he do when people began coming to the lake for summer picnics or fishing? Should he move on before then? But where? Kenji had never traveled beyond B.C.'s coast and had no idea what the rest of Canada held, or where he would be safe. He realized, also, that isolated here as he was, he would have no idea when or if the war ended—or who won! He began to think that perhaps he should have gone with his family. Where were they now? Were they thinking of him?

Slowly the days lengthened, and the sun began to gain some warmth. On a clear morning after days of rain, Kenji decided to try fishing from the small dock around the point, to see if he could entice something other than the endless small trout to nibble on his hook. First, however, he dragged his tarpaulin out into the sun to dry. It was developing small holes from the cedar's sharp twigs, and last night a steady drip of rain on his sleeping place had kept him awake and damp throughout much of the night. He stared at it, trying to imagine how he could patch it. Perhaps sap from the cedars, daubed on the holes? Maybe. He'd think about it while he fished.

A half hour later, he stood on the little dock, gazing mindlessly around while he dangled his hook into the clear water. Suddenly he wondered: who had built this dock, and why? It had not occurred to him to ask the question before, but now it seemed unlikely that it had been created at random, with no specific purpose.

He turned his head, his eyes searching up the slope that ran away from the dock into the forest. He squinted, turning his head this way and that. Was that a building far back in there, some sort of shack? Or was it just the rough-scaled trunks of the huge Douglas fir trees that marched away into the distance? He realized that in summer, the leafed-out alders and thick underbrush would completely obscure whatever it was he was seeing. No one standing on the dock in summer would have any idea there was anything back there.

His curiosity getting the better of him, Kenji wound up his fishing line and left it on the dock. Now that he was looking for it, he readily found the small trail that disappeared into the trees opposite the dock. It was twisty and mostly overgrown, but still fairly easy to follow, and he did so with growing excitement. As he drew closer, his heart began to pound. Indeed, it *was* a building—and not a small one as he had first thought!

Stumbling over a gnarled root, he sprawled onto his hands and knees. As he got to his feet and dusted himself off, he looked up to find that he had entered a clearing, and the building was directly in front of him.

It was built of wood, with cedar shake roof shingles, and it consisted of a large central hut with two longer wings stretching to each side. The windows were all boarded up, and there was no sign of habitation.

Kenji walked all the way around it, trying to peer inside, but the boarded-up windows offered no chance. He found the door, but it was closed tight with a metal hasp sporting a heavy padlock. Frustrated, he sat on the stoop and thought.

What is this and who does it belong to? he wondered. *Maybe a fishing camp, or a hunting lodge, or a loggers' camp?* It seemed to have been here a long time, from the look of the weathered boards. He'd never heard anyone in Powell River talk about it, so perhaps it had fallen out of use. It certainly looked abandoned at present.

Determined to solve the puzzle and excited by the possibility of sheltering under an actual roof, he got up and did another perimeter walk. At the far end of the right-hand wing, a huge fir tree stood close by the end of the building, and Kenji noticed that one of the boards nailed over the window at that end had rotted a bit from the constant damp of the overhanging branches. When an initial attempt to pull away the rotted board with his hands failed, Kenji found a stout fallen branch and bashed away at the soft spot until it was wide enough to allow him to insert the branch and use it as a lever.

The first branch simply snapped with a sound like a rifle shot when he leaned his full weight on it, as did the second and third branches he tried. On his fourth try, however, the branch was strong enough to push the splintering board away from the window frame, the rusty nails screeching in protest. Panting, Kenji peered inside the hole he had made.

No glass filled the space, only a wobbly piece of flyscreen. *So*, he thought, *this place is only used in warm weather, probably*. Beyond the dusty screen, he could just make out the shadowy shapes of several narrow beds lining the walls, and a table holding a wash bowl and jug. *Hmmm, no running water*, he surmised. *Must be pretty old…*

He stepped back and stood staring. How likely was it that someone was going to come back to this place? Not very, he told himself, refusing to consider the possibility that a change of season might bring its owners to the site.

Coming to a sudden decision, he picked up his sturdy branch and attacked the remaining boards. Within another half hour, he was sweating with the effort, but he had uncovered most of the window. He poked tentatively at the screen, and was startled when it tore readily, opening a ragged hole into the room.

Well, he thought, *I'm in for it now anyway if someone comes. I might as well go in and take a look.*

Tossing the branch aside and taking care not to get snagged on the remaining nails jutting out from the sill, Kenji put his hands on the window frame and hauled himself up and through. He tumbled to the floor, raising a cloud of dust that caused him to cough for a few moments as he stood up and looked around.

The space was a bedroom for six people, judging by the number of beds, and as Kenji walked down the dusty hall, he found several more bedrooms with multiple bunks. Many people—likely all men—had lived here at some point. Reaching the central square building, he peered around in the gloom, lightened only by narrow shafts of sunlight poking through the occasional gaps in the boards over the windows. Ah—here was a dining table, long and narrow, with rough-hewn benches on either side. And nearby, a basic kitchen with a plank worktop inset with a deep porcelain sink that appeared to drain outside. Some open shelves had been nailed to the walls above, and a few cupboards stood underneath. The shadowy bulk of a woodstove filled one corner of the room.

Kenji crouched down to open a cupboard door and peered inside in the gloomy light. Aha! A full set of cooking pots and pans! In the next, he found an even more exciting treasure—an old can half full of cooking oil, and a musty box of tea bags, along with several rows of canned goods with rotting labels, or none at all. *Probably beans*, he thought wryly. There was an icebox, but it stood dark and empty.

He sat back on his haunches and looked around himself. The thought of living inside, with access to a stove, cooking supplies—and an actual bed!—was strongly tempting. It was clear no one was using the cabin, he argued to himself, and he would be careful to do no harm to it. He chewed on his lip, balancing the desire to be more comfortable with his inherent sense of morality and right behaviour. He had almost convinced himself that it would be wrong to make use of the hut when his eyes, having adjusted to the dim light, fell upon a faded photograph tacked to the wall above the sink. He stood up and went to pull it from its nail, carrying it over to one of the shafts of light.

A group of *hakujin* hunters grinned up at him, their arms slung around each other's shoulders, an enormous dead elk splayed at their feet. One of the men had his booted foot propped up on the beast's side, and another gestured to its magnificent rack of antlers. Something in their expressions repelled Kenji. They seemed so sure of their place in the world, so confident of their right to kill this king of the forest. There was no hint of sorrow at the death, no sign of any remorse at the loss of so beautiful a creature. No—only triumph and celebration of their dominance over the animal.

As he gazed at the image, echoes started up in his head, taunting voices calling "Jap, Jap!" and eyes just like these dismissing him as less than themselves—as little more than an animal. His heartbeat quickened and a simmering rage rose in his throat. He dropped the photo onto the floor and raised his head. These were the kind of men who had caged his family and told them they had no right to live freely in their own country. Well, he would fight back. He would make use of their hunting lodge and reject their judgement of him. It served them right.

1942
Hastings Park, British Columbia

Asami gathered all their soiled clothing into her arms and made her way toward the communal laundry facility adjacent to the large women's washroom. As she neared the door, a horde of screeching children, Isabel among them, went scrambling past, kicking a ball some child had brought to confinement. Asami smiled wearily. At least the little ones were able to find fun and a measure of freedom here. She wondered what they'd remember of this experience, years from now.

Her smile slipped away as she thought about why these children were running around, essentially unsupervised. The government had made no provision for schooling for the children during their internment, despite education being their right as Canadian citizens. The women had asked again and again to have classes set up, but despite vague promises nothing had been done. Now a few Nikkei women with teaching backgrounds were proposing to start classes up in the high bleachers ringing the agricultural building. Where they would find books and other teaching supplies, Asami had no idea, but yesterday she'd heard that Hide Hyodo, the well-loved teacher from Steveston--and a member of the failed franchise delegation to Ottawa back in '39--had agreed to come and teach for them in the evenings after her own teaching day in Vancouver ended, at least until she, too, was evacuated somewhere away from the city. This was excellent news, and Asami felt a spark of hope that Isabel's time here would not result in a total loss of progress in her schooling.

She made her way to the laundry, a makeshift setup of rows of half-barrels set into rough wooden frames, with a water line running along each row. She piled her washing into one of these and sprinkled a handful of soap flakes over it, as the tub filled. She swished her hand through as the soap dissolved, risking either scalding or freezing: the water lines were unpredictable at best.

A woman she'd seen a few times before came to the tub opposite hers, setting down two tiny sleeping infants tucked up in a large basket first, then unloading piles and piles of soiled diapers into the wash tub with a weary expression. Asami nodded to her.

"Never ending, isn't it?" she commented sympathetically. The woman gave her a weak smile in return.

"Especially with twins," she said.

"Oh my, yes. Where are you from?" Asami asked, eager for conversation to pass the time and lighten the drudgery of scrubbing the clothes.

"Salt Spring Island," the woman replied. "My husband is a Japanese National—he had applied for naturalization, but we didn't get the papers back in time. So he was taken to the road camps, I think in Yellowhead." She laughed bitterly. "I don't even know where that is." She looked up at Asami, and her eyes filled with tears. "When they came to get him, we had his suitcase ready because, you know, we knew they wouldn't let him stay at home. He went out as soon as they came for him, all ready to go, didn't make a fuss. And as he was climbing up into the back of the truck, this soldier just—just picked him up by the back of his coat and threw him in! For no reason! He was already obeying, getting into the truck! He fell hard on his stomach, and the soldier slammed the tailgate and the truck started up. My husband—he scrambled to his feet and turned back to wave to me. 'It's all right, I am all right!' he called to me and waved and waved until he was too far away for me to see." She covered her face with her hands and sobbed into them. "And now I am alone with my two babies, and I do not know if I will ever see my husband again."

Asami dried her hands on her skirt and came around to the young woman, taking her into her arms. "It is hard. But you are not alone. I am here, we are all here together. I will help you."

The younger woman sniffed and wiped at her face with her fingers. "You are kind," she whispered. "Thank you! My name is Mary, Mary Takimoto."

"Asami Tasaka. Come, I will help you rinse the diapers and then we will hang them up outside together. It is hard to get them dry in this damp place, but we will do our best!"

The next morning, the breakfast was again thin, tasteless porridge with a drizzle of diluted canned milk over it. Isabel hated it passionately and most days she refused to eat it. Asami could not blame her, as the grey sludge was extremely unappetizing. Across the table, another mother was trying to persuade her little boy to eat it, but the child was crying and complaining of a pain in his tummy.

Suddenly, a foul stench filled the air and the mother opposite gasped in shame. Her little boy had soiled himself with diarrhea that dripped down his legs and into his shoes.

"I told you, I told you I was sick!" the boy screamed.

One of the *hakujin* staff came rushing up with another white woman dressed in a nurse's uniform.

"Come now," the nurse said. "Let's take you to the infirmary and see what we can do for you."

"Mama, mama, don't let them take me!" the child screamed, clinging to his mother.

"Now, now, it's all right, your mother can come too," the nurse soothed.

"It is just the food, he cannot eat this terrible food," said an elderly woman close by. The nurse turned to the old woman, her expression hardening.

"You should be grateful that we are feeding you at all!" she snapped. "You are here for your own protection I hope you realize. If we'd left you on the coast, who knows what would have happened to you! We are at war with Japan, you know!"

"Yes, I do know that!" replied the old woman sarcastically. "But do *you* know that we are not Japanese? We are Canadian." She stared hard at the nurse, her expression stony, until the other woman flushed and turned her face, leading the poor child and his embarrassed mother away without another word.

Asami was stunned by the nurse's words. *Is that really how they see it? That they are doing us a favour, protecting us?* She shook her head. How amazing, that people could justify their actions in such a way.

A few weeks later, Asami was sitting on her mother's bed one evening after supper, treasuring a steaming cup of their dwindling supply of green tea. It was aromatic Sencha tea, and just inhaling its scent helped her to shut out her dreary surroundings. She was grateful that Sara had thought to pack some in their hurried departure from the farm.

All up and down the rows of bunks the women had hung sheets or blankets from the bed frames in an attempt to provide a small amount of privacy and separation from one another. With all the different patterns, the effect was like a huge gathering of colourful Romani wagons, all parked in some gigantic field. Sara had draped a yellow-flowered sheet from her bunk, but at present they had drawn it back for a little air. The twice-weekly disinfectant sprinkling of dichlorine of lime had happened the day before, but the aroma of manure overlaid by the smells of three thousand women and children living in close quarters still lurked beneath the strong chemical smell.

"I saw that Mrs. Koyanagi bought her daughter a new coat and hat for her birthday," Sara said, making idle conversation. "Little Muriel looks very pretty in it, too. Purple's a good colour on her."

"Yes, although did she tell you? She had obtained a pass to take Muriel shopping, but when they got to Woodward's Department Store there was a big sign saying, 'No Japs allowed,' I guess to keep out the Nikkei who are still living in Vancouver waiting for their deportation. So she had to take another tram down to Japantown—what's left of it—to find something. They were almost late back, but I heard that the gate soldiers didn't say anything."

"Tsk," her mother said, shaking her head. "Maybe that nurse was right—maybe it would have been worse for us to stay on our farm. Who knows what people will do when they are afraid and angry?"

Then Sara looked up and a smile of joy broke out on her face. Coming towards them down the long aisle were Harry, Hoshi, and Jiro! It was the first time they had seen the men since their arrival at Hastings Park. They all rushed together and hugged, asking so many questions on both sides that no one could hear anything.

"Come," said Harry, "let's go outside, get some fresher air. It stinks in here!"

"Don't we know it!" exclaimed Asami. "Isn't your building the same?"

"No," her father replied. "It was a hockey rink before we were brought here, so it doesn't smell, at least, though it is very noisy with all the echoes."

"Lucky you," said Asami, hooking her arm through her husband's. It was so good to see the men!

They went out, showing the guards the pass that the men had obtained to visit the women's building. "All right," said the Mountie. "But remember it's just for an hour. Make sure you are back in the men's building before curfew."

They walked around the fairgrounds under the weak spring sun, quietly savouring the gentle wind and the simple fact of togetherness. There was no point in talking further about the conditions or complaining. There was nothing to be done but endure.

"Have you heard anything about our move to East Lillooet yet?" asked Asami, and her husband nodded.

"Yes, I think we will be going before the end of April. I have been told that our houses are not yet ready for us, but that they are building them."

"And what about us," Sara asked Harry. "Have you received approval for us to accompany Hoshi and Asami?" Harry nodded, but his expression was wry.

"Yes, but they have said that the strawberry farm will be leased to pay for our keep there, as it is a self-supporting camp, one of five being set up in the interior of the province. Otherwise, we must go to one of the old ghost towns in the interior—the ones that were abandoned after the gold rush was over. We even told them that we would all live together, not ask for a separate house, but they said, no, we still must pay the full amount."

Sara looked distressed but said nothing. Staying together with her family was more important to her than the farm. Who knew if they would ever be permitted to return there anyway?

"What about you, Jiro?" she asked anxiously. Her adopted son was fully as dear to her as her own daughter.

Jiro laughed and took her arm. "They don't seem to be able to make up their minds," he joked good naturedly. "One day I am a worthless blind man; the next day they think I ought to go to one of the work camps. We shall see. Don't worry, Sara, it will all work out. I will manage, either way." He patted her hand and distracted them all from their worries by telling funny stories about the young scamps in the men's building.

"They've managed to cut a hole through the wire fencing behind the guard house, right opposite the Hastings confectionary store across the street. When the guards are busy checking a vehicle coming in or out, the boys dash across the street and buy penny candy or a popsicle, and then scoot back in before the guards look around again."

"They are bored and at loose ends," said Harry. He shook his head. "A bad combination for young men."

"I also heard that one clever lad swiped a whole pile of blank passes when the clerk wasn't looking and is selling them to the other boys for five cents each. He writes whatever time they want on it—say, three hours to visit their mothers instead of the one hour that's usually allowed. I don't think the guards have caught on yet!"

They chuckled. These pranks were relatively harmless, and they felt a certain pride in seeing their young people's cleverness and determination to resist oppression, even in such small ways.

At that moment Isabel came dashing up, having spotted her father from across the yard.

"Papa!" she shouted, and Hoshi swept her up in his arms.

"Isabel," he said, hugging her close. "Have you been a good girl for Mama?"

"Yes," the child replied, and dug into her sweater pocket, pulling out a rather lumpy bit of bright red knitting. "Look, Papa, I am learning how to knit socks! This one is for you, but Mrs. Kunemoto hasn't taught me how to turn the heel yet, so it's just a tube. Do you like it?"

"It is wonderful, Isabel. I will wear it with pride when it is finished, especially if you make two of them so both of my feet can be warm!"

Isabel laughed, but then her face turned serious. "Where is Kenji?" she demanded, looking at the men. "Why didn't he come to see me too?"

"Hush!" said her father. "Remember, your brother has gone to another place. We must not talk about him. We don't want the soldiers to go looking for him!"

Isabel frowned and wriggled to be put down. "He shouldn't have run away!" she said, stamping her small foot. "I want him to be here, to read me stories and bring me another geisha doll!"

The adults looked at one another. Of course, Asami had told her mother the truth about Kenji's absence, and Hoshi had told Harry and Jiro the same.

"Yes," said Harry, crouching down to Isabel's level. "We all wish he was here too. But look, it is almost time for supper, and we must go back to the other building soon. Shall we play a quick game of rock, paper, scissors before I go?" Isabel loved this game, so she was easily distracted from her thoughts about her brother. Harry did his best to ensure that she won most of the rounds, and after a few minutes the child was giggling, her earlier pique forgotten.

They walked slowly back toward the looming buildings that were silhouetted starkly against the fading light in the sky. Asami sighed, twining her hand briefly into Hoshi's. Surely things would get better when they moved to East Lillooet—at least they would be together there. All but Kenji. She closed her eyes for a second, sending a fervent prayer heavenwards that her son was alive and well.

1942
Powell Lake

Kenji lay on one of the beds in the smallest bedroom, clad only in his underwear, drowsing as the spring dawn strengthened outside, sending faint stripes of light across his blanket through the chinks in the window coverings. He had left the windows of the lodge boarded up except for one in the kitchen that faced toward the deep forest, and the one he'd originally broken through. He thought that it was highly unlikely that anyone would notice it even if they did come to the lake and look in that direction, and the opening provided some light and air as the season rolled toward summer.

His life had improved greatly since he'd moved into the cabin. He was warmer, drier, and better fed, though the cooking oil remaining in the can was dwindling fast. He tried to ration himself, frying fish only every second day with it and making do with beans and rice in between. Yesterday, he'd gathered some tightly furled new fern fronds—called fiddleheads for their shape--in the woods and steamed them. How wonderful it had been to crunch the vigorous greens between his teeth! He could almost feel his body eagerly absorbing the vitamins he'd been missing for so many weeks. He looked forward to the coming summer, with its blackberries, salmonberries, and cloudberries. How sweet they would be.

But he was still desperately lonely. In thc past few weeks, he'd taken to using a twig of charcoal from the woodstove to write out ancient haiku that he'd memorized in school in Japan on the backs of the pages of an old calendar left behind by the hunters, to pass the time, to practice his Japanese writing, and to express his feelings of isolation. The Japanese loved poetry so much; he had been amazed how adults and children in Japan had quoted and made up poetry all the time. Even the most common person sought to put their feelings into the elegant form of the haiku or other formal structures. Kenji had developed a taste for it in his boyhood, and it offered a bit of solace now in his isolation.

Winter seclusion -
Listening, that evening,
To the rain in the mountain--Issa

An old silent pond...
A frog jumps into the pond,
splash! Silence again --Bashō

Over the wintry

forest, winds howl in rage
with no leaves to blow- Soseki

As he lay in the bed now, listening to the rising dawn chorus of birdsong, he tried to think of a poem about birds. The only one that came to him was another one by Issa, the 18th century master.

The wren
Earns his living
Noiselessly.

But that didn't suit this cacophony of sound echoing through the trees behind the hut. He closed his eyes again, playing with English words to try to capture the feeling of joyous springtime in the five-seven-five syllable haiku structure…

Spring aviary
Notes in the bright green forest
Daybreak symphony

He grinned to himself. Not bad! He'd have to write it down before he forgot it. Opening his eyes, he flung off the light blanket and froze in the act of rising from the bed. What was that sound? That was no birdsong! It sounded like a motor!

He listened for a moment or two, straining his ears. He heard nothing more, so he ran silently on bare feet to the kitchen to see if he could see anything. His eyes widened in alarm as a metallic rattling noise came from the locked front door. Before he could think to hide, run, or do anything at all, the door swung open to reveal a short chubby man silhouetted against the morning light, laden with boxes and bags stacked so high in his arms that they partially obscured his face. He stepped over the doorsill and shifted his load slightly to see where he was going.

A pair of slanted dark eyes fell on Kenji's near-naked figure, illuminated by the brilliant sunlight that poured in the open doorway. The two stared at one another in shock.

"Huh!" said the man. He walked forward to set his load down on the long dining table and turned to pierce Kenji with a stern look. "Who you?"

"I—uh—I…" stuttered Kenji, at a complete loss to explain his presence. Why hadn't he thought this through and come up with some explanation if anyone came by?

"Hmph," grunted the man, who Kenji thought was probably Chinese. "You trespasser, that who you are." He eyed Kenji up and down and evidently decided he wasn't an immediate danger. "You have more clothes?" he asked, and Kenji gaped in surprise. That was not what he'd expected to be asked! He nodded, unable to think of anything to say.

"Good," said the man. "Go put on. Come help unload supplies." Kenji stood staring for another moment. "Hurry, or I decide you criminal and tie you up!" the man said sharply, and Kenji jumped, racing down the hall to the bedroom.

As he struggled into his clothes, his mind raced with wild thoughts of escape. He could jump through the window with the broken screen where he'd first come in, run into the forest—but there was no time to gather his things, the things he'd need to survive, and obviously he wouldn't be able to return for them. He could—um, take the man's boat, for surely he must have come by boat to have brought so many supplies—and drive it away. But to where? And then he'd truly be a criminal, a thief, and the police would hunt him down. Or could he knock the man out? No, no, that was crazy, that wouldn't solve anything and besides, the man looked a lot stronger than he was himself.

By the time he was thrusting his feet into his ragged shoes, he was resigned to the only possible course of action—to help the man unload the boat and hope he didn't get tied up and delivered to the Mounties.

For the next half hour, the man said no word other than to direct Kenji in carrying the many boxes, crates, baskets, and bags from the sleek little boat tied up to the dock. Once they were all in, the man took a key out of his pocket and opened a tall cupboard in the corner of the kitchen, frowning at the evidence that Kenji had tried to open it. He extracted a crowbar and handed it to the boy.

"I see you got boards off one window, so go take rest off. Stack beside back door. I need light; start with kitchen windows."

Kenji nodded again, open-mouthed. As he got to the door, however, he turned back. "Who are *you*?" he blurted.

"I am Hu," the man said. "Cook for hunting camp, come to get lodge ready for men coming next week to hunt deer." With that, he flapped a hand at Kenji. "Windows…" he said.

By the time Kenji had removed all the window coverings, he was hot and dusty, and his arms ached from prying, pulling, and carrying. He didn't dare stop, however. This Hu seemed willing to tolerate him, but Kenji had a suspicion that it wouldn't take much to change his mind.

He went back into the main room and stopped in astonishment. It was transformed! The floor had been swept, a pail of clean water stood by the sink, a fire had been kindled in the woodstove, and the room was filled with morning light. The cook had set a block of ice into the icebox and was stacking cheese, eggs, milk, and fresh fruits and vegetables inside. Best of all, however, when Hu saw Kenji come in, he stood up and set a plate of steaming pancakes dripping with butter and syrup on the table. A mug of something that smelled wonderfully like strong coffee sat alongside. Kenji stood frozen, staring in hunger but making no move.

"What? You not hungry?" Hu said, and a smile, the first Kenji had seen from the man, creased his round face. "Sit, eat, eat!" he said, and turned back to the woodstove to serve his own pancakes. Kenji didn't wait to be told twice. He sat on the long bench and wolfed the pancakes down in two minutes, washing the sweetness down with gulps of the coffee. It was heaven!

Hu sat placidly opposite, eating his own breakfast much more slowly. When Kenji's plate was scraped clean, Hu waved his fork at the woodstove. "More there. You look like you need." Kenji gratefully re-filled his plate and polished off another huge stack of the tender griddle cakes and another large mug of coffee. He sat back, swiping at his sticky mouth with his sleeve, and sighed in gratitude.

"That was really good. Thank you," he said, meeting Hu's eyes.

"Hmmm," said the cook, sitting back and sipping his own coffee. "You Japanese, yes?"

Kenji hesitated. "Um, no, I am Chinese Canadian," he lied, frantically trying to think up a Chinese name to give. But the man opposite shook his head.

"No, you not. I found poems. All by Japanese poets."

"Oh," said Kenji, and stopped, at a loss for what to say next.

"Hiding from evac-ua-tion, right?" asked Hu shrewdly, pronouncing the long English word carefully. Suddenly Kenji, undone by the simple acts of kindness this man had shown him, found himself telling the whole tale from start to finish. Hu said nothing as he listened, only nodding his head with its thick black hair, and sipping from his cup.

"Will you turn me in?" Kenji asked when his story wound to an end. He sat trembling, awaiting his fate.

The stocky Chinese man tilted his head to one side. "You want join your family?" he asked. Kenji hesitated, then shook his head.

"No. I wouldn't know where to find them now, and I doubt the government would just let me walk in even if I did! If they caught me, I'm sure they'd send me to a road camp or even a prisoner-of-war camp for avoiding their orders. Besides, I still believe it's wrong, what they're doing. I'm not Japanese—I am Canadian!" He looked up defiantly as he said this, his old fury resurging. Hu gestured with his stubby-fingered hands, making a patting-down motion.

"All right, all right, no need to shout! Canada not exactly treat Chinese much better, you know!"

"No, I know, I'm sorry. It just makes me so mad!"

"Hmmm," said the cook again, looking thoughtfully at Kenji's face. Then he appeared to make up his mind. "You know, white men, they not tell one Asian from another. You likely pass for Chinese to them."

"Them?" asked Kenji, confused. Was Hu going to make him go back to Powell River?

"Hunters, of course," Hu said, and nodded decidedly. "I tell them you apprentice, come to help cook and clean, yes?"

"I suppose," said Kenji. Then he grinned. "At least I'll get better food than I was cooking!" He paused. "What name will you give me, a Chinese name?"

Hu considered, then gestured to the deep green trees outside the windows. "Lim," he said. "Means evergreen forest—and easy to remember." He chuckled. "So, you not tell me your real name—you are Lim, my apprentice cook. No one need to know more."

1942
Hastings Park, East Lillooet, British Columbia

April had come and gone, and most of May, before the word finally came that the family was to be moved to East Lillooet within a week. Their relief at the prospect of leaving the terrible conditions of Hastings Park was marred by the news that Jiro was not to accompany them. Harry was never able to find out who had made the final decision, though he tried again and again to appeal it. Jiro was hustled off one morning with a group of men being sent to a prisoner of war camp in Angler, on the north shore of Lake Superior in Ontario. No explanation was given. He was given only a quarter hour to gather his skimpy belongings before being loaded onto the back of a truck headed to the train station. Harry and Hoshi had but scant moments to bid him good-bye, and the women none at all. They wept many bitter tears when they discovered his absence, but there was nothing to be done. They could only hope that someday, when the war ended, he would find his way home to them.

On their last evening at Hastings, Sara and Asami followed the lines of women into the dining hall for supper as the spring light was fading. Isabel moaned when she saw the slab of dry meat loaf on the plate with not even a spoonful of sauce to moisten it or relieve its bland flavour. Sara felt anger rise in her and suddenly she lifted Isabel into her arms and whispered to Asami, "Come."

She led her bewildered daughter and delighted granddaughter outside and walked them briskly towards the guards' hut.

"Mama! It's no use complaining about the food," hissed Asami. "We're leaving tomorrow, don't make trouble now!"

"I'm not planning to make trouble," her mother replied calmly but with purpose. She paused in the shadows of a large tree near the hut and waited, watching the guards move to and fro. When they were all occupied, she grabbed Isabel's hand. "Now," she said quietly, "Follow me!"

They slipped to the back of the hut and Asami began to suspect her mother's goal. Indeed, within a moment Sara had found the hole the boys had made in the wire fence and stretched it open, wide enough for them to slip through. "Come," she said again. After they were out, she pulled the gap closed behind them.

Isabel giggled softly at being included in such an adventure, but she knew enough to keep quiet as they looked both ways along East Hastings Street and then ran across in the twilight.

"Where are we going?" Asami asked, getting caught up in the thrill of escape, if only for an hour or two. Her mother pointed down the block to where the yellow lights of the *Golden Slipper Café* glowed in the spring dusk.

"I am not going to eat one more bite of their tasteless cooking!" Sara said vehemently. "Before we go tomorrow, we're going to have a proper supper."

They opened the door of the café, setting the little chimes above it tinkling. It was empty of customers, but at the sound of the chimes a wizened old Chinese woman came out from the back and peered at them. Nodding sagely, she said nothing, just gestured the women and Isabel to a high-backed booth near the rear of the room, one that hid them completely from anyone on the street. When they were seated, Sara asked for menus, but the old woman shook her head wordlessly and disappeared through a beaded curtain into the back.

"Is she refusing to serve us?" asked Asami, worried that the old woman was going to expose them to the guards.

"I don't *think* so..." said Sara, though her voice sounded tense. They had only a moment to wonder, however, for the curtain rattled again as the old woman re-entered the café, carrying three bowls of steaming soup on a tray. She laid one in front of each of them along with small flat ladles decorated with blue Chinese patterns. She nodded to them, gestured at the soup with a small bow and disappeared again through the curtain.

"Ahhhh," sighed Sara, lifting the bowl of soup and sniffing its aromatic steam appreciatively. Thin slices of gingerroot and green onion floated in the golden broth, along with star-shaped slivers of carrot. She set the bowl down and took a spoonful, sipping it carefully. Her eyes closed momentarily in ecstasy. "It's *wonderful*!" she exclaimed. "Go on, Isabel, but be careful—it's hotter than anything you've had in months!"

Over the next half hour, they were presented with a stream of delicious dishes that more than satisfied their cravings for flavour and texture. There were plump steamed dumplings in a savoury sauce, chewy noodles in a spicy peanutty chicken and vegetable mixture, strips of tender beef smothered in a rich dark gravy, and a chow mein dish with crisp bean sprouts and crunchy fried noodles on top. When they protested that they could eat no more, the old woman brought pots of scalding green tea, and a tiny dish of ice cream for Isabel with a charming little white rabbit candy on the side, wrapped in shiny foil.

When they were finished, Sara dug into her skirt pocket and brought out a handful of coins and bills. She offered her open hand to the old woman, but the crone reached out with her gnarled fingers and closed Sara's hand over the money.

"No," she said, and it was the first word she had spoken. "Wrong, what they do to you. Our honour to feed you."

Sara's eyes filled with tears, and she bowed low in gratitude. "Thank you," she whispered. "Thank you."

They were reunited with the men early the next morning, standing with their luggage piled up around them as they waited silently for the trucks that would take them to the train station. Hoshi bent down to his daughter.

"What's that you've got there, Izzie?" he asked, glimpsing a small object held closely in her little fist. The child opened her hand to show her father the rabbit candy, still wrapped in its foil. "Where did you get that?" Hoshi asked, puzzled. Candy was never provided to the children here in the detention centre.

"From the old Chinese lady," Isabel replied quietly. She was learning that some things needed to be kept secret. Hoshi looked up at Asami, his brow furrowed.

"I'll tell you later," his wife whispered. "It's all right, as long as she keeps it hidden. Our own little rebellion, you might say." She smiled at her mother, who quirked her eyebrows in response but said nothing.

A red-coated Mountie came out of the guard house and began calling out the names of those who were to board the trucks. When he called "Sara Sato," Asami's mother answered in a clear voice.

"I am here, sir, but my name is Sakura Sato."

The guard frowned at her in confusion, but Sara simply looked back calmly. Finally, the man shrugged and gestured to her to join the others.

"Why did you do that?" asked Harry in a low voice. "You have always insisted that you be called Sara, from the minute you stepped onto Canadian soil over forty-five years ago."

"I know," his wife answered. "And I will stay Sara. But if the Canadian government will not recognize me as Canadian then I will use my Japanese name to them. Perhaps someday they will welcome us as full citizens, but for now, who knows? Japan may win this war and then we must be prepared to become Japanese once more, to survive. It may be best to have our Japanese names on government documents after all."

Harry nodded thoughtfully. "You may be right. Haruto Sato," he said firmly to the RCMP as they all climbed into the back of the truck and settled onto the rough benches.

Asami stared at her parents, aghast, as the truck began to move. It had never occurred to her than the Allies might lose the war, or what it might mean if they did. The thought horrified her, and she shuddered, pulling her shawl tightly around herself in the cool May morning.

At the quiet station, they boarded a Pacific Great Eastern steam train that stood huffing and hissing in the brightening light. Isabel was excited to board the train, and bounced on the seat, looking around with bright eyes. Watching her, Asami and Hoshi smiled a little at each other.

"It can't be any worse than Hastings Park," said Hoshi, and Asami nodded in agreement.

"And we will be together as a family," she said. After a pause she added under her breath, "All but Jiro—and Kenji." Hoshi reached out and squeezed her hand gently for a moment but said nothing. What was there to say?

It was a trip of about 150 miles, almost due north, and there was much to keep them interested as the train chugged its way out of the city, across Burrard Inlet rippling like silver in the grey morning, and up the ragged coast of Howe Sound, a deep fiord off the Georgia Strait. The mountains, always present in the distance from Vancouver, now rushed up beside them, obscuring the rising sun and casting the dark waters of the sound into shadow. As they approached the town of Squamish, they could see evidence of a lively logging industry, with huge booms of chained logs lying offshore in readiness for processing.

"Mama, I have to pee," whispered Isabel, and Asami got up to take her. As they made their way along the narrow aisle, swaying with the train's movement, Asami saw a familiar face.

"Mary!" she exclaimed. "I didn't know that you were transferring to East Lillooet! But…" she hesitated, for the young woman had only one baby clasped in her arms, and her face was thin and white.

Mary closed her eyes in pain for a moment and then spoke so softly that Asami had to bend to hear her over the rattle of the train. "My baby son—my Davy—he died at Hastings Park, of tuberculosis. They tried to save him, in the special hospital ward, but…luckily neither little Lily nor I caught it from him." She glanced at an older woman and man seated next to her. "These are my husband's parents, Mr. and Mrs. Takimoto. They have so very kindly paid for us to join them in East Lillooet." Her voice caught on a sob. "I have had no word of my husband Edward, not since he was taken…"

Mrs. Takimoto hushed her, not unkindly, taking the sleeping baby out of her arms, and Mary wiped her eyes.

"I am sorry, it is just so hard, not knowing where he is or if I will ever be able to tell him of his son's death," she said, choking back another sob.

"I am so very sorry, Mary," Asami said softly, laying a gentle hand on the woman's arm. "When we are settled, I will come to see you, see if there's anything I can do to help."

"Thank you," whispered Mary, and Asami moved away, filled with sadness for this poor young mother, left to manage her crushing grief without her husband.

When she came out of the tiny bathroom with Isabel, Asami saw that the train had moved away from the coast. They were now headed slightly east, and craggy mountains towered on either side of the narrow tracks.

"Mama, there's snow up there!" said Isabel, pointing. Asami crouched down to see that her daughter was right. Even though spring had come to the coast, here the temperatures were cold enough at night that the peaks still held a great deal of snow cover.

They passed through a few towns and Isabel read out the signs as they went through: "Garibaldi, Whistler, Pemberton…"

The section of track northeast of Pemberton wound along the very edge of the mountain, and Asami gazed with a little anxiety at the long drop down to a ribbon of turbulent water rushing far below. Looking out the other side of the car, Hoshi called out to them to come and look. A small herd of mountain goats perched high above on ledges so narrow that it seemed impossible that they could support the large woolly animals, who gazed down at the train with indifference, their sharp black horns gleaming in the sun. As they passed them, to Isabel's delight, one tiny kid leaped from ledge to ledge, following the path of the train for a time.

The sun had disappeared behind the western ridge of peaks as they arrived at Lillooet, and their long shadows cast a chill over the small station where another fleet of trucks awaited to transport the families to the internment camp. Asami peered along the road, discerning a street of storefronts in the distance and the windows of many homes glowing yellow through the gloaming. It looked quite welcoming, and a small flame of hope sprang up. Perhaps it wouldn't be too bad.

Unfortunately, the town was not their destination. As soon as their luggage was loaded into the backs of the trucks, they all climbed up to find unsteady perches among the bags and boxes. The evening wind chilled them as they drove over the trestle bridge that spanned the mighty Fraser River and linked the town of Lillooet to the internment site of East Lillooet. As they drove off the bridge, Asami saw red-coated police officers replacing the barrier behind them. Clearly, passage between the two communities was prohibited.

Night had almost fallen as they reached the camp. There was no fence—but none was needed. Steep mountains hemmed them in on one side, a steep drop to the river canyon on the other. There was nowhere to run to. They stood docilely beside their pitiful piles of belongings as a guard called out their hut numbers.

"Takimoto: number 4" he cried, and Asami saw Mary and her parents-in-law pick up their suitcases and trudge off in the direction indicated by the guard's outflung arm. He continued to call out numbers and one by one the families left to seek out their designated accommodation. Finally, he called out: "Tasaka: number 54!"

Harry and Hoshi carried the suitcases, while Sara carried Isabel and Asami lifted the heavy sewing machine case, tucking her frying pan under her arm. They made their way down a long row of shadowy dwellings, only half-visible in the rapidly fading light. Each one seemed to be the same: a small boxy shape with a peaked roof, with a small window to each side of a centrally placed door—like a child's drawing of a house.

Their number—54—was about two thirds of the way down the row, on the right. A dim light from the house next door was just enough for them to reach the steps, but then it winked out, leaving them in darkness. Hoshi groped in his pocket for a match and struck it. Their door stood open, and the inside was chillier than the cool evening outside. He saw a lantern standing on a rough table just inside the door and lit it before his match burned out.

The flickering flame revealed the paucity of their new dwelling: one room with a rudimentary kitchen, a dining table with two long benches, and three sets of bunk beds along the walls. There was no running water, no heat but a woodstove, and no toilet—a peek out back revealed a row of shared outhouses. It would be adequate, but barely. Asami's heart sank.

Beside her, her mother drew in a deep breath.

"Well," she said briskly. "It smells far better than Hastings Park, and it has a door! I'd say our lot has improved! Now, Harry, can you please see what is available in terms of firewood and get a fire going in the stove? Hoshi, can you find us some water? My big kettle is in the carpetbag, there—see if you can fill it. Asami, get Isabel into her pyjamas, she's half asleep already—find our sheets and blankets and make up a bed for her..."

Within half an hour the luggage was unpacked, the woodstove was warming, and there was a pot of water for tea heating on it. Isabel was fast asleep in a nest of blankets, clutching her geisha doll. The adults sat at the table, faces weary but more relaxed than they had been in weeks. They were here, for who knew how long. *Kodomo no tame ni.* For the sake of the children, they would make the best of it.

1943
East Lillooet, British Columbia

Asami stood up from hoeing between the rows of tall tomato plants, wiping the sweat from her brow. She had never imagined such heat! In contrast to the mild climate on the Pacific coast, where summer and winter varied more in rainfall than in warmth, the interior of the province had extremes of both temperature and precipitation.

Still, she appreciated the warmth. Their first winter in East Lillooet had been brutally cold, with both days and nights well below freezing for months. The flimsy tar-paper shacks that had been hastily built for the sixty-two families living in the camp provided poor protection from the cold. Asami had woken most mornings to find frost feathering the wall beside her bed, and icicles glistening from the ceiling where the shoddy roof failed to keep out leaks. Torrential rains, or icy hail mixed with snow, had battered them when they went to fetch water each day, and though the snow didn't accumulate much beyond a few inches, its chilly breath was bitter. The chopping of wood for their woodstove was a constant chore that never seemed to yield enough warmth for comfort, despite the smallness of the hut at only twelve feet by twelve feet.

Some of the older *issei*, the earliest immigrants, began to be more vocal in their support for Japan, openly hoping that they would win the war. Angry at their internment and shabby treatment, they began to turn against their adopted country. They cheered when rumours circulated that several Japanese submarines had fired on Canada's west coast, though apparently to no effect. Others, however—especially the *nisei*, those born in Canada and thus citizens—held to the hope of an Allied victory and maintained the belief that only by being docile and conspicuously loyal to Canada would they have a chance to repair the damage done by the war, after it was over. Tensions rose as these two factions argued, and the harsh conditions isolated one from another more and more. Those who maintained that Japan would lose the war began to be called *atama no kuroi keto*, or 'black-haired white trash' by some of the most vehement *issei*. A few of the younger people began to absorb their elders' attitudes, and when an old newsreel showing the Pearl Harbour bombings was shown as a trailer to a Fred Astaire-Ginger Rogers musical one night in the camp's community hall, some responded with shouts of *Banzai*, or *long life to the emperor*! Asami, sitting in the audience, had shivered in fear lest the guards hear this and tighten the restrictions even further.

With spring's warming weather, there was some lessening of the animosity, and the men had pooled their meagre savings to purchase timber to re-roof and re-side the little houses to make them better able to withstand the next winter. For the news of the war—the little they managed to glean from the guards--was bad, and few imagined that it would end soon enough to release them from their imprisonment before the season turned again.

The terms of their agreement in this 'self-sustaining' community meant that they were beholden to pay for everything—their food, firewood, lumber--anything they needed from the town across the bridge, and the trickle of income from their confiscated properties back on the coast was sorely needed. In January, when the B.C. government received permission to liquidate all Japanese Canadian property held within one hundred miles of the coast, everyone was both furious and bewildered. They had been assured that their property would be held 'in trust' and that the income from it would be sent to them to pay for their needs here in the camp. Word came that somehow the Custodian of Enemy Alien Property had been persuaded by a Vancouver Alderman, one Mr. Buscombe, to designate land as 'perishable property' by making the argument that maintaining it would cost more than selling it outright. This suggestion was approved after a group of dignitaries took a tour of the Powell Street area. They observed that most of the private residences lacked bathing facilities and so they—apparently ignorant of or willfully blind to the cultural custom of communal bathing in Japanese Canadian communities—declared the buildings 'unfit for human habitation' and therefore 'perishable' and subject to sale by the government. This decision was soon expanded to include both city and rural properties owned by Nikkei.

Word came, months later, that their own representative, Kishizo Kimura, who had cooperated with the government committee and tried to get the best deals he could for the impounded fishing boats, had resigned in anger over this decision. He said in *The New Canadian* newspaper, which was now being published from the internment camp in Kaslo, that he expected that the seized farmland would be given to *hakujin* soldiers after the war, as had been done after the Great War. He revealed an ambitious plan of urban renewal on the part of Vancouver real estate investors that would wipe out Japantown in its entirety. Kimura hinted that he believed that the removal of Nikkei to supposedly 'temporary' internment camps for the duration of the war was a ruse, a mere first step in removing Japanese Canadians from the coast permanently. The sale of their land, he speculated, was but another step in that direction.

There were also disturbing rumours about Etsuji Morii, a big-time racketeer in pre-war Vancouver. Morii's position was ambivalent. He was the highest-ranked Nikkei collaborator with the British Columbia Security Commission and a powerful *issei* leader. However, at the same time he was a notorious Japanese Imperial sympathizer and a member of the Black Dragon Society, a paramilitary, ultranationalist group with roots in Japan and chapters in both America and Canada. Gossip and rumour swirled around the role he may have played on both sides of the conflict, but as the gangster—who was nevertheless also a generous philanthropist in the Nikkei community—was now interned in Minto, another self-supporting camp, nothing was certain.

Harry's strawberry farm was sold without his consent or even his knowledge until the day that an envelope containing a cheque for less than one hundred dollars arrived. This—for a large working farm in good order, one that had been developed over decades to a state of robust health and arability, including all the tractors and tools, the greenhouses and packing sheds, the strawberry crates and boxes, sold for just over a thousand dollars. The deductions from the sale price were listed as 'administrative fees' and 'taxes' that had been retained by the various government offices. It was a pitiful recompense that sent Harry into a depression that lasted for weeks.

Indeed, everyone in the camp feared what would happen if they ran out of money, and discussions were held among all the families as to how to earn funds for the community. It was Harry, farmer that he was, who rallied from the blow of his own loss and offered a solution. He suggested that they dig up a large area of land south of the gravel road that ran through the camp, to plant a community vegetable garden to feed themselves, and a field of tomatoes, which he believed would grow well in the coming hot summer, for commercial sale. Accordingly, they all donated money to purchase tomato plants from Mr. Palmer, the *hakujin* farmer whose land had been leased for the internment camp. All toiled to prepare the soil and plant out the aromatic seedlings.

Those seedlings had thrived, watered by clear cold water drawn from the river and stored in the row of half-barrel water tanks that lined the field. These tanks were filled thanks to old Sadajiro Asari, who found and repaired a pump so that the Japanese Canadians were able to use an ancient wooden irrigation flume to carry water up from the muddy Fraser River to these wooden storage tanks. The plants had grown quickly in the hot sun. And it had been hot: after a temperate spring, the daily highs had quickly climbed to the one-hundred-degree mark and then edged over it. The little settlement and the gardens baked and wilted, but the steady application of water to both plants and workers prevented disaster.

Now it was August, and the globes of the tomatoes glowed red amidst the rustling greens. The Nikkei were rightfully proud of their success, for the tomatoes were large and intensely flavourful, and they had rapidly become the preferred choice of the people in the town of Lillooet. The Nikkei had even built a small tomato cannery on site and were able to can the tomatoes they didn't sell fresh. It was only the fruits of their labours that were valued, however; no traffic was permitted between the camp and the town, and the townspeople feared and disliked having the Japanese Canadians so near to them, a mere few hundred yards away, separated only by the slender bridge.

It had been Asami who had first recognized Kaye Kaminishi as he sat on the low step of hut # 51, just a few doors down from them. Ever since she'd given birth to Kenichi under the bleachers of Powell Grounds more than sixteen years before, Asami had been an avid fan of the Asahi baseball team. Even from Powell River, she'd followed their continued success, and had been saddened to hear, among all the other, more serious dislocations of the war, that the team had been disbanded. As a result, she recognized the young rookie, who had joined the Asahis as a seventeen-year-old high schooler back in 1939. She had greeted him and sat down beside him, exchanging introductions and memories of the great baseball team of *pauru gai*—Powell Street. She learned that he was here with his mother, having used his savings to pay their way, but that his family's sawmill had been sold off anyway.

"Yes, the Royston Seizai that I inherited from my father employed about one hundred Nikkei workers and was doing quite well before the war. We had a railroad line up into the mountain and other innovations. But the government declared it a wartime emergency and sold it off. We received less than one-tenth of its value." He'd shaken his head sadly and Asami had nodded sympathetically.

"I imagine that you miss playing baseball more, though," she'd said, and Kaye had nodded and chuckled a little.

"I brought my glove, bat, and ball—even my uniform!" he'd said wistfully. "I guess I still hope to be able to use them again someday."

Asami had sat silently for a moment. Then, "Why not now?" she had asked him. Kaye had looked at her in surprise.

"Here?" he'd asked. "You think so?" Asami had nodded emphatically.

"I can think of nothing better to raise everyone's spirits and lift us out of our troubles," she'd said. "I bet if you asked, you'd find more than a few men and boys have managed to bring along baseball gloves and bats. There's still room on the flat land beyond the tomato field—why don't you mark out a baseball diamond and see what happens?"

Now, as she stretched, easing the ache in her back, Asami could hear the faint calls and cheers of the men and boys practicing. Enthusiasm for the idea had been immediate, and a playing field was created in short order. A slight slope topped by tall fir trees bordered one edge, but a wooden fence had been built along the opposite side to demarcate the outfield and hold back the many spectators who watched every practice and pickup game. Two wings of a taller fence stood behind home plate, angled to shelter it. Any time it was light enough to see the ball, a gang of men and children could be found on the diamond, tossing the ball, practicing their batting, or playing a game if there were enough on hand to make up two teams. Everyone—*issei* and *nisei* alike—loved baseball and coming together to play and watch had brought the community closer than it had been for months.

Asami bent to her task again and finished the row, then went to the water tanks for a refreshing drink, replacing her hoe in the rack that had been built beside the field. She saw Mary Takimoto, her little girl, Hina, strapped to her back, nearing the end of her row as well.

"Mary!" she called. "Let's go watch the baseball for a few minutes." The other woman waved and made her way over.

"Phew, it's so hot!" she said, unwinding the straps that held Hina to her and setting the toddler down as she dipped a drink for them both out of the tank. "It's a good thing that your name means good greens, Hina, because I think you are going to grow up in the middle of a vegetable field!" Asami was glad to hear the woman make even a feeble joke. It had seemed for a time that she would never rise out of her grief over the loss of her baby boy. But time and the company of other young mothers had helped, and now she was better able to cope. She hoisted the child into her arms, and they strolled together along the edge of the tomato field to the baseball diamond.

Today Kaye seemed to be coaching the boys and men in how to bunt the ball close to home plate to foil the opposing team into chasing it while they ran for first base. Time after time he demonstrated how to hold the bat at a low angle to gently tap the ball. As he did so, he regaled them with stories of famous Asahi players like centre fielder Eddie Kitagawa, who had been a manager for the Bank of Montreal in Vancouver. Through the intervention of Eddie's brother-in-law, who was studying medicine in Ontario when war broke out, and a local pastor, a home had been found for the Kitagawa family in Toronto for the duration of the war. Eddie's wife Muriel wrote for *The New Canadian* newspaper, but Eddie was only able to find work in a laundry at thirty-five cents an hour, quite a come down from his former job.

Other players hadn't been even that lucky: Roy Nishidera, Harry Miyasaki, Tom Nichi Matoba, and young Jack Hayami had all been sent to the Angler prisoner of war (POW) camp in the cold barren land north of Lake Superior in Ontario. They had all been very active in a group called the *Nisei Mass Evacuation Group* or NMEG, mostly young Japanese Canadian men who had lived in Vancouver and rallied before the actual evacuation, lobbying for families to be allowed to relocate together, beyond the self-supporting camps. Asami wondered, hearing Kaye speak of his teammates sent to Angler, if any of them were friendly with Jiro. *He'd love that,* she thought, *getting to talk about baseball with Asahi players!* Leaning against the rough wooden fence, her thoughts strayed to her brother and then, inevitably, to her son. Where were they? Were they all right? She sighed. She could only hope so.

1943
Angler, Ontario

Jiro wound up and pitched the baseball as hard as he could to Roy Nishidera, a former Asahi player sent to Angler for his activities with the Nisei Mass Evacuation Group (NMEG). Jiro's limited vision prevented him from being a great batter or catcher, but he could pitch reasonably well. Roy swung and the bat connected with a crack, sending the ball soaring over Jiro's head to disappear across the field.

Jiro laughed and pulled off his glove, dusting off his white prisoner's uniform with its large red dot on the back of the shirt. *Makes a good target*, Jiro had thought in dismay when it was first issued to him. Now, however, he took it for granted.

"That's enough for me, Roy. You've hit every ball so far that I can't even see them to retrieve them! If you want to bat some more, you'll have to go find them yourself."

The compact man standing at the spot designated as 'home plate' laughed in turn, swinging the bat idly. "That's okay, Jiro, I'll send one of the younger fellows to search later. Let's go find a cool drink."

As they made their way toward the large, black-roofed barracks buildings, they saw many men hurrying toward the last of the eight huts.

"Huh," said Roy. "I wonder what's up. Let's go find out."

They skirted the perimeter with its triple layers of barbed wire and waved to the guards—mostly WWI veterans too old to fight overseas in the current war--at the watchtowers as they passed. Angler detention camp had been built to house German and Italian prisoners of war, but after a dramatic—but ultimately failed--escape attempt involving a one hundred-and fifty-foot-long tunnel dug through the sandy soil under the perimeter fence, the Germans had been sent to Ozada Camp 133 in the Bow Valley in Alberta, and Angler had been repurposed to house the Nikkei who had been identified as 'agitators.'

How Jiro had ended up here was unclear to him, as he'd never had anything to do with the NMEG or any other protest group, but he hadn't made any attempt to have the error corrected. In fact, he'd found himself in sympathy with the so-called 'agitators' ever since the day he was boarding the train for Angler. A woman with an infant strapped to her back and a toddler by the hand was on her knees, tearfully pleading with the RCMP officer to allow her to accompany her husband, who had just boarded the train. The officer was stone-faced, unresponsive, and Jiro had wondered how he could be so immune to such an impassioned plea. During the train trip, he had thought deeply about what was happening, questioning whether there was a real need to implement such inhumane schemes that split families apart and left women and children without protection or income. He could not come up with the answers, but since that day he had ceased to believe that all the government's motivations were either necessary or truly for the good of either the Nikkei or the rest of Canada. It was an uncomfortable feeling, to question the democracy that he had always believed in.

However, other than the simple fact of confinement, conditions were reasonably good here: the food was palatable, if skimpy, and the guards were mostly friendly. Some of them even seemed to be a bit sympathetic to the Japanese Canadians' plight—one of them had told Jiro that he'd fought with Japanese Canadians in the first war, and they'd exchanged stories of the horror of the trenches. And there were Asahi players here! Jiro was thoroughly enjoying his time with them, and he often thought guiltily of his family, hoping that they were managing all right in East Lillooet.

He and Roy entered the long building and walked between the rows of bunk beds, twenty per side, to the far end where crowd of fellows were chattering animatedly, their voices raised in questions and shouted answers. As they got closer, the group quieted to listen to Fujikazu Tanaka. Fuji was one of the *nisei* founders of NMEG, a well-educated man whose English was so good that he'd been a radio announcer for a time. At first, he had been the leader of the POW's, playing the role of liaison between the prisoners and the camp commander. But the recent influx of a group of radical *issei* from the Petawawa POW camp, after an uprising there had almost resulted in a firing squad incident, had caused some challenge to his leadership. Whereas the NMEG members were focused on improving conditions for *nisei* and their families, the *issei* were more likely to be Japanese nationalists. As well, there were continuing rumours that the road camp projects were being abandoned. The Angler men were being asked to go to other work camps set up by the government, where they would make a tiny wage of twenty-two cents an hour. There were many debates on this topic among the men, and some heated disagreements.

When the internees' election for leader had been held a month ago, Fuji had stepped aside for one of the new *issei*, Tokikazu Tanaka. Toki was older and craftier, and he encouraged the others to maintain loyalty to Japan and try to undermine the Allies, though only a few of the younger men listened to him. Despite his allegiances, he was fulfilling his role as leader successfully, and Jiro had no complaints so far. However, he had great respect for Fuji, so he leaned in to hear what he was saying now.

"The government has realized that keeping us here, paying for us to stay, when there's a critical labour shortage across Canada, isn't sensible. That is why they are asking us to leave here and join their work camps."

"Will we be allowed to go back to university if we leave?" asked one of the younger men. All Japanese Canadians had been expelled from Canadian universities after Pearl Harbour. Fuji shook his head.

"Not yet," he replied. "But if you volunteer to go to work in a camp, perhaps you will be more likely to be allowed to return later." The questioner nodded thoughtfully.

"I was at the University of Alberta. Perhaps they will let me rejoin my program if I show myself to be a loyal citizen."

Quite a few of the *nisei* were also nodding and murmuring among themselves. But Toki spoke up angrily.

"Why should we do what they want, work for them and solve their problems? They just want us off their hands—but why should we give them that? I say, stay here and make them pay our way for the duration of the war. After—well, then we will see. Perhaps Japan will win the war—or perhaps Canada will send us all back to Japan anyway."

"Oh, surely not!" exclaimed one of the youngest prisoners. "I've never been to Japan, I don't speak the language, I don't know anyone there and I feel little connection to the culture—how would I make a living? I am a Canadian citizen! They can't make me leave!"

Toki smiled, but the expression was bitter. "You think not? Well, we shall see..." He shook his head. "I, for one, am going nowhere." He strode away and most of the *issei* prisoners followed him.

For the rest of the day the debate was the sole topic of conversation, and heated arguments raged throughout the camp. Several family dramas played out, with fathers and sons having different opinions, or brothers falling out over the decision. Not wishing to engage in the arguments, Jiro kept his thoughts to himself.

The next morning, he went out early to enjoy the cool dawn and to think quietly, as he often did. He stood watching a large group of young men running laps around the perimeter of the camp, the large round red patches on the backs of their prisoners' uniforms bouncing up and down like a school of agitated goldfish. They called themselves the YMTG, the Young Men's Training Group, and they ran every morning and evening for two hours. Jiro admired their tenacity and their dedication to keeping themselves healthy and fit, but at fifty-six he didn't think he'd be able to keep up with them, and he didn't want to invoke their pity.

As the run came to an end, Jiro found himself near a young man he'd noticed before. The youth, who was perhaps just twenty, was slight and seemed shy, but he never missed a run and even Jiro could see his fitness level improving week by week.

"You are doing well!" Jiro called out on an impulse. "You are much less out of breath at the end of your run now than you were when you began!"

The young man smiled shyly and walked closer to Jiro. "Thank you!" he said, panting a little. "Why don't you join us on our runs?"

"Oh, I am too old, and my lungs are still a little scarred by mustard gas in the last war," said Jiro with a rueful smile, patting his chest with his hand. "Jiro Sato," he said then, holding out his hand to shake.

"Tamio Kuwabara, but call me Tom," said the youth, shaking hands with enthusiasm. "I am sorry to hear about your lungs, but maybe you'd like to walk with me while I cool down, anyway." Jiro nodded and smiled, and the two of them proceeded to walk in the churned trail of footsteps from the runners. Once he had regained his breath, Tom asked Jiro the first question all prisoners exchanged:

"Well, what did you do to be brought here?"

Jiro laughed. "In fact, I don't know! I didn't engage in any dissident or revolutionary activities, much less anything criminal! I thought I'd be sent to East Lillooet with my family, but at the last moment I was told to report to the train coming here. No idea why and you know, they don't take too kindly to being questioned!" He shrugged. "Perhaps I was mistaken for someone else. What about you? You seem rather young to have been a revolutionary!"

Tom smiled a little sheepishly. "It was surprising, even to me! My younger brother and I were chatting to a group of fellows from Vancouver Island the day before we were all to be sent off to join a road camp. This was in Hastings Park—you were there at some point, yes?" Jiro nodded and Tom continued, "Anyway, these other fellows said they'd decided to refuse to go. They spoke very eloquently about human rights, and the need to resist our unfair persecution and somehow—I don't know exactly how—we were persuaded to join them in their refusal! It all sounded very heroic and noble at the time," he said, shaking his head with a bitter chuckle.

"So, what happened when you refused to board the train?" asked Jiro. He didn't remember hearing about this incident back at Hastings Park, but then, no doubt the authorities had suppressed such inflammatory news from the other internees as much as possible.

"Oh, they were very angry. They tried to threaten us and get us to back down, but we kept saying '*ganbarum da zo'*—let us not give up!--to each other and eventually they took away our train tickets and registration cards. The next day they handed us over to the army, who locked us all in the Immigration Building on the other side of Vancouver. It was very barren, with just bunk beds and a dining area. There were only two small windows, very high up, and we used to fight to get a chance to look out of them." Tom's eyes were vague, and Jiro could see that he was in the past, remembering his hardships. After a moment, he looked at Jiro and smiled, once more focused on the here and now. "Visitors used to gather outside, calling up to us and trying to deliver parcels of food and other small gifts, but they were not allowed up to see us. It was during that time that my resolve to continue to resist hardened. You see, at first it was, I don't know, kind of a lark, a way to fit in with the other fellows. But as time went on, I saw things that made me very angry with the *hakujin*. One day, the guards were chasing off the crowd of visitors standing outside, and one old lady refused to go. She wanted to deliver a *bento* box of treats to her son. Nothing subversive or likely to cause any problems, right? But the guard, he drew his pistol and forced her away, step by step, waving his gun in her sad little wrinkled face! An old lady, grieving for her son!" Tom's eyes were wide with remembered shock. "What possible harm could she do? At that moment, I hated Canada and what it was doing to us. I resolved to resist in every way I could, for the duration of the war."

Jiro nodded in sympathy and comprehension. "How long were you held there?" he asked.

"About six weeks," answered Tom. "Then we were sent off to Petawawa."

"Oh," said Jiro, "you were in the group who came from there last summer, then?" Tom nodded. "Why did they move you, do you know?"

"Yes, because of an incident last July. There had been a lot of dissent among the men, just as there is here, with some arguing that we should agree to go and work in the road camps, and others trying to get them to stay, to keep working to be reunited with our families. I guess some of them decided to hold a secret meeting in the dining hall in the middle of the night, to try to decide on a strategy. As they were crossing over between buildings about two a.m., suddenly the search lights came on from the watchtowers and the guards started shooting at them from three different directions! Miraculously, no one was hit, but shots went into several buildings including the kitchen—there were bullet holes in several pots and pans next morning!" He shook his head again in disbelief. "They'd fired blanks before when they were quelling a disagreement or something, but these were live rounds! Canadians shooting Canadians—civilians who had done nothing other than passively resist unfair incarceration! Unbelievable!"

"The next morning, we all refused to go outside for roll call. We told them we would refuse until we got some explanation for the previous night's incident. Well, the camp commander met with a delegation of the prisoners and maintained that the guards were right to fire 'warning shots' as he called them because the prisoners were outside their barracks after curfew. Warning shots? Live rounds! We still refused to go to roll call, and demanded that the Spanish Consul--you know, the neutral country authority assigned to oversee the POW camps in Canada--be brought in. Usually, he came every three months to inspect conditions, just like he does here, but we said we wanted him to make a special visit to resolve this issue."

"In retaliation, the commander closed our canteen and suspended all incoming mail and newspapers and cancelled all movies. Well, that didn't deter us. For three more days we refused roll call. Then we were told to come to a meeting—this was on July 4th—where a high-ranking military officer spoke to our camp leaders. He agreed that the guards' shooting had been wrong, but he said that refusing roll call wasn't an acceptable response. If we continued to refuse, he said, the camp leaders would be rounded up and prosecuted under military law—perhaps even executed!"

"No!" said Jiro, stopped in his tracks, aghast. "Just for refusing to come out and be counted each day? Surely that's not such an important thing!"

Tom grimaced and stopped also. "Apparently it is," he continued. "There was no room for discussion; the officer just made this statement and left the room. Our leaders came out and told us—we were all standing in a big crowd outside the building, waiting to see what would happen next. There were armed soldiers standing in a line not far from us, just watching us. Toki—you know him, he was our barracks leader in Petawawa too—he came out and told us the threat, and we were furious. A big uproar started up, but this staff sergeant—I remember, he was a little short guy with a chubby face—he hollered at us and pointed to his wristwatch. He said, 'You have exactly five minutes to obey our orders and line up for roll call!' Then he gestured at the armed soldiers and the implication was obvious—line up or be shot."

"God in heaven!" exclaimed Jiro. "I have heard of nothing like this before! What did you do?"

Tom took a deep breath and blew it out before replying. "I will admit to you that I have never been so frightened in my life. I looked at those soldiers and I saw that some of them—not all of them, but enough—they just wanted an excuse to shoot. Maybe they hated Japs because of the war, and no doubt some of them had good reason—maybe they'd lost a loved one to a Japanese attack or something. Or maybe they just hated us anyway and didn't want us in Canada. I don't know. My little brother was beside me, gripping my hand and sweating. The five minutes passed in silence, and no one moved. But just as the sergeant was about to raise his hand, Toki stepped forward. I swear, Jiro, he looked like a samurai of old—noble, dignified, wise. He calmly said, 'Gentleman, please. Let us line up for roll call.' He walked over to where we usually lined up, and everyone followed him in silence. Not a word was said during the counting, but then ten of our leaders were called out and taken away in a truck to the detention room near the gate. As they drove off, one of them called out '*ganbare*—don't give up!'" Tom sighed. "Anyway, only a few days later they said we were all to be transported here. Three of the ten men returned to the camp, but the other seven were apparently sent off to be tried by a military tribunal for inciting resistance. I haven't heard what happened to them."

"That's quite a tale," said Jiro as they resumed their walk. "I had no idea that such incidents had happened. It does make you feel quite skeptical about a happy ending for us Nikkei after the war, doesn't it? And it also makes me feel that perhaps Toki is right—we should stay here and refuse to go to the work camps." A few minutes later, Tom stopped again. He gestured outside the tall, barbed wire fence they'd been following, to where a patch of little white daisies with golden centres waved in the warm breeze of the summer morning.

"You know, every day when we run, I look at those little flowers. Some days the sun is blazing down on them, and some days they are covered in frost, but almost every day, at least one flower is blooming, no matter the conditions." He looked at Jiro, and the older man was impressed by the wisdom in the young man's eyes. "All we can do, I guess, is strive to be like that little flower—to bloom wherever we find ourselves, whatever struggles we are enduring." He took another deep breath, and then his youthful face broke into an impish grin. "And Jiro, you should come to our judo club in the afternoons. I'll soon get you into better shape so you can come out and run with us!"

Small white blossoms shine
In sun, rain, cold feathered frost
Roots go deep in sand.

1944
Powell Lake, British Columbia

Kenji finished scrubbing the last of the big copper pots and wearily hung up his drying towel. It was the last meal for the current group of hunters, and he would be very glad to see them go tomorrow. Hu had been right, the *hakujin* hunters scarcely gave him a glance, for the most part accepting him without question as Hu's Chinese apprentice. This group, however, included Mr. Simpson, a man Kenji suspected was a police officer despite his casual hunting clothes. There was something about the way he held himself, some extra alertness that made Kenji very nervous. More than once, he'd caught the man gazing at him intently as he served or cleared the table, and he would be very glad to see the back of him.

Kenji had been grateful to Hu, who had even paid him a small wage for his work in addition to not exposing his true identity. When he'd closed the lodge at the end of that first autumn, he'd given Kenji a key and left some supplies for him to help him survive the winter. As a result, other than being desperately lonely, Kenji had been quite comfortable until Hu reappeared in the spring. Another hunting season and another long winter had come and gone since then. Kenji had eagerly devoured the books Hu had left for him last fall, but the cold season had crawled by, and he was fed up with having to hide.

His proud dreams of resisting, of making a statement, had faded with the long months of isolation. However, he was still afraid to expose himself. The hunters, who were older men, too old to have gone off to fight—had talked of nothing but the war, and their hatred of the Japanese was as virulent as their hatred of the Nazis. Many of them spoke disparagingly of the Nikkei and openly said they should all be shipped back to Japan, a statement that shocked Kenji to his core. It was abundantly clear that these *hakujin* were completely incapable of differentiating between enemy Japanese and those of Japanese descent born in Canada, loyal Canadian citizens. To Kenji, such an attitude was as deeply offensive as Hitler's treatment of the German Jews, the very thing Canadians said they found so repugnant. Could they not see that judging all Nikkei merely because of the colour of their skin and the slant of their eyes was just as wrong? The same arrogance, the same certainty of Caucasian superiority, was behind both, yet these men could not see it. Kenji despaired of ever being accepted, even after the war.

He pushed open the screened back door and stepped out into the summer night. He found Hu sitting, as he did most evenings, listening to his radio in the fading blue twilight. The Chinese cook looked up at Kenji's step and beckoned to him.

"Come," he said. "Something you need hear."

Kenji went near and sat cross-legged on the fir-needle-strewn ground beside the radio on its stump. He leaned in close to hear the announcer's deep voice. As he listened, his eyes grew wide, and his mouth dropped open in an 'o' of disbelief. When the broadcast ended, he looked at Hu, whose small dark eyes were full of sympathy.

"You heard?" Kenji asked quietly. "The Canadian government has announced a program to disperse Japanese Canadians throughout the country, to separate those who are 'loyal' from those who are 'disloyal,' and to 'repatriate' the disloyal back to Japan."

"Yes," said Hu. "But how decide who is loyal and who disloyal is hard question. If man is disloyal, would he say so?"

Kenji nodded. "That's a good question, Hu. I don't know. But even if we are deemed loyal, we are not to be allowed to live together, to support one another in communities, to maintain our culture and language. In short, we are to disappear into *hakujin* society. Only this will convince them of our loyalty to Canada, though no other Canadians are restricted in this way. Even the property seizures, the internments, the road camps, the POW camps—not even all of these indignities will serve." He closed his eyes and suddenly pounded his fist into his other palm in fury. "How can this be right?" he hissed. "How can this be fair? They have taken everything from us, for no reason—even the Prime Minister has confirmed that no Japanese Canadian has been found guilty of a single act of sabotage or treason!"

Hu's meaty hand landed on Kenji's shoulder and squeezed gently, though he spoke no word.

Kenji spent a restless night, tossing and turning on his narrow camp bed, thinking furiously. What was the point in hiding any further, if Canada was going to send him away anyway, even after the war was over?

Into his mind came an image of his mother as he'd last seen her, getting on the boat that would take the family to Vancouver. Did they ever get to East Lillooet? Perhaps he should just turn himself in, ask to be sent to his family. Surely they'd allow that—wouldn't they? He didn't think he could take another winter alone here in the forest. There seemed no point anymore and—tears welled up in his eyes as he pictured them—he wanted his mother and father, his little sister, his grandparents. If they were to be dispersed across the country, he'd never find them after the war. But what if they put him on the first boat back to Japan, especially if they found out he'd been raised and educated there for a time? Either choice seemed fraught with danger, and he felt paralyzed with uncertainty. His heart ached with loneliness and fear. Eventually he fell into an exhausted sleep filled with dreams of being chased.

He woke with a start as his shoulder was roughly shaken.

"Wake up!" said a deep voice, and Kenji opened his eyes to see Mr. Simpson, the hunter he suspected of being a policeman, standing over him. Hu stood in the doorway of the bedroom, wringing his hands, his face a picture of dismay.

"I tell you, he Lim, Chinese apprentice cook," Hu said, and it was clear he'd been saying this for some time.

"I don't think so," said Mr. Simpson, his face stern. "Come now boy, you are Japanese, are you not?"

"N-no, me Chinese!" stuttered Kenji, shaking his head and cowering back on the bed.

Mr. Simpson held out his hand, and in them he held a sheaf of Kenji's haiku, written in Japanese and English. Kenji blanched. Why hadn't he destroyed those, especially after Hu had guessed his origins after seeing them? How could he have been so stupid, so careless?

"Then how did you write these?" Mr. Simpson asked, obviously not expecting an answer. "Get up, boy. You'll be coming back to Powell River with me today. We'll soon find out who you are and what you think you've been doing, hiding out here." He turned and gave Hu a hard look. "And if we find out that you knew he was Japanese, well, it could go badly for you, too, harbouring a war criminal."

"No war criminal—just scared boy!" said Hu, waving his hands in agitation.

"Perhaps," said Simpson, "but breaking the law, nevertheless. Well, you are a good cook, Hu, and we'd be sorry to lose you. I'll try to keep you out of it. For now, get him packed up. We leave in twenty minutes." Turning away, he strode to the door. Even amid his terror, Kenji felt a wave of anger as he saw Simpson tuck his poems into his pocket as he left the room. What right did he have to keep them? They were private!

"I so sorry," said Hu, near to tears. "I try to say you Lim, but he no believe me."

"It's not your fault, Hu. I appreciate all you've done for me already. I was thinking about going back, turning myself in, anyway. Now I don't have to make up my mind—I have no choice."

Kenji stood up and quickly put on his clothes. For an instant he considered darting out the back door and into the woods, but Mr. Simpson seemed like a man who'd hunt him down. What was the point in running? He'd been found. Better to face the consequences like a man.

In the still air, the only sound was the rumbling of the motor as Mr. Simpson's boat glided away from the dock. Kenji sat in the stern, watching as Hu's stocky figure, his massive shoulders hunched in misery, became smaller and smaller.

Behind, the island
Morning mists hide its peak
One goat calls, farewell.

1944
East Lillooet, British Columbia

Kaye Kaminishi jumped lightly to his feet after sliding into home base in a cloud of dust. He laughed and called out, "We win!" His teammates cheered and gathered around him, while the losing team grinned ruefully and offered good-natured handshakes. It was all in good fun. No one took winning or losing seriously, though a healthy spirit of competition made them all play as well as they could. Kaye was astounded at the level of enthusiasm for his small league. Asami had been right: the activity kept people's spirits up, and engaged everyone in the community, whatever their politics.

In recent weeks, Kaye had also noticed more and more *hakujin* faces lining the fence. At first it had been just Constable Nelson propping a shiny black boot on the lowest rail and idly watching the game after his weekly inspection of the camp. He seemed to always time his visits for the day of a baseball game. Soon, a few fellow Mounties had come along to watch, and then a handful of the more senior officers. Today, for example, there were six red-coated policemen gathered at the far end of the fence.

On a whim, Kaye dusted off his uniform—the white one with the flowing red Asahi script across its chest—and strolled down to where the tall men stood, their wide-brimmed hats off to better enjoy the warm early summer breeze.

"Afternoon, gentlemen," he said, smiling affably. "Did you enjoy the game?"

"We did," said Constable Nelson, smiling back. "You little fellas play a great game. I'd never have believed it if I hadn't seen it myself."

"Yes, yes, good show," interjected an older man whose walrus moustache almost obscured his mouth. "Of course, it's one thing to play against people your own size. I think it would be quite a different matter if you were playing against—well, for example, our team."

Kaye hid a grin. "You think so, sir?" he asked disingenuously. "You may be right. What would you say to a little friendly competition?"

The officer, whose name tag identified him as Inspector Borden, bristled a bit in surprise. "What, you against us?" he blustered. Kaye nodded, holding his easy smile. "Well, I don't know. Seems a bit unfair..."

"Oh, don't worry about that, sir," said Kaye. "It's just a game, after all. It would be enjoyable for my lads here to try themselves against a different team. But perhaps it wouldn't be appropriate. I mean, what if we beat you?" He shook his head, as if contradicting himself. "No, I shouldn't have suggested it..."

"Now just a minute! I didn't say we wouldn't play you," snapped

Borden. "But not here. We'd play on our field over at the barracks; it's regulation sized."

"That would be better," said Kaye, his face serious, "but we are not permitted to cross the bridge over to Lillooet, sir, as I'm sure you know."

The inspector waved his hand negligently. "Oh, we can sort that out for such an occasion," he said. Kaye decided to press his advantage.

"That sounds fine, sir, but I hope you'll agree that it would only be fair for both sides to have cheering fans on the sidelines. Would you allow our families to come along as spectators?"

Borden was taken aback by how his casual comment had suddenly ballooned into something much larger. But he couldn't back down now; the honour of the Mounties was at stake! "Well, well…let me see what I can do. Shall we plan for—oh, two weeks from today?"

"That would be fine, sir." Kaye grinned cheekily. "After all, we're not going anywhere!"

The news soon spread, and the community was thrown into a state of delighted chaos. In the school, which the Nikkei had built in the second summer of their detention, classes became impossible. Miss Hide Hyodoko, the beloved young teacher, had encouraged them to build the school. Detained herself in the ghost town of New Denver, she'd learned that the B.C. government did not intend to honour its responsibility to ensure schooling for Nikkei children during the internment. Furious and determined, she had obtained permission to recruit and train a group of high school graduates in each internment camp to teach all grades, so that the young children's education should not lag during this enforced detainment. Hide had traveled tirelessly from one camp to another to help set up and maintain classes in each location—always with a guard, of course.

She happened to be here in East Lillooet this month, but even she could see that trying to keep the children focused on schooling in the face of such excitement was futile. Instead, she sensibly suggested various educational tasks associated with the upcoming game: math problems having to do with score keeping and gathering player statistics; language assignments such as writing up the play-by-play; science questions to do with the physics of the arc of a thrown ball; and art projects such as drawing the various players. Then she let the children go, watching them run screaming across to the baseball diamond where the newly dubbed 'East Lillooet Tigers' were practicing intently, day after day.

When word came that, indeed, spectators would be allowed into the town to watch the game, excitement reached a fever pitch. It would be the very first time any of the Nikkei had been allowed to walk across that high wooden suspension bridge that divided Lillooet from the East Lillooet camp. Almost the whole camp intended to go.

Constable Nelson was at their end of the bridge early in the morning on the designated day, smiling as the baseball team approached, followed by a large crowd. With a bow, he ceremoniously pulled aside the barriers and waved them through. Kaye Kaminishi stepped out onto the bridge first and walked slowly to the centre of the span. There, he stopped for a minute, gazing out over the Fraser River below, then at the detention camp behind. His expression was serious, and everyone went silent, watching him, conscious of the importance of this moment. The slight young man looked at his fellow internees, and all those dark eyes gazed back at him: hobbling grannies and stooped grandpas; mothers packing infants and fathers with toddlers on their shoulders; grinning teens and bouncing children. His people: Japanese Canadians, determined and resilient, surviving and even thriving despite being isolated, despised, suspected, demoralized. He swiped the back of his hand over suddenly moist eyes and then grinned.

"Let's go play some baseball!" he shouted, and the crowd roared in agreement. He turned and continued walking, feeling the tramp of their footsteps behind his. A feeling of freedom and pride welled up in his chest. However the game played out, his people had already won. Their bodies may be imprisoned, but their spirits were strong.

It was a near thing, but they won the game. Making the most of the 'brain ball' tactics Kaye had taught them, the novice Tigers managed to outsmart the taller, stronger Mountie players. They didn't even try to out hit them. They bunted and ran like greased lightning while the bigger men were fumbling to grab the balls that trickled and rolled off the Tigers' bats. They whipped the ball back and forth between bases, squeezing the Mountie players between the two until they were tagged out. They made use of every strategy Kaye had drilled into them, and it paid off.

Packed tight along the sides of the field, crowded into the hastily extended bleachers, *hakujin* and Nikkei spectators groaned and cheered, laughed and jeered side by side. As the game went on, even white fans began to root for the clever Nikkei players and when the youngest of the Tigers scored the winning run, the entire crowd erupted into pandemonium.

The teams lined up to shake hands and Sergeant Borden came out onto the field to congratulate the Nikkei team. He shook his head ruefully.

"Well, Mr. Kaminishi, I guess you could say, the bigger they are, the harder they fall! We underestimated you badly and we've paid the price. I can hardly believe it. So, we never did set the terms of the wager—what would you have as your prize?"

Kaye was prepared for this moment, having given it considerable thought.

"Inspector Borden, I hope that you've seen today that I and my fellow Japanese Canadians are not criminals. We are just ordinary folks trying to make our way the best we can in difficult circumstances. I'd like to ask if we could have permission to come into Lillooet, just a few at a time, do some shopping, go to the cinema, maybe eat in a restaurant alongside your good citizens." He gestured at the tall, inhospitable mountains surrounding them. "There's no way for us to run, and no place for us to go even if we could. Can you trust our parole, sir, and allow us a little freedom, a little dignity for the remainder of our stay here?"

Borden hesitated, but his shrewd mind saw benefits to acquiescence. The town of Lillooet was struggling, with its main labour force off fighting the war, and money scarce at home. These Nikkei—he knew they had money to spend. If he let them into the town, well, it would help boost the local economy. He chewed the tips of his luxuriant moustache for a moment longer and the tension grew, but Kaye held his eyes steadily. Suddenly Borden thrust out his big hand and engulfed Kaye's small one, nodding and grinning.

"I think we can agree to that," he said loudly, and a delighted gasp was followed by loud cheering from the crowd. A few *hakujin* faces frowned in dismay, but the positive feelings engendered by the game swept most of them up in the wave of friendliness. Under cover of the chaos, Borden leaned in close.

"One problem, and you'll all be back on your side of the bridge before you can say *sayonara*!" he growled. Kaye, his heart pounding at his audacity and what he'd achieved by it, nodded.

"Yes sir," he said. "But there will be no trouble, you'll see."

1945
Angler POW camp, Ontario

Jiro and Tom walked briskly along the fence line in the August sunshine, enjoying its rays on the red-dotted backs of their uniforms. They knew too well that summers were short in this northern forest. September would bring cooler temperatures and in no time, they'd be waking up to the first dusting of snow on the fir trees that stretched away from the camp. For now, on August 10th, it still felt like summer, and they flexed their sore shoulder muscles in the warmth.

Tom had persuaded the older man to join the judo and the kendo clubs, as well as the haiku club. Jiro continued to be impressed with this young man's determination to make use of his incarceration to improve himself. He had taken both English and Japanese language classes, shorthand classes, drawing classes, and was active in every physical fitness group, sumo wrestling as well as the running, judo, and kendo clubs. He said that all these activities kept him from brooding, and he had taught Jiro the deep abdominal breathing technique he used to combat anxiety or insomnia. Jiro was grateful for Tom's friendship. Without it, he probably would be lounging inside every day, playing cards and gossiping with the old men, getting depressed and soft. He'd even taken several classes himself: calligraphy and bookkeeping.

Today, however, no breathing technique would calm them, for their thoughts and conversation were focused on the war. For weeks, tensions had risen in the camp. The war in Europe had ended with Germany's unconditional surrender at Reims in May, and Hitler's suicide had convinced everyone that Germany and its Axis allies were truly defeated. But the war in the Pacific continued, and many of the die-hard *issei* in the camp had stubbornly insisted that Japan could still win. They lauded the success of Japan's balloon bomb offensive. Over the past year, thousands of unpiloted balloons with skins of lightweight paper had been sent out to float from Japan to North America on the 'divine wind,' the westerly river of air at 30, 000 feet. Using ropes attached to the balloons, the military mounted incendiary devices and high-explosive bombs rigged to drop over the US and Canada, hoping to spark massive forest fires that would instill panic and divert resources from the war effort. Though many of these bombs had sunk in the Pacific, some had reached their targets—one explosion had killed an innocent family picnicking in Bly, Oregon—and achieved their aims.

Jiro was horrified by these tactics, but he understood the *issei*'s close-mindedness—many of them were Japanese nationals who fully intended to return to the fatherland as soon as they could. If Japan lost, where would that leave them?

Abruptly, Jiro said, "Have you ever read the report that Kunio Hidaka wrote before the war, listing all the Canadian laws that discriminate against Japanese Canadians?" Tom shook his head. "I think he wrote it when he was studying at the university in British Columbia. A learned man in my community in Haney brought it to our attention once at a meeting of the farmers' association. Along with the obvious, that we aren't allowed to vote and therefore can't work in any professional capacity like medicine or law, Hidaka also lists exclusion from admittance to a home for the aged, and that we aren't allowed to work underground in any mine. We also can't be hired for any public works contract and any timber company given a license to log on Crown Lands can't hire any Japanese. We can't sell liquor, and our people can't employ white women in their businesses or rent them lodgings."

"Do those laws only apply to Nikkei?" asked Tom.

"Some of them apply to Chinese and Indians—what they call Hindoos—as well," admitted Jiro. "But some of them are specific to us." He shook his head. "I don't know. Some days I think that if Canada really hates us that much, maybe we *would* be better off returning to Japan. I can't believe I'm even thinking that—Canada has been my home since I was ten years old! I haven't seen or even heard from my family since the day I left Japan's shores. I don't even know if they survived the war. But how can Canada justify excluding a whole segment of its legitimate citizens from so many things that others take for granted?" Sighing deeply, he walked on, with Tom keeping pace silently by his side.

As they passed the guard hut at the bottom of the gate watchtower, they saw an unusually large number of guards huddled around the radio. Suddenly the group erupted with a yell, waving their arms in the air in jubilation. Jiro and Tom stopped, nonplussed.

Donald, one of the guards who treated the prisoners well and was quite friendly with them, saw them standing there.

"It's over! Japan has surrendered!" he shouted to them.

Jiro and Tom froze, open-mouthed, astounded. The guards ran around the camp yelling the news, and prisoners poured out of the buildings, gathering to hear the details. Of course, they had received news of the devastating atomic bombs dropped by the Americans on the city of Hiroshima on August 6th and then on Nagasaki just two days ago, on the 8th. All the POWs, whatever their allegiance, had wept as the images arrived on the newspapers' front pages. The two cities were utterly destroyed by this new weapon of unprecedented power, and the suffering of the Japanese people was heart-scalding. Women, children, elders, none of whom had signed up to fight, were dead, maimed, scarred for life, homeless, penniless, wandering in a radioactive wasteland.

Though he had left them behind in Hiroshima decades ago, Jiro had wept as he thought of his birth family's destruction on that day when fire and death had fallen from the sky.

Jiro had been wrenched by the images, but he understood the American's action. Japan had refused to surrender, had fought fiercely and relentlessly, recently deploying suicide missions to destroy Allied naval ships with fighter planes that plummeted from the sky—*kamikazes*, they were called—killing thousands. The tradition of death rather than defeat, capture, or shame was deeply entrenched in Japanese military culture; one of the primary values in the samurai way of life and the *bushido* code was loyalty and honour until death.

Their absolute unwillingness to compromise, their determination to fight to the bitter end, had left America with little choice, Jiro thought. He had just never imagined that the killing strike would be upon civilians. After the bombs, it had been clear that the end had to be near. Then Russia had declared war on Japan as well, and swiftly overwhelmed their forces in Manchuria. Japan was cornered and broken.

And now surrender had finally come. Emperor Hirohito had agreed to the American General MacArthur's demands and said that he would sign the Potsdam Declaration, giving the Allied Forces control of Japan. The papers noted that Hirohito's surrender tried to stipulate that he would maintain his powers as Emperor, but Jiro doubted that this would be accepted. Japan was in no position to negotiate.

The war was over, but camp life continued much as before. Snow came late in September and the temperatures dropped. Another winter was coming; everyone wondered what it would bring.

In November, the newspapers reported that the repatriation of Japanese would begin in the new year. Despite his status as a naturalized Canadian, Jiro realized that there was a distinct possibility that he'd be sent to Japan along with the other POWs. They'd all heard about the Canadian government's new Order in Council that gave them the 'right' to determine a Japanese Canadian's loyalty or disloyalty. *I guess all prisoners of war are labeled as disloyal,* he thought morosely, *even if they didn't do anything to be put here*. His failure to protest his placement at the start now seemed like a very bad decision, though at the time it had seemed easier to just go along with it. He brooded on his future. What would he find to do in devastated Japan? He had spent two-thirds of his life in Canada and all his allegiance was to his Canadian family, his adopted country. He spent many hours thinking about Harry and Sara, the only parents he really remembered. He wondered how they, and Asami, Hoshi, and the children were doing. They'd exchanged a few letters over the past years, but these were so heavily censored that he knew almost nothing other than their location in East Lillooet.

Jiro sat on his bunk and opened the wooden box that Harry had made for him decades ago, when he first came to stay on Galiano Island. He took out the carved figures, examining them one by one. Warriors, kings, soldiers, dragons—even a maiden to be rescued. So many hours of pleasure these had provided—how loved they had made a lost boy feel. As he replaced the toys carefully back in the box and cushioned them with the scrap of silk Sara had given him long ago, Jiro wept. How he longed to rejoin his family, and how he feared that he might never see them again.

At the end of the first week of December, Jiro was greatly relieved that the directive changed. Now it seemed that each Japanese Canadian was to be given a choice: stay in Canada, but live east of the Canadian Rocky Mountains, or go back to Japan with a two hundred dollar per person stipend. Even prisoners of war were to be permitted to make a choice--he could find the others and stay in Canada!

However, no Nikkei were to be permitted to return to the west coast. Jiro wondered if that was because the *hakujin* had taken over all the farms, businesses, and fishing rights the Japanese Canadians had had before the war and didn't want to give them back or compete with Nikkei again. He couldn't think of any other reason for banning Nikkei from their former homes in British Columbia now that the war was over, and it was clear that no spying was happening. In his election campaign, B.C. Member of Parliament Ian Mackenzie proposed a slogan for British Columbia: 'No Japs from the Rockies to the sea.' Clearly, anti-Japanese feelings were still entrenched on the coast.

There was also pressure from the government, saying that Japanese Canadians should disperse and not form new communities, to avoid trouble in the future. *They must really hate us*, Jiro thought sadly, remembering the lively community of Powell Street, the joy and sense of belonging they'd all shared there. *Are we truly citizens if we aren't even allowed to choose where we can live in our own country?*

This new rule sparked more furious debate. A few stubbornly refused to change their intent to return to Japan, but most of the men in the camp were afraid to try to build a life in that war-torn country. Tom and his younger brother told Jiro that they would abide by their parents' decision once they received mail from them from the New Denver camp.

"But I hope that they decide to stay in Canada," confided Tom as he and Jiro cooled down after judo practice just before Christmas. "I will go to Japan if they insist, but I think our chances are better here despite the attitudes towards us. I don't imagine that the native Japanese will be very welcoming of those who abandoned them years ago, so it will probably be just as hard or even harder there. Japan has enough to do, trying to rebuild and support their own citizens." Jiro agreed and was immensely grateful that he had been given a chance to choose, despite the restrictions.

1945
Vancouver, British Columbia

Mr. Simpson was indeed a retired police officer, and he still had friends on the force. Kenji had spent one night in a sparse cell in Powell River, and the next morning was escorted onto a steamer leaving for Vancouver, with a red-coated Mountie by his side. He hung his head, avoiding the curious or outright hostile glances of his fellow passengers. Inside, his guts were writhing. What would they do to him? What was his best course of action: silence, or confession? Should he tell them his real name and hope they reunited him with his family in East Lillooet, or refuse to identify himself? He was now eighteen, old enough to be prosecuted as an adult rather than a juvenile. What would they charge him with? His mind spun in an endless loop of all these questions, but no answers presented themselves.

When they reached the city, he and his guard rode in the back of a van to the Oakalla Prison south of Vancouver, an enormous red brick building with a high cupola in the centre and two sweeping wings to the sides. It was a model farm, designed to engage prisoners in rehabilitation, but as Kenji peered out the small window in the van, it looked anything but welcoming. He was issued a prison uniform and escorted to a small cell with two narrow beds against the walls, a toilet, and a sink. It was bare and cold, and it brought a lump of fear and sadness to his throat. He had done nothing wrong—nothing but staying in his native country, in his home. How could that be an imprisonable offence?

As the door lock rattled closed, he sagged down onto the thin mattress and stared at his cellmate, a young *hakujin* probably about his own age. The fellow had red hair and a thick scattering of freckles all over his face. This colouring, and his large and prominent ears, gave him the look of an innocent farm boy, and Kenji wondered what on earth he had done to land in here.

"Hi, I'm Harry, Harry James," said the other, standing and offering his hand.

Without thinking, Kenji gave his real name as he reached out and shook hands. "Kenichi Tasaka. Call me Kenji," he said, and then looked up anxiously, wondering if the guards could overhear. Harry grinned.

"Don't worry, they don't monitor us much in here. It's a minimum-security prison." He flopped back down on his bed. "So, whatja do to get put in the slammer?" he asked casually.

Kenji shrugged. "Not much of anything, really. I just refused to be put out of my home for no reason. Obviously, I'm Japanese Canadian—and I just—didn't go to the interior when they said I had to."

"Whoa, that was years ago," said Harry, raising his bushy red eyebrows high. "Where ya been since then?"

"Hiding out at a hunting camp in the bush." When Harry looked impressed, Kenji felt he should clarify. "The Chinese cook let me stay, passed me off as Chinese. For a while, anyway."

"But the war's over—they can't keep you out of B.C. now, can they?"

"Seems as if they mean to--we'll see," said Kenji. Then he jutted his chin at his cellmate. "What about you? How come you're in here?"

"Ah, bad luck, mostly," said Harry, shrugging in his turn. "A fella tried to come on to my girlfriend and I slugged him hard. Too bad for me that he hit his head on the curb when he fell and died. Manslaughter, ten years. Only nine left to go!" From the guard station down the hall came the sudden sound of music, and Harry laughed, jumping up from the bed. "Say, you like music? I love Glen Miller…listen!" He started to move, snapping his fingers. "You know how to jitterbug, Kenji? C'mon, I'll show you!"

Unable to resist Harry's energy and friendliness, Kenji took the offered hand and found himself whirled and twisted around the small cell, laughing. Laughing! It seemed a century since he'd laughed. When the song ended, they heard shouts of "Keep it down, will ya?" from other inmates and the guard turned the radio down. They collapsed on their beds, still chuckling.

Kenji realized, to his great surprise, that he felt better. He decided that, whatever happened, he would try to face it with grace and humour. He was blessed to have been given such a friendly soul as a cellmate. He listened to Harry's stories over the next several hours, feeling the first peace he'd felt in years.

When the guard came to get him, Kenji followed him readily, doing his best to maintain the calm acceptance he'd achieved over the past weeks. Harry had proven to be an amusing and good-natured companion, and Kenji had been able to talk about his family, his time in Japan, his flight and escape from internment, his solitude in the woods. Harry had been amazed that he'd survived so long on his own.

"Man, I couldn't do that—I'd go crazy alone in the forest! How did you pass the time?"

"Fishing, mostly. Writing a bit of poetry."

"Poetry! What on earth for?" Harry had grinned, sure that Kenji was pulling his leg.

"Oh, it's a thing Japanese people do. It's fun."

"I'll take your word for it," Harry had said, shaking his head. But after Kenji had recited a few haikus for him, he'd looked thoughtful. "Huh. Yeah, I kinda get it. I can see what you're talking about, it kinda paints a picture, doesn't it?"

Kenji was expecting to be locked into a cell with a bare bulb and accused of all kinds of criminal activities, so he was astounded when the guard escorted him into a civilian part of the building and ushered him into the Prison Warden's office. Inside was the warden, a middle-aged man with a bad leg who walked with a cane, and another man who was wearing a military uniform. They invited Kenji to sit down in an armchair opposite the warden's desk.

"Well, young man, you've gotten yourself into some deep trouble."

"Yes, sir," answered Kenji quietly, without arrogance but also without cowering.

"Hmmm, I'm told you were found masquerading as a Chinese apprentice cook," said the warden, piercing Kenji with his pale blue eyes. Kenji nodded. The soldier picked up a sheaf of papers from the warden's desk that Kenji recognized as his poetry.

"You wrote these?" he asked, and Kenji nodded again. "Both the English and Japanese, these are your words?"

"Mostly," said Kenji. "Some of it is just me writing out ancient Japanese poems that I know."

"And where did you learn those?" asked the soldier.

"At school in Japan," answered Kenji. "I was sent there as a child to become my uncle's heir when he was unable to have children."

"Then why aren't you still there?" the man demanded. Kenji shrugged a little.

"I am not Japanese. Canada is my home and I wanted to come back to it. So I ran away and returned to Powell River, where my parents were."

The men exchanged glances and sat silent for a moment. Kenji did his best to sit still, though his heart was pounding. What was the point of all these questions? He had broken the law—what more was there to say?

"You have no loyalty to Japan, then?" asked the warden suddenly. Kenji looked up, surprised.

"No sir, none at all. When I ran away to return to Canada four years ago, my uncle was very angry and disinherited me. I have not spoken to my relatives—or anyone else--in Japan since then. As I said, I am Canadian."

There was another long silence and again Kenji remained still. It seemed, somehow, as if he was being tested. Finally, the man in the military uniform spoke again.

"What you have done is an imprisonable offence, I hope you realize." He paused to let that sink in for a moment, then spoke again. "If we gave you a chance to serve in the British military, working in Japan, would you take it?"

"Instead of jail?" Kenji asked, astonished. The man nodded. "Well, yes, sir, but, if I may ask, why the British military? Why not Canada's?

The man seemed discomfited by the question and blustered a little. "That's just the way it is—that's the offer, take it or leave it."

"But—what would I be doing in Japan, sir?" Kenji asked.

"Military intelligence," he replied. "Interviewing former prisoners, translating documents, facilitating communication between our forces and the Japanese government and military. You can speak, read, and write both English and Japanese, correct?"

"Yes, sir, fluently."

"Well, that's the job. Are you interested?"

Kenji thoughts skittered frantically. Back to Japan—a Japan that had been bombed, devastated by the war—not a rosy prospect. But to work for the military intelligence, doing a legitimate job, proving his innocence and loyalty to Canada—what an opportunity! He gave a fleeting thought to his parents and grandparents and had a vision of himself returning to Canada as a hero, wearing a military uniform—maybe even a medal! They'd be so proud of him—instead of angry and ashamed as he assumed they were now. His anger at Canada's treatment of the Nikkei had not gone away, but his young man's ego couldn't resist this chance to do something meaningful, to contribute to the war effort. He rose to his feet and put out his hand to the soldier.

"Yes sir, I am interested. Tell me what you need, and I'll do my very best not to disappoint you."

"Good," said the man, and shook his hand with a firm grip. "All right, now, sit down and I'll explain the mission…"

Kenji felt a lurch in his stomach at the word 'mission.' Just what had he agreed to? Well, anything was better than staying in jail--he hoped.

1946
East Lillooet, British Columbia

Asami was humming quietly to herself at her sewing machine as she worked on a fancy high school graduation dress for one of the neighbourhood girls when she was startled by the front door banging open, letting in a gust of late winter wind and snow.

"Mrs. Tasaka! Come quick, come quick!" screamed the boy who appeared in the door. It was little Jack Kosaka, one of the gang of children who ran around together whenever school was out. He was Isabel's best friend in the camp, and the urgency in his face galvanized Asami into action.

"What is it? What's happened?" she asked as she grabbed her coat and thrust her feet into her boots. It was frigidly cold outside, but a bright sun was shining on the deep snow that came in late October and stayed through to April here in the cold shadow of the surrounding mountains. The children had been happily sledding on sheets of cardboard down the long hill and onto the gravel road that bisected the camp since midmorning, but now as Asami stepped outside, pulling on her thick mittens, she could hear screams—screams that she recognized as Isabel's!

"It's Isabel," confirmed Jack. "She was going so fast that she couldn't swerve when the policeman's car stopped on the road—she slid right underneath and we can't get her out! She's stuck and I think she hurt herself too."

They ran as fast as they could, awkward in the deep snow, until they reached the scene. The Mountie, a young man unfamiliar to Asami, was on his knees, peering underneath his car and pleading with Isabel to stop screaming so they could help her. Asami fell to her knees beside him and squirmed her way to her daughter. She was appalled to see sheets of blood cascading from Isabel's head. Yet her mouth was open in an ear-piercing shriek, so obviously she hadn't been knocked unconscious by the collision.

"Ma! Ma! Help me! Get me out! It was the bad arsyempy! He should have seen me! It wasn't my fault!!" Isabel cried out.

Asami didn't even smile at Isabel's reversion to her childhood name for the Mounties.

"Isabel, Isabel, hush, I'm here. Never mind whose fault it was for now. Be quiet for a moment so I can see what's happened and decide how to get you out," she said, raising her voice to be heard over her daughter's howls. Isabel's screeches turned into sobs of terror, as she squirmed frantically and reached out a still-mittened hand to her mother. Asami sighed in relief. If she could move her arms and legs, she hadn't broken her neck, at least. She turned her head to speak to the fidgeting officer as he crouched beside the car.

"Can you please get Dr. Miyazaki to come right away? Isabel has cut her head badly and will need stitches for sure."

"Should I take the car?" the young Mountie asked, his eyes so wide the whites showed around the blue irises.

"No, of course not!!" said Asami sharply. "Don't you have a radio in your car?" The man nodded. "Then radio up to ask him to come as fast as he can," she said, exasperated at his stupidity. Why hadn't he radioed for help already?

She stayed underneath the vehicle, speaking soothingly to Isabel, and trying to staunch the blood with her woolen mittens, but they were soaked through in moments. She could hear the scratchy squawk of the police radio, and then more and more voices as people arrived, anxious to help. Finally, Hoshi's bulky form squirmed in next to her. Someone must have run to get him where he was cutting wood up on the edge of the forest. He spoke quietly to Isabel, who cried harder, as he assessed the situation.

"I think we need to pull her out," he said to Asami. "But we'd better take her out opposite to the way she came in, so she doesn't cut her head even more. See, she's scraped her scalp on this piece here." He reached up and touched a sharp part of the car's undercarriage, his fingers coming away sticky with blood.

Asami nodded. "All right Isabel, your father and I are going to go around to the other side and pull you out. We'll be just a minute, all right?"

"No, no, don't leave me! I'm scared! It's going to hurt!!" screeched the child, clinging to them. It was clear that no amount of persuasion was going to help. Hoshi and Asami exchanged a look and began to work their way backwards as quickly as they could. As they came out from under the car, Asami was relieved to see Dr. Miyazaki's car trundling across the bridge.

The tall, slender doctor had been such a godsend to the community. An osteopath and surgeon by profession, he had been permitted to come to Lillooet from his internment in the Bridge River camp last year when the only doctor in Lillooet had died unexpectedly. Needing a coroner as well as a general physician, the town had petitioned for the Nikkei doctor to be moved, and he had quickly established himself in Longford House, the old Phair mansion, where a doctor's office and living quarters had been readied for him and his family. Since then, he had delivered babies, signed death certificates, set broken bones, stitched up lacerations, and treated various illnesses on both sides of the bridge as well as in all the local Indian reserves. The poor man was run off his feet, but his calm manner and obvious expertise soothed all his patients,

Nikkei, *hakujin*, and *dojin* alike. When there was a smallpox scare a few months ago, he vaccinated all seven hundred members of the D'Arcy, Seton, Portage, Shalalth, Lillooet, Cayoosh, Neskip, Bridge River, Fountain, and Pavilion Reserves. As a result, the Indians refused to be treated by anyone else and would travel for miles to see the Nikkei doctor. Asami had wondered if the town would ask him to stay on even after the war. If they did, she'd thought he probably would choose to do so, as he seemed quite happy here.

"Wait," Asami said to Hoshi. "Let's see what the doctor says." She pointed to the doctor's car, now approaching along the gravel road.

A moment later the middle-aged doctor stepped out of his new Plymouth—a great improvement over his rickety old Hudson Terraplane that had broken down on regular occasions--adjusting his black-framed glasses as he hefted his doctor's bag out of the back seat.

"Well now," he said calmly as he came up. "What's happened here?" Quickly the situation was explained, and the doctor jackknifed himself down to his knees in the snow to look in at Isabel. In but a moment he stood up again, dusting the wet snow off his trousers. "Yes, we need to get her out," he said. "She has a serious head wound and I need to get the bleeding stopped as quickly as possible. I can see that she's moving well, so I don't fear a neck or back injury but even if I did, we can't leave her under there for much longer." He glanced at Asami, recognizing her as Isabel's mother. "Head wounds bleed a lot," he said reassuringly. "They often look much worse than they really are. However, we do need to get it stitched up soon."

Hoshi and Harry, who had arrived as well, went to the far side of the car and crawled under to grasp Isabel's shoulders, steadying her head and neck as they pulled and pulled to get her out from under the car. Isabel's screams resumed and she struggled and squirmed as they tugged.

Finally, the child's head emerged, and the crowd gave a collective gasp. A large piece of her scalp had been nearly sliced off her skull! No wonder she had been screaming! A trail of bright red blood stained the snow as she was dragged fully out from under the car, although it was no longer streaming from the wound. Hastily the men created a stretcher out of someone's coat, and four of them lifted Isabel onto it and placed her gently in the back of the doctor's car, her lacerated head cradled in her mother's lap on someone else's folded jacket. Hoshi slid quickly into the front seat. The doctor turned the car around in a whirl and sped back over the bridge.

When they arrived at the office, Dr. Miyazaki went in ahead to prepare the surgery as Hoshi and Asami carefully carried Isabel in on the coat sling. The child was quiet now and seemed almost drowsy. The doctor gestured for them to place her on the surgery table and asked them to steady her head as he began to clean away the clotting blood and gently replace the scalp tissue. Isabel began to shiver violently.

"Go into the house and ask Mrs. Miyazaki for some extra blankets, please," the doctor asked. "We must keep her warm."

The next two hours seemed like fifteen hours to Asami, as the doctor painstakingly clipped and shaved her hair and stitched Isabel's torn scalp back together. He had injected some local anaesthetic into the edges of the wound, but still Isabel cried out and had to be held still as he stitched and stitched, seemingly endlessly, at the ragged flesh. Asami and Hoshi spoke soothingly to her but still she sobbed. When the stitches were done, he washed it one more time with antiseptic and then wound layers and layers of clean white bandages around the little head. Finally, when the child was weeping quietly in exhaustion, Dr. Miyazaki stood and stretched his back. He picked up a clean cloth and wiped his hands, smiling down at the child.

"Well, Miss Isabel, I think you have won the prize for the most stitches I have ever placed on a patient—thirty-two! That's quite a cut you gave yourself!"

"Will she be all right?" Asami asked anxiously. The doctor nodded wearily.

"Yes, I think so. You must keep the wound clean and dry, and I'll give you some antibiotic pills for her. Thank goodness we have those now! Only a few years ago, this kind of wound would likely have become septic and poisoned her bloodstream. But the penicillin should keep that from happening. If there's any sign of a fever, call me immediately. Otherwise, I'll come by to check her in a few days. It will take some time for her hair to grow over the scars, but eventually I think they'll all be hidden." He looked down at Isabel, whose eyes looked huge in her tiny face surmounted by the bulky white bandage, and waggled his forefinger at her. "No more sledding for you this winter, young lady," he said with another smile. "Let's protect that head for a while, all right?" Isabel nodded wordlessly, finally too tired to make a fuss.

As Asami wrapped Isabel in the blankets to go home, the doctor took Hoshi to the outer office, where the bookcases held years of issues of the yellow-edged National Geographic magazine. Distracted, Hoshi remembered that Dr. Miyazaki had told him that the Society had recently rescinded his membership because of his Japanese heritage, a source of great disappointment to the kindly doctor, who loved to read the magazines in his few idle hours. He'd also mentioned to Hoshi that even the B.C.A.A., the automobile association, had refused to accept his membership this year for the same reason. But the doctor was speaking to him, and Hoshi wrenched his tired and anxious mind back to the matter at hand.

"We are fortunate," the doctor was saying. "Only a little longer, and she would have bled to death or at least gone into hypovolemic shock. The nearest place to give her a blood transfusion is forty-five miles away in Lytton and it's a treacherous, winding road. I'm not sure I could have gotten her there in time in my car in this snow, even with my home-made tire chains."

Later that year, when Dr. Miyazaki persuaded the Lillooet town council to stage a fundraiser to finance an ambulance, Isabel's family was among the first to donate. And when the Red Cross announced its plan to build a three-bed outpost hospital in the town in the coming year, they were glad to hear it. By that time, however, they were readying themselves to leave.

Word had come to East Lillooet that, with the end of the war in the Pacific, Japanese Canadians in internment and POW camps were to be given a choice: return to Japan or settle east of the Canadian Rockies. They were advised not to gather in communities, to relocate as individuals, but for most Nikkei, the idea of living separate from their fellows was very daunting, especially given the closeness that had been generated through the internment camp experience. The adults had discussed the possibilities long into the night, turning over the benefits of every option. None of them wanted to go to Japan. Harry and Sara had been gone from there for over sixty years, and Hoshi had left his native country behind for good when he'd emigrated. Even should they have considered a return, news of conditions in the war-shattered country would have discouraged them. They weren't even sure they had any family alive after the bombings. No—nothing was left for them there, and despite their treatment in recent years, they considered themselves Canadians. Asami, a native-born Canadian, had no doubts. Canada was home.

East Lillooet camp stayed open even after most of the other internment camps closed, providing a temporary stopping place for Nikkei not yet sure of their plans. As some people left, others arrived. Newcomers spoke of various places they'd been interned or worked during the war. One family, also named Tasaka though Hoshi could not determine if they were related, spoke of working at the Finlay sugar beet farm in Elie, Manitoba, just west of Winnipeg. Those not able to pay for a self-supporting camp had been given the choice of a government internment camp or work on various farms or road works, and many had chosen to work on farms in Manitoba to keep their families together. They said that old Mr. Finlay was a good man, welcoming and fair to all his workers, including Japanese, Dutch, German, Ukrainian, and all others.

And with so many internees leaving to settle elsewhere, there was a need for more workers.

"I would like to end my days on another farm," said Harry quietly. He did not speak of the loss of his own strawberry farm, of everything he'd worked for, for so long and so hard. "I'd rather do that than move to a city and work in a factory."

Asami's heart clenched as she looked at her father's wrinkled face, his stooped eighty-six-year-old body. How could he work on a farm? Sugar beet farming was a brutally exhausting job, requiring physical strength and great stamina. But she understood; he'd rather drop in the traces like a tired old workhorse than die in a soft bed, far from the fields.

"I will write to Mr. Finlay and inquire," she said. "And if we are hired, I will see if I can arrange for Jiro to meet us there." She was rewarded with a brilliant smile from her mother.

"That would be very good," said Sara.

If only she knew how to make the same arrangement for Kenji, Asami though sadly. Where was her son now? Would they ever find him again? Was he even alive?

1946
Angler, Ontario

Jiro stood beside Tom Sando and his young brother, watching the small group of men huddled around their luggage, shivering in the cold wind that carried flecks of snow and belied the April date on the calendar. These men were leaving the camp for transport to Japan. Both the men leaving and the ones staying behind had tears on their cheeks. They had been together in this place for over four years and had grown close; for some, closer than family. It was hard, very hard, to say goodbye, especially to these men who had chosen to return to Japan. One of those leaving was Koyanagi, their beloved judo teacher. It was very unlikely that they would ever see one another again, and they were all despondent.

The truck that would transport the departing prisoners to the train station rumbled up and the men climbed into the back, tossing their suitcases and bags ahead of them. As they moved away toward the gate, Tom raised his hand, waving and shouting after them. "*Ganbari ya*, my dear friends; never give up!"

After the truck was out of sight, they dragged their feet back to the bunkhouse to get warm. Tom lay down with his face turned to the wall. Jiro thought that this separation was going to be very hard for his young friend. Tom and Shig were going to work in a pulpwood bush camp near Winnipeg, Manitoba, to earn some money before rejoining their parents. Jiro had been overjoyed to get a letter from his sister, Asami, inviting him to join the family at the Finlay farm. So they would all be traveling together for a while yet. Shig seemed quite eager to be gone, but Jiro worried that the loss of his routine and the companionship of his fellow prisoners was going to be a difficult change for Tom. He could only hope that the physical and emotional fortitude he'd gained while in the prison camp would serve him well in his new life.

The sun was warmer on April 29th as Jiro and the others made their way out of the bunkhouse for the last time. Jiro glanced back as he exited, looking for the last time at the rows of empty bunks and forlorn bookcases. He was happy to leave, eager to reunite with his family, yet a strange melancholy had taken hold of him. He, too, would miss the various classes, the camaraderie of these other men, the quiet routine. Now he'd have to take responsibility for his own life again. The thought was a little daunting.

They entered a large warehouse building near the gate and were given their old suitcases that had been piled up there for the past four years. They pulled out their original clothing and exchanged their red-target-marked uniforms for outdated suits and musty-smelling shirts. Jiro tried to punch his squashed fedora hat into shape but gave up—it was ruined beyond repair. They laughed for a moment at Shig—his sleeves ended three inches above his wrists and his trouser legs barely grazed his ankles; he had grown a lot in four years! They were each given a train ticket to Winnipeg and eleven dollars as spending money for the trip, and then they, too, climbed into the back of a truck for the trip to the station. The gate clanged shut behind them. Jiro wondered why the sound didn't make him as joyful as he'd expected.

Jiro saw Tom glance aside as they drove alongside the barbed wire fence, to where the patch of wild daisies still bloomed in the sandy soil. *Yes*, he thought, *we must be like the daisies. We must find a way to bloom no matter where we find ourselves, no matter how difficult the circumstances*. He placed his hand on Tom's shoulder and was rewarded with a nod and a slight smile. They, too, would survive.

On the train to Manitoba, Jiro picked up a recent issue of *The New Canadian* that another passenger had discarded. In it, he read an article about the creation of eight 'hostels'—temporary communal housing sites for Nikkei who were still seeking permanent accommodations and employment east of the Rockies. Some of the residents there had refused offers of unsuitable employment and also refused to be evicted from the hostel despite miserable conditions. One old *issei* explained his stance:

In pre-war days I owned a small business in Vancouver. Into this business I put my life savings. The business was bad for years, and I was forced to work in a sawmill while my wife looked after our little store, but for years my paycheque also went into the business. It was just before the outbreak of war that my business turned profitable. An Official of the Custodian of Enemy property came to take my business away. At this time, he promised me and my family that as soon as peace was restored my business would be given back to me. After doing this, the RCMP visited me and told me to leave my family and go to work in the Rockies making roads at 25 cents an hour. This employment I refused for the simple reason that it was impossible for me to leave my family and children, not knowing where they would be sent after I left. I was taken into custody by the RCMP and shoved into a concentration camp. For four years I have been behind barbed wires and this life was none too good. What did I do to deserve all this punishment? Was I guilty of something? If I was, why didn't the government give me a trial or tell me that I am guilty?

One day an official of the Department of Labour came to the camp and told me and the other inmates that we are moving to Moose Jaw. We did not have any choice. We are called 'die-hard internees' but that is not true. I have every intention of moving out of here and I would like to go and start life again just like every other evacuee family has done. But with all the misery and hate that I have gone through under democracy, it makes me so mad that I don't know whether to laugh or cry. But one thing I would like to say is that with my family of three children, with the biggest fifteen years old and me getting close to sixty, I've got to get more security or financial help, or I just can't figure out how I could live and start life anew again. The employment they offer is mostly farm work--sugar beet or wheat farming. It is impossible for me to accept this type of employment, especially with three girls, all young, and with four years of concentration camp life I am physically and mentally unfit. The Department of Labour is only trying to get rid of us; they don't care how they do it.

I would like to ask: who is responsible for us? Who was responsible for the misery I went through behind barbed wire for four years? What did I do to deserve all this punishment? The sooner the government gives me a satisfactory deal, the sooner I will get out of this place. My store has been sold without my consent. My life savings are gone. Is this democracy?

Next, the article described the attitude of another man who was refusing to leave the hostel. Masumi Mitsui was a WWI veteran who'd been awarded the Military Medal for bravery among other symbols of recognition of his service. When he was stripped of his Port Coquitlam poultry farm and directed to appear before the Security Commissioner, Mitsui threw his military medals on the floor, demanding "What good are these?" A third old *issei*, Yasuzo Shoji, had also served in the Canadian military in WWI with the Princess Pats, and been wounded twice during the war. He had lost a nineteen-acre chicken farm, developed on land that he had purchased under the Soldiers' Settlement Act after his return from his European service. The farm, including his two-storey house, four poultry barns, an electric incubator and twenty-five-hundred chickens, was sold for $1,492.59. Mr. Shoji received a cheque for $39.32. The deductions were, according to the article, for 'taxes and sundry expenses.'

Jiro refolded the paper and sat staring at the landscape sliding by the window, thinking about his own experiences in the Great War, and the loss of his family's strawberry farm. Spring had come to the prairies and the green of new shoots made the wide fields into an endless emerald carpet. It all looked so promising, so fresh and fertile. Would that promise hold true for him and his family here? Would they ever regain their former wealth and status?

1947
Brantford, Ontario
Vancouver, British Columbia
Myitkyina, Burma

Not long after his recruitment, Kenji discovered why the Canadian recruiter had insisted that Kenji and the other Japanese Canadians be placed under British command—Botan, one of the other *nisei* soldiers, had whispered it to him one night in the barracks in Brantford, Ontario, where they were undergoing four months of basic training together.

"It's so we aren't qualified to vote when we return to Canada," Botan said bitterly. "Remember, World War I veterans got the franchise? Well, they don't want any more Nikkei qualifying. They'll let us serve, but they won't give us our rights as citizens afterwards."

Basic training, however, was delivered by the Canadian Army, and recruits were issued Canadian uniforms for its duration. Arriving in Brantford, Kenji was astonished to find a whole platoon of Japanese Canadians. Most of them were British Columbians but had been recruited from across the country, pulling them from wherever their families had fled or been imprisoned, to serve as translators and assistants in post-war Japan and other Far Eastern countries. They were here to learn basic military skills before going on to specialized language training in Vancouver.

Although they had bitter and horrifying stories to tell of internment, all the *nisei* that Kenji met were nevertheless delighted to have finally been given a chance to prove their loyalty to Canada through military service, even though the war was over. Most of them, however, expressed a preference for combat service over the specialized language duties they were being offered. They wanted no special treatment or covert operations; they wanted to be seen to be fighting on the ground, defending the Allies from the Axis. Kenji heard many of them say that they hoped that they'd encounter pockets of resistance so they could engage in real combat.

The Canadian government had prevaricated for months about allowing *nisei* to serve at all, despite increasingly strident requests from both the Australian and British Armies for recruits who could fulfill their specialized needs. Even as some of the *nisei* soldiers were enroute to their basic training, they had received letters from the B.C. Security Commission, asking them to consider repatriation to Japan. Their response had been unanimously negative—one soldier told Kenji that he had not only torn the letter to shreds, but he had also torn up his wartime 'Japanese registration' card at the same time.

The *nisei* soldiers were determined to prove their prowess as well as their loyalty. Colonel Corey, their commander, was heard to remark that the *nisei* were "in many ways, the most intelligent of the lot and the best platoon we've ever had at Brantford. They are quick, smart, pick up their work easily, and we've never had a deserter among them, never a crime, no shirking or malingering."

Time and time again, the *nisei* platoon was selected to go on display as exemplary: the mounted the new guard for a ceremony of the changing of the guard during an inspection by Major-General Potts, then again at the investiture of the 48th Highlander Pipe Band, and yet again they were chosen for a ceremony honouring Major John Aiso, a Japanese American officer of the US Army. Their immediate superior, Lieutenant Marion, commented that he thought that their smart appearance and impeccable behaviour was a result of their pride, long delayed, at finally being allowed to serve their country. He wasn't surprised, he said, to find that every single *nisei* soldier voted when a Canadian federal election was staged in June of that year. They were thrilled to be allowed to vote, and they followed the campaign with keen interest, especially each politician's views on the 'Japanese problem.'

Their commanding officers had only one cause for complaint about their new recruits: their fluency in Japanese was far lower than had been expected.

"I don't know why they're so shocked," Botan had muttered. "We're Canadians, for heaven's sake, not Japanese! When are they going to realize that?"

When initial tests showed limited fluency in speaking and even less facility in reading and writing Japanese, intensive training began. Still, by the time they finished their basic training, only a quarter of them had achieved a rating of 'good' on both written and spoken Japanese. They knew they'd have to work very hard at the language school to be ready for deployment overseas.

Basic was grueling and taught Kenji just how out of shape he'd become during his months of indolence at the hidden hunting camp. He was very glad when it was over and sixty of them from the S-20 division were shipped to Vancouver, where they took language training at the Canadian Army Japanese Language School. It was very strange to be the only Japanese Canadians in Vancouver. One evening, Kenji and Botan, careful to wear their uniforms and carry the documents identifying them as legitimate soldiers, walked along Powell Street past block after block of empty storefronts. A few addresses had been re-occupied by *hakujin* stores, but for the most part unlit Japanese signs loomed darkly over dim spaces. Even the ballpark was deserted. The whole area was like a ghost town, and Kenji shivered as they left. Would his people ever be permitted to return? He thought it unlikely and was glad to leave the melancholy place behind.

Though they stayed mostly within the school's boundaries after that, there were a couple of distressing incidents that showed that, despite their status as Canadian soldiers, ill will was still to be found among the general populace of Vancouver.

The first incident took place at a radio broadcast hosted by Reverend D. Howard Norman, one of the S-20 instructors. It was part of a series of 'Town Halls of the Air' staged by local station CJOR. The title of this session was "What about our Japanese Canadians?" and three *nisei* soldiers, Tom Shoyama, Roger Obata, and George Tanaka, were selected to represent the *nisei* alongside Bob McMaster, a lawyer, and Reverend Norman himself. Huddled around the radio in the barracks to listen, Kenji was told that Shoyama was the editor of *The New Canadian* newspaper, the one Nikkei newspaper that had been allowed to continue throughout the war, to act as the official communication channel to Nikkei across Canada. Tom had kept the paper going even after being interned in the camp at Kaslo. He was well-known and well-liked by Nikkei and many *hakujin* as well, but on the other side of the debate were two who detested Shoyama and all he stood for: Austin Harris, a truck driver from Steveston, and J.H. Fletcher, representing the Japanese Repatriation League which had been actively campaigning for all Nikkei to be sent to Japan after the war.

Kenji was surprised to find, as he listened to the debate, that most of the people in the studio audience seemed to be in support of the Japanese Canadians. The lawyer's and minister's presentations were reasoned and persuasive; the two opposing speakers' arguments were both illogical and illegal.

"The Japanese must be sent back to Japan because of the terrible atrocities they have committed. They do not deserve to stay in Canada," said Fletcher.

"What about the Germans in Canada?" asked one of the audience members.

"We can't deport Germans, because they're like us..." Fletcher replied, to catcalls from the audience.

The debate devolved into heated argument. Towards the conclusion of the event, Reverend Norman asked Tom Shoyama, who had been standing quietly at the back of the room wearing the King's uniform, what race he belonged to. "The Japanese race, sir," replied Tom, which is what the Reverend had wanted him to say, to draw attention to the *nisei*'s loyalty and service. Angry at some of the remarks he'd heard, however, Tom didn't stop there. He went on to defend his newspaper, and the next day received a sharp reprimand from the Colonel.

The second incident, which occurred after the S-20 had been

moved to Ambleside Camp in West Vancouver, again involved J.H. Fletcher. One day, several *hakujin* corporals wandered into town and stood outside the Hollyburn Theatre, perusing the films on offer. Several *nisei* soldiers joined them. The cashier called out to one of the corporals, asking if the other soldiers were 'Japs.' The corporal explained that these were Japanese Canadians stationed at Ambleside. The cashier called the theatre's manager, who happened to be the same Mr. Fletcher from the radio show, and Fletcher made it clear that 'Japs' were not to be admitted to the premises.

"We don't want them to come into the theatre whether they are wearing the King's uniform or not!" Fletcher stated emphatically.

The next evening, Corporal David Watanabe, who hadn't heard about the incident the previous day, went to buy a ticket to the movie. He was told that the movie was full, so he bought a ticket for the next showing and went to a nearby coffee shop to wait. When he returned, the cashier told him that she had to refund his ticket. When Watanabe asked why, she said she'd been directed to do so by Mr. Fletcher. Watanabe refused the refund, and the embarrassed cashier called the manager. Fletcher, in turn, called the West Vancouver Police Force and insisted that Watanabe be removed. Although the policeman who arrived pointed out that Fletcher had no legal basis on which to refuse Watanabe's admission, he did suggest that Watanabe accept the situation quietly, which the soldier did.

The incident did not end there, however. While he acknowledged Fletcher's racist and illegal actions, the Colonel ordered all the *nisei* soldiers not to attempt to enter the movie theatre. The *nisei* were incensed at this condoning of outright discrimination, and a few nights later several of them again tried to enter the theatre and were again refused entry. The problem escalated up the chain of military command and began to be debated in the local newspapers. *The Lion's Gate Times* supported Fletcher and called the presence of the *nisei* an "affront to the municipality." Even though the Vancouver *Sun* came out in support of the Japanese Canadians, tempers flared, and more overt signs of discrimination began to appear, such as cafés refusing entry and buses not stopping for the *nisei*. White members of the language school wrote to the papers, expressing their outrage over the treatment of their fellow soldiers, and a local high school planned a demonstration in their support, though this was cancelled for fear of danger to the students.

Both the military and Dave Watanabe himself considered legal action against Fletcher, but in the end, the order to stay away from the theatre was upheld. The *nisei* realized reluctantly that, while the citizens of Brantford had been friendly, Vancouver was still 'enemy territory' for them. Though it left a sour tase in their mouths, nothing further came of it.

These distractions apart, most of the recruits were still working hard to improve their Japanese, especially the specialized vocabulary needed for military investigations, Kenji's own English and Japanese were fluent, so they trained him in basic Korean and Chinese instead. At the end of the training, he was shipped overseas to join the British Forces Southeast Asia Command (SEAC) in Burma.

Though he thought that Botan's suspicion about the reason for it had probably been correct, Kenji wasn't unhappy to be under British command. Major General Rich, in overall command in Burma, was a tall, impressive fellow with a handlebar moustache under a bladelike nose and piercing blue eyes. Kenji took care not to come under that fierce gaze any more than he had to. His immediate commanding officer was Lieutenant General Sir Philip Christison. Christison was a Scot whose many years of military experience in both wars had given him a world-weary but not unkind expression and so far, Kenji had no cause for complaint, though some of the lower-ranking officers looked sideways at him, eying his Japanese features. One had spit at him as he passed, but Kenji had ignored the insult, and nothing more had come of the encounter.

Now Kenji wiped the sweat from his face, then straightened the fountain pen and notebook on the desk in front of him, trying hard not to show his nervousness as he waited for his first interviewee to come through the door. He cleared his throat a little and brushed miniscule particles of dust off the lapels of his smart Canadian army uniform, marveling again that he was wearing it. In a surprise turnaround just before their deployment, the Canadian government had changed its mind, determining that the Nikkei recruits should be issued Canadian uniforms even though they'd report to the British commanders. Kenji had never found out what had been behind that last minute reversal, but he was proud to be wearing the uniform, nevertheless.

His job today was to interview the few women who had been found in an *ianjo*, a so-called 'comfort station,' in the city of Myitkyina.

Kenji, still a virgin himself and with little experience of women other than his sister, mother, aunts, and cousins, had been utterly shocked when the purpose of these places had been explained to him. He had been hard-pressed not to show his reaction on his face, and he suspected his fellow recruits had felt the same way.

The practice had begun after the 1937 overthrow of Chinese Nanking by the Japanese. When news of the massacre of its citizens and the mass rape of tens of thousands of its women had leaked out, the international community had been sickened. Emperor Hirohito, concerned that such behaviour would not only tarnish Japan's international reputation but also lead to the spread of venereal disease, had ordered the army to recruit Japanese prostitutes to follow the armies and supply 'comfort' to the soldiers so far from home. He hoped this would reduce the rape of women in conquered territories and control the spread of disease. Sadly, not only had the practice not achieved these aims, it had instead resulted in the kidnapping, deception, and enforced sex slavery of thousands upon thousands of innocent girls and women.

In the late 1930s, preparing for war, Japan had stopped using established Japanese prostitutes as *ianfu*—comfort women. Instead, it had begun deceiving and collecting ordinary women from conquered countries and territories, including China, Korea, the Philippines, and Burma, as well as Japan itself. Offering education and promising jobs in nursing, restaurant work, or other service industries, along with fair wages and good working conditions, recruiters from the Japanese military deceived poor women and young girls into signing contracts that were worthless. Some girls were eager to go, to escape harsh fathers who denied them schooling or a chance to work outside the home—sadly, this was a common situation, Kenji knew, given the strictly patriarchal system in traditional Japanese families. Some fathers, beaten down by extreme poverty and with whole families to support, agreed to sell their daughters, not knowing--or choosing not to know--what would happen to them.

By whatever route they had ended up in this plight, the girls—some as young as ten years of age—had hoped it would be a chance to improve their lot. Instead, they found themselves imprisoned in miserable accommodations, with inadequate food and water, subjected to brutal rape and endless sexual services all day, every day. They were moved with the army, herded and transported like cattle from place to place. As the war continued, the military stopped even the pretense of contracting these women; girls sent to the store for milk or working in a field would be grabbed up and thrown into the back of a truck, never to be seen by their parents again.

Few of these poor girls and women had survived the war. Subjected to endless and brutal penetration, most had suffered vaginal or other internal wounds. Forced abortions had left other scars. Poor food and inadequate housing had resulted in nutritional deficiencies, viral illnesses, bacterial infections. Sexually transmitted diseases had caused sterility or worse. Physical abuse had left the women with broken bones that had healed poorly, head injuries, blindness, or deafness. The imprisonment and unending tortuous treatment had driven numerous women insane, and many had committed suicide at the first opportunity. Those too old, too ill, too broken to serve had been summarily beheaded, their bodies left by the roadside or buried in mass graves along with the other battle dead. When the war was lost, many were executed and buried in mass graves to prevent them from telling their sad tales. Others were simply abandoned to their fates, as had happened at Myitkyina.

Now Japan was denying the whole sordid mess, saying that the women were professional prostitutes who had voluntarily signed on to do their patriotic duty. They maintained that the women were proud to be part of this 'Imperial gift' provided to motivate the soldiers and insisted that the practice was normal and necessary for military success. The comfort station in Myitkyina had been managed by a Korean man eager to curry favour with the Japanese overlords, whom he was sure would win the war. When interrogated by the Allied military after Japan's surrender, he had insisted that the *ianfu* had been housed in comfort, allowed outings and picnics, sports and art supplies, tenderly cared for to keep them in the best of health. Christison was skeptical of the man's reports, and he'd detailed Kenji to interview one of the three women remaining in the station.

Clearing his throat again, Kenji glanced down at the paper before him. Akiko Okuma, from the Nagasaki region of Japan. He wondered if she felt lucky to have escaped the site of the second atomic bomb, or whether she wished she had been killed along with her family. He checked her birthdate and blinked: the girl was only fifteen! She'd been in sexual servitude for three years—since she was twelve.

He shook his head. It was hard to imagine a people who would do this to their enemies, let alone to their own countrywomen. The stories coming out of the Japanese POW camps were equally appalling—the torture of captured Allied soldiers was almost too awful to believe, flouting all international standards for the treatment of prisoners of war. It was one of the reasons why Kenji had fled from Japan as a teenager. Their cultural values—this tendency to do all manner of inhumane things as a way of displaying their masculinity--just didn't mesh with his own, those of his family. His heart burned with hatred of the Japanese Imperial Army—to think he might have had to serve within it! He had never been so glad to be Canadian.

The door opened and a slight girl was ushered in by a nurse in a Red Cross uniform. She led the girl by the arm to the chair in front of the desk and gently sat her down, speaking quietly to her before nodding at Kenji and leaving the room.

Akiko sat motionless, her head down so that her long, unbound black hair obscured her face. The hair had been recently washed, but months of neglect had left it dull and straggly. The nails on her slender fingers were ragged and chewed, and she twisted the sash of her soiled kimono uneasily between her hands.

Kenji had been advised to be extremely kind, not to frighten, threaten, or otherwise upset the girl, while at the same time obtaining as many details of her experience as he could. He wasn't sure how he was supposed to achieve these incompatible goals. Clearing his throat again, he reached out to pour a glass of water from the carafe on the desk, pushing the filled glass toward her.

"Drink," he said quietly in Japanese. "Please," he added, then waited.

Her hand reached out to grasp the glass, and Kenji stifled a gasp at the sight of infected rope burns around her wrist. What had been done to her while those were confining her movements? It made him feel sick to imagine. She took the glass and took one sip from it behind the cover of her hair. Then she replaced the glass on the desk and returned to her motionless waiting.

"Akiko," he finally said. "Miss Okuma. Can you look at me?"

She raised her head slowly, pushing her hair aside with the back of her wrist. Kenji's stomach lurched. Her face was a wreck. She had been badly beaten, her left eye swollen shut with blackened flesh, and other bruises that distorted her cheeks and lips. She stared at him, her visible eye filled with fear at his Japanese appearance even while she held her head high and met his horrified gaze.

"I am so sorry," breathed Kenji. He swallowed hard. "I am so sorry for what you have endured. I am Kenji Tasaka, a Canadian serving in the British military. I was born in Canada, do you understand? I am not Japanese."

He saw an expression of wary relief flit across her face.

"I am here to ask you about your experience, your story. We wish to know if what the Korean manager of this *ianjo* says is true."

Her ruined face changed from impassivity to fury in an instant, and she spit to the side from her swollen lips.

"That *jaakuna hito*—that evil one--he lies," she hissed.

"All right. You tell me, then—how did you come to be here?" Kenji sat back and picked up his pen, vastly relieved that Akiko seemed willing to speak to him. She pushed her hair further back, raised her head to gaze up at the small, high window, and began to speak in a monotone, as if reciting some history that had nothing to do with her. As Kenji scribbled notes, increasingly appalled, he realized that this was the only way she could bear to tell the tale.

"One day in June, in 1944, when I was twelve, I had to prepare lunch for my parents who were working in the field. I went to the village well to fetch water. A Japanese garrison soldier surprised me there and took me away, so that my parents never knew what had happened to me. I was taken to the police station in a truck, where I was raped by several policemen. When I shouted, they put socks in my mouth and continued to rape me. The head of the police station hit me in the face because I was crying. After 10 days or so, I was taken to the Japanese army garrison barracks. There were around 400 other young girls with me, and we had to serve the Japanese soldiers as sex slaves every day - up to 40 men per day for each of us. If I resisted, they hit me or stuffed rags in my mouth. One held a matchstick to my--private parts--until I obeyed him." She glanced at Kenji, her unswollen eye blazing with fury. "Private parts! Huh! There has been nothing private about them since the day I was taken!" She breathed in deeply through her nose and turned again to the window. After a moment she continued.

"One of the Korean girls who was with us—most of the girls were Korean or Filipino-- objected to serving so many men. To punish her for her questioning, the Japanese company commander Yamamoto ordered her to be beaten with a sword. While we were watching, they took off her clothes, tied her legs and hands and rolled her over a board with nails until the nails were covered with blood and pieces of her flesh. In the end, they cut off her head. Another soldier told us, 'It's easy to kill you all, easier than killing dogs.' He also said, 'Since those girls are crying because they have not eaten, boil the human flesh and make them eat it.'" Kenji felt his bile rise and swallowed it down with difficulty. Could such an atrocity really have happened?

"One girl caught a venereal disease from being raped so often and, as a result, over 50 Japanese soldiers were infected. To stop the disease from spreading and to 'sterilize' the girl, they stuck a hot iron bar in her private parts."

"Once they took 40 of us on a truck far away to a pool filled with water and snakes. The soldiers beat several of the girls, shoved them into the water, heaped earth into the pool and buried them alive. I think over half of the girls who were at the garrison barracks were killed. Twice I tried to run away with another girl, but both times we were caught after a few days. We were tortured even more, and I was hit on my head so many times that it has never stopped aching. They also tattooed me on the inside of my lips, my chest, my stomach, and—other parts. I fainted from the pain. When I woke up, I was here. I have been here ever since."

Kenji paused and offered the water glass again, and Akiko drank it to the bottom this time. He refilled it and she picked it up again, avoiding his gaze.

"And since you arrived here—what has it been like?" he asked after a moment, hating to force her to expose her pain, her shame, but knowing it was these details that his commander required. She shrugged, turning the glass in her hands.

"More of the same," she said. "Many, many men, every day. No rest, no freedom, little food or water. Punishment for any defiance. And since Japan surrendered, American soldiers have used us as well." She looked at Kenji. "They are a bit nicer than the Japanese. Maybe

Canadians are nicer, too." Kenji felt his face flushing a little. Americans? Visiting Japanese comfort stations? He found that hard to believe but he wasn't about to challenge the girl. He put his head down and recorded what she'd said.

"What happened to provoke this latest beating?" he asked next. Her face twisted in a curious expression both wry and proud.

"I stole some extra food for us," she said. "The commander had me brought to his tent and after—when he fell asleep, I gathered up all the food from his table and hid it in my clothes. Of course, it was discovered that I had taken it, and I was beaten." Her hand gestured vaguely to her face, but also at the rest of her body. Kenji tried not to think of what they might have done to her. Then she looked directly at him, and her mouth moved in a travesty of a smile. "But by then we had eaten all the food. It was more than we'd had in a week, so it was worth the beating."

"So, no picnics, no outings, no medical care..." Kenji said, consulting the notes from the Korean manager.

"Picnics! Ha!" Akiko spat again. "Maybe for a few girls, the ones assigned to officers. I think maybe they get better treatment, nice clothes, more food, maybe even medical treatment. But for us, the *pi,* medical care consists of killing any girl who gets sick. So, sure, I guess that means they keep us healthy—the ones they allow to live, anyway."

"*Pi*?" Kenji asked. "I don't think I know that word." Akiko smiled sarcastically with her broken mouth.

"Good, it's good that you didn't know it," she said. "It's a very rude Chinese slang word for a woman's—you know, vagina. That's all we are to them—a place to put their..." She trailed off and looked away again, her expression remote.

Kenji sat back and laid his pen down on the desk, gazing at this girl whose spirit endured despite what she had suffered. He had experienced only loneliness and mild discomfort. How had she come through such torture, defilement, imprisonment for so long? He had to know.

"How did you survive?" he blurted out. She smiled again, more genuinely this time.

"By imagining a better day to come," she said softly. "Whether through death or an end to this war, I didn't know, but I decided to believe that this horror could not last forever, that someday it would end. And every morning when I woke up, I thought to myself, 'Perhaps today is the day.' And now that day has come. And I am still alive. I am still me."

Kenji saw Akiko once more before his unit moved on to other duties. She was crossing a courtyard, carrying two pails of water. Her hair was neatly tied back, and her head was up. Her bruises had faded, her black eye had lost its puffiness, and Kenji could now see that she was beautiful, a fact that had been totally obscured by her injuries. She would have walked by him, but he stopped her with a gesture.

"Miss Okuma. How are you feeling?" She smiled faintly.

"A little better, thank you, sir. It is very good to be free and have enough to eat."

"And will you be staying here?" asked Kenji, not sure what had prompted the question. The girl shook her head.

"No, sir. Soon I will go back to Japan, to stay with my cousin who lives in Tokyo. I hope I can find some work there. Something honest and decent." She shook her head, her expression troubled. "But I don't know. Everyone will blame me for what happened to me. No one will want to speak to me for the shame I have brought to my family. My cousin, she says I can only stay with her for a short while, until I find work. Then I must make my own way."

Kenji frowned. "But how can it be your fault? You were taken and held against your will!" Akiko's still-swollen lips twisted, and a harsh laugh came from her throat.

"You truly are not Japanese, sir, if you say this. My family has disowned me. They are ashamed that I did not find a way to kill myself to avoid the defilement."

Kenji stared at her, appalled all over again. Although his own parents would perhaps be angry or ashamed of his running away rather than be interned, he was certain they wouldn't disown him. He wasn't sure where they were now, but once he returned to Canada he fully intended to look for and reunite with them, knowing they would welcome him. What would it be like to have your family turn its back on you? Suddenly he took his small notebook and pencil from his pocket and held them out to Akiko.

"Can you write down your cousin's address? And—would it be all right if I wrote to you there?"

She looked at him, confusion in her eyes. "Why would you want to do that, sir?" she asked, wary. Kenji shrugged, embarrassed and half regretting his impulse.

"It's Kenji—Kenji Tasaka—not sir. And I don't know. Just—I guess--so you know that someone hasn't disowned you, maybe…" He trailed off, his cheeks burning. Then he looked into her eyes. "It's not what you think. I don't expect anything from you. I just thought maybe you'd like to have a friend."

She continued to stare, biting her lip. Then she slowly reached out to take the notebook and pencil, writing down an address.

"I only have a little reading and writing, sir—Kenji. So don't use a lot of big words, all right?" A ghost of a smile appeared on her face and was as quickly gone. "I must go, they are waiting for the water."

Kenji nodded, tucking the notebook back into his pocket. "Of course. But I will write to you, and I hope you'll answer. I'll put the address for the unit on my first letter, so you'll know how to reach me—they'll get your letters to me wherever we are." She nodded and bent to pick up her pails, moving away but glancing back several times with a puzzled expression.

Kenji watched her until she stepped inside a building and disappeared. Then he walked away, whistling and feeling inexplicably better than he had in months.

1948
Elie, Manitoba

Isabel was excited to be on the rails again—she barely remembered the train that had brought them to East Lillooet six years before. Now an almost-grown-up young lady at fourteen-and-a-half, she sat demurely on the seat, clutching her new purse, but inside she wanted to kneel up and stare out the windows just as she had at age eight. The fast-moving landscape passing outside distracted her from the lingering sadness she felt at leaving her friends back at the camp. The Nikkei families were scattering everywhere across Canada—many to Toronto, Ontario and a few to Montreal, Quebec. A couple of other families were also traveling to Manitoba on this train, but none of them were Isabel's close girlfriends. She wondered if she'd ever see them again. These sad thoughts had been muted as they traveled east through the Rocky Mountains: the terrifyingly skinny bridges over deep gorges, majestic peaks, and soaring eagles had distracted her. Now they were past Calgary and the land had flattened out into rolling prairies. It was a lot less dramatic than the mountains, and Isabel's mind wandered. She looked at her reflection in the smeared train window, patting her hair into place to be sure that her scar wasn't showing. She sighed, thinking about the friends she'd left behind.

On their last night together, Isabel and her five closest friends had sworn to initiate a Hanky Exchange as soon as they were settled in their new homes. This pastime had become popular in recent months. It was sort of like a chain letter, but in with the letter you wrote and sent to the girl whose name was at the top of the list, you enclosed a handkerchief, hemmed and embroidered with your initials in one corner. Then you sent copies of the original letter, with the top girl's name removed and your name at the bottom of the list, to six new girls. If no one broke the chain—and everyone swore on their lives that they wouldn't--then each girl should end up with dozens—no, hundreds of handkerchiefs! When she'd excitedly showed the letter to her mother, Asami had scoffed.

"Those things never work, Isabel! I would take weeks and thousands of letters going out for your name to even get to the top of the list! It would be better if you all just agreed to send a nice handkerchief to each of your six friends and forget all the rest." Isabel had been infuriated by her mother's response but when she secretly did the math in her bed that night, she'd realized that her mom was--annoyingly—right. The next day, she'd persuaded her friends to agree to just send each other hankies, though she didn't give Asami the credit for exposing the holes in the scheme. Anyway, she now had five fine cambric squares tucked into her purse along with needle and thread and a hank of pretty blue embroidery floss. She planned to hem and embroider all her hankies by the time they reached Winnipeg and get them out in the first available post so that hers reached her friends first. They'd be so impressed! In fact, she should start now.

She took the supplies out of her purse and shut it with a satisfactory snap. It was her first grown-up handbag, purchased in Lillooet just before they left. She set it beside her, admiring its smooth leatherette surface and shiny clasp. She measured out a good length of white thread and held up her needle to thread it. Several minutes and many frustrating attempts later, she huffed in exasperation and thrust everything back into her bag. It was impossible to thread a needle on a moving train! It was also making her feel quite sick to her stomach, trying to focus on the tiny eye of the needle. She'd have to thread a really long length at the first stop and see if she could hem the hankie's edges despite the swaying.

A wide field of brilliant yellow came into view in the distance and Isabel craned her neck to look. As they came nearer, she leaned over to tap her mother's knee.

"Look Ma, isn't that pretty? What is it?"

"Mustard," her father replied when Asami shrugged. "There are acres and acres of it in Alberta and Saskatchewan. I'm glad you think it's pretty, Izzie, because you're going to see a lot of it over the next few days!"

Indeed she had. Isabel was thoroughly sick of the brilliant yellow as they neared Winnipeg and swore to herself that she'd never, ever, buy anything yellow again in her life.

She was also feeling quite disgruntled that she hadn't managed to hem a single handkerchief. Every time she tried, the train's unpredictable movements jostled her hands and ruined her stitches. Elizabeth Sakimoto was sure to beat her in sending her hankies out! Elizabeth was always trying to outdo all their friends and it galled Isabel to let her triumph.

They stayed overnight in an army barracks just outside the city and although it was dusty and drafty, Isabel was too glad of a stationary bed to do anything but close her eyes as soon as her head hit the pillow. At least she was pretty sure the bed was stationary; her body insisted on telling her that she was still moving even when she wasn't. It was quite disconcerting.

The next day started early. They washed and dressed and made their way to the breakfast buffet supplied by the army cooks. Isabel enjoyed the selection and had eggs, bacon, toast, waffles and fruit, far more than they'd ever had for breakfast in East Lillooet! Then they carried their suitcases into a large empty warehouse space where other families stood in huddled groups. The door swung open and some roughly dressed farmers came in, chatting and laughing.

They walked around the room, speaking to the Nikkei families and eyeing the age, size, and number of their children. Families with infants or toddlers were passed over repeatedly; not only couldn't the children work in the fields, but the mother's labour would also be unavailable. Families with healthy, strong looking teenagers, especially boys, were selected quickly and disappeared out the door. Isabel began to feel as if she was watching a cattle—or worse, a slave—market, and was glad that they had already been selected by Mr. Finlay for his sugar beet farm. She wished he'd show up soon. It was so embarrassing to stand around, not being chosen—worse than picking teams for games at school!

The door opened again and a tall, husky young man of about twenty stepped into the room, drawing all the women's eyes. He was blond, blue-eyed, and very handsome—and after a brief pause to scan the space, he strode right over to where they were standing!

"Mr. Tasaka, right? I'm so sorry to be late," he apologized, shaking Hoshi's hand. "One of the trucks got a flat tire halfway between here and Portage Le Prairie and it took me awhile to get it sorted out. I'm David Finlay—my dad told me to come and get you folks and bring you out to the farm. Can I help you with your luggage?"

Within minutes they were squashed into the cabs of two rather muddy farm trucks, their belongings piled into the open backs. Isabel was pleased that she ended up in the back seat of the truck David was driving—an old Japanese man drove the other. Her mother sat sedately in the front passenger seat, making stilted conversation with David as they pulled away from the city and headed back westward on the highway toward Elie. Isabel tried furiously to think of some clever question she could ask to get David's attention. Finally she thought of one that she genuinely wanted an answer to.

"Excuse me, but how did you know which family in that warehouse was us?" she inquired, leaning forward to make herself heard. Beside her, her grandmother hid a smile by looking out the window.

David turned his head to smile briefly at Isabel. "It was easy," he said. "I was told to look for a group with an older gentleman and his wife, a middle-aged man and his wife, another single man, plus a teenage girl. Your family was the only group that fit that description."

"Oh," said Isabel, flushing and sitting back. She'd thought it would be something much more interesting.

But now that he was talking to her, David continued. "You've arrived at a good time. The first weeding of the sugar beets has just finished, and there won't be another for almost a month. You'll have lots of time to get settled in, meet the other workers, before the field work really gets going again."

"I understand that you have many different nationalities among your employees," said Asami. David nodded, flashing a white-toothed smile over at her that caused Isabel's heart to do a little flip-flop. *My, but he's handsome!* she thought. She couldn't wait to write to her friends and tell them all about him!

"We do," he said now, responding to Asami's comment. "My father doesn't think it's right to judge people by their backgrounds, but rather by the work that they do. If a worker does an honest day's work, pulls his—or her—weight and gets along with the others, that's good enough for Dad. There are a lot of people coming to Canada now to try to make a better life, people displaced by the war, or who've lost their homes in Europe. We've got Ukrainians, Dutch, French, Polish, even a few Germans who disagreed with the Nazis and don't want to live in Germany anymore—or Jews who got out when they could. We'll take anyone who's willing to work hard. Because I do need to warn you, it *is* hard work! The seeds are planted by machine, but then we thin the seedlings by hand—that's a backbreaker, let me tell you—those shoots are small and low to the ground! Then there's first hoeing—that's been done—and then second hoeing, that'll be in August. With each row half a mile long, it takes a looong time to hoe!" He grinned at Isabel's reflection in the rear-view mirror. She was afraid she was looking aghast. Half a mile long? What had they signed up for? She'd be in school in the fall, but this second hoeing thing—it sounded awfully as if she'd be expected to help with that. David was still talking as she tuned in again.

"But it's the harvest that's the toughest. The sugar beets are big and heavy—around a foot long and up to five pounds each. We leave them in the ground as long as we can to get the maximum sugar content, so the ground is freezing up by the time we pull 'em in late September or early October. We plough the ground alongside to loosen them up a little, but you still have to pull 'em out, bang the dirt off 'em, then slice the leaves off the top with a big machete. We pile the beets in long rows and then drive along slowly while everyone throws them up into the back of the truck. Your arm muscles will get very strong before we're done," he said, catching Isabel's eye again.

"But I'll be in school by then!" she protested.

"Sure," David replied, "But the teachers let you out at two o'clock in harvest time so you can help in the fields for a couple of hours before dark. Everyone pitches in. If we're too slow, the beets freeze and go mushy; then they're no good for processing." He must have seen Isabel's dismay, for he grinned again. "Don't worry—you'll be okay," he said. "I bet you're stronger than you look."

Isabel wasn't sure whether to be insulted or complimented by this last comment. She sat back and turned her head to stare out the window where a seemingly endless field of brassy yellow mustard plants streamed by. Again.

It was hard work. But surprisingly, it was also fun. By the time harvest came around, Isabel had made good friends with David's younger sister Cathy, who was in her grade at school. Somehow when the boss himself and all his family members worked alongside you, it didn't feel so much like work, so onerous. There was time for play, for singing along with the truck's radio, having a spontaneous food fight with the cut-off beet tops, or racing to see who could get their row finished first or haul up the biggest beet.

Isabel liked it best when David was in their row, his good-natured teasing keeping them all going. His farmboy good looks only got more appealing as the summer went on, bronzing his muscled arms to gold and bleaching his hair to almost white. Isabel was entranced and could hardly speak in his presence. Cathy laughed at her.

"Izzie, forget him. He's way too old for you and besides, he's interested in Karen Okaida, you know, the girl who works at the telephone office."

"I know," Isabel said, tossing her head. "I don't care, I was just looking."

"Uh-huh," said Cathy, nudging her friend with her elbow. "Well, just don't get your heart broken over my big brother!"

So she had been warned—but it was still a blow to arrive at school one morning just before Christmas to find Cathy so full of excitement that she looked likely to explode. Her friend grabbed her elbow and hauled her deep into the coatroom.

"Ow!" said Isabel. "What is the *matter* with you? Your fingers are like pincers!"

"Sorry--but never mind that," hissed Cathy. "You'll never guess what's happened!"

"Well, I won't even try then," said Isabel in exasperation, rubbing her elbow.

"It's David! He and Karen eloped yesterday!"

"They what?" gasped Isabel, her stomach sinking. Oh yes, she knew she was far too young for David, but still...something in her had hoped, just a little, that maybe he'd wait for her?

"I know—isn't it so romantic?"

"I guess," said Isabel, frowning. "But why? Didn't Karen want a nice wedding with lots of guests and a cake and dancing and all? Did she even have a wedding dress?" Isabel's own wedding fantasy was fully developed; she knew exactly what kind of dress she wanted, and the cake was clear in her imagination. If the groom's face was a little fuzzy at present, well, there was lots of time to figure that out. Cathy shrugged.

"I guess not. I don't know, maybe they were afraid people would talk, you know..." she trailed off, her cheeks heating.

"Talk about what?" Isabel asked, confused.

"Well, you know—with Karen being Japanese and all..." said Cathy, looking down. Isabel scowled harder.

"She's not Japanese! She's Canadian!" she retorted, and Cathy nodded quickly.

"I know, I know, but, well, some people will say it's not right to mix races."

"Oh, for heaven's sake," said Isabel. "We're all part of the human race! What difference does it make?" Cathy shrugged again, uncomfortable.

"None to me, you know that, and obviously none to David and Karen—David always says 'Love is an itch in your heart that you can't scratch'--but, well, some people..."

"Is your dad one of those people?" Isabel asked. David and Cathy's mother had died birthing their youngest brother, Calvin. Cathy's head came up, her eyes ablaze.

"No, of course he isn't! You know my dad doesn't hold with discriminating against people because of things like that! Look at all the different kinds of people on our farm! How can you even ask that?" Now it was Isabel's turn to shrug.

"It's one thing to allow people of another 'race' to work for you. It's quite another thing to allow your eldest son to marry one. I just thought maybe that could be why they ran off and eloped instead of having a proper wedding." Cathy shook her head.

"No, I'm sure it wasn't that. But maybe they just didn't want to cope with all the gossip that's sure to start up about them."

"It'll happen anyway, if what you say is true," Isabel answered.

"Yes," said Cathy, "but now that they're married, maybe it won't be such a big deal. Maybe people won't bother to make a fuss."

"I hope that's true," said Isabel. "I'm glad for them," she said, belatedly. "I hope they're happy."

When the new Mrs. Finlay birthed a healthy eight-pound girl just over seven months after the elopement, people had something else to gossip about. Karen's Japanese Canadian heritage seemed to be the least of the scandal. However, Isabel was to discover just how deep anti-Japanese Canadian attitudes still ran when she wrote an essay for school about her internment camp experience. The teacher called her in for an after-school discussion and accused her of making things up.

"Those camps provided better living conditions than you people had on the coast," the teacher, a grey-haired matron named Mrs. Campbell, said. "And better nutrition, too! And I'm sure that the conditions weren't as bad as you say in your essay, Isabel. It's important to stick to the truth!"

Isabel was stunned. "I am sticking to the truth! I was there! And Mrs. Campbell, no disrespect intended, but you were not! How would you know what the conditions were like?"

The teacher drew herself up and retorted, "I saw that documentary, *Of Japanese Descent,* that came out in 1945! It showed the hovels your people lived in in B.C., and the awful food you ate! Why, you didn't even have bathtubs in your houses! And besides," she finished triumphantly, "the film showed happy children in the camp, playing baseball and attending a Scout meeting!" She glared at Isabel, daring her to disagree.

Isabel was, unusually for her, struck speechless. How could she even begin to combat the biases inculcated by that government-commissioned film? She'd seen it, too, and been appalled at how selective the filmmakers had been, showing a single dilapidated house that had been abandoned when the family were interned, left to ruin. As for the food, the film implied that 'good white bread' was superior to rice, though no justification for this statement was offered. And baths—oh, there it was again, that *hakujin* misunderstanding of the communal bathing habits of the Nikkei. Baseball, yes, they had indeed played that—Isabel hid a smile at the memory of their team beating the RCMP—and the Scouts? That had been permitted only after years of struggle to be recognized as capable of running their own program. She wanted to argue, to convince Mrs. Campbell that her narrow vision of the camp conditions had been shaped by one very biased source, in contrast to Isabel's own childhood experiences. But as she stood there, the teacher's superior expression and absolute confidence in her right to correct Isabel stopped her tongue. She was close to graduation. Would anything be served by antagonizing this woman who had control over her grades, her future? Pushing down her anger, her desire to slap the smirk from her teacher's face, Isabel picked up the essay from the desk.

"May I write another essay on a different topic?" she ground out between clenched teeth. The teacher bent her head in gracious assent.

"You may," she said, as if granting a huge favour to an errant child, "but be sure you tell the truth this time!"

"Yes, ma'am," Isabel said, and strode out, barely containing her fury.

She submitted an innocuous essay on some bland topic and received a miserly 'C' grade. But by that time Isabel was facing a more momentous change in her life. The whole family had saved as much as possible from their farm labours, and her parents were looking for a small house to buy in Winnipeg. It was time for Grandpa Harry to stop working so hard, and Isabel's mother hoped to take up her language teaching again. As soon as Isabel graduated from high school, she'd be leaving her friends here in Elie behind. She was conflicted—she'd miss Cathy and the others here on the farm, but she was also excited by the opportunities offered by the city. Finally—finally—possibilities seemed to be on the horizon. She could hardly wait.

1949
Fraser Valley, British Columbia
Tokyo, Japan

Harry stood, supported by a walking cane, gazing out over the lush field where rosy globes of ripening strawberries peeked out between ruffles of scalloped leaves. The spring breeze caressed his wrinkled old cheeks. He breathed deeply, savouring the hint of fruity sweetness on the air.

Asami stood beside him, watching her father enjoy her eighty-ninth birthday gift to him, this trip back to their old farm. Now that the Canadian government had finally—after much lobbying and politicking on the part of the Japanese Canadian Association and others--lifted the restriction on Nikkei living west of the mountains, they were able to travel back to their old home, though the family had no plans to relocate from Winnipeg. Hoshi had found work at a box factory—not perfect, but a start--and Asami was again teaching in the local language school. Isabel had applied to attend business college, intending to train to be a secretary. Sara stayed at home to look after Harry and manage the household. There was a growing community of Japanese Canadians in Winnipeg, and they had made some new friends. Things were better, and they seldom spoke of the hardships behind them. It was time to look ahead.

On Harry's other side, Sara shaded her eyes with her hand, looking out over the fields where they had toiled together.

"It was a good place," Harry said, sighing. Asami nodded and took his free hand.

"It was, Dad," she said softly. "I had a wonderful childhood here on this farm. I'm sorry we lost it."

Her father turned to smile at her and shook his head. "Ah, well, that money kept us fed in the camp, and the very last of the cash from the sale was little Isabel's high school graduation gift. I consider it a fair trade." But then he sighed again. "I do wish I could have left it to Jiro, but now that he has found a job in the city as a bookkeeper, I don't feel so bad. It is better for him not to have to work so hard out on the land anymore. He is getting old—sixty-three!"

Asami thought of Kenji with the deep pain that always accompanied any reminder of her missing son. Perhaps he would have wanted to buy back the strawberry farm. But no word had ever been received from him, and they did not speak of him. That did not stop Asami and, she assumed, Hoshi, from thinking about him in the dark hours of the night. She wondered if her husband still had hope that Kenji would reappear one day, as she did. Every time she dusted Isabel's room and saw the old geisha doll standing on the bookshelf in her faded pink silk kimono, she whispered a little prayer. Someday…someday.

But now Sara chuckled, distracting Asami from her sad thoughts. "I can hardly believe that scrawny little ten-year-old we took in on Galliano Island is almost an old man! It makes me feel very old myself."

Harry turned his smile to his wife. "Ah, you have years yet! You are only seventy-two—I was cutting sugar beets in my eighties!"

Sara's face turned sad. "That should not have been. You should have been able to spend your eighties at ease, not labouring in the beet fields." But Harry shook his head as he let go of Asami's hand and reached out to place his arm around Sara's bent shoulders.

"No regrets, dear wife, no regrets. We did what we had to do for the sake of our children. *Kodomo no tame ni."*

On the other side of the ocean from the river valley where they stood, a huge steamer was slowly leaving the Tokyo dock, headed for Vancouver. Inside a modest cabin, Kenji lay on a bunk, gritting his teeth through the rounds of burning and chills that shook his emaciated body. He was going home. He had to hang on until he got there! He had to tell his parents that he'd become a soldier, that he'd made something of his life. He had to introduce them to his wife, his adopted child.

Akiko's small hand was cool on his forehead and the girl—still only a teenager-- shook her head, reaching for the bottle of quinine tablets on the tiny washstand nearby.

"Your fever is up again," she said quietly, then lifted Kenji's shoulders so he could swallow the tablets that did so little to treat the malaria that got worse and worse each time it recurred. As he struggled to sit up, Kenji tried to smile at baby Kaiya at the foot of the bed, but she just stared solemnly back at him with huge brown eyes. Sitting down beside her baby, Akiko curled her legs beneath her and felt a sense of wonder that they were really on their way to Canada. It seemed impossible and as she watched Kenji closely, she replayed in her mind the circumstances that had brought her to this place.

Soon after Akiko settled in her cousin's house, she discovered that she was pregnant by some unknown soldier, possibly the last one to make use of her 'services' before the *ianjo* was closed for good. She was enraged that she would be forced to bear a child of what she considered rape, a child who would remind her every day of her shame, her pain, her defilement. Her cousin was horrified and insisted that Akiko get an abortion or leave her house immediately. Akiko made the appointment, determined to rid herself of this burden.

But on the scheduled day, she found herself hesitating at the bottom of the dark stairway. Another backroom abortion could scar her forever, make her barren for the rest of her life. Akiko knew many *ianfu* who had had this happen. And this child was innocent. Yes, the baby was the product of some nameless soldier—Akiko remembered that her last customer had been American, but she wasn't sure if he was the father—but it was also Akiko's child. Something of her own, something no one would take from her as all else had been taken. She stood there, one foot on the stair, one hand on the rickety banister, chewing her lip, unable to decide.

At that moment, a nun in a sweeping black habit came around the corner and saw Akiko standing there. The woman approached her, glancing up the stairs as if she knew exactly what went on in the squalid rooms at the top.

"You have a choice," she said quietly in accented but understandable Japanese, laying a gentle hand on Akiko's arm. "There is a place, a place of safety, where you may bear your child. There are many families in other countries who are looking for babies to adopt, who would give your child a good home, a good life."

Akiko found herself snatching her arm away from the nun. "No one is going to take my child from me!" she hissed, crossing her arms protectively at her waist, and backing away. The nun raised an eyebrow, glancing again up the stairway.

"So you do not wish to have the child cut away from you after all?" she asked bluntly and Akiko was surprised to find herself shaking her head fiercely. The nun nodded.

"Very well then," she said firmly. "Do you have a place to bear your child, to raise him or her in safety?" Akiko shook her head again, unable to lie. She had nowhere, no one.

The nun held out her hand. "Then come with me," she said, and her expression was kind. "As I said, there is a place. And if you wish to keep your child, you may. But if you change your mind, we can help you with that as well. Come."

When her daughter was born months later, Akiko looked at her and knew she could not give her away. She had no idea how she was going to make her way in the world with a tiny infant, with no family, no friends to help. But this little scrap of life deserved something from her—and in the crumpled little face Akiko saw, to her surprise, a chance at redemption, a way to lift herself above the filth and ugliness of the past four years. She named her Kaiya—which means *forgiveness*.

She was allowed to remain in the Catholic shelter for unwed mothers for only a few weeks after Kaiya's birth and in desperation she wrote to Kenji. They'd exchanged a few stilted letters over the past year, but she had not told him of her pregnancy. Now she confessed it and described her newborn daughter to this Canadian soldier she barely knew, but who had been kind. She asked if he could help her make her way to America, to find a home and work. She had no idea how she would earn her passage—perhaps she could work on the ship at something?

Weeks had passed with no reply. She'd given up hope and was thinking she might have to sell her body on the streets again, perhaps even give Kaiya up for adoption after all, as the nuns kept urging her to do--when one of the nuns came to say that a man, a soldier, was asking for her at the door.

It was Kenji, but a sadly altered man from the one she'd met in Myitkyina. He was desperately thin, his cheeks hollowed out, and he stood shakily, leaning on a walking cane. It was malaria, he told her, from an infected mosquito in Burma. It came and went—today was a bad day, he said with a grimace—but he'd been invalided out, was going home to Canada in a week.

"Come with me," he said simply, and her mouth gaped open.

"Why? Why would you do such a thing for me?" she stuttered. Kenji looked down for a moment, silent. Then he looked into her eyes.

"Because I know what it is to be forced into a situation you never planned to be in," he said. "To be innocent of any crime and yet imprisoned, to be alone. Along the way, a few people helped me, offered me a chance at something better. I want to do that for someone—for you."

Akiko narrowed her eyes, unable to trust in the intentions of any man, however kind he seemed to be. "If I said yes, what would I be agreeing to? To be your comfort woman?"

Kenji laughed bitterly. "Akiko, I am in no shape to make use of a comfort woman. I may never be well enough again. But if that situation ever presents itself, I promise you I will never touch you without your permission, and I will shoot any other man who tries to do so."

Somehow Akiko believed him. She nodded, but then had another question. "What about Kaiya, my daughter?" Akiko demanded.

"Well," Kenji said with a better laugh, though his knees were trembling badly. "If you'd let me come in and sit down, I'd be happy to meet her." Then he reached out with his free hand and touched her cheek tenderly. "Akiko, I will marry you, if you agree. I will take you home as my wife, and your little girl as my daughter. I have had enough of this war, enough of these horrors. Let us start afresh together."

Come, let us sail east
Into a rosier dawn
We three, a new life.

Now, as her new husband slept uneasily, Akiko looked again at the two precious papers she always kept on her person. One was her marriage certificate, proving that she was legally married to a Canadian citizen. The other was Kaiya's official adoption certificate. Akiko had insisted that both processes be completed before she boarded the ship. Who knew what might change between Japan and Canada? A woman had to look after herself, so matter how nice a man was. Akiko had learned this lesson down to her bones and she would never forget it.

PART III

1981-1982
Winnipeg, Manitoba

Isabel Ikeda, formerly Tasaka, now forty-seven, sat in the darkened auditorium, stunned by what she was hearing. On a whim, she'd decided to attend an information session presented by the Manitoba Japanese Canadian Citizens' Association (MJCCA), called "Coming of Age: the role of Japanese Canadians in Canadian Society," about Nikkei war experiences and their consequences for today.

As the presentation went on, Isabel was shocked to learn of the unfairness and hardships experienced by *issei* and *nisei*, including her own parents, during the war. Yes, she had vague memories of the internment camp, especially the toboggan accident when she'd slid underneath the RCMP cruiser! Even now, she had to comb her hair carefully to hide the white scar that zigzagged around her scalp. But her memories were of fun times with a gang of kids, racing around the camp, playing in the tomato fields, watching baseball—she had never considered why they were there, or what her parents had lost because of Canada's treatment of the Nikkei during the war. It had all seemed so long ago and irrelevant to her current life, but this session was really opening her eyes to the reality. By the time the lights came up, she knew she had to confront her mother with what she'd learned. Not one to procrastinate, she drove straight to her mother's small house, where Asami lived alone now that Hoshi was gone.

"Ma, why didn't you ever tell me about how hard it was for you during the war years?" she demanded in the forthright way she had.

Asami, eighty-one and struggling a little to control the tremor in her hands as she poured out the green tea, set the teapot down carefully and shrugged a little. "What would have been the point?" she asked, pushing the filled teacup over to her impatient daughter. "It was over. There was nothing to be gained by raking over the coals again and again. We focused on the future, on rebuilding our family. Your grandfather, your great uncle Jiro, and your father—they all worked very hard on the sugar beet farm until we had enough money to move into the city, buy this house, start over. No one wanted to keep talking about those difficult years."

"But Ma, it was wrong, what the Canadian government—especially the B.C. government—did to all the Nikkei. Did you know that Japanese Americans got their property back after the war, and that they did not have to pay for their own internment? They were also free to live anywhere they wished in the U.S., unlike Nikkei here who were forced to choose between deportation to Japan or dispersal east of the Rockies!

Grandpa should have been given his strawberry farm back after the war."

"Yes, yes, you are right, of course. But he didn't get it back. So we had to make do with what we had."

"It's still wrong," Isabel repeated stubbornly. "And there are some people who think Canada should pay the money back to all the Nikkei they stole it from. They're calling for some form of financial redress, and a public apology."

Asami sipped her hot tea and then set the cup back into its saucer, rattling it a little as she did so. "Well, good luck to them, I suppose. But I'm not sure it's a good idea to stir all those things up again. There was a court case in 1944, you know, trying to get compensation for our lands and possessions being sold off for below their value, but we lost it. The judge said we couldn't question the actions that the government took, because of the War Measures Act. But we did get the vote finally, in '49, after all."

Asami hesitated, looking warily at Isabel to see if she would argue. After a moment, she continued, "You know, it took Japanese Canadians a long time to get our fellow Canadians to stop seeing us as the 'yellow peril,' to stop suspecting us of spying or worse. I'm sure you don't remember, Isabel, but long after the war ended, maybe 1952 or 53—your father and I took a trip to Seattle, in Washington state. We had no trouble getting over the border into the US, but when we came back into Canada, the border guard wasn't satisfied with our answers to his questions. He made us pull over to the border station and they tore apart our car, looking for I don't know what. And when they didn't find anything suspicious, they took us inside and…and…" She hesitated and looked away, becoming agitated.

"And what, Ma? What happened?" Isabel demanded, concerned.

Asami twisted her hands in her lap. When she looked back, her eyes were filled with tears.

"They strip-searched me and your father. For no reason other than that we were of Japanese descent. I've never been so humiliated in my life, not even when we were taken into internment." But before Isabel could express her fury that such a thing had happened to her parents, Asami wiped her eyes and insisted that things like that were all in the past. "It was a long time ago, years and years. Things have changed for the better. I don't want to go back to the way it used to be! It's better to let it go."

Isabel, appalled at her mother's story and even more by her seeming acceptance of the experience, snorted. "What? They treated you like criminals, but we're supposed to just keep our heads down, never object, be model citizens? I know, I know--*deru kugi wa utareru*—the nail that sticks up gets hammered down. But that just won't do any more. It's time to tell the truth about what happened, to make Canada admit that what they did was wrong." She emptied her cup in one long swallow and stood up, slinging her leather bag over her shoulder as she did so, then stooped to place a quick kiss on her mother's wrinkled old cheek. At the door, she turned back and spoke more quietly.

"Because, you know, Ma, it really was wrong. We were Canadian citizens who had done no wrong, and our wealth and livelihoods were taken from us for no reason. Such things should not be swept under the rug and forgotten. Because if it can happen once and no one objects, it can all too easily happen again to us or to someone else."

A few months later, Isabel smoothed the full skirts of her striped peasant style dress and checked the curled bangs of her new, short hairstyle in a nearby shop window before pushing open the door of the small office where the MJCCA had its headquarters. She'd started volunteering here soon after attending the information session that had so shocked her. Satisfied with her appearance, she swung through the office door and set her bag down on the desk where she usually sat, calling out hello to Randy Kawasaki, another volunteer. Randy looked up with a smile from the adjacent desk.

"Hey, Isabel. How are you doing?" He waved the book he held in his hand, his thumb inserted between the pages to keep his place. "Say, have you read this yet? This *Obasan* by Joy Kagawa? It's amazing. Really gets inside the internment experience."

Isabel nodded as she smoothed her skirt under her and sat down. "Yes, I have, and I loved it. But have *you* read Ann Sunahara's new book *The Politics of Racism?* I couldn't put it down. She talks about the connection between racism and political expediency, showing how a lot of the things that happened to us were controlled by a small group of politicians who scapegoated the Nikkei just to keep power for themselves. I was shocked to realize how easily Canadians allowed themselves to be manipulated. Those politicians really played on the *hakujin*'s fears and war hysteria to achieve their own ends. And she uses the government's own documents to prove her points!" She looked thoughtfully over at Randy and continued, growing more and more impassioned as she spoke.

"Did you know, for example, that it would have been illegal to 'intern' the Japanese Canadians, because the Geneva Convention act that governs the internment of people—which Canada signed--is applicable only to actual aliens—which, as citizens, we are not? Our government got around that by not *officially* interning us. In the formal documents, we were 'detained at the pleasure of the Minister of Justice' throughout the war and beyond! And those prisoners of war in Angler and other places? If they'd known enough to invoke the writ of *habeus corpus*, demanding that they be brought before a judge and actually accused of a crime, they would have been let go! But, of course, they didn't know that—they were fishermen, farmers, not lawyers." She laughed cynically. "Of course they weren't lawyers—you can't be a lawyer, or any other kind of professional, without the right to vote! And we all know that was denied to Nikkei at the time. And don't get me started about the War Measures Act—what a carte blanche that is, allowing the feds to do anything they want without reprisals or even investigation! And it's still in our laws—remember, Trudeau invoked it during the October crisis in 1970 to have the power to incarcerate people involved in the separatist movement in Quebec, after the FLQ kidnapped and murdered James Cross, that British diplomat. I know we need to have the ability to act decisively in emergencies, but the way that Act is worded—it is much too broad, and it undermines the human rights of citizens. It needs to be revised, I think! For example, in the US, once the war was over, interned Japanese Americans were free to return to their former homes and livelihoods; here in Canada the Act was extended and extended, for years after the war ended, to justify the government's agenda to disperse Japanese Canadians throughout the country and specifically away from British Columbia. That Liberal politician in B.C. at the time--Ian Mackenzie—he has a lot to answer for!" She took a breath and smiled a little, recognizing that she was preaching to the converted. "Anyway, Sunahara's book provides a really good case for redress. Has Mr. Miki read it, do you know?"

"Probably," Randy replied, "We should ask him, make sure he has. But it needs to go beyond the MJCCA—this is something the National Association of Japanese Canadians needs to take on."

"Yes, I know," replied Isabel, taking the cover off the typewriter, and preparing to type up the letters that had been left beside it for her to transcribe. "And I really hope Mr. Miki takes the idea forward next time he attends an NAJC meeting. It needs to be done, and that's his job as our president," she finished emphatically, and then the clatter of her typewriter keys precluded any further conversation.

When Isabel arrived home hours later, her twenty-two-year-old daughter Michelle was already making supper. A tempting aroma of frying onion and garlic wafted out as Isabel opened the door.

"Mmm, spaghetti?" she asked as she slipped off her shoes and went into the kitchen.

Michelle nodded her dark-haired head, unwrapping a package of ground meat as she did so.

"Yup, hope that's okay. I had late classes today, so I just got home myself." Michelle was studying law at the University of Manitoba, hoping to practice civil law after graduation.

"Your dad not home yet?" asked Isabel as she poured herself a glass of red wine and sat down at the table.

"No, but he should be...ah, there's his car now," Michelle answered, ducking to peek out the window toward the street. A minute later, the front door opened again, and Dan Ikeda came in, smiling as he saw his wife and daughter in the kitchen.

"There they are, my two favourite women in the world," he said genially, reaching for a wineglass in the cupboard and asking Michelle with a raised eyebrow if she'd like one. At her nod, he took two and poured for them both. Isabel felt a twitch of shame that she hadn't thought to offer Michelle a glass when she'd poured her own. But that was Dan, always so courteous, so kind, so attuned to others' needs. *Heaven knows, it's probably the only way he can stand living with me!* Isabel thought guiltily. Dan was the most patient, the kindest, the least argumentative person she'd ever known. From the moment he'd sat down beside her on a bus over twenty years ago, he'd responded to her often-irritable personality with calm good humour. His Tizzy Izzie, he called her affectionately as he waited out the storms. As Dan and Michelle chatted, Isabel reminisced about meeting her husband, and the revelations that had emerged as a result...

On the day they met, Isabel was on her way to her classes at Robertson College, a private vocational institute, where she was training to be a secretary. Dan, who had studied mechanical engineering at the University of Manitoba, was on his way to the local camera store where he repaired the complicated single-lens reflex cameras recently launched by Canon, a Japanese company. When she took Dan to meet her parents for the first time, Isabel noticed a small reaction to the name of the cameras he worked on, quickly covered over. After Dan went home, she asked her mother what that had been about.

"Oh," Asami said, waving her hand as if to dismiss the question. "It's nothing. Just—your father's elder brother worked for Precision Optical Instruments, the company that made the Kwanon camera, as it was called then, before the war. Maybe he still does, I don't know."

"Why don't we ever see or talk to the family in Japan?" Isabel asked, wondering this for the first time. Her mother turned her face away.

"We had a—a falling out, I guess you would say—before the war."

"Over what?" Asami was silent for long moments. Just when her daughter thought she wasn't going to answer at all, Asami turned back and spoke so quietly that Isabel barely heard her.

"Your brother, Kenji."

Isabel sat down hard. Her brother! Yes, she'd had a brother! Long forgotten memories flooded in, and she stared back at her mother, wide-eyed.

"Kenji! He brought me that geisha doll from Japan, right?" Asami nodded with a sad smile. "I loved that doll! Do we still have it somewhere? And where is Kenji? What happened to him. Why don't we ever talk about him?"

Over the following hour, Isabel learned the hidden history of her family, things she had completely forgotten. At the end of it, she made a vow to her mother.

"I'll find him, or at least what happened to him. There must be some record..." Asami waved her hands again, shaking her head.

"No, no, we have tried, Isabel, don't you think we have tried? There is nothing, no record of him after we left Powell River that day. It is better if we don't stir it all up again. It is too painful. Even if he lives, perhaps he does not want to be found. I have reconciled myself to his loss—it is almost twenty years now—please leave it alone."

Of course, Isabel could not leave it alone. She poked and prodded and researched, wrote letters and made telephone calls. She finally found a record of Kenji in the Powell River jail for a single night in 1944, and a former guard there suggested that perhaps her brother had been recruited into the military as some Japanese Canadians had been at the end of the war. So she scoured the military records, spending hours peering at faded old microfiche copies in the Winnipeg library, but no Kenichi Tasaka was listed in any unit of the Canadian Armed Forces for that time period. In the end, frustrated, she too gave up, concluding that her brother must have died in some jail. It wasn't an encouraging or comforting conclusion, and so she never spoke about Kenji to her mother or father again. Over time, his memory faded from her mind as well, and she never thought to tell her own daughter anything about her lost uncle as she grew up.

But all that had happened more than two decades ago and half an hour later, over the spaghetti and salad, talking about her lost brother was the last thing on her mind despite her earlier reminiscences. Instead, she was full of opinions and ideas about the need to petition the Canadian government for redress for the wrongs of the war.

"What would you think would be appropriate redress?" her daughter asked, serving herself more salad. Isabel shrugged.

"I don't know, some monetary payment, I guess. Some say that we should ask for a lump sum to be used for programs for Nikkei across Canada, but I agree with those who think we should press for individual payments."

"Would Grandma Asami get something, then, Mom, and you, too?"

"Yes, as would you and your parents, Dan." Her husband nodded thoughtfully.

"That would be helpful to my folks, I'm sure. But I wouldn't get your hopes up too high, Isabel. It will take a lot to persuade Prime Minister Trudeau, I think."

"Then we shall have to come up with a lot!" replied Isabel, topping up her wine glass.

A year later, Isabel sat on the couch between Dan and Michelle, watching an episode of CBC's *The Journal* titled *A Call for Justice*. The program began with announcer Russ Froese explaining that the footage and interviews had been created at a recent 40-year reunion of Nikkei dispersed from the Fraser Valley, revealing the truth about their wartime experiences and setting the stage for a call for redress. The story was supported by wartime photos and footage, including clips from the 1945 film *Of Japanese Descent* that had so thwarted Isabel's ability to defend her high school essay. She snorted when these appeared, but then clapped when they were framed as racist, biased propaganda. There were several interviews with former government employees—former alderman Halford Wilson and former Custodian of Enemy property Glen McPherson. Journalist Barbara Frum interviewed Wilson, quoting some statements that had been commonly believed by whites at the time of the war.

"I'd like to know if you still agree with these statements about the Japanese Canadians in B.C., Mr. Wilson: they undercut white wages; they monopolized farming in the Fraser Valley, forcing white farmers out; they fished without a care for conservation; they broke white fishermen's strikes against canning companies; they practiced unscrupulous business practices, staying open all hours; their homes smelled; and they stuck to themselves."

"I agree with them completely," said Wilson without hesitation or qualification. Isabel shouted in indignation but was hushed by Michelle, who leaned forward to increase the volume on the television set.

Frum next interviewed members of a group she introduced as the 'Sansei Redress Committee,' and again Isabel objected. "It's called the Japanese Canadian Centennial Project Redress Committee," she said, and again was shushed so they could hear Randy Enomoto, one of the committee members.

"A crime has been done," an emotional Enomoto stated to a sympathetic Frum. "There's been a miscarriage of justice. That's a central fact that cannot be lost sight of. The enormity of that just stands there, and it rankles and festers; it's there, and it's becoming more so there in the Canadian consciousness, and it *has* to be dealt with…" He broke off, wiping at his eyes.

Frum's questions clarified that Japanese Americans had already received a redress settlement of $25,000 each. Enomoto pointed out that Japanese Canadians had been held for four years longer than the Americans and had not been allowed to return to the west coast until 1949. He read from an American commission report that stated that *'the promulgation of Executive Order 9066 was not justified by military necessity, and the decisions which followed from it—detention, ending detention, and ending exclusion—were not driven by analysis of military conditions. The broad historical causes which shaped these decisions were race prejudice, war hysteria, and a failure of political leadership*.' Enomoto suggested that the same could be said about the Canadian experience.

The overall tone of the program was clearly supportive of the redress movement, and when it was over and the television dark, Isabel was jubilant.

"I told you the tide was turning!" she crowed triumphantly, raising her glass of wine.

"I hope so," Dan answered after sipping from his own glass. "But there is still a long way to go. I think most Nikkei believe that redress will never come—and some believe that to push for it will undo their efforts over the past forty years to blend in, to rebuild their lives."

Isabel set down her glass and stared at her husband, who was usually so amicable. "Do *you* believe what we're doing is wrong?" she demanded. Dan hesitated, then shook his head.

"No," he said. "It must be done, for the good of the country as well as the Nikkei. But it will not be easy, and it will not be quick, Isabel. It will take patience and perseverance, and just plain guts. Luckily," he said, smiling and raising his glass again, "you have two of those in abundance—not so sure about the patience part!" He laughed and stepped over to hug Isabel's shoulders. "To redress!" he said, and they all drank to that.

1984-1988
Winnipeg, Manitoba
Ottawa, Ontario

Isabel was beside herself with excitement. She vibrated with energy as she helped to unpack boxes of documents in the new office Art Miki had rented as his centre of operations for the National Association of Japanese Canadians (NAJC). She been delighted when Art was elected president of the national body, and even more thrilled when he'd asked her to help staff the new office alongside well-known activists such as Harold Hirose, Henry Kojima, Lucy Yamashita, Fred Kaita, Alan Yoshino, Carol Matsumoto, and Joy Ooto. Although her role was only secretarial, Isabel nevertheless was very pleased to have an insider seat during this important time.

Taking minutes at their inaugural meeting a few hours later, Isabel learned that the divisions among the Nikkei community were even more complex than she'd realized, despite the boost the CBC program had given the movement.

As Dan had warned, some still felt that the whole issue should be dropped. Like Isabel's mother, they had no desire to stir up the old racist attitudes and bring attention to themselves after so many years of effort to integrate into Canadian society. For many, talking about the past brought up feelings of shame, humiliation, and embarrassment. These feelings were especially prevalent amongst the older *nisei*. Others felt that seeking redress was a futile effort. The Nikkei only numbered about 60,000 people and they had very little political influence. It seemed hopeless. Some supported asking for an apology but not financial compensation from the government, feeling that would be enough to satisfy their honour.

Even among those who supported a financial redress effort, opinions were divided as to what form that should take. While the NAJC supported both individual <u>and</u> community compensation, opposing groups wanted only community compensation, feeling that approach had a better chance of success and would also be more equitable to all. Art listened to everyone's ideas and then, in his calm and thoughtful way, suggested that the group conduct a survey of all surviving internees and see how the majority wanted to proceed.

Accordingly, the committee began drafting the survey questions while Isabel started compiling a list of addresses. It was straightforward clerical work, but she felt that she was involved in a critical historical event and went to work with a will.

It took a year to get the survey out and back, but the committee was not idle in the meantime. They drafted a brief titled 'Democracy

Betrayed' and submitted it to the federal government in 1984. In it, they referenced the *Canadian Charter of Rights and Freedoms*, saying, "*As a visible minority that has experienced legalized repression under the War Measures Act, we urge the Government of Canada to take such steps as are necessary to ensure that Canadians are never again subjected to such injustices. In particular, we urge that the fundamental human rights and freedoms set forth in the* Canadian Charter of Rights and Freedoms *be considered sacrosanct, non-negotiable and beyond the reach of any arbitrary legislation such as the War Measures Act.*" Isabel's heart had swelled with pride as she'd typed those words. As she'd said to her mother, this *was* an important thing, a decision that would affect all Canadians for generations to come. It was worth all the effort and slog-or at least she hoped it would be eventually.

As a result of the brief, Prime Minister Pierre Trudeau offered to make a public apology and establish a community fund. Isabel thought that the NAJC would accept the offer. Art and his closest advisors discussed it for days. In the end, they rejected it, opting to hold out for more. On Trudeau's last day in office as PM, in June 1984, Leader of the Opposition Brian Mulroney chided him for his unwillingness to properly compensate Japanese Canadian internees. It was a statement that would come back to haunt Mulroney soon enough, when he and his Conservatives swept to a majority government—the biggest majority in Canadian history--in September of that year. Now it was up to his government to make good on his promises.

Such public debate caused the issue to gain traction in communities across Canada. Small groups of Nikkei began to gather for information sharing. Stories from *issei* and *nisei* began to be revealed and collected.

Another important book was published in 1985. *This is My Own: Letters to Wes and other Writings on Japanese Canadians, 1941 – 1948*, based on a series of letters between Muriel Kitagawa and her brother Wes Fujiwara during the war years, cast more light on the events of the time. The Nikkei experience was coming out of the shadows, and even some *hakujin* began to feel troubled by Canada's mistreatment of its own citizens.

By the end of 1985, the survey count was in, and it was clear that despite some continued rumblings of disagreement, there was a strong majority of internees in favour of moving ahead with a request for individual redress for each Japanese Canadian interned during the war.

So now they had a clear mandate. But how to go about achieving it? Isabel found herself developing a great admiration for the political savvy and tenacity of Art Miki and his committee members. They made redress a national issue by developing close relationships with the media. They contacted supportive politicians, especially within the opposition parties, and kept them updated on what was happening. Every time the NAJC staged a national meeting to discuss redress, Art would direct Isabel to arrange a press conference and ensure good media coverage. Art himself appeared on many talk shows in different provinces and once on the CBC program *Front Page Challenge,* which gave the issue national exposure.

Of course, not everyone was supportive of their efforts. Their campaign for redress meant that they were asking for monetary compensation, which, inevitably, some Canadians opposed. However, Art cleverly placed the emphasis on a negotiated settlement. He rarely talked about the sums involved but focused more on the process. This approach did seem to temper some of the reactions from the public, but Isabel still opened a lot of angry mail, especially from *hakujin* veterans' groups.

It took patience, fortitude, and determination to persist in their efforts as the years ground on and the players changed. They dealt with a carousel of federal Ministers: David Collenette, Jack Murta, Otto Jelinek, and David Crombie. Again and again, these officials offered lump sums to the Nikkei community. Again and again, Art had to insist on fair and equal compensation for each individual internee, as mandated by the survey of his constituents. "But how much would be fair?" asked the government. Who had a definitive calculation of how much the Japanese Canadians had lost? No one, it seemed.

So the NAJC undertook to develop just such a calculation, at their own expense. In 1986, they engaged the well-respected accounting firm Price-Waterhouse to study the records and recommend a fair recompense. The resulting report, which calculated that approximately 443 million dollars' worth of goods and property had been seized from the internees, was rejected by Minister Crombie on behalf of the government. He made what he said was their final offer, again a community lump sum.

Isabel spent a dejected Christmas, depressed about their lack of progress, almost ready to give up the effort. She expected Art to accept the offer, unsatisfactory as it was. She was surprised when she learned that the committee had opted to reject the government's offer yet again.

Over the next two years, the NAJC redoubled their efforts to make redress a human rights issue. Isabel was kept busy writing letters, reaching out to major unions, churches, mayors, Members of Parliament, and academics across Canada. As a result, they gathered over four thousand signatures on a petition demanding individual redress. Well-known Nikkei published opinion pieces in newspapers across Canada.

In the *Winnipeg Free Press*, Frank Moritsugu wrote a paragraph that, for Isabel, summarized her own feelings well: "*A sense of incompleteness gnaws at me. I need to feel right about my country. I need this to happen while I am still around to appreciate it. What would finally ease the bitter memories and deep hurts that simmer inside me is for the government in Ottawa to take the high road in producing a Redress settlement. It should not only satisfy Japanese Canadians but also assure all Canadians that, despite temporary aberrations, our country guarantees that the rights and privileges of citizenship cannot be taken away, for whatever reason.*" *Exactly*, thought Isabel, and cut out the article for her files.

On a beautiful April day in 1988, Isabel marched amid five hundred other Nikkei up the steps of Parliament Hill in Ottawa. Her daughter Michelle, now a full-fledged lawyer, strode beside her. They carried signs that advertised their position: 'Redress in our time!' 'Erase the shame!' 'Justice Now!' One woman's sign read 'I was labeled an Enemy Alien at six months of age!' Isabel's own sign displayed the title of Ken Adachi's seminal 1976 history of Japanese Canadians, *The Enemy that Never Was*, a work that could be said to have been the first step in the re-emergence of the Nikkei in Canada's consciousness. Michelle's said simply 'Justice for my grandparents.' Spirits were high, and a sense of determination united them. It was time to press harder for a resolution to this issue that had dragged on for years.

Again, they were offered a lump sum community payment, and yet again Art Miki stood his ground. They would not come to the negotiating table at all, he said, unless individual payments were on offer. They waited. Many prominent Canadians came and spoke on their behalf and Isabel was encouraged to see that not all of them were Nikkei.

The day wore on, and the group began to lose its energy as a cool wind came up and the sun began to decline behind the towering buildings. Suddenly, however, a new person appeared: the new Minister of State for Multiculturalism, Gerry Weiner, came to the microphone and invited the negotiating team to the table. Individual redress, he said, would be discussed. Against a background of wild cheers, Art Miki agreed that they would begin talks the following morning.

Of course, it didn't happen immediately. Negotiations continued for weeks—months—the crowds returned home, waiting, watching, hoping for a settlement.

1988
Vancouver, British Columbia

Isabel, Dan, and Michelle stood close beside Asami in the warmth of the early August sunshine in Vancouver's Stanley Park, in a ring of spectators encircling the Japanese Canadian War Memorial. In the crowd were many elderly Nikkei in wheelchairs or leaning heavily on canes. Close by the tall column sat the guest of honour, Sergeant Masumi Mitsui, one of the last surviving World War I veterans.

While she waited for the ceremony to begin, Michelle opened the pamphlet she'd been handed and read the history of the monument. It had been funded by the Nikkei community and dedicated on April 9, 1920, the third anniversary of the opening day of the Battle of Vimy Ridge. The Canadian Japanese Association, who also funded the training of 227 soldiers in Vancouver from January to May 1916, erected the memorial in memory of the victory at Vimy Ridge, the loss of 54 men and the 168 surviving Japanese Canadian Veterans who returned to Canada. The column, placed on gravel in what was then an open field, had been designed by James Anderson Benzie in 1919. On top of the column, she read, a Shinto pagoda form contains a Japanese lantern symbolizing the unification between Canada and Japan. The 12 "polygons" of the base suggest radiating chrysanthemum petals, emblematic of the Japanese imperial family, but also a symbol of lamentation or grief.

On the next page Michelle read about the many cherry trees encircling the column and she lifted her gaze to look up at their encompassing branches. She was astonished at the deep symbolism represented by these beautiful trees.

After the memorial was dedicated, cherry trees were planted, including the shirofugen *in 1920,* ojochin *in 1925, and* shirotae *in 1932. The cherry trees serve many symbolic interpretations that relate to the fallen soldiers. In 1958, as a symbol of the friendship between Canada and Japan, 300 additional cherry trees were donated by the Japanese consul Muneo Tanabe. In 1977, two of the last surviving Japanese Canadian Veterans of the First World War planted* akebono *cherry trees at the memorial.*

In addition to differences of colour, the cherries selected for the memorial display a variety of tree shapes and follow a different blooming sequence. The landscape incorporates symbols of regeneration for traumatized humanity, reinforcing the remembrance of and reverence for the war dead. This landscape speaks eloquently to the devotion of Japanese Canadians to the memory of the brave soldiers who fought and died on behalf of their compatriots, and the obligation of survivors to honour their service and sacrifice through these moving symbols of death and restored life.

Realizing that the ceremony was about to begin, Michelle closed the pamphlet and tucked it into her purse. It would make a good souvenir of this happy occasion. Supported by his family, Sergeant Mitsui raised his head and spoke in his thin old voice.

"In 1942, this flame was extinguished when Canada labeled Japanese Canadians as 'enemy aliens.' Today, so many years later, Canada has recognized its error and agreed that this eternal flame, an emblem of our love for our country, our willingness to fight and die for her if need be, should be rekindled. Let us hope that it is never extinguished again."

At his hand signal, the flame at the apex of the column sprang into life, waving gently in the summer breeze. Quiet applause echoed through the cherry grove, and not a few of the elderly folks wiped tears from wrinkled cheeks, Asami included.

"Oh, Hoshi and Jiro would have been so pleased to see this," she whispered as they stood looking up at the flame. "They were heartbroken when it was put out. It seemed to them that their sacrifice, their willingness to serve Canada, had been rejected, forgotten. I am so glad to see it burning again." She raised a trembling hand to her lips, kissed her fingers, and gestured to the sky, as if to send a blessing to her long-dead husband and brother.

It was another month before Prime Minister Mulroney signed the final redress settlement. On September 22, he formally apologized in the House of Commons to all Japanese Canadians. In addition to the apology, the government also offered $21,000 to each individual directly affected by the internment, the creation of a community fund, pardons for those who had been wrongfully imprisoned during the war, and Canadian citizenship for Japanese Canadians and their descendants who had been wrongfully deported to Japan at the war's end. The agreement also promised $24 million towards the creation of the Canadian Race Relations Foundation, whose purpose would be to work for the elimination of all forms of racial discrimination in Canada.

Back in Winnipeg, Isabel sat at her desk in the NAJC office, staring at the stacks of documents surrounding her. There was much to do—programs to be set up, people to help. But after so many years, so much effort, they had won! The critical work was done. She nodded to herself with satisfaction. *See, sometimes it pays off to be cranky and stubborn*, she thought to herself with a small smile. Then she pulled the cover off her typewriter and set to work.

PART IV

2000
Winnipeg, Manitoba

"All right, Mom, time to explain. Who the heck is Uncle Kenji and why don't I know anything about him? And don't try to tell me that Grandma Asami was hallucinating!"

They were seated at Michelle's small but comfortable kitchen table, where the winter sunshine poured in over the bright orange tablecloth. Michelle had practiced civil law in a not-for-profit organization for six years after articling, but the grind of struggling for fairness and equity for an endless roster of underprivileged clients had taken its toll on her health, both physical and mental. The unending hours of research, writing briefs, arguing for social justice with little success--all had prevented her from amassing the personal wealth most people assumed that lawyers had, and she had found little time for socializing despite her mother's constant nagging about her single status at age forty-one. Recently she'd accepted a teaching position at the University of Manitoba, and she hoped this would prove less strenuous and more rewarding. Time would tell. In the meantime, this modest apartment was all she had to call her own.

Isabel set down her coffee cup, her eyes wary. She knew that she should have told Michelle this piece of family history long ago, and she geared herself up to defend her position. It wasn't an easy case to make, considering that she herself had harangued her mother about sweeping uncomfortable war stories under the rug. And she didn't want to admit that the main reason was simple forgetfulness. She just hadn't thought about her lost brother for many years. That didn't seem very loyal or caring, but it was the truth.

"Well, you have to remember that I was a very young child when he disappeared," she began, "and my parents never talked about him after he ran off just as we were boarding the steamer to Hastings Park."

"But that's the part I don't understand," interrupted Michelle. "*Why* didn't anyone talk about him? You've told me stories of the internment, but you never mentioned a brother."

"At first it was because we didn't want to alert the authorities about him, because he'd avoided the evacuation. We didn't want to put the police on his trail. I remember being told not to mention him and that went on for so long that I forgot that I'd ever had a brother. He was raised mostly in Japan, you see, and had only returned to Canada a short while before war broke out."

"Wait, what? Why would one child be raised in Japan and the other in Canada?" Michelle asked, confused. Isabel did her best to explain the family situation, but she didn't really know all that much either.

"It was something about needing an heir to inherit family property, I think. And it wasn't that uncommon back then, to send Nikkei children back to Japan to be educated. But I don't really know. I was only an infant when he went to Japan and then, years later, he suddenly returned home. I barely knew him."

"Okay, but why didn't Grandma and Grandpa go looking for him after the war ended?"

"I'm not really sure. I guess, as the years went on and he didn't turn up, well, maybe it was less painful for my mother and father not to dwell on his absence. They probably assumed he was dead. I think, too, they might have been a little bit ashamed that Kenji had broken the law, disobeyed the RCMP sent to herd us to internment." Isabel paused thoughtfully. "And I don't know, maybe they were embarrassed that they hadn't prevented him from escaping—or maybe I'm wrong, maybe they were proud that he did get away but didn't want to say so in public." She shrugged. "I never thought to ask them why they kept silent and in recent years, well—to be honest, Michelle, I haven't thought about him much. I've had a lot of other things to think about, what with my association work and all." She picked up her cup and sipped again to cover her discomfort over the admission. Then she looked keenly at her daughter, turning the conversation away from her lapse. "And I don't want you pestering your grandmother about it either, you hear? She seems to have forgotten all about him again and that's for the best. There's no point in upsetting her when there's nothing to be done."

"Yes, I'd figured that out all by myself, Mom," said Michelle with gentle sarcasm. "But you said to Grandma that you had tried to find out what had happened to him. When was this, and where did you look?"

For the next half hour, Michelle grilled Isabel on every source of information she'd tried. Eventually, to her mother's gratification, Michelle had to admit that she couldn't think of any other avenues Isabel might have investigated.

"But," she concluded, rising to rinse out their coffee cups, "these days the databases are all online and connected. Maybe I'd have better luck."

Her mother stood up and put on her stylish coat, then turned to peer into the little mirror by Michelle's door, smoothing on a layer of bright red lipstick. Michelle had to smile. Isabel was sixty-six, but she always looked so put together, so elegant. *More than I ever do,* Michelle thought wryly, thinking that maybe she'd have a bit more time to think about her appearance now that she'd left her law practice.

"If you want to, go ahead," Isabel said, giving Michelle a brief hug. "But if not, don't worry about it. If Kenji had wanted to find us, I'm sure he would have. Maybe we just have to let him go."

Michelle didn't argue, but long after the sound of Isabel's high heeled boots had faded down the hallway beyond her door, she found herself still thinking about her uncle. What *had* happened to him? Had he tried to find them? Perhaps this summer when she had some time off from teaching— holidays, what a novel concept!—she'd do a little digging of her own.

2000
Vancouver, British Columbia

Juggling her filled breakfast plate, a napkin rolled around a set of cutlery, a cup of coffee, and her conference bag, Michelle made her way from the buffet to the closest vacant seat at one of the small tables set up in the lobby of the massive library at the University of British Columbia, where the glass ceiling soared four stories overhead. As she tried to slip the handle of the bag over the back of the chair, she tipped the coffee cup in her other hand too far. A large male hand shot out and grabbed the cup, righting it before it could spill. Michelle gasped slightly and looked up to meet a pair of tilted dark eyes and a set of very white teeth peeking out in a grin from a curly-bearded face set atop a pair of shoulders that could pass for a wrestler's.

"Oh, thanks!" she said, managing to seat herself with no further mishap. "Trying to carry too many things at once..."

"No problem," her rescuer said, setting her coffee within her reach. "They probably should have provided trays." He shrugged a little. "Guess they can't think of everything."

It was late August, the first morning of a conference on teaching in higher education, and Michelle was really looking forward to the sessions she'd selected. She had discovered, over her first term of teaching, that the profession was a lot harder than it seemed. She'd known the legal content, of course, and had spent a lot of time preparing her lectures. But what she hadn't even thought about was how to plan her lessons to be interactive, engaging, how to ensure that her students actually *learned* what she was presenting, instead of just sitting there passively. It was unexpected—it seemed a lot of things had changed since her own university days. Now, she was expected to know about educational theory, conduct research on teaching and learning, and keep an active course website as well—all this on top of having her content ready to deliver, grading tests and papers, and serving on campus committees. It was all a lot more work than she'd expected—nearly as much as being a practicing lawyer—but she had also discovered that she loved it. She was very keen to learn more teaching techniques and evaluation strategies from the conference and was also pleased to be back in Vancouver. She'd spent only a little time here when the Veterans' Memorial flame had been re-lit back in '88 and hadn't had a chance to visit since.

After unrolling her knife and fork from the napkin, she put out her hand.

"I'm Michelle Ikeda. I teach law at U. Manitoba in Winnipeg."

"Hiro Mackenzie," said the genial fellow, shaking Michelle's small hand firmly with his big one. "That's H-i-r-o, not H-e-r-o, but I suspect you knew that already." Michelle smiled, forking up some scrambled eggs.

"Well, I might be more likely than most to get it right. I bet you have to explain it a lot, though." Hiro nodded with a dramatic sigh and shrugged his burly shoulders again.

"Yup. Not many recognize me as a hero on first meeting." He grinned again. "Mostly I go by Mac, to tell you the truth. Kinda avoids the whole confusion. But I figured you might get it. You're *sansei*—third generation, am I right?"

Michelle nodded, her mouth full. After she'd swallowed, she gestured at his full beard, highly unusual on a person of Japanese descent.

"Between that and the surname, I'm thinking there's something other than Nikkei in your background."

"My father, James Alistair Mackenzie, proud Scottish Canadian," he replied. "I'm just happy I avoided the red hair. The beard's confusing enough with these Asian eyes—but can you imagine them with red hair and beard?"

Michelle put her head on the side, considering Mac's long dark hair, which he wore pulled off his face in a knot at the back of his head. Inwardly she thought that his unusual combination of racial features was not only striking but very attractive. *Other than the beard,* she thought, *he could pass for an ancient samurai with his hair and build.* "Well, it would certainly be memorable!" she said, eyes twinkling. "But what and where do you teach, Mac?"

"Computer Science, right here at UBC. It's a growing field."

"I can only imagine," said Michelle and asked a few questions about his work as she finished her breakfast. The conversation turned to teaching and they found that they had both signed up for the same session after the opening plenary. It was natural for them to gather their things and make their way to the auditorium together, chatting easily as they walked.

Although she met and conversed with dozens of other fascinating educators over the course of the conference, Michelle found herself glad whenever her path crossed with Mac's, and he seemed equally pleased to see her, ensuring that they sat at the same table or walked together between sessions. When they had a few hours free between the afternoon sessions of the second day and the evening banquet, he sought her out with a suggestion.

"Have you ever been to the Nitobe Memorial Garden here on campus?" he asked. She shook her head. "It's within walking distance. Would you like to see it? It's quite lovely."

She readily agreed and they made their way through the slanting late afternoon sunlight to the modest entrance to the gardens. Michelle paused to read the information plaque and learned that the original garden had been created in 1933 to commemorate the work of Dr. Inazō Nitobe, a very accomplished gentleman who dedicated his life to being a 'bridge across the Pacific' to strengthen ties and understanding between the Eastern and Western worlds. After the Second World War, with anti-Japanese sentiments tainting the attitudes toward Japanese Canadians, the garden had fallen into neglect.

In the late 1950s, under then-UB.C.-president Norman Mackenzie ("No relation, I assure you," said Mac as he watched Michelle read this section of the description), a decision was made to expand and restore the gardens with the cooperation of Japan. Kannosuke Mori, a renowned landscape architect from Chiba University, was selected by the Government of Japan to design the garden. Mori arrived in 1959 and spent 14 months designing and building the garden with the help of local Japanese Canadian gardeners. Boulders, rocks, and stones from around the province and a combination of native plants and plants shipped from Japan were carefully chosen for the garden. Not only did Mori place each rock and plant individually, but he taught the workers proper maintenance and construction techniques for the future preservation and maintenance of the garden.

Everything was done to express Dr. Nitobe's valuing of *bushido* ('the way of the warrior'), the ethical code that governed the samurai warrior class before its demise and which continues to influence the modern Japanese psyche. Nitobe wrote that to live by the code of *bushido* was to embody the traits Japanese people held in highest regard: courage, rectitude, benevolence, politeness, sincerity, honour, loyalty, and self-control.

Michelle sighed a little, thinking of the frustrations of her work in social justice. "Wouldn't it be wonderful if everyone really lived up to those qualities?" she said sadly.

"It sure would," answered Mac quietly. "That's why I like to come here as often as I can. It helps me to re-focus on expressing those qualities in my life." He gestured her through the gates and into the tranquil green space.

The garden wasn't large, and it was extremely simple, not much more than a path that circled a still body of water, winding through mossy expanses under whispering trees, with the occasional Japanese stone lantern placed as a quiet accent to the natural scene. Eventually they came upon a traditionally styled tea house and sat down inside, enjoying the artful views framed by its open windows.

After a few moments of silent contemplation, Michelle sighed in a different way than she had at the gate and leaned back, savouring the tranquility of the space. She realized that her shoulders were more relaxed than they had been for days—perhaps weeks. She smiled over at Mac, whose large frame was also completely relaxed on the seat opposite.

"It's beautiful. Thank you so much for bringing me here."

His white teeth flashed in the dim interior of the tea house. "My pleasure," he said. "Michelle, I wanted to ask--are you returning to Winnipeg right after the conference?"

"I had planned to, but there's no great hurry. My classes don't start for two weeks yet. Why?"

"There's another place I think you might like to see. It's the new Nikkei National Museum and Cultural Centre out in Burnaby, just south of Vancouver. It's not actually scheduled to open until the third week of September but, well, my mother's on the staff so I could get you in to see it if you're interested."

"Sounds very interesting." She paused, a new thought occurring to her. "Tell me, do they have records of Nikkei from the war years?"

"I think maybe they do; I know one of the major permanent exhibits will be a history of the internment. Why do you ask?"

"I'm looking for someone—my uncle—who disappeared during the war years..." She went on to explain the circumstances and the research her own mother had done back in the sixties. Mac listened attentively, not interrupting with questions. When she stopped, gesturing palm up with her hands to indicate that she wasn't sure how to proceed, he bent forward to take her hands in his.

"I think my mom would be a great resource for you, Michelle, and she'd love to meet you. She knows a lot about this stuff and is more than keen to talk about it. I'd love it if you stayed for a few days, went with me out to the Centre. Heck, I'll even take you out to the best Japanese restaurant in Vancouver for dinner if you'll stay."

Michelle hesitated. She was certainly enjoying Mac's company and there really wasn't any compelling reason for her to rush home. *Oh heck, why not?* she thought to herself. *Take a chance for once in your life, Ikeda. Who knows what might come of it? Besides,* she reasoned, *it's research—maybe I* will *figure out what happened to Uncle Kenji.*

Michelle stood at the entrance to her hotel, waiting for Mac to pick her up for the drive to the Nikkei Centre. She felt warm in the late August heat and wondered again why Mac had insisted that she wear jeans, a jacket, and closed-toe shoes for the trip to Burnaby. *Maybe the Centre is still a construction zone, and you have to wear these to tour it?* she thought. Mac had refused to answer any questions, just asking her to comply and then walking off with a teasing smile. Oh well, she'd find out soon enough.

In the distance she heard the deep rumbling roar of a motorcycle coming along the street. She ignored it, having little interest in bikes, but it came closer and closer and then the Harley turned into the hotel's curved entrance drive and pulled up right in front of Michelle. She took an involuntary step back, wondering if she should wait inside the lobby. She really didn't know anything about Harley bikers other than what the media said, but because of that coverage she did feel a trifle nervous about coming face to face with one.

The large man, his features completely obscured by his face shield, swung a long leg over the low-slung seat of the bike and reached up to undo the helmet's strap, facing her directly. As he lifted it off, Michelle gave a startled laugh. It was Mac! Now the requirement for long sleeves and pants and closed shoes became clear. Her heart sped up a little: she'd never ridden on a motorcycle!

"Good morning!" Mac called out, laughing at her expression. "Ready for a ride?"

"Um, no!" she said, shaking her head but laughing as well. His good humour was infectious. "But I guess I'll have to put my life in your hands!"

He unstrapped a second helmet from the back of the bike and came toward her with it in his hands. For a moment he looked at her, his expression becoming serious. "Are you really uncomfortable with the idea? I can go back and get my car if you really don't want to do this."

Michelle hesitated, but then her spirit of adventure kicked in. She smiled and reached for the helmet.

"There's a first time for everything!" she said, pulling the heavy covering over her head. Mac helped her to tighten all the straps, carefully checking the fit. When he was satisfied, he gestured for her to zip up her jacket to her throat.

"I know you feel warm now, but once we're moving the wind can feel quite cool. Plus, it's better protection against stray bugs that accidentally bash into you. It's amazing how much force can be expended by a bee at 100k!"

Once she was ready, Mac put his own helmet back on, remounted the bike and directed her to climb aboard behind him, showing her where to place her feet on the foot pegs. He reached back to pull her arms around his ample waist, crossing her hands in front with a gentle pat as if to say, 'stay,' then started the bike up with its deep-throated roar.

"Just relax your body and move with the bike, okay? Don't try to lean in any particular way or sit rigid. Just go with it," he called back to her. "I promise I won't let you fall!"

Michelle's heart was still racing, but the high back of the seat felt solid behind her, and Mac's big form protected her in front. She felt surprisingly secure as he wheeled the bike out to the street and turned out onto the road.

Within twenty minutes they were out of the city and making good speed on the highway southeast toward the Fraser Valley. Flat fields of late berries, cut hay, and ripening pumpkins unrolled on either side as Michelle turned her head to the left and right. Reading the road signs, she suddenly found herself with a lump in her throat. This was her family's land! Somewhere out here was the strawberry farm where her great grandfather Harry and his wife Sara had made their living after they moved to the mainland from Galiano Island, where Grandma Asami and her foster brother Jiro had grown up, where Grandma had met her husband, Grandpa Hoshi. She was surprised at how emotional she was to see these fields, criss-crossed by dikes and canals built to control the flow of the tributaries of the great Fraser River. A ring of craggy mountains surrounded the flat plains. Mac reached back and tapped her thigh, pointing to draw her attention to the majestic bulk of snowy Mount Baker, hundreds of kilometers away to the south in the state of Washington, but as clear as if she could reach out and touch it.

To her surprise, Mac took an exit off the highway and drove into a roadside coffee shop, parking and pulling off his helmet. He helped her off the bike and then got off himself.

"I confess that I've taken you quite a bit further than we needed to go," he said with a smile. "Burnaby's back closer to Vancouver, but I couldn't resist showing you the valley. Your people came from here before the war, right? I thought maybe you'd like to see it."

"Thank you, it's beautiful and yes, it's wonderful to see where my grandparents farmed. I've never been here before."

"Good. Besides, they make great cappuccinos in here. Ready for one?"

After their coffee stop, Mac wheeled the bike back onto the highway going back in the direction they'd come. Fifteen minutes later, he took them into a suburb in Burnaby, finally parking on the street a little way past the almost-completed Nikkei Centre. Michelle tidied her hair, mussed from the helmet, and took off her jacket. She'd been glad to have it on the ride, but it was nearing midday and getting warm.

They walked a winding pathway through a Japanese style garden where some graceful maples were being planted and checked in with a guard wearing an orange vest near the entrance, giving Mac's mother's name. The guard called in on his radio, and they were then allowed into the spacious lobby of the large but discreet building tucked in between tall apartment buildings in this quiet neighbourhood. Michelle gazed up, admiring the elegance of the two-storey space with its curved walls lined with horizontal strips of caramel-coloured Douglas fir. Several large paintings of the sea were just being installed on the only straight section of wall, which topped a long window framing a green view of the surrounding vegetation. A set of wide shallow steps led up from the lobby and a Nikkei woman in her sixties was descending them, smiling.

"Mac, there you are. I expected you half an hour ago!"

"Oh, we took a little side trip, sorry we're late. Mom, this is Michelle Ikeda, from Winnipeg. Michelle, this is my mother, Susan Mackenzie."

Michelle reached out and shook Mac's mother's small hand. The contrast between this diminutive woman and her towering son was striking; no one would guess they were even related but for their dark Asian eyes. "I'm so grateful that you've allowed us this visit, Mrs. Mackenzie. I'm not sure when I'll be back in this area, and I'm very interested in what you're developing here."

"It's Susan, please—hearing Mrs. Mackenzie always makes me look around for my mother-in-law! I'm very pleased to meet you, Michelle. Mac has told me a little bit about you—your family spent the war at East Lillooet, right? Come on upstairs and I'll show you the exhibit we're installing about all the internment camps."

At the top of the stairs, they paused to read the large information board that gave the overall history of the Nikkei evacuation. Alongside, a clear shadow box frame held samples of Japanese Canadian identity cards that all Nikkei were required to carry after 1941. Michelle felt sad to see this early evidence of differential treatment, but she knew worse was to come. As they walked slowly along the hall, they came to a section titled *The Perseverance of the Issei.* It included a photo of the first Japanese immigrant to Canada, Manzo Nagano, with his family; one of a group of Nikkei men standing by a small fishing boat, proudly showing off several enormous fish; and an exterior view of the Steveston cannery.

"My great grandfather Haruto worked there. Mr. Nagano was his partner in several businesses," said Michelle.

The next section had photos of family groups labouring in the fields. One of them depicted a large field of strawberries. Michelle leaned close to peer at the faces of the farmers, but she couldn't tell if any of them were her family members.

"They could be your family, or neighbours," said Susan when Michelle explained her connection. "We found many old photos stuck away in the backs of drawers or in attics. Most of the people were unidentifiable by that time, but many of the old folks told us stories. I remember one woman telling us that they had to put tarpaper over all the windows of the farmhouse for the blackout, you know? This was at the beginning of the war, when they were still in the Fraser Valley, before they were taken to be interned. She said that one night the police came pounding on the door and accused her father of being a spy. Apparently there was a tiny hole in one of the pieces of tarpaper, and the police saw a light winking out through it as the paper moved in the draft—they were convinced that it was a signal sent in Morse Code to someone out on the river."

"It was a very suspicious time," said Michelle. "I can't imagine living with that kind of fear."

Another panel traced the growth of farming cooperatives in the Fraser Valley, initiated by Yamaga Yasutaro.

"Hey, I remember Grandpa Hoshi talking about him! He was a friend of my great grandparents, I think," said Michelle, getting a sense of just how much had been taken away from the Nikkei community in the valley when war broke out.

Scenes of fishing and farming abruptly gave way to scenes from the war years.

A photo of the women's and children's building at Hastings Park brought tears to Michelle's eyes. Rows of rude bunks draped with a medley of patterned sheets and blankets flanked channels down which had run animal manure in the building's previous incarnation. A quote from internee Mary Kitagawa was featured nearby: "The whole place was impregnated with the smell of ancient manure and maggots…"

"I can't imagine how awful that must have been," said Mac quietly. "How terrified, how furious they must have been, to be treated so awfully just for being of Japanese descent. I don't think I've ever really grasped that before now," he said, his usually genial face solemn and a bit angry. He gazed for a long time at a photograph of men waving good-bye to women and children who hung out of train windows. The anguish on the adults' faces was obvious even though the children looked ready for an adventure.

"You were born in a camp, weren't you, Mom?" he asked. Susan nodded.

"Yes, Tashme, fourteen miles east of Hope. It was the last camp to be built, and the largest. My mother gave birth to me a few months after we arrived there. My father was sent to a road camp in the north, where he died of pneumonia brought on by the harsh conditions."

"Your poor mother," said Michelle sympathetically. "It must have been terrible for her, a new mother, in such a place."

Susan nodded. "But she always said that it was her own mother, who was there with her, who kept her going. My *Obaasan* was a tough old bird," she smiled in reminiscence.

"Oh, it's good that your mother and grandmother were at least in the same camp," said Michelle. "Tashme, that's a strange name. Was it some First Nations word?" To her surprise, Susan laughed.

"Not at all," she said. "It's made up from the first few letters of the names of three commissioners of the B.C. Securities Commission that oversaw the internment: Taylor, Shirras, and Mead. Ta,sh,me, see?"

Moving on, Susan pointed out the enlarged photograph that provided the backdrop to information about the internment camps, depicting rows of small tarpaper shacks on a windswept plain encircled by tall mountains. "That's East Lillooet," she said, "The way your grandparents and mother would have found it when they first moved there, before they made any improvements."

Michelle stood gazing at it, for the first time able to imagine the shock and hardship her elders had had to endure. She knew about the evacuation, of course, but her mother's stories had been mostly about childhood games and experiences and, listening to her, Michelle had not envisioned this bleak, inhospitable, prison-like scene.

She turned to Susan. "I think it's so important, what you're doing here. My generation, and the ones to come after us, we need to see this, to remember, to realize that we must not become complacent. My mother was very active in the redress movement because she felt the Nikkei needed to be compensated for the things they endured. That was important, and I'm very glad it was finally paid out but still, we shouldn't pretend the internment never happened. Or it could all happen again to us or to some other group that are suddenly vilified for no good reason."

Susan nodded soberly. "I agree. When the pressure's on, the veneer of civilization cracks pretty quickly. Unless we keep these memories alive, help Canadians remember what was done here and how wrong it was, it could indeed happen again, all too easily."

They turned to walk back down the hallway, looking at the photos and panels on the opposite side. One big image brought a smile to Michelle's face, and she chuckled aloud.

"That's the baseball game in Lillooet, where the cobbled-together team of Nikkei beat the RCMP team! Look, there's Kaye Kaminishi, the Asahi who made it all happen. My Mom loves telling that story."

"Yes, we're hoping to have Mr. Kaminishi at our opening next month, in fact. He's seventy-eight, but still very lively. He's donated his Asahi uniform and glove to us as well. Someday we'll have an exhibit of them, I'm sure," said Susan. "But come back to my office. Mac said you had some questions that perhaps I can help you with."

They followed her down a side hallway and into a small office, where she gestured them to take chairs in front of her desk. It was a tight fit for Mac, but he grinned as he squeezed in.

"I'm just not your typical Nikkei size!" he exclaimed. "You shouldn't have married a Scottish giant, Mom!" His mother rolled her eyes at what was obviously a well-worn joke and turned on her computer.

"The man you are looking for—it's your uncle?"

"Yes, my mother's older brother," said Michelle, and provided Uncle Kenji's full name and birthdate, plus the avenues of research her mother had already undertaken. "We've placed him in the Powell River jail on one night, August 28th, 1944, but nothing after that. We think it's possible that he was recruited into the army to help with post-war investigations, as he was fluent in both English and Japanese—we know a handful of Nikkei were recruited for that purpose around that time. But my mother scoured the Canadian military records and found nothing."

"Oh," said Susan absently, clicking and scrolling as she spoke, her eyes on her screen, "that would be because those recruits weren't in the Canadian army. They were placed in the British army."

"What? Why?" asked Michelle. Could this be the missing bit of information that had stymied their search?

Susan looked at her with a wry expression. "The Canadian government didn't want any more Nikkei to be eligible to vote—remember, the WWI vets had successfully campaigned for the franchise—so they asked the British to take them on. No Canadian military service—no vote, see?"

Michelle huffed out a breath and exchanged a wide-eyed look with Mac. "Well, that changes everything! Do you have access to the British records?" She was crestfallen when Susan shook her head.

"We don't. But don't give up hope. I have some connections who might be able to help…" She turned away from the computer. "It will take time, though, and may not be successful. I have your uncle's information now, anyway, and I'll see what I can do. I'm sorry I couldn't be of more immediate help."

Despite Susan's apology, Michelle felt excited about their progress as she leaned against Mac's broad back on the ride into Vancouver. She was amazed at how relaxed she already felt on the bike; in fact, the warm sun, and the good lunch they'd had in the Japanese restaurant attached to the Nikkei Centre, lulled her so much that she even dozed off for a second, her helmet bumping against the back of Mac's. She jerked at the feel of his hand delivering a sharp slap to her thigh.

"Stay awake back there," he hollered. "Can't have you falling off!"

"Sorry!" she shouted back and sat up straighter. Behind the helmet's visor, she found herself grinning. Who'd have thought she'd be feeling confident enough to fall asleep on the back of a Harley by the end of the day? And at least she now had a lead on her uncle, a previously unexplored possibility. Things were looking up!

2001
Winnipeg, Manitoba
Vancouver, British Columbia

Michelle and Mac exchanged emails and the occasional telephone call over the school year, but the demands of teaching left little time for socializing and no time at all for researching anything to do with her uncle. As the end of the spring term approached, however, Mac invited Michelle to consider coming back out to Vancouver for an extended holiday.

I don't know if my mom has found any solid leads yet, he wrote, *but if she does, I expect you'll still need to dig around in archives and records here in Vancouver. I know, I know, most of them are digitized these days but isn't it more satisfying to be on site? Maybe we could go visit Steveston or take a ferry up to Powell River—actually, I think that involves two ferries, but anyway. I guess what I'm saying, Michelle, is that I'd like to spend some more time with you. The search for your uncle is just a great excuse! What do you think?*

When this email arrived, Michelle had just finished grading a large set of assignments from her first-year students. She was exhausted but satisfied; most of the students seemed to be grasping the critical concepts she'd tried so hard to present to them. Oh, there were still a few who tried to get by on a wing and a prayer, but their lack of success had a lot more to do with their lack of effort than anything Michelle was doing. She was especially pleased with how well some of her in-class activities had gone this term. That conference had really inspired her to try more creative approaches, and her efforts seemed to have paid off. But she was definitely ready for a break.

She sat back in her desk chair, picturing Mac on his motorcycle, imagining the two of them driving off on an adventure together. It made a tempting picture. Michelle had worked so hard to establish herself as a lawyer, and then as a university professor, that she'd neglected her social life almost entirely. She was forty-two. Not precisely an old maid—if that term even had relevance these days—but not exactly a spring chicken either—yech, another outdated saying! She hadn't had a relationship other than the occasional short-lived fling in the past ten years. Did she intend to spend the rest of her days living alone in her little apartment? Well, no…not if she had a better choice.

Impulsively, she fired off a succinct response. *Yes!* she said simply. *When?*

Walking from her gate into Vancouver's YVR airport on a warm day in the last week of July, Michelle appreciated anew its beautifully designed traveler experience. Pulling her small carry-on suitcase behind her, she passed by murals and sculptures incorporating indigenous designs and breathed deeply as she descended on an escalator beside a cascading waterfall where the water flowed over a wall of natural pebbles to foam into a lifelike streambed at the bottom. It was all designed to immerse her in the vibe of Canada's west coast before she even left the airport, and she found her spirits rising as she neared the exit. Even though she loved Manitoba, something about this place was very enticing.

Her excitement increased at the sight of Mac's tall form looming over the small group of people waiting to pick up passengers. Grinning, he slipped through the gate and engulfed her in a bear hug that almost took her breath away. He concluded his greeting by lifting her entirely off her feet and giving her a smacking kiss on her lips, their first. It should have surprised her, but somehow it felt entirely natural. They'd exchanged enough life history over the past months that she felt she really knew him now, and she'd allowed him to get to know her, as well. Without any formal discussion, they'd moved to another level of relationship.

Laughing, Michelle slapped his arm. "Put me down, you great lummox! And yes, I'm happy to see you, too."

"I'm so glad you're here!" Mac replied, undeterred by her response. "Did you bring checked luggage?"

"Certainly not," she said. "What's the point in bringing things I can't pack into the saddlebags on a motorcycle?"

His smile grew wider. "Excellent choice, though I did bring the car just in case," he said, and they moved toward the exit doors. Stepping out, Michelle drew in a deep breath.

"Ah, the scent of the coast," she said appreciatively. "I've missed it. All right, where to first?"

"My parents have invited us to dinner. Hope that's okay?"

"Sure, but can I have a shower and get changed first? I'm a bit travel worn." As she said this, her belly did a little flip-flop. She'd consented to stay with Mac at his condo near the university. This next hour would be a test of just what that agreement meant.

In the end, it was just as natural as that first kiss. Michelle came out of the ensuite bathroom modestly wrapped in a towel, seeking fresh clothes from her little suitcase, and Mac came up behind her. He touched her bare shoulder, turning her to him, and pulled her in for another kiss, this one much longer and with clear intent. Michelle found herself responding eagerly and within minutes they were on the bed, her towel unwrapped. Almost an hour passed before she even thought about fresh clothes again.

It was Mac's turn to draw in a deep breath as they lay entwined on the bed. "I've been wanting to do that for months," he said.

"Me, too," she replied. They smiled at each other and then Mac glanced lazily at his wristwatch.

"Shit!" he said, jumping up. "We're going to be late! I'm always late! I promised my mother I wouldn't be this time."

"Well," Michelle replied, "we're going to be even later now, because I need another quick shower—and so do you, likely. Why don't you call your mom while I get started? If she knows we're delayed, at least she won't be trying to keep dinner hot or anything."

"Good idea," he said but then gave her a look. "But don't get out of the shower until I get there, okay?"

She gave him a mischievous grin. "What, and be even later for dinner? Not on your life—I'm hungry!" She scampered into the bathroom and shut the door, still laughing.

Susan Mackenzie showed no sign of pique at their late arrival. She hugged Michelle warmly and drew her into the elegant living room, where wide windows overlooked English Bay. A man with red hair cut short and a matching beard trimmed close to his jawline was standing by the windows. Despite these differences, he was such a near replica of Mac that Michelle would have known the man for his father even without the context.

"James Mackenzie," he said, striding forward to shake hands but ending by sweeping her into a hug nearly as encompassing as his son's. "Sorry," he said, pulling back. "It's just that Mac's been telling us so much about you that I feel as if I know you already."

She smiled, warmed by their enthusiastic welcome. They made small talk over drinks and an appetizer of smoked salmon and then moved to the dining table for a meal that blended Asian and Western influences in a delicious medley. When dessert—a tart lemon mousse—was served and everyone's wine glasses topped up, Susan's face became serious.

"Michelle," she said softly. "I didn't want to spoil our meal with this, but I don't want to delay any further. I recently found out some information about your uncle."

"Oh," said Michelle. "I get the feeling it's not good news." Susan shook her head.

"It's not, I'm afraid. Your uncle Kenichi was indeed recruited into the British army, and he was sent overseas to Japan and other areas of the South Pacific as a translator and investigator of war crimes, for about four years. But he was invalided out late in '49 and shipped back home to Canada. I'm sorry to say that, according to the military records, he died on the voyage of complications of malaria. He was buried at sea."

"Oh," said Michelle again, and sat back, feeling stunned and disappointed by this news. She struggled to smile at Susan. "Thank you for your efforts, Susan. Of course, it's not the news we'd hoped for, but it does provide some closure."

"I know, and I'm sorry not to be able to bring you happier news. However," she paused, as if uncertain as to whether to continue.

"Yes?" asked Michelle. "It's all right, Susan; whatever it is, I want to know." Mac's mother nodded and set down her glass.

"Yes, of course you do. All right, then. The records show that your uncle was traveling with a wife and child when he died--a Japanese woman he'd married just before they left Japan." She paused again. "And the child, a girl, was adopted by him at the same time, though the child's birth certificate lists the father as 'unknown.'"

Michelle raised her eyebrows and fell silent for a moment, considering. Then she asked the obvious next question. "Do we know where this woman and her child are now?" Susan shook her head.

"I have their names and the fact that they disembarked at Vancouver at the end of the voyage, but that's all. It will take quite a bit of sleuthing to track them down, so many years later—if they are even still in Canada. They may have returned to Japan."

"And what are their names?" Michelle asked.

"Akiko and Kaiya Tasaka," Susan replied.

"I've been thinking," said Michelle, accepting the steaming cup of coffee Mac offered her as she sat with her back against the headboard of the bed in Mac's condo the next morning.

"About me, I hope?" asked Mac with a smile. Michelle rolled her eyes, realizing as she did so that she was already mimicking Susan's affectionate tolerance for Mac's teasing.

"No, why would I be thinking about you? You haven't done anything in the last—oh, say, ten seconds—to make me think about you, have you?" She grinned up at him, then became serious. "Thanks for the coffee, Mac. And everything else. It's wonderful to be here with you."

"The feeling is more than mutual," he replied, setting his own coffee down on the bedside table and climbing back under the sheets to give her a quick kiss. "Ok, teasing aside—what have you been thinking about? How to find Akiko and Kaiya, I would guess."

"Exactly," she replied, blowing across the coffee, and taking a sip. "Oh, this is *good* coffee, Mac! I must say the coffee culture in Winnipeg doesn't compare with the coast's! Anyway—I'm wondering if we could start by reviewing deaths in B.C. and then further across Canada and see if either name turns up. If we don't get any hits on that, maybe we could try searching for Kaiya in school records?"

"Yes, to the death records," Mac replied. "Maybe to the school records. Few of them are digitized and they're not linked to an overall database yet as far as I know. But we have to start somewhere. We might also see if anyone in *Paueru Gai* has any memory of them."

"*Paueru Gai*? What's that?"

"Powell Street," Mac answered. "That's where Akiko and her child would most likely have gone first, where the few remaining Japanese Canadians lived in Vancouver. In the last few decades, people of Japanese descent—Nikkei—have been reclaiming the area where pre-war Japantown stood. It started in 1977, the centennial year of Manzo Nagano's arrival on B.C. shores. The Japanese Canadian Volunteers' Association—*Tonari Gumi*--organized a festival of Japanese culture on the street. It's been staged every year since. In fact," he said, glancing at the calendar hanging by the bed, "I think it might be on this coming weekend. It's usually on the long weekend of August. Let me grab the newspaper and check."

He came back to the bed holding the entertainment section of the *Vancouver Sun* and nodding. "Yes, it is this weekend," he said. "I know it's a long shot, but just maybe we can find someone who might point us in the right direction."

By the time they arrived at the Powell Street Festival the following Saturday, they knew a little more. They'd scoured the B.C. death records and, with mixed emotions, found an Akiko Tasaka listed as having died in Vancouver in 1956 at only twenty-four. The age matched Kenji's wife's birthdate listed on the marriage certificate. Michelle was excited to think they may have located the right Akiko but saddened to think of the woman having died so young. And if this was her aunt, what would have happened to Kaiya when Akiko died? The child would have been only eight when she lost her mother.

They'd also discovered that there was a Japanese Canadian elders' housing unit, *Sakuro-So*, and a drop-in centre at the headquarters of *Tonari Gumi*, which had recently moved from Powell Street to new offices on East Broadway. Both might be good places to investigate. The Volunteers' Association did much more than stage the annual festival, they'd learned. They offered a wide variety of services for the few remaining *issei*, the *nisei*, and every generation of Nikkei since. They also helped new immigrants from Japan to find their way in Canada. Like the Cultural Centre and Museum in Burnaby, their goal was to celebrate and uphold Nikkei history and culture. As well, however, they had the express purpose of helping individual Nikkei to connect to an ongoing supportive community. If anyone could help them find someone who might remember Akiko and Kaiya, they surely would.

Of course, the offices were closed today—everyone was at the street festival. And it wasn't hard to find! The rolling thunder of *taiko* drumming, the characteristic plucking of the *koto* stringed instrument—these were audible from several blocks away as they walked from where they had parked the motorcycle. At the entrance to the venue, a smiling volunteer handed them a printed schedule that listed presentations of music, dance, theatre, and martial arts throughout the day. There was an *ikebana*--flower arranging--exhibition, and a place to sit and fold origami. The aromas of traditional Japanese street food—along with a few distinctly modern additions such as candy floss—assaulted Michelle's nose. The sharp tang of wasabi, the smoky earthiness of soy, the enticing smell of sizzling meat on skewers—it all made her mouth water.

"Oh, my goodness—where to start?" she said, dazzled by the many choices.

"Let's just walk around a bit first," replied Mac, and she was happy to accept his suggestion. They couldn't resist buying some *takoyaki* to share, the crisp golden fried batter enclosing a mix of savoury octopus, ginger, and green onion tamed by a squeeze of mayonnaise and topped by dried seaweed and fish flakes.

"They're so hot!" cried Michelle, blowing madly on her fingers as she tossed the steaming treat from hand to hand. "But so good!"

Mac nodded, his mouth full, then pointed to a vendor selling *kakigori*—shaved ice flavoured with a variety of syrups. He bought them a lemon-flavoured one and they shared spoonsful of the sweet cold concoction to cool their mouths.

A few minutes later they came upon the origami tables. There were a couple of available seats, so they sat down.

"Hi," said a woman staffing the station. Her name tag read Olive Kawamoto. "Would you like to fold a crane or a Daruma?"

"I'm not sure," said Michelle. "I've never tried origami—which one is easier?"

"Oh, the Daruma, maybe, to start," Olive replied. She passed over a square of paper that was red on one side and blue on the other. "Do you know the story of the Daruma?" she asked. Michelle shook her head. "It's based on the legend of a famous Indian monk, Bodhidharma, who brought Buddhism to China over fifteen hundred years ago. Later, of course, Buddhism expanded to Japan as well. One story about Bodhidharma tells how he sat in meditation for almost ten years, his legs wasting away to nothing. So the Daruma doll—and the origami version--resembles a red-robed monk with no legs. They are also always eyeless so that the person making the Daruma can make a wish by folding in one of the eyes. Legend has it that the Daruma, wanting the other eye, will help the wish to come true. In gratitude for the wish being granted, the recipient of the wish must fold in the other eye."

"Sounds good," said Michelle. "I do have a wish in mind, in fact." As Olive began to instruct her in folding the paper, Michelle could see Mac's big hands out of the corner of her eye, deftly folding up a paper crane without instruction. She felt a small pang of envy for his familiarity with this traditional Japanese craft. Her mother had been very keen on activism for Nikkei rights, but she'd never had any interest in teaching Michelle the traditional Japanese arts. Michelle had a vague memory of Grandma Asami showing her how to fold a crane once in her childhood, but it was too long ago to help her now.

She made a few mistakes, but eventually she created an acceptable little folded monk. Her instructor smiled at it.

"You're welcome to keep it, of course, but we are also collecting Darumas for a *kuyō*, a ritual burning next January. It's a Shinto ritual that offers the final transformation towards healing as well as honouring the ancestors of the land. You can make as many as you like if you want to donate some."

"Are you collecting cranes as well?" asked Mac, holding up his perfectly folded little bird.

"Always," replied Olive with a smile at Mac, who promptly started folding another bird.

"I know the cranes symbolize something to do with the nuclear bombings," said Michelle. "But I'm afraid I don't know exactly what."

"They are a symbol of peace," said Olive. "The connection between paper cranes and peace can be traced back to a young Japanese girl named Sadako Sasaki. She was two years old when she was exposed to the bomb, though she had no apparent injuries and grew into a strong and healthy girl. However, nine years later when she was in the sixth grade, in 1954, Sadako was diagnosed with leukemia, quite likely caused by her exposure to radiation, and was admitted to the hospital. Believing an old legend that said that if you folded 1,000 paper cranes the gods would grant you a wish, she started folding them, but after an eight-month struggle with the disease, she passed away. Her death triggered a campaign to build a monument to pray for world peace and the peaceful repose of the many children killed by the atomic bomb. The Children's Peace Monument that stands in Peace Park in Hiroshima was built with funds donated from all over Japan. Later, this story spread to the world, and now about 10 million cranes are offered each year at the monument."

"What a lovely tribute," said Michelle. "Can you teach me how to fold one of those as well, please?"

At that moment an adolescent girl joined them, seating herself beside Olive and looking so much like her that the relationship was obvious. The girl was wearing an elaborate kimono and her hair was styled in a traditional way.

"Oh, hi, sweetie, there you are," said Olive. "How did the dance performance go?"

"Okay," said the girl, reaching out and folding a Daruma with nimble fingers.

Her mother rolled her eyes a little at Michelle. "Typical teenage response!" she said teasingly. "So many details! This is my daughter Amanda." Amanda nodded politely to them but didn't speak, concentrating on her folding. Michelle was astonished at how quickly the girl completed each piece.

A few minutes later, Michelle held up her latest attempt at a Daruma. "Well, he's still a little wonky, but I guess that's as good as he's going to get. Now, how do I go about making this wish?"

"Well, you're supposed to say it aloud, but you don't have to," replied Olive. "And fold down one of his eyes as you say it."

"I don't mind saying it aloud—in fact, I'm hoping that someone here can offer me as much help as my little Daruma here." She folded down the origami's right eye. "I wish that I could find out what has happened to my cousin Kaiya Tasaka, who came to Vancouver from Japan as an infant back in 1949."

"Hmmm, so she'd be, what, early fifties by now?" Michelle nodded. Olive was quiet for a few minutes, then she shook her head. "I'm sorry, I can't think of anyone by that name. Do you know anything else about her?"

"Only a little," said Michelle. "Her mother's name was Akiko, and she came to Canada on the same ship, but we think Akiko died in 1956. She was married to my uncle Kenji, but he died on the way home, sadly. My family is trying to locate Kaiya—we only found out about her existence a few days ago!"

Olive shook her head again. "I'm sorry I can't help but you might try…" She was interrupted by her daughter.

"I might know her," the girl said. Olive turned to her in surprise.

"Really? You know a middle-aged woman named Kaiya Tasaka?"

"Not exactly," Amanda amended. "But I have a girl in my class at dance school whose mother's name is Kaiya, and I'd say she's about the right age. I've seen her a couple of times when she comes to pick up Beth—and Beth's last name is Tasaka."

Olive frowned in puzzlement. "But how do you know her mother's name is Kaiya?" she asked. Amanda widened her eyes at her mother as if questioning her intellect.

"Because it says so on the name tag that she wears on her Save-On Foods uniform!"

"Oh," said Olive, giggling a little. "That makes sense." She turned to Michelle. “This could be the woman you’re looking for, I guess—what a lucky coincidence that Amanda was here when you asked!”

“Or maybe my little monk here had something to do with it,” said Michelle, delighted by the promising lead. She held up the lopsided figure and folded down his other eye. “Thanks, Daruma!” she said, and grinned at Mac.

2001
Vancouver, B.C.

"I don't know, maybe we should have tried to call her ahead of time?" Michelle asked nervously.

"Maybe," agreed Mac, "but we're here now. Let's just give it a try, ok? She may not even be the right woman. Nothing ventured, you know..."

It had taken them a few days to get this far. The street address in front of them, a modest and somewhat ramshackle single-story house on East 13th Street in the Commercial Drive district of the city, matched what Amanda's dance teacher had given them. She'd been a little reluctant to provide the information at first, but eventually she'd become convinced of Michelle's authenticity and genuine interest in finding her cousin. They'd checked the city records just to confirm the information, and that's when they'd discovered that the house was not listed under Tasaka but a different name: Mr. Richard Emerson. But that didn't mean that Kaiya and Beth didn't live there, Michelle had reasoned.

Now that they were here, she was having second thoughts. How would she feel if some stranger knocked at her door and announced that she was her cousin? She hoped that she would be willing to listen, at least. Taking a deep breath, she managed a weak smile at Mac and made her way up the uneven path through the overgrown grass to the front door. There was no doorbell or knocker, so she rapped sharply on the door itself.

For a long time, there was no answer, but eventually they could hear footsteps approaching and the door cracked open a little. A very pretty adolescent girl peered out, her iPod in her hand and an earphone plugged into one ear. She didn't offer any greeting, just stared at Michelle. When her eyes flickered over to Mac, she pulled back and almost shut the door.

"Wait," said Michelle quickly. "Are you Beth Tasaka?" The girl nodded once, still saying nothing. "Ok, good. Your friend Amanda from dance class gave me your name—I'm Michelle Ikeda and this is my friend Mac--I mean Hiro Mackenzie." She realized that she was babbling a little in her nervousness. "Um, is your mom home? I'd like to speak to her. I think we might be cousins."

The girl finally spoke. "She's home but she's sick. She can't come out to talk." Despite the girl's words, Michelle heard another voice calling from inside the house, asking who was there. Looking a bit irritated, Beth called back over her shoulder. "It's a lady saying she might be your cousin."

A moment later a Nikkei woman came slowly up behind Beth, a

faded housecoat clutched around her thin body. Her long dark hair was carelessly pulled into a knot behind her head, and her eyes were wary. There was a dark bruise on her left cheekbone.

"Who are you?" she asked, and Michelle repeated her own and Mac's names.

"Are you Kaiya Tasaka?" she asked, and the woman nodded slowly.

"Yes," she said. "But how do you know my name?" Michele explained their research, ending with a description of their encounter with Amanda and her mother at the festival. "So, if I'm right, your mother Akiko was married to my uncle Kenji, and we're cousins."

The woman chewed on her lip and glanced quickly behind herself into the house. Her expression was conflicted, anxious.

"Maybe," she said. "Um, I can't invite you in right now, but maybe we could meet somewhere later—maybe in a few days?"

"Of course," said Michelle and pulled out one of her business cards from U. Manitoba. "Here's the number where I can be reached..." Grabbing a pen from her purse, she wrote Mac's phone number on the back of the card.

Kaiya took the card and was reading it when a car pulled into the driveway. At the sight, she flinched and stepped backward, slipping the card quickly into the pocket of her housecoat. Young Beth, who had been crowded in beside her mother following the conversation curiously, disappeared back into the house. A white man in late middle age slammed the car door as he exited and strode up to the stoop where they stood.

"Whatever you're selling, we don't want any," he said loudly as he approached. "And if you're those goddamn Jehovah's Witnesses, you had better get off my property before I call the cops."

"Hang on," said Mac, holding out his big hands placatingly. "It's nothing like that..." but the man wasn't listening.

"This is my house, whatever she's told you," he said threateningly, "and in my house, it's my rules. So leave now." He stepped rudely in front of them and shoved Kaiya aside roughly as he entered the house.

"I'm so sorry," Kaiya whispered, but she closed the door in their faces.

Back in Mac's condo, they sat glumly at the kitchen table, nursing cups of green tea. Mac had chosen the tea over coffee, feeling that they needed comfort more than stimulation at this point.

"Do you think she'll call?" Michelle asked. Mac shrugged his big shoulders, twisting the cup around and around in his hands.

"I'd say likely not," he said after a few minutes. "Women like that—

they've learned not to talk to outsiders." Michelle frowned.

"What do you mean, women like that?" she asked. Mac looked at her, his expression serious.

"Abused women," he said shortly. Michelle inhaled sharply. Of course. Mac was totally right. How had she, who had worked for years with legal aid, missed the signs? The bruise, the wary eyes, the protective posture, the hesitancy, the fearful reaction to the man's arrival...*I guess I was more focused on the possibility that she was my cousin. But I should have seen it for myself.*

"How do you know about that?" she asked. Mac was silent, looking down. She waited. If he didn't want to tell her about whatever experience he'd had, that was his right. But she was conscious of a little flicker of disappointment, a little drawing back, in her emotions. She'd thought they were becoming really close, but...

"It's okay," she said, getting up to rinse out her cup. "If you'd rather not say..."

"No, stop," said Mac, reaching out to catch her wrist and drawing her gently to him. He wrapped his arms around her hips as she stood beside him. With his face in her stomach, his voice emerged muffled. "I'm just a little afraid to tell you how I know, in case you think differently about me when I do."

Michelle's heart sped up. Was he going to tell her that *he'd* been an abuser at some point? She could hardly believe that possible but, well, some men were really, really good at hiding their tendencies. She pulled out of his arms and looked down into his face. She was conscious of a spurt of relief when he didn't try to hold her against her will, and that realization frightened her.

"You need to tell me how you know what an abused woman looks like, Mac, or I'm walking out of here right now."

His eyes widened in an expression of dismay. "Oh God, no, not me! Lord, is that what you think? No, no, it's not that. Okay, just sit down, wait, I have something to show you." He jumped up and went toward the bedroom.

She sat down again, her hands clasped on the table before her, her heart still pounding. She looked over to where her purse sat, near the door. Should she just go now? She rubbed her face with her hands, hardly believing she was even having these thoughts. This was Mac—she'd had sex with the man only a few hours ago for heaven's sake! Nothing he'd done or said from the moment she'd met him had suggested any tendency toward violence. But how well did she really know him?

At that point in her fearful ruminations, Mac came back into the kitchen wearing a sleeveless black leather vest over his T-shirt. It had a red and white badge on the front depicting a clenched fist thrust forward.

The letters B.A.C.A. were printed on the knuckles. He turned to show her his back, and she recoiled at the frightening image of a skull that leered out at her.

"You belong to a biker gang?" she asked, horrified. He spun around again.

"No, no—agh, this is just what I was afraid you'd think! Please, read it more carefully."

She took a breath and looked again. Arching over the skull were the words "Death to child abuse." The embroidered badge with the fist said, "Bikers Against Child Abuse." Her heart began to slow down, and she sat back in her chair.

"Okay, I'm listening. You'd better tell me what this is all about." He blew out a breath and sat down heavily.

"A few years back, a buddy of mine—his sister was killed by her husband, and it turned out that their daughter was being abused as well. At the trial, the little girl was accompanied by two members of B.A.C.A. and I got curious about what they were doing there. To be clear, it's not a vigilante justice group, okay? Look, read this." He handed her a printed pamphlet filled with photos of smiling children wearing small replicas of Mac's vest, surrounded by towering men and women similarly attired. She flipped it over and read the initial text:

Bikers Against Child Abuse, Inc. (B.A.C.A.) is a non-profit, tax-exempt organization that exists to provide aid, comfort, safety, and support for children that have been sexually, physically, and emotionally abused. We are dedicated to the principle that one of the basic rights of childhood is to be safe and protected, and when the child's family or environment have failed them, we stand ready to provide it to them. B.A.C.A. is a strong organization of dedicated individuals who are willing to sacrifice any and all in order to protect and secure a child's basic right to a happy childhood.

Next, she read the explanation of the images on Mac's vest:

According to the founder of B.A.C.A., and Rockit, the B.A.C.A. International Trademark Specialist Officer and originator of the B.A.C.A. patch, the following areas hold significance:

Red represents the "blood shed by wounded children"
White represents the "innocence of the children"
Black represents the "dark times the child goes through"
The fist represents "our commitment to stop child abuse"
The skull and crossbones are the symbol of "death to child abuse"

The chains represent "our united organization."

"We only intervene after we confirm that the case is already in the legal system as a case of child abuse. We get referrals from lots of people—teachers, police, social workers, lawyers--but we can't do anything until the parent or guardian—or the province--presses charges against the abuser on behalf of the child. And we are committed to non-violent interventions. Any B.A.C.A. member who becomes violent in the course of his or her duties is subject to serious investigation and consequences—usually termination of membership. It's about protection—being a barrier between the child and his or her abuser—not punishment. Usually, the knowledge that we're on the kid's side, that we'll come to his or her rescue, is enough to keep the abusers away. They're bullies, you know, preying on the weak. They don't want to tangle with someone tougher than they are," Mac explained as Michelle kept looking at the brochure.

She read that anyone seeking membership had to go through a thorough background check and volunteer for a year before being confirmed as a member by a unanimous vote of the chapter's leadership. Only then were they given training on intervention and allowed to commit to the protection of a needy child. She noted that there were chapters across the U.S. and Canada and that the organization had been in existence since 1995. She looked up to see Mac watching her anxiously. She smiled a little and reached out to give his hand a squeeze.

"Okay, I'm starting to get it. You're not a member of Hell's Angels. I'm surprised that I didn't know about this already, given the legal aid work that I did. But I see that there isn't a Manitoba chapter, so I guess that's why I didn't encounter it." She waved the pamphlet at him. "Does this take up a lot of your time?"

"Sometimes," he replied, sitting back and beginning to relax. "Some months it'll be nothing but a chapter meeting, and then the next month I could get called out half a dozen times to patrol in front of a kid's house. In fact," he said, looking anxious again, "I'm supposed to go to a Level 1 intervention on Saturday. Would you be willing to come along, see for yourself what it's all about?"

"I'm not sure—would that be appropriate? What's a Level 1 intervention—do you confront the abuser? I don't think..."

"No, it's not like that at all. We ride out in a small group to the child's home and have a—well—sort of an adoption ceremony, I guess you could say. It's all very casual and fun—seeing the expression on the kid's face when she—it's most often a girl, though not always—gets her vest and meets her new biker family—that's priceless, believe me. You'd be welcome if you're with me."

Michelle thought for a minute. It was well out of her comfort zone but if this was an important part of Mac's life, then she wanted to know about it. And she certainly agreed with the principles. It would be an interesting experience if nothing else!

2001
Vancouver, British Columbia

Riding in the middle of a pack of fifteen motorcycles was an entirely different experience than riding with Mac alone, Michelle concluded. For one thing, the sound was deafening, the deep-throated roar of the bikes—most, but not all, Harley-Davidsons—vibrating in the muscles of her chest and belly. She could understand its appeal to some people—it most certainly drew attention and established dominance—and she also admitted that she had been frightened by it in the past. Even now, as she peered through the tinted visor of her helmet at the bikers riding beside them, she felt a bit nervous and a whole lot out of her depth. For one thing, they were big, like Mac himself, and some of them had the stereotypical pot bellies, shaved heads, tattoos, and biblical beards portrayed in movies. Together, the 'ride' as they called a group traveling to an intervention, was quite intimidating. And, she guessed, that was its point.

There were a few women in the ride, however, including one whose name tag identified her as the Licensed Mental Health Professional required to be involved in each B.A.C.A. case. Michelle had been introduced to Judy Lamont, child psychiatrist, as the ride convened in a local parking lot. She was tall and lean, with close-cropped hair and a no-nonsense air. Michelle had asked her whether she thought that the B.A.C.A. interventions were effective.

"Absolutely I do," Judy had replied with an emphatic nod. "The two major gaps in our child welfare system are, one, providing for the safety of the children and, two, providing funding for their therapy. Even with court involvement to protect children from further abuse through protective orders, and by removing perpetrators from neighborhoods, the perps sometimes still manage to access and wound the children. The police can't protect these children from their abusers on a continual basis—it's just not practical. That's where these guys come in. And many children who are abused don't qualify for therapy funding because their cases don't meet the basic requirements for evidence. For example, it might be clinically obvious that a child has been abused, but the kid might be too scared to provide enough evidence for the case to be pursued. The biker family helps the child feel safe, and children who feel safe are more capable of telling the truth. They might still feel threatened by the abuser, but this is offset by the presence of dedicated bikers who are on her side."

Michelle's own experience with legal aid confirmed everything Judy said. She was beginning to wish that she'd had a B.A.C.A. chapter in Winnipeg to call upon back then—things might have gone better in quite a few cases she could recall.

At the signal to mount up, she'd climbed back onto Mac's '95 Heritage Softail and settled herself behind him. His bike looked a bit less threatening than many of the others. It had gold fenders and tank and whitewall tires, in contrast to the unrelieved black fittings of most of the others. To her relief, even the toughest looking riders had greeted Michelle courteously and seemed focused on the task at hand. She had also been surprised not to hear any rough jokes or foul language--things the media portrayal of bikers had led her to expect.

Now they were veering off an exit ramp, the bikers being careful to maintain a safe distance from one another as they did so. They roared through the suburban streets and pulled up with a flourish outside a white ranch house in a modest but well-kept neighbourhood. At the noise of their arrival, the front door opened and a young mother with her daughter, a slight child who looked to be about ten or so, stepped out of the house onto the front step. The girl looked very anxious, but her mother bent down and spoke reassuringly to her. They came down the front path to the street and stood there uncertainly.

Judy Lamont, the psychiatrist, took off her helmet and went to meet them. She was obviously a familiar figure to the girl, who seemed to relax a little at her arrival. Judy crouched down and spoke to the child at length, gesturing behind her to the bikers, who had now all removed their helmets and were standing in a loose group a few feet away, facing the house.

One of the bikers, a burly man whose B.A.C.A. vest identified him as Pipes, likely for his massively muscled arms, stepped forward with a smile. He held a small-sized vest in one hand and he, too, crouched down to be at the girl's eye level.

"Hey there, I'm Pipes," he said quietly. "I've been told that the name you've chosen as your B.A.C.A. family name is Sugar. Can you tell me what made you choose that?"

The girl brushed her dark curls out of her eyes and looked solemnly at Pipes with large brown eyes that hadn't lost their anxious look. She hesitated, but Pipes just waited patiently. Eventually she spoke up in a voice that Michelle could barely hear.

"Because I like sweet things," Sugar almost whispered. Pipes smiled again.

"Well, me too. My favourite's chocolate; what about you?"

"Caramel," she answered, a bit louder.

"Oh, yeah, that's super good too. I especially like it on ice cream sundaes. So, Sugar, we've made you a vest just like ours, see?" He shook out the denim garment so that she could see the B.A.C.A. badge with its outthrust fist, and Sugar, her chosen name, opposite. "See where it says Sugar?" Pipes asked, and the little girl smiled for the first time, reaching out a tentative finger to touch the raised embroidery.

"So, what this means, Sugar, is we're part of your family now. You can wear the vest anytime you want to, though you don't have to if you'd rather not. But because you're our family now, we'll help to protect you from bad things happening. If you need us, you or your mom can call us, and we'll come right away. We'll be right here outside your house if you feel scared or if you think your stepdad is nearby. You can see that we're pretty big and tough, eh?" He gestured to the bikers arrayed behind him. "Think we're tougher than the guy who's been hurting you?"

Sugar nodded, her eyes still wide but looking a little less scared than before.

"Okay, good. Now I'm going to introduce you to two people who are going to be your special protectors; we call them 'primaries,' okay? This here's Zoomer, she's your first primary, and this is Mac—that's his B.A.C.A. name but would you believe his real name is Hiro? Now, it's spelled with an 'i' instead of an 'e' but you can count on him to be your own personal hero."

Sugar bumped fists with Zoomer, a well-muscled Black woman in her late forties whose graying hair was arranged in multiple long braids, and then with Mac.

"Want to try your vest on, Sugar?" asked Mac in a gentle voice. The girl nodded and held out her thin arms for Mac to slip the vest on. She looked up at her mother, grinning now, and twirled to show off her vest.

"Okay, now let's get some pictures of you with your new family, Sugar," Pipes called out, and the riders arranged themselves behind the child, assuming exaggerated poses to make her giggle. Judy took a handful of shots and promised to drop off some prints to Sugar the next day. Zoomer took the girl's hand and spoke softly to her.

"So, Sugar, you keep one of those photos handy and if anyone tries to hurt you, you show it to them and say, 'This is my family, and you don't want to mess with them 'cause they're really tough!' Right?" Sugar nodded. "Okay, good. Now, would you like to go on a short ride on my motorcycle? I brought a helmet just your size."

Sugar's eyes lit up. "Can I, Mom?" she asked, and at her mother's nod she ran over to Zoomer's bike, eagerly reaching for the helmet. Mac smiled at Michelle.

"I'll go with them, too—be right back, okay?" She nodded.

As Zoomer and Mac rolled out slowly, with Sugar behind Zoomer, clutching her waist, the others broke up into informal groups, chatting. Michelle stood near Judy, who was speaking with the girl's mother. She saw that the mother was wiping away tears.

"You can't know what this means to me," she said. "It's the first time she's been willing to do something without me for months. And that's the first real smile I've seen in I don't know how long! It's been tough for her, so tough."

Judy reached out and patted the woman's arm. "I know it has, but I do think these guys will be a help to her. And remember, if you want them to be in court when Sugar has to testify, we can apply to the judge for permission."

"Yes, I remember Pipes told me that when I first met with him," the woman said. "It's such a relief to know we have someone we can count on, someone to call if we need help. I was afraid I was going to have to give up my house, maybe move us into a women's shelter, if we couldn't do something. My ex-husband, he just will not leave us alone even with the restraining order. I was so afraid that he was going to somehow manage to get hold of her, spirit her away somewhere, to punish me or something." She took a deep breath. "But I don't think he'll dare show his face around here once he knows we've got protection."

"Right," said Judy reassuringly. "And he will be informed that B.A.C.A. is on the case, rest assured."

A few minutes later, Mac and Zoomer returned, and Michelle was delighted to see that Sugar's face was glowing. She ran to her mother, chattering excitedly like a normal, healthy child. Michelle noted that a few of the bikers were surreptitiously wiping their eyes at the sight.

"And *that*," said Mac, coming up behind Michelle, "is why I'm involved in this."

2001
Vancouver, British Columbia

Michelle was surprised and pleased when Kaiya did call several days later. She still sounded hesitant, but she agreed to meet them at a coffee shop near the grocery store where she worked on the following day.

Michelle and Mac got there before her and sat in a corner booth near the back, watching the door. Kaiya came in timidly, her eyes darting around until she saw them, but she looked a little better than the first time they'd seen her. She was wearing her grocery store uniform. Its bright green colour made her skin look sallow, but her hair was neatly braided down her back and the bruise on her face was fading.

Mac waved to her and stood. "What can I get for you?" he asked as she approached.

"Oh, a large double double would be nice, thank you," Kaiya said with a blush as she slid into the booth. As Mac went off to purchase the quintessentially Canadian sweet, milky coffee, Michelle thanked Kaiya for coming.

"I know this has come out of the blue," she said. "Believe me, if we'd known about you before, we would have sought you out years ago. My mother did search, back in the sixties, but she didn't realize that my uncle had been with the British military instead of the Canadian army, so she never found his records." As Mac returned with the drink, she went on to explain how Mac's mother had supplied the vital clue and helped them track down Kenji's presence on the ship with Akiko and baby Kaiya. Kaiya listened quietly, sipping her coffee, but then spoke in an agitated tone.

"You do realize that I am not your uncle's natural daughter, right? I'm not truly any relation at all." Michelle nodded.

"We do know that," she said. "But he adopted you, and that makes you family to me."

Kaiya smiled weakly, but then sighed. "I wish you had found us sooner. My mother struggled a lot, from what I can remember. She spoke almost no English and hardly anyone would believe that her Japanese marriage certificate was real, that she was Canadian by marriage. Eventually she found work in a Chinese laundry, I think it was run by a Mrs. Sang. She let us live in the back of the shop, to watch it overnight, but we had just a little corner with a cot. I was only eight when my mother died. She was twenty-four. I'm not sure what exactly she died of, but she was always in pain, I do remember that. I think she'd had a really hard time in the war, you know?"

Michelle and Mac exchanged glances. By perusing the details of Kenji's military service record—now that they'd found it—they suspected that he'd met Akiko in one of the 'comfort stations' set up by the Japanese army to service its soldiers. But they weren't sure, and they didn't want to offend Akiko's daughter with what she might take as a slur on her mother.

"Many Japanese women had a terrible time during the war," Michelle said neutrally. "But what happened to you when she died, a child alone?"

Kaiya's face twisted in a complex expression that mixed sadness, anger, and shame. "Foster care," she said. "At first, I was put into an orphanage, and then in a series of foster homes. Some weren't too bad, but some…" she fell silent, leaving the details to their imaginations. "When I turned eighteen, I moved out, got in with a few other girls. Things got better for a while. I found regular work and eventually I met Beth's father. He's white. But he was already married," she said, glancing at them out of the corner of her eye as if not sure how they'd take this bit of information. "Anyway, he visited me regularly for a long time--years. He helped me a bit with money, made it possible for me to get my own apartment. Then I accidentally got pregnant with Beth and, well, he wasn't having that. No way would he divorce his wife and marry me, and he swore he'd deny that the baby was his if I insisted on having it. He accused me of getting pregnant on purpose, of trying to manipulate him. I guess I had ignored all the ways that the relationship was to his benefit, done his way. He insisted that I have an abortion but, I don't know—I was forty by then, and I figured this might be my only chance to have something of my own, someone who wouldn't leave me, you know? So I kept her, and he disappeared. I have no idea where he is now."

"That must have been a challenge, raising your daughter on your own," said Mac sympathetically. Kaiya nodded.

"It has been, but we make do."

"And have you been with your current husband long?" asked Michelle, probing as gently as she knew how. Kaiya laughed, a short, bitter laugh.

"Oh, Richard isn't my husband. He's another one like Beth's father, except he's not married to anyone else. No, he just likes having me in the house—*his* house, as he told you—to do his bidding, whatever and whenever he wants it." She sighed, "I stay because I keep hoping that things will get better. That's what my name means, after all—forgiveness. And there are some benefits. I wouldn't be able to provide as nice a place for Beth, things like her dance lessons, on my own."

They sat for a few moments in silence as Kaiya finished her coffee. They'd only just met the woman—what right did they have to question her life decisions or probe into her relationships? As Kaiya glanced at her watch and stood up, Michelle stood as well. "Here," she said, passing over a piece of paper, "that's my address in Winnipeg, and my home phone number—the one I gave you the other day is Mac's number. Kaiya, you're my cousin—one I never knew I had—and I'd like to get to know you and Beth. My family in Winnipeg would also be thrilled to meet you, especially our grandmother. Do you think there's any chance you could come for a visit? We'd be happy to host you and—well, pay for your tickets if needed. I don't mean to imply anything or offend you..."

Kaiya shook her head with a sad smile. "You haven't offended me, Michelle and you're not wrong--I would have to ask for help if we were to visit. Let me think about it. It's not easy for me to get time off work and, of course, Beth has school. Maybe some day..." she trailed off and shrugged. "But thank you—thank you both—for being interested in us. It's nice to know that I have family somewhere, even if I never meet them. A grandmother—who knew?" But she sounded defeated, and her shoulders were hunched.

Mac stood up as well, his tall form towering over Kaiya's slight one. He hesitated, but then spoke very quietly. "Kaiya, I live here in Vancouver, as you know. If you should ever need help—you or Beth—for anything at all, please call on me. I may not be an official cousin, but I live a lot closer than Michelle does and, well, just keep that card, for if you ever have an emergency."

Kaiya nodded with a faint smile and thanked them again before slipping out the door. They watched her trudge back towards the grocery store, her green uniform bright in the sun but her dark head bent, her steps slow.

Michelle and Mac made the most of the rest of her visit, going back to visit the Nikkei Centre, visiting the fishing village of Steveston where so many Japanese immigrants had begun their lives in Canada. They even took a car and ferry trip up the coast, stopping briefly in Powell River to explore the Museum and Archives. Michelle read the exhibit related to the pulp and paper industry with great interest, peering closely at the photographs of the employees, hoping for a glimpse of her grandfather Hoshi. She couldn't see him anywhere, though the text did mention that the mill had employed some Japanese immigrants. She had an interesting conversation with the gentleman who was volunteering at the desk, an old man full of stories he was keen to share.

"Oh, yes," he said, shaking his grizzled old head sadly, "sure I remember when the Japanese were sent away. Not all of us agreed with that, you know. Those fellas were hard workers. I had no argument with 'em, anyway."

Michelle nodded, but she couldn't help thinking how many people said this. In fact, you'd think no one ever had any prejudice against the Nikkei at all—*Oh, no, not me!* they all said. It was like people who said that if they'd been German, they'd have stood up against the Nazis in support of the Jews. *I guess we all hope we'd have been better, braver, stronger, more principled,* she thought. *Every one of us.* There was no point in arguing.

"Did you ever hear of any Japanese Canadians staying in B.C., hiding out, avoiding the internment?" she asked. His wrinkled old face puckered in thought.

"Well, I do know that the owners of the hunting camp up on Powell Lake had a Chinese cook back along the way. Somebody said he had a Japanese apprentice, but I don't know if that was true."

"When might this have been, if it was true?" asked Mac.

"Oh, I'm not sure, a long time ago—could have been during the war, but I'm not sure."

"Is the camp still there? Who owns it now?" asked Michelle.

"It's a retreat lodge now," the man replied, "People coming for a rest, massage, meditation, organic food, you know—kind of New Agey stuff if you ask me, but lots of folks love it and who am I to argue? Up until '96, it used to be owned by McMillan Bloedel, the paper mill owners. They used it as a place to take the top execs, y'know, show 'em a good time—fly 'em in for fishing, hunting, drinking. Burned down in '52 but they rebuilt it a lot bigger, fancier. But like I said, now it's a private lodge—I think they call it Rainbow Lodge, for all the rainbows on the waterfalls. Pretty place...haven't been there in years..." he trailed off, his rheumy eyes full of memories. They thanked him and walked off to look at some of the other exhibits.

It was all very interesting, especially the exhibits about the First Nations, but they didn't find anything else related to Kenji's story. Just as they were about to leave, however, the old fellow called out to them.

"Hey, I just remembered—Mr. Simpson, he was one of the fellas who once owned the original hunting camp—he did say something to me once about bringing a Japanese into the jail. I'd forgotten all about that until you asked."

"Is he still around?" asked Mac and was disappointed when the man shook his head.

"Oh, no, no, he died years ago. His grandson works as a clerk at the mill, though. Not likely he'd know anything but if you want to speak to him, go to the main office and ask for Kyle Simpson."

They thanked him again and made their way down the hill to the main plant. An inquiry at the reception desk brought a young man out from the inner offices, looking inquisitive.

"I'm Kyle Simpson," he said. "What can I help you with?" When they'd explained, he shook his head. "I don't remember anything about that, but my grandma might. She's up in the nursing home. She's almost a hundred now, but her mind's still pretty sharp most of the time. And she'd love to have a visitor, even if she can't help you." He pointed out the window and gave them directions.

So up the hill they went again, wondering if anything would come of their efforts. Michelle shrugged as they opened the door to the nursing home.

"Well, I may never come back here, so I guess it's worth a try anyway."

The nurse led them to a small room facing the sea, where a wizened figure sat hunched in a wheelchair at the window.

"Mrs. Simpson—Maude!" the nurse almost shouted. "You've got some visitors!" She turned to Michelle and Mac and spoke at normal volume. "I'll see if I can get her to put in her hearing aids—she's not too fond of them."

The old lady resisted at first, but seeing Michelle and Mac, her curiosity got the better of her ill humour and she allowed the nurse to put in the aids.

"*What* do you want?" she asked, unable to follow their complicated explanation.

"Did your husband ever bring a Japanese man to the jail here, during the war?" Mac asked loudly, simplifying the query. The wrinkled face lifted into an expression of pride.

"He sure did!" she crowed. "Caught him hidin' out at the hunting camp, he did! Dragged him back and put 'im where he belonged—in jail! Imagine the cheek of that Jap, refusing to be interned. My Henry put that right, yes he did."

Well, thought Michelle with a hint of amusement, *here's one at least who'll admit to her racism! And never mind that I'm obviously of Japanese descent—no false politeness here.*

"They were the enemy, you know," Mrs. Simpson continued, warming to her topic and ignoring the nurse's horrified remonstrations. "Oh, they were sly, crafty—pretended to be working here but all the time they were plotting our downfall! Planning to burn our forests and homes down around our ears! Oh yes, they had those radio machines, y'know, and they were in constant contact with their homeland! If the government hadn't taken their boats, they'd've barricaded the coast, cut us off from help from the sea!" She nodded emphatically. Michelle had to hide a smile at the thought of the Japanese fishermen creating a blockade against huge naval vessels with their small fishing boats. Then her smile faded. It wasn't funny, really—people had truly believed this propaganda—some of them still believed it, if this lady was any example.

Mrs. Simpson beckoned them closer with a bony hand. As they leaned in, she whispered conspiratorially. "I heard that some Japanese men were masquerading as women, too, to hide out among us. ‘Cause they’re so small, see, you couldn’t tell ‘em apart.” She tapped her temple with a gnarled finger. “Clever, very clever, they were.” She nodded sagely. “But do you know how my Henry knew he was a Jap? It was the poems, them haykoos, y’know? The fella had ‘em all over the place.” She nodded triumphantly once more and then abruptly lost interest in them, turning away to gaze out the window, her expression becoming vague.

The nurse, her face crimson with embarrassment, ushered them out, apologizing. “The old folks, they kind of lose the thread, you know? She’s not a bad sort, really, but...” she shrugged helplessly. “I’m so sorry that she was so offensive.”

“It’s okay,” said Michelle. “At least she told us what we wanted to know, with no equivocation. I think the man her husband brought in might have been my uncle. He ended up in the British military, investigating Japanese war crimes. So, in the end, being brought to the jail here was a blessing in disguise. He got a job and avoided criminal charges.” She looked directly into the woman’s eyes. “We’re quite proud of him, actually. He did his best to resist an unfair practice and served on the side of the Allies in the end.”

The nurse’s face went an even deeper shade of red. “I’m sure, yes, that’s good...” she babbled, obviously mortified. Michelle relented, thanking her for her help, and they left the building.

“Do you think it was really him?” Mac asked her as they walked back to the ferry dock.

“It seems likely,” she answered. “The dates fit what we know about when and where he was recruited, and he had to have been hiding somewhere. We’ll never know for sure, I guess, but it gives me some satisfaction. I wish I could find the Chinese cook—I’d like to thank him for helping my uncle—but he’s likely long gone, and I guess it’s not very important. At least we know that he lived through the war and did some good. After all, he rescued Akiko and Kaiya in the end, gave them a chance at a better life even though that’s not really how it turned out for poor Akiko.”

“I’m not sure about that,” said Mac. “If she’d stayed in Japan, who knows what might have happened to her? The comfort women were reviled, shamed, many were rejected by their families. It would have been very hard for her to manage alone with Kaiya there. At least here in Canada she found honest work. It’s just so sad that Kenji died before they could make a home together. Her life—and Kaiya’s—would have been so different if he’d lived. You know, with no English, she wouldn’t even have known that she could have applied for a pension as the widow of a deceased serviceman.”

“If anyone would have believed that the Japanese marriage

certificate was authentic," Michelle reminded him, and he nodded. They fell silent a moment, thinking about the vagaries of luck and its impact on people's lives. Then Michelle chuckled.

"'Haykoos' was it? It's nice to imagine my uncle in the Canadian forest, writing haikus about its beauty. At least I hope that's what they were about. What a shame they were lost."

"Perhaps someday you'll write some of your own," said Mac, taking her hand.

2002
Vancouver, British Columbia

In the end, it wasn't Kaiya who telephoned Mac. It was Beth.

"I'm sorry, I don't know if you'll even remember me," she said, her voice distraught. When Mac reassured her that he did indeed remember her, she went on in a burst. "It's my mom, she's hurt, and I don't know what to do! She always kept Michelle's card inside her coin purse, and I remembered that your number was on the back. Please, I didn't know who else to call!"

"Of course I'll help you," said Mac. "Tell me how she's hurt." When he learned that Kaiya was unconscious and bleeding from several injuries inflicted by her common-law husband, who had driven off into the night leaving fourteen-year-old Beth to cope alone, he ground his teeth in fury.

"Beth, I'm going to call an ambulance, all right? Then I'm going to come over. Stay with your mother, keep her warm, and I'll be there as quickly as I can. If the ambulance gets there first, tell them I'm on my way to be with you."

As he thrust his arms into his leather jacket, Mac had another thought. He grabbed the phone again and dialed another number.

"Pipes? I've got a favour to ask…" He explained the situation quickly. "I know she's not one of our cases, but I could use a little back up in case the stepdad takes it into his head to come back and give the poor girl trouble."

"On my way," Pipes assured him. "And Mac, I'll see if Judy can come along too—might be good to have a psych with us."

The ambulance was on the street when Mac pulled up, its lights flashing silently in the darkness. He parked the bike and went up to the door, reaching it just as the paramedics were loading Kaiya's limp form onto the stretcher for transport.

"Beth," he called out to the frightened teen, who stood against the wall, her arms crossed tightly across her chest, her glossy dark hair spilling over her shoulders.

"Mac!" she said, her face crumpling in relief. "Thank you for coming. I know I had no right to call you…"

"Hey, hey, we're practically family!" Mac said, putting a gentle arm around the girl's shaking shoulders. He couldn't help but notice how she stiffened immediately, so he dropped his arm and backed up a step. He filed that observation away for later. "How's your mother?" he asked.

"They say she'll be all right, but they have to take her to the hospital to check for concussion, and they think maybe her arm's broken too."

"Do you want to go along?" Mac asked, but Beth shook her head.

"They said to stay here, that they'll call me to come later when she's conscious. They said there's nothing I can do for her right now and I wouldn't be allowed to stay with her."

Mac nodded. It made sense.

"Would you like me to stay, and then take you to the hospital later?" Beth hesitated, looking at him anxiously. "Listen, I've asked a couple of friends of mine to come along, to help out in case your stepdad comes back. One of them—I hope she's able to come—is a psychiatrist. Would you be comfortable telling her what happened?"

"I guess. She's not, like, gonna take me away and lock me up or anything, right?"

"No," said Mac seriously, despite his inner amusement. The ideas people had about psychiatry! "No, nothing like that. She'll just be here if you need to talk."

"Okay," said Beth and at that moment two more motorcycles drove up and parked nearby. "Is—is that them?" she asked, her eyes wide. "Are they, like, biker gang people?"

Mac shook his head. "No, not biker gang people at all. Wait until you meet them. I think you'll like them. But if you don't, they'll leave. It's up to you." He was relieved to see that one of the figures coming up the walk was Judy. This girl needed a woman to talk to.

As the ambulance drove off, Pipes and Judy came into the house and shut the door. Mac introduced them to Beth just as friends of his, here to help.

"What do you say to some tea?" asked Judy. "I think we could all use something calming." She went into the kitchen with Beth, and Mac filled Pipes in on the little he knew about the situation.

"I don't know this for a fact," he concluded, "but I have a strong hunch that the guy isn't just abusing Kaiya, his wife—or common-law partner, whatever. I think he may have had a go at Beth as well, one way or another."

"Oh yeah?" said Pipes grimly. "Well, Judy will try to find out and if that's the case, she'll walk the girl through her options for charging the guy. The wife—Kaiya?—might also want to press charges. Sounds as if she's been beat up pretty bad this time."

Several hours later, they heard from the hospital that Kaiya did have a severe concussion and would be kept in for at least several days, probably longer. They suggested that Beth wait until morning to come and visit. Judy asked Beth what she wanted to do, as they sat around the table sipping their latest cup of tea.

"You can't stay here alone," she said, "because you're a minor. Do you have a friend you could stay with, or any family here in the city?" Beth shook her head, tears trembling on her lashes.

"I don't have any friends close enough to ask such a big thing. Richard—my so-called stepdad--he wouldn't let me stay over at a friend's house or have friends here. He tried to stop me from having friends at all. And there's no family—except Mom's cousin Michelle, but she's in Winnipeg! I don't really know her, and I don't want to be so far away from Mom."

"Well, we could arrange foster care..." Judy began, but Mac broke in.

"Beth, if Michelle could come here, would you want that?" The girl nodded uncertainly.

"I couldn't ask her, though—she barely knows us."

"Let me call her," said Mac, checking his watch. "Hmm, it's the middle of the night there. I'll call her in the morning. Judy, would it be possible for you to stay here tonight? Or should we call for social services? I don't think it's appropriate for me to stay with Beth alone..." Judy picked up his implication immediately and said she could stay.

"I think we should all try to get some sleep now—it is getting very late," Judy added. "Beth, you can sleep in tomorrow morning. Don't worry about school—I'll give them a call first thing."

Pipes took his leave, telling Mac to call him again if he needed him. Mac tried to make himself comfortable on the sagging sofa in the living room but barely slept, one ear cocked in case Richard returned to trouble them again.

Next morning, Mac reached Michelle just as she was waking up and she immediately agreed to come.

"Give me an hour to make arrangements about my classes, and I'll catch the next flight," she said. "Mac, it's so good of you to help out. I hope it hasn't made things too difficult for you."

"No, I actually don't have classes today," he said reassuringly. I'll pick you up at the airport. Bring your boots and a warm jacket. I've got the bike."

"Is Kaiya going to be all right? And what about Beth, what will happen to her?"

"Lots of possibilities," said Mac. "Let's talk about it when you get here, okay?"

"Yes, of course. That bloody man—he'd better not come anywhere near either of them!"

"I couldn't agree more," said Mac. "See you soon."

Mac hung up and went downstairs to search out a cup of coffee. As he neared the kitchen, however, he saw Judy and Beth talking earnestly at the table. Judy, facing him, shook her head minutely and waved him off with a twitch of her fingers that Beth, weeping into a sodden tissue, didn't notice. Mac nodded and slipped silently out the front door, turning right to seek out a coffee shop on Commercial Drive.

He returned an hour later and peeked cautiously into the kitchen to find Judy sitting there alone, her phone in one hand and a notebook in the other. She spoke a few more words into the phone and then thumbed it off. She stood up and stretched her slim body, twisting her back to relieve the tension.

"Beth?" Mac asked and Judy pointed upstairs.

"Sleeping again, I hope. It's been a very tough time for her."

"Any word on Kaiya?"

"Awake, but in pain and suffering confusion from the concussion. She maintains she doesn't remember how it happened. Broken arm, cracked ribs, bruises, contusions—the usual, unfortunately."

"Hmmm. And Beth, what does she say?" asked Mac. Judy sighed deeply and sat down again, drawing her notebook toward her.

"She says plenty, and none of it good," she answered. "She says that the perpetrator—her stepfather Richard—has been sexually abusing her for several years, threatening that he'd throw her and her mother out of the house if she told. Recently the abuse escalated from heavy petting to actual penetration, and Beth, scared she'd get pregnant or diseased, broke down and told her mother what had been happening. Kaiya rather foolishly confronted Richard instead of getting the heck out of the situation and, as you might imagine, all hell broke loose. He beat her to the point of unconsciousness and then, maybe scared he might've killed her, took off. Beth came home from her dance class just as he ran from the house and drove off—that's when she found her mother and called you."

Mac sat down heavily at the table. "Is she willing to press charges?" he asked.

"Maybe," said Judy. "She wants to talk to her mother first, see if she plans to charge him for her own injuries."

"Understandable," said Mac. "I just hope Kaiya doesn't decide to live up to her name yet again."

"Her name?" asked Judy, puzzled.

"In Japanese, it means forgiveness," answered Mac

2002
Vancouver, British Columbia
Winnipeg, Manitoba

As Kaiya and Beth had their tickets checked by the guard at the entrance to the security gates at Vancouver's YVR airport, Michelle stood close to Mac, saying goodbye.

"I can't thank you enough," she began, but he laid a finger to her lips.

"You *have* thanked me enough," he said with a smile. "I'm just glad they'll have a chance to start over in Winnipeg with family nearby. I do wish they'd decided to press charges against that slimeball Richard, but I understand not wanting to expose themselves to all the public scrutiny that would bring."

Michelle saw that it was almost her turn to have her documents checked.

"Mac," she said impulsively. "Would you like to come to Winnipeg in December? Get an experience of a real snowy Canadian Christmas for once?"

His immediate grin warmed her heart. "Sure!" he answered. "My sisters and all their kids will keep my folks happy—they won't even know I'm gone! And you know, I've been wanting to check Winnipeg out anyway—they could use a B.A.C.A. chapter there and Red River College has got some very interesting computer programs launching. Let's talk soon, okay?" He smoothed her hair back from her forehead and gave her a quick kiss, laughing at the surprised speculation in her eyes. "Now go!"

She took her place in line, was allowed through, and turned back to wave one more time before disappearing behind the doors. Mac gazed after her for a moment, then turned, humming a little, to return to the parking lot.

"You should take the window," said Michelle to Beth after they'd stowed their hand luggage in the bins above. She'd been saddened to find that everything Kaiya and Beth owned could be packed into one large and one small suitcase each. Everything else in the house belonged to Richard, and Kaiya wouldn't take a single item. It had taken her a few days to make the decision to relocate to Winnipeg at Michelle's invitation, but once she had, she'd never looked back. Since leaving the hospital, she had been very quiet but resolute. What she hadn't been able to do to protect herself, she found the courage to do for her daughter's sake.

Beth, in contrast, was like a bird let out of a cage. Her natural exuberance had come to the surface upon hearing that they were to leave the city, leave Richard behind, start again in a new place where she had new family to meet. It had been a relief to both Mac and Michelle to see her recover from her trauma so quickly, though they both knew that the scars were still there and would probably resurface in time. Now, however, the young teen was fairly bouncing in excitement.

"Oh, can I? You're sure you don't mind? It's really your seat, Michelle—won't we get into trouble if we switch?"

"No," smiled Michelle, "It's okay. You enjoy the view. I've seen it many times—just a few days ago, in fact!" The girl smiled back, then turned to gaze raptly out the window at the busy activity on the tarmac beside the plane. Kaiya turned to Michelle and spoke softly.

"You are really sure that your mother and father won't mind us staying with them? It will only be for a short time, until I can find a job..."

Michelle waved her hand. "If I know my mother—and believe me, I do—she won't let you leave for a very long time! She is so excited that we have finally found you and that she'll have the chance to get to know you properly. My mom—well, she's a bit of a force to be reckoned with. You may have to fend her off or she'll try to run your whole life!"

Kaiya smiled wryly. "Believe me, Michelle, it will be such a novelty to have someone look after us that I may never leave!"

The flight--just over two and a half hours—went smoothly, with Beth exclaiming every few minutes as a new vista opened up beneath the plane. Michelle was glad that it was a sunny day; the aerial view of the Rocky Mountains really was astounding, especially the first time you saw it. Kaiya, still recovering from her concussion, slept much of the way, but awakened as they began their descent. Despite Michelle's reassurances, she was nervous and fidgety as they stood in the aisle, waiting to get off the plane.

A large middle aged white man reached past Kaiya to access his hand luggage above her. In the process, he pushed against her small form, forcing her hard against the row of seats. It was obviously very uncomfortable and embarrassing for her, but she said not a word. Michelle, however, was having none of it.

"Sir," she said firmly, placing a hand on his arm "You are hurting my cousin and there's no point in rushing. Please be patient and we'll be happy to get out of your way momentarily."

"I need to get my bag..." blustered the man, not backing off.

"Hey buddy, I can reach your bag for you—is it this green one?" a young fellow further back called out. He met Michelle's eyes and nodded in a friendly way. Pulling the bag down, he passed it forward and the owner took it, stepping away and turning his face aside as if nothing untoward had happened. Michelle was tempted to ask for an apology, but she didn't want to embarrass Kaiya. Suddenly Beth spoke up loudly from behind her.

"And you could say you're sorry for hurting my mom, too!" Her young voice carried, and the man stiffened in embarrassment but still didn't turn his head or speak. Several other passengers glared at him, but he ignored their animosity. At that moment the doors opened, and the line began to move. The man with the green bag pushed his way forward, tutting impatiently as other passengers gathered their belongings, blocking his way. As the young man who'd retrieved the bag came abreast of Kaiya, he spoke in a loud voice, intending for the older man to hear him.

"I'm so sorry you had to suffer such rudeness," he said to her. "I don't know whether that guy's racist or misogynist or just plain ignorant, but anyway--would you like to complain to the steward?" Kaiya shook her head, mortified by the unwanted attention. "All right but you know, you don't have to put up with people treating you like that." The fellow smiled at them, then passed on and out of the plane.

A few minutes later, as they stood waiting for their luggage at the carousel, Beth turned to her mother and spoke quietly but intensely.

"That guy was right, you know Mom. We don't have to put up with that kind of treatment from men. Not you or me. From now on, I'm going to stand up for myself! And you should, too!" Kaiya nodded but said nothing, looking even more stressed. Silently Michelle applauded Beth's statement and the evidence it provided of her resilience.

At that moment their suitcases came into view, and they loaded them onto the two carts they'd snagged. A few minutes later they exited through the sliding doors into the arrival court. There, close by the door, stood Isabel and Dan. Michelle's mother looked as smart as ever in a bright red suit, and she rushed forward, calling out to them.

"Kaiya, Beth! Oh, how glad I am to finally meet you both!" She flung her arms around Kaiya and hugged her warmly. At that, the poor woman's nerve broke, and she burst into tears, burying her face in Isabel's elegant suit jacket. Beth stood by uncertainly, eyes wide as she watched her usually in-control mother weep in this stranger's arms. Dan Ikeda stepped forward and spoke quietly to Beth.

"She'll be all right in a few minutes, Beth. It's all a bit overwhelming just now. I'm your mother's aunt's husband, which makes me your great-uncle, I think. You can call me Dan, or Uncle Dan if you want."

Beth looked up at his kind face. "Uncle Dan," she whispered, tears coming to her eyes as well. He enfolded her in a quick hug, then stepped away.

"Uncle Dan it is then," he said jovially. "Now, let's get all these bags to the car, shall we?"

A week later, they all entered Asami's room at the nursing home.

The old lady was dozing in her wheelchair but wakened at Michelle's gentle touch on her shoulder.

"Grandma, we've brought you some visitors," she said as the bleary old eyes opened. She crouched down on her haunches and waved for her cousin to approach. Kaiya knelt beside her, bringing her face level with Asami's. "This is Kaiya, Grandma. Her mother was married to Uncle Kenji. Do you remember Kenji—Kenichi, your son?"

"Kenji? MY Kenji? Yes, of course I do! But he's gone, isn't he? Lost…" The old lady's face fell in sorrow.

"Yes, he is gone, Grandma, he died a long time ago, just after the war. But do you know what? He died a soldier, serving the Allies." Michelle didn't try to explain the details of Kenji's assignment to the British military despite his Canadian citizenship. She wasn't sure she even understood that part herself.

Asami's eyes opened wide, and she looked at Michelle in astonishment. "He was a soldier?" Michelle nodded.

"Yes, he was. You can be proud of him, Grandma. And he married a Japanese woman, her name was Akiko. She had a daughter, Kaiya—and this is her. She's another granddaughter for you."

Asami reached out and touched her fingertips to Kaiya's cheek.

"My granddaughter?" she quavered, and Kaiya nodded, her face again streaked with tears. She had finally been convinced by Isabel and Michelle not to even try to explain her real relationship as Kenji's adopted daughter. As Michelle had said, it didn't make any difference—she was family—and it was likely to confuse Asami needlessly.

"I'm glad to meet you, Grandma." She reached out and drew Beth nearer. "This is my daughter Beth, your great-granddaughter."

Asami smiled wonderingly. "So pretty!" she said, patting Beth's hand. Then her eyes sharpened, and she beckoned to Isabel, who stood nearby, her eyes suspiciously moist. "Ichika, get me my box."

"What box, Mom?" asked Isabel, deciding, for once, to ignore the use of her original Japanese name—one she still detested. The old lady gestured querulously.

"The pink one, in the drawer over there, under the television. The pink one, pink one, you know!" Isabel shook her head in mystification but obediently opened the indicated drawer and pulled out a rather large pink box, battered with age. She brought it over to her mother and laid it carefully in her lap.

Asami untied the fraying ribbon and pulled off the lid, revealing a nest of discoloured tissue paper. She thrust into it with her gnarled old hands, pushing it aside impatiently. After a moment she smiled triumphantly, lifting out the object beneath the tissue. It was a porcelain geisha doll, her pink silk kimono a bit faded but still whole, her glossy hair still in its elaborate chignon.

"My doll!" exclaimed Isabel. "I had no idea you still had that, Mom!"

"Yes, yes, your doll, the one your brother brought to you from Japan. I kept it to remember him by, all those years when we didn't talk about him. But now, it is for this young one." She handed the doll carefully to Beth, who received it reverently into her hands.

"Really, from Japan? From my grandfather?" she said, looking around at them all with wide eyes, and Isabel nodded, her eyes brimming now.

Isabel came closer, showing Beth and Kaiya how the kimono's sash was tied in a complicated 'morning glory' knot at the back of the doll. Michelle, wiping her eyes, rose and stepped away to stand beside her father over by the window.

He put his arm around her shoulders and hugged. "It's a good thing you've done here, love," he said quietly. She nodded.

"Yes, I'm very glad that it has all worked out." They were quiet, watching the happy scene. "Dad," she said after a time. "I've heard some Nikkei say that they think that the internment and the forced dispersal was actually a good thing, that it forced the Japanese Canadians to integrate better into Canadian society. You went through it all, but I've never asked you. What do you think?" Her father was silent for several minutes.

"I'm not sure that our success is all to do with our war experiences," he said finally. "Nikkei are pretty focused and hard-working anyway. We don't dwell on negative things. Our attitude is *shikata-ga-nai,* meaning 'it can't be helped, move on,' so I think it's likely we'd have made our way regardless." He paused. "But over time, I've developed a different reason to be thankful for the way our people were treated during the war."

"Thankful? Really?" asked Michelle. Dan nodded.

"If we had not been interned, if we or our fathers had been recruited to go and fight, many of us would have died. In most *hakujin* families, one or two of the sons in nearly every family lost their lives in the war. Now, if you were told that by suffering internment and the loss of your property you could protect your children, keep them all alive, wouldn't you choose to do that? I know that I would. So, yes, I'm grateful that my father got to stay alive, and his brothers and uncles and my grandfather—your mother's family too. Yes, we suffered—but so did everyone else in that terrible war."

"Huh," said Michelle. "I've never thought of it that way." She paused and then spoke again. "That doesn't make it right, though. All Canadian citizens' rights should be protected, even during wartime, whether they choose to serve in the army or not." Dan nodded.

"You're right. I'm not denying that. That's why it's so important that our stories be told, over and over again, so they are not forgotten.

That Nikkei Museum and that Powell Street Festival you told us about, those are good things. They keep our heritage alive in us and teach us to be vigilant, to never take our citizenship for granted. Because it could happen again. Maybe not to us, but to some other group who seem to threaten the status quo." Then he laughed. "But the Nikkei, in a few generations we will disappear. Your Mac—he's half *hakujin*, and you say both his sisters married white men, diluting the Japanese blood further. That's happening more and more—I read the other day that over 75% of Japanese Canadians marry whites. Soon it won't be possible to identify a Nikkei by looking at him or her. And that's likely a good thing. Whatever our heritage, we are Canadian. That's what we all need to remember, to protect."

Beside him, Michelle nodded in agreement, feeling a warm glow that had nothing to do with her father's philosophical musings. *My Mac, eh? We shall see…*

Raindrop falls in sea
Joins with the rushing waters
Who can find the rain?

Author's Notes

This book was sparked by a chance exposure to a news article about the discovery of Japanese artifacts (sake bottles, broken dishes of Japanese design) in a remote location in the forests above North Vancouver. One of the investigators speculated that perhaps this had been the site of a camp inhabited by Japanese Canadians who were avoiding the internment order. I had a little bit of awareness of the internment story, having written a short episode in my second book, *Those Who Stay*, in which Japanese Canadian families were removed from the Pender Harbour area (did you catch the alternate perspective on that scene, in this book?). The news article, however, gave me an idea for a situation in which a family member refused to be interned, thus splitting the family, perhaps irrevocably. Certainly this had happened in reality, as men were often sent to remote road work camps, and their wives and children were sent to ghost town internment camps. Not all were reunited after the war. So, I began my research into the Nikkei experience, wanting to expose and explore this troubling episode in Canadian history. Trawling the internet for related information, I found one short blog post that mentioned that similar vintage artifacts had been found adjacent to Powell Lake, northeast of the town of Powell River. I had found my Sunshine Coast connection—fictional, but plausible!

A few comments on language are necessary: first, Nikkei (a term meaning persons of Japanese descent not residing in Japan), wasn't actually popularized until the 1950s (very early Japanese immigrants were more likely to call themselves *nihonjin,* or people of the rising sun), but I elected to use it throughout for simplicity and to avoid wearying the reader with the repeated use of 'Japanese Canadians'—a rather long and unwieldy term in the context of a novel. I have also integrated the use of some words in the Japanese language: *hakujin* (whites), *dojin* (indigenous people of Canada), *issei* (first generation immigrants from Japan), *nisei* (second generation, born in Canada), and *sansei* (third generation), as these were and are commonly used by Nikkei. Some resources that I reviewed capitalized these words; others did not. I have elected to go with italics but no capitals (see the glossary for all Japanese words/phrases used). In a few instances, I have used the derogatory term 'Japs' which was sadly common during the first half of the twentieth century though it is now considered a very racist and unacceptable slur. It appears in my novel only to illustrate historical attitudes and its use here should not, of course, be construed as any support for its continued use in contemporary times. In the same way, the use of 'Indian' sometimes refers to First Nations characters (as they were called that at the time), and sometimes it means immigrants from the country of India, though these were also likely to be referred to as 'Hindus' or 'Hindoos' [sic] at the time of the novel.

Early in my research, I found a statement that Manzo Nagano, accepted as the first officially recognized immigrant from Japan to Canada in 1877, encountered five Japanese men fishing for salmon in the mouth of the Fraser River when he and his partner fisherman were blown north by a storm in the early 1880s. Four of these men were identified, and I've used their true names in my book. The fifth was not identified, so I took the liberty of inserting my fictional Haruto Sato into the vacant slot. Thus began the story of Michelle Ikeda's great-grandfather's arrival in Canada.

Next, an issue of the *Island Tides* bulletin (Sept 22-Oct 5, 2011) came to my attention and provided the idea of placing Harry and Sara on Galiano Island early in their marriage. There is ample evidence of Japanese-style charcoal making there (and on Salt Spring Island) in the pre-war decades, and several pit kilns have now been restored. In 2002, Galiano native and then Lieutenant-Governor Iona Campagnolo presided over the placement of an information board and shelter at the site of one of the kilns on Galiano which has been restored by Steve Nemtin, a dedicated local amateur anthropologist. Learning about fine charcoal production and use was a most interesting sideline in my research!

I was delighted to find digitized copies of the Powell River Pulp and Paper Company's newsletter, *The Digester*, from the forties, as it provided a reliable insight into the attitudes, popular topics of discussion, and language of that time and place.

My research was greatly assisted by the efforts of contemporary Canadian Nikkei to record and celebrate their history and culture. A *sansei* in my neighbourhood (after whom one of the main characters, Michelle, is named), hearing of my interest, generously loaned me her copy of *Honouring Our People: Breaking the Silence*, the 2016 publication by the Greater Vancouver Japanese Canadian Association. This wonderful collection of first-person memoirs spans the diversity of the Nikkei wartime experience and was extremely helpful. I later had the honour of interviewing Michelle's mother, Doreen Campbell, a charming woman in her late seventies who was born and spent her early childhood in an internment camp (New Denver). The interview was attended by her grandson, who was hearing these stories for the first time—a wonderful example of art supporting life, I hope!

Unfortunately, my desire to attend the Powell Street Festival in Vancouver was scuppered by Covid-19 during the writing of this book, but their excellent website provided useful details. I did visit the Nikkei National Museum and Cultural Centre (NNMCC) in Burnaby and accessed many of their artifacts, photos, records, books, and newsletters, all of which provided a wealth of detail related to my story. For example, one newsletter issue (*The Bulletin,* April 2021) provided the real-life equivalent of my character Harry James, the fictional Kenji's cellmate. Harry *Jones* was the actual cellmate of Akihide John Otsuji (who preferred to be called John), a Nikkei who returned to Vancouver while the ban was still in effect and was repeatedly jailed for the infraction. Sadly, John's story did not end well; he died of dementia in 1988 after a difficult life on the streets struggling with drug abuse—but the real Harry remembered John's love of jive dancing, so I gave that trait to Harry himself in my story. The NNMCC website and the Vancouver Island University website also provided a deep archive of primary source video interviews with *nisei* that allowed me to present the Nikkei with, I hope, authenticity and respect.

At the NNMCC, I purchased a slim booklet (*Karizumai: A Guide to Japanese Canadian Internment Sites*, 2019) that describes the various types of internment sites, identifying their locations. Included in the booklet is a hand drawn map of the layout of the East Lillooet camp, drawn from memory by Taka Tsuyuki and Terry Yamashita in 1991. Having already chosen Hoshi's surname (Tasaka) at random and having also decided that the fictional family would be interned at East Lillooet, imagine my surprise and pleasure at finding the name 'Tasaka' neatly lettered beside cabin #54 on the camp map. It amazes me how often such coincidences crop up while writing historical fiction! Of course, *my* 'Tasakas' are fictional and bear no relationship to the actual family interned there.

As I had in my research for my previous books, I found that Canada's National Film Board site proved a fruitful resource, with several films specific to the Nikkei experience. It was here, in *Sleeping Tigers, The Asahi Baseball Story* (Osborne, 2003), that I was first introduced to the Vancouver Asahi, a lost but well-loved pre-war baseball team, and watched interviews with the real Kaye Kaminishi (who really did persuade the Lillooet RCMP to play against the internees, thus opening the bridge for the remainder of their internment). Being indifferent to baseball myself, I had to rely on my Blue-Jays-mad husband to explain the intricacies of the game to me, as well as gathering details from Norio Goto's book, *Story of Vancouver Asahi: A Legend in Baseball* (2016; trans. Masaki Watanabe). So now I know what a bunt and a squeeze play are! Linda Ohama's NFB film *Obachan's Garden* (2001) not only provided insight into the life of a Japanese 'picture bride' but also the idea for a secret about missing family members (in her case, two daughters left behind in Japan) kept by an *issei* grandmother and only discovered by her family members when she was in her very old age.

Jiro's experiences in the Angler POW camp were greatly informed by Tom Sando's *Wild Daisies in the Sand*, a memoir of his wartime experiences at Hastings Park and Angler. I am most grateful to his daughter Annette Desgagne and all the family for permission to include Tom by name, as well as episodes and comments from his book, in my fictional account. I was also inspired by Tom's haikus, but the poetry throughout the book is my own unless otherwise attributed.

Dr. Masajiro Miyazaki's memoirs (*My Sixty Years in Canada*, 1973) inspired Isabel's sledding accident. The real child was a boy, and the location wasn't East Lillooet, but otherwise the story is the same, including the number of stitches required! This doctor worked tirelessly for all the cultural communities of the region for many years, traversing very challenging conditions with inadequate transportation, and doctoring all manner of ailments and accidents in, at times, the most primitive of circumstances. In 1950, Dr Miyazaki became the first Japanese Canadian to hold public office when he was elected to the Town Council. In honour of his many achievements and contributions, he was invested into the Order of Canada in 1977. Prior to his passing in 1984, Dr. Miyazaki gifted the former Phair mansion to the Village of Lillooet to be used as a museum. It is now known as Miyazaki House and his office is preserved as he left it. He was very well loved and accolades to him can be read at the museum.

The Tasaka family's experience with sugar beet farming in Manitoba is based on the true story of the Tully beet farm, where Mr. Tully welcomed a 'United Nations' of workers to his fields during and after the war. Many Nikkei worked there and spoke very highly of the generosity, fairness, and opportunity given to them. The eldest Tully son did indeed elope with a Nikkei girl who was interned on the farm, and their children and grandchildren still live there. Terry Tully said (in a video interview in 2021) that he wasn't aware until his teenage years that his parents' elopement had caused a local scandal; he had never been made to feel 'different' or 'less' in the community and he feels that his mixed-race heritage has never limited him—a good news story amid so many painful ones. I have, of course, fictionalized their story for the purposes of my narrative.

An update in relation to Canadian law: many, like my character Isabel, argued that the *War Measures Act*, which enabled much of the treatment of the Nikkei during the war, was too broad and potentially contravened the human rights of Canadian citizens. In 1988, not long after redress was granted to the Nikkei, the *War Measures Act* was repealed and replaced by the *Emergencies Act*. The *Emergencies Act* differs from the *War Measures Act* in two important ways: first, a declaration of an emergency by the Cabinet must be reviewed by Parliament and second, any temporary laws made under the act are subject to the *Charter of Rights and Freedoms*. These are important revisions, ones that, I hope, would be invoked to prevent a repetition of our history should such a situation arise again. During the writing of this book, Prime Minister Justin Trudeau made use of this *Act* to disperse the truckers' protest in Ottawa (February 2022), just as his father (Pierre Trudeau) used it to manage the FLQ crisis of 1970.

Having my character Kenji recruited by the British army allowed me to tell the tale of these dedicated and loyal *nisei* who were indeed called into service after Japan's surrender (having been rejected from military service for the duration of the war). As I reviewed Roy Ito's detailed book, *We Went to War* (1992), coincidence struck again—for there, grinning in the third row of a photo of an S-20 platoon, was a "K. Tasaka"—my fictional character made flesh! I sincerely hope that the real soldier had a happier postwar life than my character does. I was also interested in exploring the sordid tale of Japan's comfort women. My understanding of this shocking phenomenon was greatly enhanced by Sarah Soh's (2008) nuanced and scholarly examination of the complex factors enabling the rise of such a horrible system. It is not as simple as it seems, and yet its existence exposes the deep divide between patriarchal societies of the first half of the twentieth century and our modern expectations of the rights of women. The NFB film *The Apology* by Tiffany Tsiung (2016) provides heart-wrenching first-person accounts from three remaining comfort women, now given the respectful term 'grandmother' by their communities. Their long crusade to achieve an apology and restitution for their suffering—and their harassment by some contemporary Japanese and Koreans--is revealing and saddening.

You can find these and more opportunities to delve into the real history of the Nikkei experience in the Selected Resources list which follows.

I was inspired to include an episode involving B.A.C.A. (Bikers Against Child Abuse) by a visit of the Vancouver chapter to the Sunshine Coast several years ago. Unfortunately, I missed their presentation, but I was intrigued by the resulting article in our local newspaper. As the daughter, sister, wife, mother-in-law, and grandmother of dedicated motorcyclists, I am perhaps more tolerant than some of the noisy 'rides' of large groups of bikers on our highways (though not at all tolerant of the bad business that true 'biker gangs' get up to). It was great to learn that perhaps such a ride might have a humanitarian purpose. The work of B.A.C.A. has been endorsed by many child protection, law enforcement, and mental health professionals in North America, and I respect them for the work they do on behalf of abused children. Their characterization in my novel, including the 'level one intervention' scene, is based on their informative website at bacaworld.org.

Anyone who knows me from my career in college teaching

will recognize the emphasis on active learning and the integration of educational technology in Michelle's university teaching experience. Her attendance at a conference on teaching in higher education, where she meets Mac, is based on many fond memories of similar conferences I attended during my own teaching years. Thank you, Educational Developers Caucus!

One final reference: the scene in which Kaiya is bullied by the man on the plane to Winnipeg was modeled on a similar experience recounted by Isabel Wilkerson, the highly accomplished Black scholar and author of *Caste: The Origins of Our Discontents* (2020) among other excellent works, all of which I highly recommend. It was included to show that overt racism and misogyny is far from absent in our modern world—Ms. Wilkerson's incident took place in the first-class section of the plane, on an American flight. In Wilkerson's case, sadly, no other passengers spoke up or attempted to help her and the (Black) flight attendant also did nothing to assist her, for fear of reprisal by the white passenger.

Like all writers of fiction, but especially historical fiction, I am always keenly aware that I am presenting fictionalized versions of characters and events of which I have no personal experience. After all, if writers did not write stories about things other than their own experiences, all we'd have is autobiographies! I do my best to make my characters and stories authentic, though I am always aware that I *am* writing fiction. When the story involves characters whose ethnicity, culture, and experience is very different from my own privileged British, white, immigrant, middle class, educated identity (as this one does), I work hard to ensure that I research deeply and check my narrative with those whose identity closely resembles that of my characters. Although I never expect my reviewers to act as representatives of an entire ethnic or cultural group, I do value and try to integrate their individual responses to my story. Therefore, I am very thankful to my draft readers (Doreen Campbell, Chris Fliesser, Ken Oka, and Michelle Smart) for their insights and suggestions, as well as their encouraging comments on the book as a whole. Remaining errors are, of course, my own.

I am, yet again, very grateful to Charmaine Bayntun for another beautiful cover image, based upon photos she took on the shore at Powell River. As well, my daughter Ellen Syracopoulos provided her stellar design and editing services again, and my husband Frank Rodgers provided support, ideas, and lots and lots of cups of tea, as always: thank you both so much!

There may yet be stories to tell in my Sunshine Coast Series, but for now I am seeking other hidden tales of Canadian and world history to bring to life for today's readers. Thank you for reading my work.

Ruth Rodgers lives and writes on British Columbia's Sunshine Coast, where she enjoys exploring lesser-known aspects of Canada's history through fiction.

Selected Resources

Adachi, Ken. *The Enemy That Never Was*. Toronto: McClelland and Stewart, 1976.

Broadfoot, B. *Years of Sorrow, Years of Shame.* Don Mills: General Publishing, 1977.

Enomoto, R., Ed. *Honouring Our People: Breaking the Silence.* Burnaby: Greater Vancouver Japanese Canadian Citizens' Association (GVJCCA), 2016.

Fukawa, M. and Fukawa, S. *Spirit of the Nikkei Fleet: BC's Japanese Canadian Fishermen*. Madeira Park: Harbour Publishing, 2009.

Goh, K. and Kage T. "Akihide John Otsuji," *1928-1988. The Bulletin*, April 2021. Burnaby: Greater Vancouver Japanese Canadian Citizens' Association (GVJCCA), 2021.

Goto, N. *Story of Vancouver Asahi: A Legend in Baseball*. Translation by Watanabe, M. Vancouver: Asian Canadian Studies Society, 2016.

Grant, D. *People of the Fraser Valley: Mennonite and Japanese*. The Reach Gallery Museum. Abbotsford, n.d.

Ito, R. *We Went to War: the story of the Japanese Canadians who served during the First and Second World Wars.* Stittsville, Canada's Wings, 1992.

Kagawa, J. *Obasan.* Toronto: Lester and Orpen Dennys, 1981.

Kitagawa, M. *This is My Own: Letters to Wes and Other Writings on Japanese Canadians, 1941-1948*. Vancouver: Talonbooks, 1985.

Lambert, B.A. *War Brides and Rosies: Powell River and Stillwater, B.C.* North America: Trafford Publishing, 2012.

Martin, H. "Honouring Galiano's Japanese Heritage" *Island Tides*, Sept 22-Oct 5, 2011. Pender Island: Island Tides Publishing, 2011

McDonald, S. *The Way of the Warrior: The Japanese-Canadian Veterans of the First World War and the Russo-Japan War*. Burnaby: Nikkei National Museum, 2016.

Miki, R. *Redress: Inside the Japanese Canadian Call for Justice*. Vancouver: Raincoast Books, 2004.

Miyazaki, M. *My Sixty Years in Canada*. Kamloops: Overland Press, 1973.

Nikkei National Museum. *Karizumai: A Guide to Japanese Internment Sites*, 5th edition. Burnaby: Nikkei Museum and Cultural Centre, 2019.

Nikkei National Museum. Ed. Stanger-Ross, J. and Sugiman, P. *Witness to Loss: Race, Culpability, and Memory in the Dispossession of Japanese Canadians.* Montreal: McGill-Queen's University Press, 2017.

Sando, T. *Wild Daisies in the Sand.* Edmonton: NeWest Press, 2002.

Soh, C. S. *The Comfort Women.* Chicago: U. of Chicago Press, 2008.

Takashima, S. *A Child in Prison Camp*. Toronto: Tundra Books, 1971.

Takata, T. *Nikkei Legacy: The Story of Japanese Canadians from Settlement to Today*. Toronto: NC Press Ltd., 1983.

Thomson, G.E. *Chiru Sakura: Falling Cherry Blossoms*. Toronto: Caitlin Press, 2021.

Waite, D. *Maple Ridge and Pitt Meadows: A History in Photographs*. Waite Bird Photos, Inc, 2008.

Ward, W.P. *The Japanese in Canada.* Ottawa: Canadian Historical Association, 1982.

National Film Board Features

Daly, Tom. *Gateway to Asia*. NFB, 1945.

Hsiung, T. *The Apology.* NFB, 2016.

Lerman, J. *Enemy Alien*. NFB, 1975.

Osborne, J. *Sleeping Tigers: The Asahi Baseball Story.* NFB, 2003.

Ohama, L. *Obachan's Garden.* NFB, 2001